Wordsworth in American Literary Culture

Wordsworth in American Literary Culture

Edited by

Joel Pace
Assistant Professor of English
University of Wisconsin, Eau Claire

and

Matthew Scott
Departmental Lecturer in English Literature (1740–1830)
St Catherine's College, University of Oxford

palgrave macmillan

First published 2005 by
PALGRAVE MACMILLAN
Houndmills, Basingstoke, Hampshire RG21 6XS and
175 Fifth Avenue, New York, N. Y. 10010
Companies and representatives throughout the world

PALGRAVE MACMILLAN is the global academic imprint of the Palgrave Macmillan division of St. Martin's Press, LLC and of Palgrave Macmillan Ltd. Macmillan® is a registered trademark in the United States, United Kingdom and other countries. Palgrave is a registered trademark in the European Union and other countries.

ISBN 1–4039–0133–3

This book is printed on paper suitable for recycling and made from fully managed and sustained forest sources.

A catalogue record for this book is available from the British Library.

Library of Congress Cataloging-in-Publication Data
Wordsworth in America literary culture / edited by Joel Pace and Matthew Scott.
p. cm.
Includes bibliographical references and index.
ISBN 1-4039-0133-3 (cloth)
1. American literature–English influences. 2. Wordsworth, William, 1770-1850–Appreciation–United States. 3. Wordsworth, William, 1770-1850–Influence. 4. American literature–History and criticism. I. Pace, Joel, 1972- II. Scott, Matthew (Matthew E.)

PS159.E5W67 2005
821'.7–dc22 2004051746

10 9 8 7 6 5 4 3 2 1
14 13 12 11 10 09 08 07 06 05

Transferred to digital printing 2005

For our parents:

Jane and Geoffrey Scott, Sharon and Joseph Pace

Contents

List of Figures

Foreword

Stephen Gill

Wordsworth has always been associated in my mind with America and Americans. When I first visited Dove Cottage in the mid-1960s to work at the Wordsworth Trust Library in Grasmere, a big push in Wordsworth scholarship was gathering momentum and the advance guard was largely American. The first volume of the *Letters of William and Dorothy Wordsworth* was about to appear, edited by Chester Shaver from Oberlin College. Mark Reed of the University of North Carolina at Chapel Hill was completing the first volume of his *Chronology*, the result of analytic labour on manuscript and other materials, the intensity of which awed me as someone new to work of this kind at this level. John Finch, an Englishman, true, but then at Cornell University, was in the early stages of planning a fantastically ambitious project, the presentation of all of Wordsworth's poetic manuscripts down to the last crossing-out and all his lifetime printed texts. What was to become the Cornell Wordsworth Series was taken over at Finch's tragic death by Stephen Parrish, also at Cornell, and it is due to his extraordinary commitment since the appearance of the first volume in 1975 that this indispensable scholarly resource now approaches completion.

Although the American scholars were numerous, the products of this sustained endeavour were actually the result, of course, of Anglo-American collaboration. That much was obvious from a glance into the small library where, poring over manuscripts of *The Ruined Cottage*, Jonathan Wordsworth might be rubbing shoulders with James Butler – literally, there was only one small table and for a long time only a single table-lamp – or Carl Ketcham talking about the dating of John Wordsworth's letters with Robert Woof. I knew that I was very lucky to become a member of this group at such a tremendously exciting moment in the history of Wordsworth scholarship. What I did not know then was that this late-twentieth-century collaboration had a noble and many-branched ancestry.

To trace one line, we might begin with a comment from one of the very greatest of American scholars of British and European Romanticism. In the Preface to *Natural Supernaturalism* (1971), M.H. Abrams envisioned an ideal place for writing on Romantic literature, 'a study in a commodious old university building' where 'a minute's stroll distant there would be a major research library with a notable collection in the age of Wordsworth, reached by a path commanding a Wordsworthian prospect of hill, wood, lake, and sky.' It was a graceful tribute to a reality, not a vision of one. Cornell University's Olin Library has a magnificent Wordsworth holding and it too is the product in some degree of Anglo-American co-operation. Cornell's Wordsworth collection has its origins in the collection amassed by Cynthia Morgan St John (1852–1919). By her early 30s she was being assisted in her search for American and English Wordsworth editions and Wordsworthiana by, as George H. Healey puts it, 'a widening circle of friends, most of them British, all of whom seemed to enjoy doing favours for the extraordinary young woman with the dactyllic name who lived in an American city called Ithaca'.[1] Those who helped her were Edward Dowden, John Ramsden Tutin, James Dykes Campbell, Thomas Hutchinson and William Knight, a roll-call of the late Victorian editors and bibliographers whose remarkable work is the foundation of all later scholarship.[2] Knight sponsored Cynthia Morgan St John's membership of the Wordsworth Society; she contributed the American bibliography to Knight's 1896 edition of Wordsworth's Poetical Works. Many of the items in Cornell's collection are there because of Anglo-American help and trust, and it is not a case of American money trumping all bidders. Cynthia Morgan St John was not wealthy. Tutin, Knight and the others helped her because they warmed to a fellow Wordsworth enthusiast, one who valued Wordsworth as a transatlantic property.

Such a valuation is shared by all the contributors to the present volume, and so it takes its place in the distinguished line I have been tracing of Anglo-American scholarly exploration around the cultural phenomenon 'Wordsworth'. It is particularly to be welcomed, I suggest, for two reasons. The first is that the essays in this collection meet one of our most pressing wants, namely, the need to know more. American friends, especially the many who visited Rydal Mount, mattered to Wordsworth in his later years, and the *idea* of America as a limitless space for the diffusion of the English language mattered even more.[3] How much, though, and in what ways, did Wordsworth matter to America? Fine survey essays by Carl Woodring and David Simpson marked out the terrain some time ago,[4] and much good work has been done since then, but it is the case that the names, dates and facts they deployed still constitute much of the data in accounts of Wordsworth and America. The time has come for more excavation of the material itself in libraries and archives and for reconsideration of the narratives it permits. In this collection, fresh evidence is presented about the meanings Wordsworth had for such canonical figures as Thoreau, Whittier, Whitman and Dickinson, and new and fascinating perspectives are opened on to Wordsworth's relation to educationalists, churchmen and cowboys. May this point the way for more digging.

The second reason for welcoming *Wordsworth in American Literary Culture* is that it is such a heartening example of scholarly practice. All of the writers convey a sense of the intellectual excitement of trying to contribute to a new phase in the exploration of cultural traffic. While remaining close to text and fact, each essay responds to the allure of speculating beyond the strictly demonstrable about the variety of ways in which Wordsworth entered American culture and the cumulative effect of such agile and suggestive exploration is to indicate that the subject is being opened up, not closed off. This is, in fact, a thoroughly Wordsworthian volume: it keeps faith with the past while opening up avenues to the future.

Notes

1. George H. Healey, 'Cynthia Morgan St John and Her Collection' in *Bicentenary Wordsworth Studies*, ed. Jonathan Wordsworth (Ithaca, NY and London: Cornell UP, 1970), 377–92. Until the completion of Mark Reed's comprehensive bibliography, currently in preparation, Healey's catalogue, *The Cornell Wordsworth Collection* (Ithaca, NY and London: Cornell UP, 1957), remains the nearest thing we have to a Wordsworth bibliography.
2. For further details on their activities, not always collaborative, see my *Wordsworth and the Victorians* (Oxford: Oxford UP, 1998).
3. Tribute should be paid here to the pioneering work of Alan G. Hill, whose footnotes to the five volumes of the Wordsworth letters are packed with information, supplementing his still indispensable article, 'Wordsworth and his American Friends', *Bulletin of Research in the Humanities* 81 (1978): 146–60.
4. Carl Woodring, 'Wordsworth and the Victorians' and David Simpson, 'Wordsworth in America', both in *The Age of William Wordsworth: Critical Essays on the Romantic Tradition*, ed. Kenneth R. Johnston and Gene W. Ruoff (New Jersey, NJ: Rutgers UP, 1987).

Acknowledgements

In addition to our contributors whose steadfast support was integral to this volume's inception and completion, we would like to thank Eleanor Birne and Paula Kennedy, our editors at Palgrave, for their help and patience. Both editors owe a deep debt of gratitude to Jennifer Hamm and Keith and Mary Povey without whose editorial assistance this volume would never have taken shape. We thank the Harvard University Press and the Trustees of Amherst College for permission to quote from the poems of Emily Dickinson, and the Wordsworth Trust for permission to quote from Wordsworth MSS. Every effort has been made to trace all copyright holders, but if any have been inadvertently overlooked, the publisher will be pleased to make the necessary arrangements at the first opportunity. Individuals who deserve much more thanks than this simple mention are numerous: Stuart Andrews, J. Drummond Bone, Joyce Botelho, Fred Burwick, Isaac Castillo, David Chandler, Jeff Cowton, Michael Darigan, Valerie A. Dodd, Alex Dunwoodie, Michael Eberle-Sinatra, Ken Eklund, Paul Giles, Marilyn Gaull, Diane Long Hoeveler, Will Kaufman, Chris Koenig-Woodyard, Allen Kurzweil, Maurice Lee, Sohui Lee, Michael Macovski, Heidi Macpherson, Paul Magnuson, John Mahoney, Harry McDermott, Bob Nowlan, Curtis Odom, Omni, Michael O'Neill, Machiste Rankin, Alan Rice, Nicholas Roe, Laura Roman, David and Robin Shih, Fiona Stafford, Michael Suarez, Judith Thompson, Nicola Trott, Michael Turner, Astrid Wind, Marty Wood, Robert and Pamela Woof, Jonathan and Jessica Wordsworth and Duncan Wu. Meredith Oakes and Tom Sutcliffe Frank and Amy Pace, Raymond and Leslie Camero and the Camero family all deserve our gratitude.

The editors are both grateful for the invaluable comments of the anonymous readers, without whom this volume could not possibly have been able to accomplish the full scope of its aims.

We would like to thank the staff of Brown University's John Nicholas Brown Center for the research fellowship that allowed this transatlantic editorial duo to meet in the same place in the setting of a first-rate university, lively and encouraging Fellows and excellent collections and helpful librarians (special thanks to the staff of the John Hay Library). For hosting panels and papers on Wordsworth in America, we thank North American Society for the Study of Romanticism, British Association for Romantic Studies, International Conference on Romanticism, Symbiosis, The Coleridge Conference, the Wordsworth Summer Conference, the Wordsworth-Coleridge Association, the Wordsworth Trust, the British Association of American Studies and the Transatlantic Studies Conference. Joel Pace would also like to thank Marcy Tanter for her help with the volume, the University of Wisconsin-Eau Claire (UWEC) Office of Research and Sponsored Programs for the University Research and Creative Activity Grant awarded for the fall of 2003, as well as the Duyfhuizen family for establishing the Duyfhuizen Professorship of English, the award of which was crucial to the completion of work on the volume. Thanks also to his colleagues in the UWEC Department of English; the students who enrolled in the 'Wordsworth in America' seminar in the fall of 2002; the brethren and faculty of Blackfriars, Oxford; and the owners and staff of the Acoustic Café, Menomonie, Wisconsin.

The editors would like to thank Seamus Perry for his continuing support on this prject and for being the first to suggest that Palgrave may have interest in it.

There is a precious debt that both editors owe to their respective families, a small amount of which is repaid in the dedication to this volume.

And, lastly, for love and support we thank Caldwell Camero and Lana Asfour.

JOEL PACE
MATTHEW SCOTT

Notes on the Contributors

Richard E. Brantley is Professor of English and American literature at the University of Florida and author of *Wordsworth's Natural Methodism* (1975), *Locke, Wesley, and the Method of English Romanticism* (1984), *Coordinates of Anglo-American Romanticism: Wesley, Edwards, Carlyle, and Emerson* (1993) and *Anglo-American Antiphony: The Late Romanticism of Emerson and Tennyson* (1994). He has published articles in *Eighteenth Century Studies, Harvard Theological Review, Studies in English Literature*, and *Studies in Romanticism*.

James A. Butler is Professor of English at La Salle University. He is editor of the Cornell Wordsworth Series editions of *The Ruined Cottage* and *The Pedlar by William Wordsworth* (1979) *The Excursion* (forthcoming) and co-editor of *Lyrical Ballads, and Other Poems* (1992). He is also the editor of Owen Wister's newly found (and published) novel *Romney* (2001). He has published articles in various journals, including *Huntington Library Quarterly, Journal of English and Germanic Philology, Nineteenth-Century Literature, Princeton University Library Chronicle, Studies in Romanticism, Studies in Philology* and *Wordsworth Circle*. He is a contributor to *The Cambridge Companion to Wordsworth* (2003).

Elizabeth Fay teaches British Romanticism at the University of Massachusetts-Boston, and is co-editor of *Working Class Women in the Academy: Laborers in the Knowledge Factory* (1993). She is the author of *Eminent Rhetoric: Language, Gender, and Cultural Tropes* (1994), *Becoming Wordsworthian: A Performative Aesthetics* (1995), *A Feminist Introduction to Romanticism* (1998), *Romantic Medievalism: History and the Literary Ideal* (2002), and articles in *European Romantic Review, Nineteenth Century Contexts, Publications of the Modern Language Association (PMLA), Romantic Circles Praxis Series* and *Romanticism on the Net*.

Stephen Gill is Professor of English Literature at the University of Oxford and Fellow of Lincoln College. His books include *The Prelude* (1970), and the Cornell Wordsworth Series edition of *The Salisbury Plain Poems of William Wordsworth* (1975), *The Prelude* (with Jonathan Wordsworth and M.H. Abrams, 1979), *William Wordsworth: A Life* (1984), *William Wordsworth* (1984), *Wordsworth and the Victorians* (1998) and *The Cambridge Companion to Wordsworth* (2003). He has published articles in the *Centennial Review, Essays in Criticism, Journal of English and German Philology, Review of English Studies, Studies in Romanticism* and *Wordsworth Circle*.

Bruce Graver is Professor of English at Providence College. He is the editor of the Cornell Wordsworth Series edition of *Translations of Chaucer and Virgil* (1998) and co-editor of an electronic edition of the first English and American editions of the *Lyrical Ballads*. He has published articles in several journals, including *European Romantic Review*, *Profession*, *Romanticism on the Net*, *Studies in Philology* and *Wordsworth Circle*.

Richard Gravil is the founding editor of *Symbiosis*, the first journal of Anglo-American literary relations. Previously, he was Reader in English Literature at the College of St Mark and St John, Plymouth, and has taught at the Universities of Victoria, BC, and Otago, New Zealand. He is the author of articles in *European Romantic Review*, *The Wordsworth Circle* and *Romanticism on the Net* as well as two books, *Romantic Dialogues: Anglo-American Continuities 1776–1832* (2000) and *Wordsworth's Bardic Vocation* (2003), and co-editor (with Nicholas Roe and Lucy Newlyn) of *Coleridge's Imagination: Essays in Memory of Pete Laver* (1985). He has also edited collections on Swift, Wordsworth, and the English Novel.

Karen Karbiener teaches at New York University and was previously Visiting Assistant Professor of English at Colby College and has also taught at Columbia University. She has written on Transatlantic Romanticism in *Symbiosis*, 'Cross-Cultural Confessions: America Passes Judgement on Thomas De Quincey', and her Columbia University dissertation contains an extensive treatment of Wordsworth (and other Romantics) in America. She is presently editing *The Encyclopedia of American Counterculture* as well as editions of *Leaves of Grass* and *Frankenstein*.

Susan Manning, Grierson Professor of English Literature at the University of Edinburgh, has published widely on British and American eighteenth- and nineteenth-century literature. Her research centres on Scottish and American literary, religious and philosophical relationships, and she has a special interest in the writing of the Scottish Enlightenment and its influence in Europe and America. She has also written extensively on the poetry of Emily Dickinson. She is the author of *The Puritan-Provincial Vision: Scottish and American Literature in the Nineteenth Century* (1990), and has published editions of Walter Scott's *Quentin Durward* (1992), Washington Irving's *The Sketch-Book of Geoffrey Crayon, Gent*. (1996), and Crèvecoeur's *Letters from an American Farmer* (1997). She has also edited *The Works of Henry Mackenzie* (1996) and Mackenzie's *Life of John Home* (1997) and *Julia de Roubigné* (1999). She is currently editing Hawthorne's *The Marble Faun* for Oxford World Classics. Her most recent book is a Scottish/American comparative study *Fragments of Union* (2002).

Lance Newman is Assistant Professor of American and British Literature in the Department of Literature and Writing at California State University, San Marcos. He holds the PhD from Brown University where he completed a dissertation on ecological criticism, class politics and poetics in the works of American and British Romantic writers, including Wordsworth, Carlyle, Thoreau, Emerson and Fuller. His articles have appeared or are forthcoming in *American Literature, New England Quarterly, Romanticism on the Net, Nineteenth Century Prose, Interdisciplinary Studies in Literature and the Environment, Concord Saunterer* and *Review*. He has two books forthcoming: *Intelligence with the Earth: Transcendentalist Nature and the Politics of Ecocriticism* and *Transatlantic Romanticism: An Anthology of British, American, and Canadian Literature*, co-edited with Chris Koenig-Woodyard and Joel Pace.

Joel Pace is Assistant Professor of Transatlantic Romanticism at University of Wisconsin-Eau Claire and a former Fellow of the John Nicholas Brown Center for the Study of American Civilization at Brown University. He gained a Master's degree and a DPhil at the University of Oxford, where he completed a doctoral thesis on the publication, reception and influence of William Wordsworth in America. He is co-editor (with Lance Newman and Chris Koenig-Woodyard) of *Transatlantic Romanticism: An Anthology of British, American, and Canadian Literature* (forthcoming) and reviews editor of *Symbiosis: A Journal of Anglo-American Literary Relations*. His essays on Romanticism's Anglo-American literary and cultural exchanges have appeared in the following books and journals: *The Cambridge Companion to Wordsworth* (2003), *Parodies of the Romantic Age* (1999), *Wordsworth Circle, Romantic Circles Praxis Series, Providence Magazine, Symbiosis, Allen Review* and *Romanticism on the Net*.

Adam Potkay is Professor of English at the College of William and Mary where he is also associate editor of the journal *Eighteenth-Century Life*. He was formerly Visiting Professor at Columbia University. He is the author of *The Fate of Eloquence in the Age of Hume* (1994), *The Passion for Happiness: Samuel Johnson and David Hume* (2000), and *An Education on the Delaware: St Mary's Hall and Doane Academy, 1837–2000* (2000). He is co-editor of *Black Atlantic Writers of the Eighteenth Century: Living the New Exodus in England and the Americas* (1995), and has published numerous articles on eighteenth-and nineteenth-century literature (including Wordsworth) and philosophy in *PMLA, Raritan Eighteenth-Century Studies, William and Mary Quarterly, Nineteenth-Century Literature, Studies in Early Modern Philosophy* and the forthcoming *Oxford Encyclopedia of the Enlightenment*.

Matthew Scott is Departmental Lecturer in English Literature (1740–1830) at the University of Oxford, and a Lecturer at St Catherine's College. He was previously Fellow of the John Nicholas Brown Center, Brown University, and Kennedy Memorial Scholar and Research Fellow at Harvard University. He has published articles and reviews in *Romanticism, Wordsworth Circle, Charles Lamb Bulletin* and *Romanticism on the Net*. Among his recent projects was a series of translations of eighteenth-century German and French texts for *The Faber Book of Opera* (Faber and Faber, 2000).

A Note on Texts

The system of citation utilized throughout this essay collection is as follows: the initial reference to (or quotation from) a work is cited in full in the corresponding endnote. All subsequent citations are abbreviated, parenthetical, given in the main text of the essay, and directly follow the paraphrase of or quotation from the source initially cited in the endnote. The parenthetical citation includes the author's or editor's surname followed the page number of the prose work, or the line number of the poetical work, being cited, save when there is more than one work by the same author(s) or editor(s). In this instance, the full (or abbreviated) title is substituted for the last names of the editor(s) or author(s). If the name of the work, editor, or author is stated in the sentence(s) preceding the parenthetical citation, then the citation will consist solely of the page or line number.

We have standardized all references to Wordsworth's works, quoting and citing from authoritative volumes that should be readily accessible to readers by virtue of their being in the collections of most libraries. We use the Norton text of the 1850 *Prelude* because its text most closely resembles the 1850 American edition (New York and Philadelphia: Appleton), which the American authors and thinkers of the time read. With the exception of Owen and Smyser's *Prose Works* and Hill's *Letters*, all editions of Woodsworth are (co-)edited by contributors to the present volume. For the (prose and poetry in) *Lyrical Ballads*, we use the Cornell editions. Unless otherwise indicated, all other quotations and citations of Wordsworth's poetry refer to Stephen Gill's Oxford edition, and all quotations of his prose are taken from Owen and Smyser's *Prose Works*. All parenthetical citations of Wordsworth's poetry refer to line numbers, and all parenthetical citations of his prose refer to page numbers in these editions.

Abbreviations to these editions are as follows:

LB *Lyrical Ballads and Other Poems, 1797–1800*, eds. James Butler and Karen Green (Ithaca, NY and London: Cornell University Press, 1992)

Prose *The Prose Works of William Wordsworth*, ed. W.J.B. Owen and Jane Worthington Smyser, 3 vols (Oxford: Oxford UP, 1974)

TP *The Prelude: 1799, 1805, 1850*, eds. Jonathan Wordsworth, M.H. Abrams and Stephen Gill (New York, NY and London: Norton, 1979)

WL *The Letters of William and Dorothy Wordsworth*, 8 vols (Oxford: Oxford UP, 1967–93). Individual volumes are as follows: *The Early Years: 1787–1805*, ed. Chester L. Shaver (1967); *The Middle Years*, pt. I: *1806–1811*, ed. Mary Moorman (1969); *The Middle Years*, pt. 2: *1812–1820*, ed. Mary Moorman and Alan G. Hill (1970): *The Later Years*, pt. I: *1821–1828*, ed. Alan G. Hill (1978); *The Later Years*, pt. 2: *1829–1834*, ed. Alan G. Hill (1979); *The Later Years*, pt. 3: *1835–1839*, ed. Alan G. Hill (1982); *The Later Years*, pt. 4: *1840–1853*, ed. Alan G. Hill (1988); *A Supplement of New Letters*, ed. Alan G. Hill (1993). The edition is referred to serially as *WL*, I–VIII.

WP *William Wordsworth: The Oxford Authors*, ed. Stephen Gill (New York, NY and Oxford University Press, 1984)

Introduction

Joel Pace and Matthew Scott

Harold Bloom has written that only two writers have truly altered the course of western poetry: 'Petrarch, who invented Renaissance poetry, and Wordsworth, who can be said to have invented modern poetry, which has been a continuum for two full centuries'.[1] One may well take issue with this characteristically controversial statement, but it is hard to deny the enormous impact of Wordsworth's writing upon the literary and cultural world that followed him. The thrust of Bloom's thesis is comparatively uncomplicated: concerned to throw off the influence of Milton and to clear some ground for his own poetic ambitions, Wordsworth conceives of an epic of the mind. In poems such as 'Tintern Abbey', 'Michael' and *The Prelude* there is a perceptible turn inward to focus on the self that, being unprecedented, casts a shadow over the subject-centred poetic tradition that follows. This was, on his account, nowhere more marked than in the American tradition in which, for writers such as Emerson, Whitman and Stevens, Wordsworth provided an anxiety-inducing model. Such a theory of influence was itself for so long influential partially because it suggested that critics were themselves undergoing a Bloomian reaction to an influence theory, which of course must have caused no small amount of anxiety. With regard to Wordsworth, this theory suggested that poets who came after him were unavoidably engaged in response to the aspects of his poems that explore human consciousness. Thus to write after Wordsworth is to be aware of his way of describing subjective experience in poetry.

This collection of essays worries the implications of Bloom's statement somewhat with a view to describing both the necessity and difficulty of moving beyond its basic declaration. In moving forward, we ask how influence functions between British authors and their American contemporaries and successors. That the reception history of Wordsworth has a place in answering this question is clear from the enormous impact of his writing upon the American reading public of the nineteenth century – an impact that is felt in environmental studies as well as the history of radical politics, religion, education and publishing. These essays acknowledge that impact and attempt to convert a generalized impression into useful and scholarly literary history. Our aim is simple: through especially commissioned essays, we will explore the influence of Wordsworth's writing upon American writers of the nineteenth century, suggesting in turn the importance of his legacy for the American reading public as a whole.

Wordsworth in American Literary Culture assesses the poet's role in issues such as education, social reform and the formation of an American literary canon. Inevitably, Wordsworth's legacy in America is the history of literary influence, but while we attend closely to his importance for major figures, we contend that this cannot be the whole picture. To describe Wordsworth's literary influence is also to describe the history of the reception of those later writers who were influenced by him. This is, moreover, to engage with his wider social, political and artistic legacy in nineteenth-century America. Our contributors have this in mind as they engage with topics as diverse as Wordsworth's presence in Dickinson, the Wordsworthian notions of civic humanism that underpin the foundation of the Boston Public Library, and Wordsworth's reception among the Episcopalians of the Delaware valley. These essays incorporate allusions and references as one indicator of international intertextuality; they also gesture beyond empirical source-study by exploring the larger historical and socio-political significance of Wordsworth's legacy.

The original impetus for this collection of essays came from Stephen Gill's *Wordsworth and the Victorians*, which states that '*the* book waiting to be written' is on Wordsworth in America:

> Wordsworth's poetry was being freshly set by American printers from as early as 1802; his first editor, during his lifetime, was an American, Henry Reed; *The Prelude* and Christopher Wordsworth's *Memoirs of William Wordsworth* were better received in America than in Great Britain; American admirers contributed substantially to the Wordsworth memorial in Ambleside Church; the greatest private collectors of Wordsworth books and manuscripts were (and still are) Americans.[2]

We believe that the Wordsworth that is revealed in this collection is indeed a writer whose widespread influence upon American literature and society has, until recently, been unduly neglected. For mid-twentieth-century scholars of the American Renaissance, who urged us to see American literature as a tradition entirely independent of Britain, it was something of an embarrassment that American writers looked over their shoulders at models from an earlier tradition. Despite groundbreaking early work by Annabel Newton, Wordsworth's role in the formation of American literature continued to be overlooked by most scholars in the first half of the twentieth century.[3] Her work was not expanded upon significantly until the century's end when articles by John Beer, David Bromwich, Alan G. Hill, John Mahoney, Mark Reed and David Simpson, among others, began to reconstruct Wordsworth's transatlantic dialogue with poets and religious reformers.[4]

The larger picture of what scholars have come to call Transatlantic Romanticism and the exchange formative for literature on both sides of the Atlantic, began to be filled in by the very early work of Perry Miller and more recent articles by Lawrence Buell and Tony Tanner as well as books by Leon Chai and, especially, Robert Weisbuch, who has indicated the importance of Wordsworth to writers like Whitman, Emerson and Thoreau.[5] Weisbuch applied Bloom's *Anxiety of Influence* to explain the precarious state of the American author.[6] Writers were conceived as attempting to inaugurate a literary tradition that was not British but specifically American, and this provided a valuable insight into the quasi-postcolonial stance of the writers of the American Renaissance, based on the idea that American authors needed to distance themselves from a foregoing tradition that was largely British. This essay collection continues to explore not only notions of anxiety of influence, but also *complicity of confluence*, setting transatlantic engagement with Wordsworth within the context of an American cultural scene that was obsessed with the poet from the early years of the century and focusing upon the ways in which American writers received Wordsworth upon their own terms by applying his social vision to their own circumstances. Our contributors suggest that literary influence is a pervasive force in the construction of American literary identity, but that British Romanticism is remade by the American reading public so that influence cannot be seen to be solely literary, as a Bloomian model would lead us to believe, but must be cultural as well.

Wordsworth's reception in America now needs to be seen in the context of recent, important work in the burgeoning field of Transatlantic Studies. In North America, scholars such as William Keach and Richard Brantley (whose essay in this volume continues his long-standing engagement with Anglo-American literary and religious studies) have done much to overturn dated preconceptions.[7] Key to the discipline in Britain is the work of Paul Gilroy and Paul Giles as well as that of two of our contributors: Richard Gravil and Susan Manning.[8] Anglo-American literary relations is also the focus of the journal *Symbiosis* and is enjoying considerable academic recognition with a number of Modern Language Association (MLA) teaching posts in graduate and undergraduate programmes devoted to its study. William Keach's 'A Transatlantic Romantic Century' notes that recent scholarship has 'opened up fresh kinds of transatlantic connections that make all forms of habitual national one-sidedness a serious barrier to critical advance' (31).

Keach's manifesto serves us well. It is clear that to discuss issues in social or literary history in isolation is to see only a partial picture. The poet's significant influence and legacy can only be recovered by revising existing scholarship to consider the transatlantic dialogue that shaped Romanticism. Such an approach requires not only bridging literary traditions that published scholarship and university curricula have separated, but also connecting approaches to literary criticism that are practised, more often than not, with mutual exclusivity. The application of critical theory to bibliographical and archival research is necessary to bring scholars on both sides of the Atlantic into dialogue and to open up the conversation to scholars all over the world.

Wordsworth first enters the American cultural environment through the publication and dissemination of primary texts printed both in America and Britain, and in anthologies, imitations and parodies. A secondary, critical level of engagement emerges in the material of reviews and articles devoted to the poet, including visits to and reports on him (such as Emerson's). A third level could perhaps be traced through the presence of Wordsworthiana in public and private collections of books, manuscripts, paintings, images of the poet and so on. Even in terse summary, this rich legacy contributes to the creation of Wordsworth as a cultural presence (in nineteenth-century America) whose specific local influence is hard to assess, even if we aim simply to trace it along lines that could satisfy the demands of traditional source study. In fact, the term 'influence' itself becomes problematic because it seems to suggest that the poet can only have a legacy as he is seriously read and studied by individuals. The evidence of our contributors suggests by contrast that varied reading communities created 'types' of Wordsworth (political, religious, philosophical) according to region and period. Moreover, on a meta-level, as a cultural presence in the intellectual and emotional space of nineteenth-century America, Wordsworth is seen to stand for certain qualities and ideas that can themselves be associated in retrospect with broader movements of diverse kinds, such as Anglican/Episcopalian theology, feminism, civic humanism, and environmentalism.

Wordsworth certainly provided a model for many American writers who read him, but our contributors wish to go beyond those individual relationships in order to demonstrate the ways in which social and political forces underpinned his attraction for the reading public by providing an early history of his reception in America. We clarify the groups of authors and readers who were drawn to his social vision and indicate how the growing corpus of Wordsworth's writing was edited and disseminated. Through examining the changing cultural climate that responded to his work, we hope to emphasize the need to re-conceptualize the theories of influence available to us in order to accommodate the impact of such a considerable figure as Wordsworth and suggest that neither of the recently dominant theories of cultural presence – those of Harold Bloom and Pierre Bourdieu – adequately accounts for the continuing weight of a figure like Wordsworth.

Bloom's revisionary ratios give an account of literary influence that has six developmental stages. The history of Wordsworth's influence in America, however, is one in which the narrative fragments, doubles back on itself, and multiplies, creating several points of departure and intersection. '[T]o follow the complex course of descent is', in the words of Michel Foucault,

> to maintain passing events in their proper dispersion; it is to identify the accidents, the minute deviations – or conversely, the complete reversals – the errors, the false appraisals, and the faulty calculations that gave birth to those things that continue to exist and have value for us ... [W]e should not be deceived into thinking that this heritage is an acquisition, a possession that grows and solidifies; rather, it is an unstable assemblage of faults, fissures, and heterogeneous layers ... The search for descent is not the erecting of foundations: on the contrary, it disturbs what was previously considered immobile; it fragments what was thought unified; it shows the heterogeneity of what was imagined consistent within itself.[9]

Before New Historicism was a critical *modus operandi*, comparative transatlantic work dealt with an imagined uniformity among the communities of interpreters on either side of the Atlantic; earlier influence studies were at leisure to deal solely with allusion and reference, as if there were little difference to the contexts informing an American author's decision to reference or allude to a British author. Studies of Anglo-American literary relationships that are solely based on textual allusion and authorial anxiety are certainly valuable, but only, we would argue, when they pay sufficient attention to the pervasive impact upon the local culture of uniquely American constructs of Romantic authors. Recent influence studies are being undertaken, in the words of Lance Newman, by 'a cohort of scholars for whom the internationalism of Romanticism is no longer a hypothesis, but an axiom'.[10] Once allusive, influence is now elusive, as we begin to acknowledge not only the gaps between reading communities on either side of the Atlantic, but also our own historical gap as we review these readings at over a century's distance.

Not only does the publication and reception of British authors change in America, but even the Atlantic call and response among works in the same genre begins to distort as the genres themselves change with each re-articulation. David Richter notes:

> [J]ust as living organisms evolve, so do genres. When the cultural environment that produced the niche changes, the genre must change ... [T]he birth of new genres out of the old, cannot be explained in purely formal terms, as the opening and exhausting of structural possibilities. Such changes must have been at least the result of a complex interaction between producers and consumers, between authors on the one hand and audiences and publishers on the other.[11]

And so we are left with a more accurate understanding, to adopt Richter's metaphor, of the critical symbiotic, predatory and parasitic relationships and ecosystems that form among authors, cultures, literary works and nations. Recent work in Transatlantic Studies is heavily indebted to postcolonial theory, as it crosses national and cultural borders to show how transnational and multicultural points of contact, contestation and exchange were and continue to be formative for literature. The narrative history of national literature becomes complicated by transnational cultural, ideological and literary exchanges. Cities like London and Boston that were formerly viewed as national publishing centres become sites of transnational transmission and re-signification.

The diversity of approaches in this collection of essays begins to articulate a theory of influence that provides a way of examining the relationships between distinct, yet linked, literary cultures. Some essays in this volume deal more with the interplay of allusion among authors, placing Wordsworth in distinctly American contexts and engaging with as well as redefining Bloomian influence theory in the process, while others focus less on literary figures and more on examining America's Wordsworth(s) as cultural constructs. The result of these varied treatments as a collective (or collection) is a more thorough examination of nineteenth-century America's Wordsworth than has ever been undertaken. Robert Weisbuch rightly identified Transatlantic Romanticism as a field that would take a generation of scholars to define. In keeping with his words, our contributors hope not only to provoke more thought about America's Wordsworth (and Wordsworth's America), but also about influence in the context of transnational cultural and literary exchange.

The collection fragments what was previously assumed to be a coherent tale, and a critical understanding of fragmentation is, as Susan Manning has demonstrated, essential to understanding Atlantic-rim connections. Manning's *Fragments of Union* examines, among other things, ways in which the writing of Scotland and America paradoxically contains both expressions of discrete national identity as well as notions of unified identity with the colonizing country. Such seeming *doublethink* is essential for circum-Atlantic writers who simultaneously identified with their country of birth and with other countries to which they travelled, these countries often being interdependent culturally, economically and politically. For example, writers of the black Atlantic – such as Olaudah Equiano, who was kidnapped, enslaved and taken to colonies on the Atlantic rim – construct narratives that contain hybrid national and cultural identities, yet maintain a critical distance by critiquing Atlantic institutions, such as slavery, from within. Another example is Jefferson, who declares American independence from Britain while drawing heavily on English, and especially Scottish, enlightenment philosophy to frame his declaration. As Manning shows, Scottish Enlightenment philosophy itself attempted to reconcile notions of political union and separateness, an endeavour not wholly foreign to a young America that was striving to embody the motto *E Pluribus Unum*.

In Susan Manning's essay in this volume, '"Grounds for Comparison": The Place of Style in Transatlantic Romanticism' (Chapter 1), she continues the work begun in *Fragments of Union* by applying its theories to the study of Wordsworth in America.[12] In so doing, Manning develops a comparativism that not only focuses on the discursive and ideological level of poetry, but also demonstrates the importance of a simultaneous focus on the pulse of poetry – its rhythm, grammar and syntax. Manning bridges ostensibly mutually exclusive critical practices by combining Formalism's attention to textual and syntactical patterns with the political and historical contextualization of New Historicism and the theoretical sophistication and linguistic play of Poststructuralism. Additionally, she theorizes Transatlantic Romanticism by emphasizing the connotations, denotation and etymological roots of the prefix *trans*. As Romanticism moves *across* the Atlantic and is *translated* into different cultures, nations and regions along the Atlantic rim, it undergoes land and sea changes that are not fully accounted for by Bloomian influence theory. For instance, influence moves vertically in its Bloomian conception because it obeys an authorial hierarchy in which a young poet, an *ephebe*, strives to reach the height of his established predecessors. Manning posits a horizontal motion of influence as it moves *trans*atlantically and *trans*nationally by bridging the Atlantic. Although this essay primarily treats Wordsworth and American writers, such as Margaret Fuller, its conclusions have ramifications for all comparatist work on transatlantic literary relations and lay the groundwork for a new theory of transnational influence.

In 'The Wordsworthian Metamorphosis of Natty Bumppo' (Chapter 2), Richard Gravil examines the role Wordsworth's writing played in the development of James Fenimore Cooper as a novelist and the evolution of his most famous character, Natty Bumppo. Indeed, it takes Cooper's Natty

Bumppo two decades of reconfiguration to complete the transition from unconscious 'inmate of this active universe' to 'prophet of nature'. Those two decades – from 1823 to 1843 – were of course the ones in which Wordsworth's American reputation gradually attained ascendancy over Byron's. This essay traces this development, attending to Bumppo's final configuration (in *The Deerslayer* and *The Pathfinder*) as a figure who embodies the values of 'Tintern Abbey'. The essay also examines the debt owed to Burke's theories of the sublime and beautiful in this transition. Cooper utilizes the Burkean sublime to describe the vastness and ruggedness of an American landscape that was problematically made more sublime by its associations with American Indian removal. Gravil makes passing reference of Cooper's debt to Emerson and suggests that such unacknowledged borrowing is fair exchange. For in 'The American Scholar', Emerson had quite shamelessly usurped Cooper's prior role as an advocate of literary and cultural independence. Paradoxically and perhaps inevitably, the mantle of independence on both writers cloaks a figural dependence on *the* poet of 'National Independence and Liberty', and this essay argues that it is Wordsworth's influence that we must keep in mind in the construction of an American Romantic canon.

Bruce Graver's essay, 'Discord at Pennacook: Whittier and the Problem of American Picturesque' (Chapter 3), continues the discussion of how American writers attempted to adapt British aesthetics to American landscape. Particularly, Graver focuses on how John Greeenleaf Whittier uses conventions of the Picturesque to describe the landscape of his native New England. In 'The Bridal at Pennacook', Whittier examines the difficulty of mapping British poetic conventions onto an American landscape that is, he asserts, more beautiful than England but also more deeply imbued with a genocidal past. Like Wordsworth (whose 'Michael' is an important model for this poem), part of his interest is in finding ways to fit unusual-sounding place-names (Kearsarge, Winnepiseogee, Uncanoonuc, Pennacook) to the patterns of English metre. Since these are American Indian names, Whittier uses them to evoke the brutal conflicts between indigenous and European cultures that constitute so much of the early history of New England, and which were generated largely, he says, by Yankee greed. Whittier's aim is to preserve a native heritage that has all but disappeared (beyond place-names), and to alter the way in which picturesque tourists perceive natural beauty by reminding them of the violence that made their wealth and leisure possible. Wordsworth sought in 'Michael' to revise the picturesque by investing insignificant details of the landscape – insignificant at least to Gilpin – with profound moral significance; his means of doing so was narration rather than description. Similarly, Whittier uses his narrative to transform the way his tourists view picturesque landscape, but his American setting forces him to revise Wordsworth's revisions.

Continuing Richard Gravil's and Bruce Graver's essays concerned with Wordsworth, American landscape and race, and in line with Susan Manning's discussion of influence, Joel Pace's 'Transatlantic Gothic and Race: Wordsworth, Hawthorne, Poe, Chopin, Cable and Chesnutt' (Chapter 4) expands the geographical scope of Gravil and Graver's discussion by examining gothic's engagement with (and contribution to) pseudo-scientific discourse on race published on both sides of the Mason-Dixon line as well as the Atlantic. Tracing these authors' use of gothic conventions – such as ruined structures and the inclusion of an interpretive community that (re)frames the narrative – the essay argues that these elements buttress racial constructs that are responsible for a haunting guilt at the heart of the gothic tradition. Running a counter- (and complementary) narrative to reception histories that show the role played by Wordsworth's poetry in American reform movements, this essay examines alternative readings of the poet formed by communities of interpreters who were alive both to the notions of race that can be read into Wordsworth's verse and to Transcendentalist interpretations and appropriations of his work.[13] The essay uses the notion of interpretive communities to indicate the point where any attempt to trace a single narrative of the influence of Wordsworth on America fragments into directly opposed American interpretations of his poetry, each reading modifying the previous one until the poet's line of influence becomes lost in the complex web of the countless intertextual exchanges of which it was a part.

Adam Potkay, in 'Wordsworth and Bishop Doane: High-Church Romanticism on the Delaware' (Chapter 5), continues Pace's discussion by focusing on another community of interpreters who defined themselves in contradistinction to the Transcendentalists and Unitarians of Massachusetts: the Episcopalians of the Delaware valley. On 6 June 1851, Theodore Parker wrote:

> Wordsworth was a dear old granny, with a most hearty love of mankind, especially the least attractive portions of it – *beggars*, and *fools*, and Bishop Doane, who he thinks was a great and good man. Wordsworth heard him preach once at London; saw him at his house, and liked him much. If Wordsworth had lived a little in London, and felt the presence of some one who was manly and differed from him, it would have done him service.

Parker's derisive remarks concern George Washington Doane (1799–1859), second Episcopalian Bishop of New Jersey and founder of the early female seminary, St Mary's Hall, in 1837 (the year Mary Lyons established Mount Holyoke). Parker, Unitarian and urban, considered himself the very antithesis of the rural, High Church, Tractarian Bishop

Doane – and it is no surprise that the two men held, in their respective images, two very different versions of the value of Wordsworth. Bishop Doane made Wordsworth's poetry one of the bedrocks of his curriculum at St Mary's Hall: for example, his pupils were assigned compositions on Wordsworthian topics such as daffodils, 'the pansy at my feet', and clouds. Meanwhile, commencement addresses routinely exhorted graduates to conform to the model woman of Wordsworth's 'She was a phantom of delight'. This essay examines the historical phenomenon of Doane's High Church Romanticism in relation to both the more general late Victorian reception of Wordsworth (building on work done by Stephen Gill), and the biographical details of Doane's relationship with William and Christopher Wordsworth. (Doane spent the summer of 1841 at Oxford and London, and visited William at Rydal Mount.) Finally, it addresses the influence of Doane – as well as Henry Reed of the University of Pennsylvania – on Wordsworth's Ecclesiastical Sonnets, and the influence, in turn, of those poems on Doane's ecclesiology, and on his sense of the mission of St Mary's Hall.

Lance Newman's 'Henry David Thoreau as Wordsworthian Poet' (Chapter 6) revisits Massachusetts and builds on Potkay's examination of responses to the Wordsworth of Emerson and Parker by showing a critique from within: Thoreau's moving from underneath the shadow of Emerson's Wordsworthian Transcendentalism.[14] The appearance of Wordsworth's *Yarrow Revisited* (1835) sparked a flurry of reviews in American magazines, in which critics simultaneously called into existence and attempted to explain a sudden explosion of interest in the poet and his works. The Yarrow sequence may be read as exclusively concerned with uncontroversial observation of scenes of the Scottish border country. However, in New England, it was read for its bearing on the question of how the beleaguered Federalist élite should respond to both the increasing militancy of the new trade unions and the Jacksonian Democrats' ongoing occupation of Washington. Most élite New England readers, looking for a restoration of their social and political authority, were fascinated by Wordsworth's discovery of the schoolroom of natural republican sentiments in the rural Scottish landscape. Others disagreed strongly, arguing that he spoke not in the accents of a true 'spirit of democracy' but in those of a condescending Tory with a human face. The bourgeois radicals, especially those associated with the Transcendentalist movement faced a crucial problem: how to invent a self-definition that would allow them to critique the deepening class divisions in the new cities. They based their image of themselves on claims of a close relationship to nature. In this context, Wordsworth, the 'Poet of Nature', came to stand as the foremost example of the appropriate functions and demeanour of the cultural critic. It was in relation to this touchstone that the young Henry David Thoreau built his initial sense of himself as a poet. For ten years he worked with and against a distinctly Wordsworthian persona and poetics. Furthermore, the habits of thought that he acquired during those formative years strongly shaped his great prose narrative, *Walden*.

Continuing this volume's engagement with Wordsworth's influence on American poetry, Karen Karbiener's 'Intimations of Initation: Wordsworth, Whitman, and the emergence of *Leaves of Grass* (Chapter 7), like Newman's essay, examines the neglected early work of a major American author and places it on a continuum with the substantial autobiography (*Walden*, or in this instance 'Song of Myself') with which the author made his mark on American letters. Karbiener attributes, for the first time, a short piece in the *Brooklyn Daily Eagle* to Walt Whitman, and demonstrates how it shows an early and previously undiscovered debt to Wordsworth. In the preface to the first edition of *Leaves of Grass*, Whitman wrote of his literary beginnings: 'I continued, years ago, elaborating the plan of my poems and continued turning over that plan, and shifting it in my mind through many years (from the age of 28 to 35)'. At the earliest budding of *Leaves of Grass*, then, Whitman was at the peak of his journalistic career: from 1846 to 1848, he was the editor of the *Brooklyn Daily Eagle*. As such, Whitman basically served in every capacity, not only as printer and distributor but also as the writer for most of the paper's copy. The book reviews, poems, essays and articles that appear in the *Eagle* during this time thus serve as largely untapped sources of Whitman's poetic beginnings.

Careful to keep up appearances, expert in the art of concealment, Whitman led his audiences to believe that he travelled far and wide, that he sired illegitimate children, that he did not write those flattering 'anonymous' reviews of *Leaves of Grass*. Through his reticence regarding Wordsworthian matters, Whitman also managed to convince his readers that he lacked interest in, or even knowledge of, this formidable literary precursor. But is Whitman yet again 'far different' from what we have supposed, as he writes in 'Whoever You Are, Holding Me Now in Hand'? His stony silence may well have been his defence against the anxiety of influence, or soundproofing for a busy interior dialogue he maintained with Wordsworth. A young man aspiring to become the 'Adam' of American literature would certainly not want to facilitate the making of any connections or comparisons between the ageing English poet and himself. Perhaps, then, Whitman's omission of Wordsworth is even more telling than any direct mention of him might have been. This seems most true when one looks at the places where Wordsworth might have been mentioned, but is not – as in several of Whitman's pieces for the *Eagle*, in which he worked out ideas and styles he would use for the next five decades. For example, an *Eagle* sketch that clearly anticipates some of the philosophies espoused in 'Out of the

Cradle Endlessly Rocking' is actually a cleverly altered prose transcription of Wordsworth's 'We Are Seven'. Examinations of Whitman's early, covertly imitative works enable us to view his alleged 'originality' and his 'Americanness' from new perspectives, and to question whether there was another Preface to Whitman's 'Preface', a *Prelude* to his 'Song of Myself'.

Richard Brantley concludes the volume's treatment of American poetics with a discussion of a topic without which no examination of the influence of Wordsworth on American poetry would be complete. 'The Wordworthian Cast of Dickinson's Romantic Heritage' (Chapter 8) demonstrates how Dickinson's 'wise passiveness' makes her as much Wordsworth's prime legatee as, for instance, Whitman's 'self-reliance' makes him Emerson's. The naturally experiential 'world / Of all of us, the place in which, in the end, / We find our happiness, or not at all', joins with spiritually experiential 'moments in the being / Of the eternal Silence', to inform the synthesizing imagination of the Myth of Amherst, so that her eyes and ears become her spiritual sense. This natural/spiritual dialectic conditions the mysterious relationship between her external and internal experience.

At the heart of Dickinson's poetics, and consistent with such quotations from Wordsworth, there is an empirical/evangelical dialogue. This Anglo-American Romanticism seals the dynamic identity of her broadly experiential vision. Throughout this essay on eighteenth-and nineteenth-century Anglo-American cultural poetics, Brantley is concerned to show how Dickinson stands on broadly experiential ground common to British empiricism, Anglo-American evangelicalism and Wordsworthian Romanticism. Her contribution to the empirical/evangelical dialectic of Romantic Anglo-America finds its proper *locus classicus* in the poetry of Wordsworth, who nurtures her wisest tone, and perhaps even inspires her most optimistic import.

In 'Wordsworth, Bostonian Chivalry and the Uses of Art' (Chapter 9), Elizabeth Fay shifts our focus from the influence of Wordsworth's poetry on American cultural poetics to the influence of Wordsworth's prose, specifically the Preface to *Lyrical Ballads*, on Boston's architecture, artwork and institutional attempts to realize civic humanism. The late Victorian use of chivalry as translated into Boston's architectural/institutional forms reflects Ruskin's interpretation of the gothic, but begins earlier with the impetus of high art during the Romantic period to transform the chivalric code into civic humanism. Edwin Austin Abbey's 1901 mural sequence on the 'Quest for the Holy Grail' for the Book Delivery Room of the Boston Public Library and the stained glass of Harvard University's Sanders Theatre use chivalric narratives and emblems in public spaces dedicated to inspiring public-spirited individuals. Such spaces, palpably refined into male-oriented ones through such visual narratives, translate the viewer's internal drive of individualism into the external drive of civics through a chivalric spiritualization of the self. In doing so, these narratives carry out the high purpose of Wordsworth's 1802 Preface to the *Lyrical Ballads*, which is inherent in his theoretical defence of his poems. There, Wordsworth describes the character of the poet in knightly terms, and challenges the reader to interpret his medieval-inspired ballads as other than manly, public-spirited and spiritually elevating. The contract Wordsworth makes with his reader in the Preface mediates the social contract with the knight's vows to produce an obligation on the reader's part that raises him to a higher level of civic duty than the private act of reading and the detachment of the social contract normally convey. The reading performance of the public library is conducted under the auspices of this obligation, visually imposed, to read for the higher good. Moreover, one of the most important works that they are reading is the *Lyrical Ballads*, first published in America in 1802.

A century after the *Ballads* was printed in Philadelphia, Owen Wister published *The Virginian*. It has been estimated that during the first half of the twentieth century more Americans read this work than any other novel. In 'Home (at Grasmere and "On the Range"): Wordsworth and Owen Wister's *The Virginian*' (Chapter 10), James Butler notes that when queried by a stranger about his favourite poems, Wister listed a few poems which 'hit [him] most intimately and left the deepest marks'. These include Wordsworth's 'The world is too much with us' and 'The Daffodils' (unpublished letter, 10 July 1910). 'The world is too much with us' aptly describes the sentiments of Wister, one of the bluest of blue-blooded Philadelphia aristocrats, who – agreeing with Wordsworth that 'getting and spending we lay waste our powers' – felt truly happy only on extended trips away from the city into the wilds of Wyoming. Of man as he found him there, Wister wrote, 'It is not the dollars that played first fiddle with him ... [but] to be out of doors ... to enjoy independence of mind and spirit' ('Evolution of the Cow-Puncher', 1895). As in Wordsworth's 'Daffodils', Wister in *The Virginian* recreates not present reality but his memory of it: 'It is a vanished world. No journeys, save those which memory can take, will bring it to you now' (Preface to *The Virginian*).

Like Wordsworth's Preface to *Lyrical Ballads* and his 1801 letter to Charles James Fox, Wister's main theoretical statement – 'The Evolution of the Cow-Puncher' (1895) – celebrates rural people and the language they speak. Wister's palpable anxiety over what his social class had become ('merchanting themselves upwards to the level of family portraits and the cut-glass finish') finds relief through fellow feeling not with the well-off but with the heroic common man ('though rude and rough, though life's forces run over the edge of their bowl ... yet place before them a poor man who needed their aid, a defenseless woman, they melted into sympathy and charity at once'). 'Men who do not wear fine cloaths can feel deeply' argues Wordsworth, and Wister asserts the same for those who 'put aside their ... New York suits for tribal dress'. Equally, the language spoken by these Wisterian equivalents of the Lake District 'statesmen' is not to be denigrated: 'Ordinary words and phrases, freshened to novelty by the cow-puncher's wits, show his unpremeditated act of brevity, varying in aptness, but in imagination constant'. Wister's long, appreciative discussion of Western diction concludes that the evocative language of the cow-punchers – some of the words perhaps 'of long standing and archaic repute' – has an eloquence which only 'that prudery which we carry as a burden along with the benefits of academic training' prevents from finding more general use.

Wister married his cousin in 1898, shortly before he began assembling his Western stories in *The Virginian*. To these adventure stories he added a well-born New England 'schoolmarm' and love interest, Molly Stark Wood. Wister's wife Molly Channing Wister, a civic leader of national significance, also became one of the first women to serve on the Philadelphia School Board; when she died while giving birth in 1913, she was praised by the Governor of Pennsylvania as 'a great leader of educational thought'. Her educational theories pervade *The Virginian*, and a national tradition still survives among Wister descendants that she was an active collaborator on the book (as she definitely was in shaping the 1903 stage version). There can be no doubt, however, about the source of Molly Channing Wister's educational theories in the writings of her great-grandfather William Ellery Channing, author, proto-Transcendentalist, and 'apostle of Unitarianism'. Channing acquired a copy of *The Excursion* shortly after publication and 'never read anything but Shakespeare more'. Finding in Wordsworth 'a fountain of spiritual life', Channing ranked Wordsworth and Coleridge as the principal poets of the age, visited Wordsworth at Rydal Mount in 1822 (producing a written account of their conversation), and corresponded extensively with the poet. Another way in which Romanticism in general, and Wordsworth in particular, influenced *The Virginian* was therefore through the educational theories bequeathed by William Ellery Channing to his talented great-granddaughter Molly Channing Wister.

Like Butler's chapter on Wister, Matthew Scott's essay, 'An Ethics of Wonder and the Cure of Poetry: Wordsworth, William James and the American Reader' (Chapter 11), draws connections between the nineteenth- and twentieth-century American reception of Wordsworth. In keeping with the interdisciplinary and international focus of this volume, Scott examines the extent to which present-day discussions of sympathy such as those of Geoffrey Hartman and Susan Sontag can be be usefully read alongside nineteenth-century debates such as those articulated in Wordsworth's 'The Old Cumberland Beggar' and William James's Wordsworth-influenced essays on philosophy and psychology. James, like so many other American readers, read Wordsworth's poetry as an elixir of mental health, as a salve for life's most serious emotional wounds. As such Wordsworth's poetry is linked to a sense of healing through sympathetic acts of imagination. Scott's essay also examines the failure of sympathy, as is evinced in the inability of the speaker in 'We Are Seven' to comprehend the child's consolatory notion of afterlife. This volume's discussion of transatlantic literary, cultural and political relations is concluded with consideration of present-day Anglo-American politics and failure or near complete absence of our own capacity for sympathy.

This volume hopes to show that the political relevance of nineteenth-century America's Wordsworth was transmuted into fresh debates that emerged as the century progressed and readers of Wordsworth turned interpretation to their own ends. His poems were as much a source of strength to the mid-century New England Federalist élite as they were to certain feminists; they were worried by writers concerned with the Native American question, and were a source of inspiration to the growing environmental movement and to educationalists. Meanwhile, they provided guides for Emerson, in search of a national canon, and were to be models of a foregoing tradition to the great innovators, such as Henry David Thoreau, Walt Whitman and Emily Dickinson. These essays also hope to promote a sense of dialogue that may help us to understand how such a writer can be seen to be key to the construction of a literary canon in America, while also exerting a wide-ranging and indirect influence upon education, theology and counter-cultural movements like feminism and environmentalism.

It has been the result of the partiality of literary history that we have tended to see Wordsworth as simply a literary forefather and nothing more, despite his obvious importance as such. The culture industry that lionized Wordsworth at home and abroad has been, we will argue, the model upon which America has based the construction of its own literary canon. And yet, even as we rightly challenge the stability of 'the canon', we continue to uncover the (not wholly unproblematic) influence of Wordsworth in unexpected and previously unimportant areas. This sense of pervasive influence is a result of the high profile enjoyed by Wordsworth's reputation by virtue of his marketability. However, the very strength of his literary reputation transcends this, and the human themes to which he addresses himself as a writer are themselves universals that have become embedded in the American cultural consciousness. The field that comparative studies opens up is relatively new in terms of the many undocumented connections (in editions, letters and reviews) that exist in Anglo-American literary relations with reference to Wordsworth in America. This study is not meant to be the final word on the subject but, rather, it hopes to offer points of contact, contestation, intersection and departure.

Notes

1. Harold Bloom, *The Anxiety of Influence* (Oxford: Oxford UP, 1970); *A Map of Misreading* (Oxford: Oxford UP, 1975); *The Western Canon* (London: Macmillan, 1995).
2. Stephen Gill, *Wordsworth and the Victorians* (Oxford: Oxford UP, 1998), 9.
3. Annabel Newton, *Wordsworth in Early American Criticism* (Chicago, IL: University of Chicago Press, 1928).
4. See John Beer, 'William Ellery Channing's Visit to the Lake Poets', *Review of English Studies* 42, no. 166 (May 1991): 212–26; David Bromwich, 'From Wordsworth to Emerson', *Romantic Revolutions: Criticism and Theory*, eds. Kenneth Johnston, Gilbert Chaitin, Karen Hanson, Herbert Marks (Bloomington, IN: Indiana UP, 1990); Alan G, Hill, 'Wordsworth and His American Friends', *Bulletin of Research in the Humanities* 81 (Summer 1978): 146–60; John L. Mahoney, 'The Rydal Mount Ladies' Boarding School: A Wordsworthian Episode in America', *Cultural Interactions in the Romantic Age*, ed. Gregory Maertz (Albany, NY: State University of New York, 1998); Mark Reed, 'Contacts with America' in *William Wordsworth 1770–1970*, ed. Nesta Clutterbuck (Grasmere: Trustees of Dove Cottage, 1970) and 'Wordsworth and the Americans: Two New Letters and Visits', *Emerson Society Quarterly* 33 (1963): 70–2; David Simpson, 'Wordsworth in America' in *The Age of William Wordsworth: Critical Essays on the Romantic Tradition*, ed. Kenneth R. Johnston and Gene W. Ruoff (Jersey City, NJ: Rutgers UP, 1987). For more on Wordsworth in America, see David Bonnell Green, 'William Wordsworth and Lydia Huntley Sigourney', *New England Quarterly* 37 (December 1964): 527–31; Scott Harshbarger, 'Transatlantic Transcendentalism: The Wordsworth-Peabody-Hawthorne Connection', *Wordsworth Circle* 21, no. 3 (Summer 1990): 123–6; John Michael, 'Emerson's Chagrin: Benediction and Exhortation in *Nature* and *Tintern Abbey*', *Modern Language Notes* 101, no. 5 (December 1986): 1067–85; John Brookes Moore, 'Emerson on Wordsworth', *Publications of the Modern Language Association* 41 (1926), 179–92; Margaret Neussendorfer, 'Elizabeth Peabody to William Wordsworth: Eight Letters, 1825–1845', *Studies in the American Renaissance* (1984): 181–211; Joel Pace, 'Wordsworth, the *Lyrical Ballads*, and Literary and Social Reform in Nineteenth-Century America', *Romantic Circles Praxis Series* (Fall 1999): n. pag. Online. Internet: http://www.rc.umd.edu/praxis/lyrical/pace/wordsworth.html, and '"Lifted to Genius"?: Wordsworth in Emerson's Nurture and Nature', *Symbiosis* 2, no. 2 (October 1998): 126–40, and '"Gems of a Soft and Permanent Luster": The Reception and Influence of the *Lyrical Ballads* in America', *Romanticism on the Net* (February 1998): n. pag. Online. Internet: http://www. erudit.org/revue/ron/1998/v/n9/005782ar.html; Roberta F. Weldon, 'Hawthorne's Old Apple-Dealer and Wordsworth's Leechgatherer', *Nathaniel Hawthorne Journal* (1977): 249–59.
5. Lawrence Buell, 'Postcolonial Anxiety in Classic US Literature' in *Postcolonial Theory and the United States*, ed. Amritjit Singh and Peter Schmidt (Jackson,

MS: University Press of Mississippi, 2000); Leon Chai, *The Romantic Foundations of the American Renaissance* (Ithaca, NY: Cornell UP, 1987); Perry Miller, 'Thoreau in the Context of International Romanticism', *New England Quarterly* 24 (June 1961): 147–59; Tony Tanner, 'Notes for a Comparison Between American and European Romanticism', *Diverging Parallels: A Comparison of American and European Thought and Action*, ed. A.N.J. Hollander (Leiden: Brill, 1971). For more on transatlantic studies, see Janet Beer and Bridget Bennet, eds. *Special Relationships: Anglo-American Affinities and Antagonisms, 1854–1936* (Manchester and New York: Manchester UP, 2002); Michael Durey, *Transatlantic Radicals and the Early American Republic* (Lawrence: University Press of Kansas, 1997); Stephen Fender, *Sea Changes: British Emigration and American Literature* (Cambridge: Cambridge UP, 1992); Heidi Slettedahl Macpherson and Will Kaufman eds, *Transatlantic Studies* (Lanham, NY, and Oxford: University Press of America, 2000) and *New Perspectives in Transatlantic Studies* (Lanham, NY, and Oxford: University Press of America, 2002); James McKusick, *Green Writing: Romanticism and Ecology* (New York, NY: St Martin's, 2000); Christopher Mulvey, *Transatlantic Manners* (Cambridge: Cambridge UP, 1990); James Raven, *London Booksellers and American Customers* (Columbia, SC: University of South Carolina Press, 2002); W.M. Verhoeven and Beth Dolan Kautz, eds. *Revolutions and Watersheds: Transatlantic Dialogues, 1775–1815* (Amsterdam and Atlanta: Rodopi, 1999) and W.M. Verhoeven, ed., *Revolutionary Histories: Transatlantic Cultural Nationalism, 1775–1815* (Basingstoke and New York, NY: Palgrave, 2002).

6. Robert Weisbuch, *Atlantic Double-Cross: American Literature and British Influence in the Age of Emerson* (Chicago, IL: University of Chicago Press, 1986).
7. Richard Brantley, *Coordinates of Anglo-American Romanticism* (Gainesville, FL: University Press of Florida, 1993) and *Anglo-American Antiphony: The Late Romanticism of Tennyson and Emerson* (Gainesville, FL: University Press of Florida, 1994); William Keach, 'A Transatlantic Romantic Century', *European Romantic Review* 11, no. 1 (Winter 2000): 31–4.
8. Paul Giles, *Transatlantic Insurrections: British Culture and the Formation of American Literature, 1730–1860* (Philadelphia, PA: University of Pennsylvania Press, 2001); Paul Gilroy, *The Black Atlantic* (Cambridge, MA: Harvard UP, 1993); Richard Gravil, *Romantic Dialogues: Anglo-American Continuities, 1776–1862* (New York, NY: St Martin's, 2000); Susan Manning, *Fragments of Union: Making Connections in Scottish-American Writing* (Basingstoke and New York, NY: Palgrave, 2002).
9. Michel Foucault, 'Nietzsche, Genealogy, History', trans. Donald F. Bouchard and Sherry Simon, in *Language, Counter-Memory, Practise: Selected Essays and Interviews*, ed. Donald F. Bouchard (Ithaca, NY: Cornell UP, 1977), 139–64.
10. Introduction, 'Transatlantic Romanticism', a special issue of *Romanticism on the Net*, eds Joel Pace, Lance Newman and Chris Koenig-Woodyard (forthcoming, 2004).
11. David Richter, *The Progress of Romance: Literary Historiography and the Gothic Novel* (Ohio State UP, 1996), 117–18.
12. These chapter summaries were written in conjunction with the author of the chapter being described.
13. This essay is meant to complement and build upon the following essays: Joel Pace, 'Wordsworth and America: Reception and Reform' in *The Cambridge Companion to Wordsworth*, ed. Stephen Gill (Cambridge: Cambridge UP, 2003)

and 'A Publisher's Politics: *Lyrical Ballads* (Philadelphia, 1802)', *Symbiosis* 7, no. 1 (April 2003): 35–55.

14. Newman also builds upon his own published scholarship: 'Wordsworth in America and the Nature of Democracy', *New England Quarterly*, 72, no. 4 (December 1999): 517–38.

1
'Grounds for Comparison': The Place of Style in Transatlantic Romanticism

Susan Manning[1]

I

Consider two extracts: the first canonical, from one of the foundational poems of British Romanticism:

> like a roe
> I bounded o'er the mountains, by the sides
> Of the deep rivers, and the lonely streams,
> Wherever nature led; more like a man
> Flying from something that he dreads, than one
> Who sought the thing he loved ...
> ....
> The sounding cataract
> Haunted me like a passion: the tall rock,
> The mountain, and the deep and gloomy wood,
> Their colours and their forms, were then to me
> An appetite: a feeling and a love,
> That had no need of a remoter charm,
> By thought supplied, or any interest
> Unborrowed from the eye. – That time is past,
> And all its aching joys are now no more,
> And all its dizzy raptures ...
> ....
> For I have learned
> To look on nature, not as in the hour
> Of thoughtless youth, but hearing oftentimes
> The still, sad music of humanity,
> Nor harsh nor grating, though of ample power
> To chasten or subdue. And I have felt

> A presence that disturbs me with the joy
> Of elevated thoughts. (*LB*, 'Tintern Abbey', 68–96)

The second comes from Margaret Fuller's *Summer on the Lakes* (1844):

> [A]ll great expressions, which, on a superficial survey, seems [*sic*] so easy as well as so simple, furnishes, after a while, to the faithful observer its own standard by which to appreciate it. Daily these proportions widened and towered more and more upon my sight, and I got, at last, a proper foreground for these sublime distances. Before coming away, I think I really saw the full wonder of the scene. After awhile it so drew me into itself as to inspire an undefined dread, such as I never knew before, such as may be felt when death is about to usher us into a new existence. The perpetual trampling of the waters seized my sense. I felt that no other sound, however near, could be heard, and would start and look behind me for a foe. I realized the identity of that mood of nature in which these waters were poured down with such absorbing force, with that in which the Indian was shaped on the same soil. For continually upon my mind came, unsought and unwelcome, images, such as never haunted it before, of naked savages stealing behind me with uplifted tomahawks; again and again this illusion recurred, and even after I had thought it over, and tried to shake it off, I could not help starting and looking behind me.[2]

Each of these pieces records a tour made through the writer's own country at the boundaries of familiarity (figured in topographical terms, respectively, as the Wye valley on the border where England meets Wales, and Niagara, the outer edge where America, in a sublime geologic disjunction, becomes Canada). Personal testimony and the representation of memory work to dramatize poetic presence across both space and time. Generically 'Tintern Abbey' is located in a culturally authoritative British loco-descriptive tradition which includes works like Denham's 'Cooper's Hill' and Thomson's 'Summer'. It responds to the conventional prompting to piety of the backdrop of the ruined artefact in the landscape, provoking reflections on humanity and mortality which recall parallel moments like Johnson's meditation on Iona in his *Journey to the Western Islands of Scotland*, while the measured tread of its blank verse inherits both power and harmony from Milton. These associations locate the poem's self-reflexivity within authoritative frames of reference.

Fuller's words also address the educative interpenetration of nature and consciousness, but she construes the personal voice in different registers: generically hybrid, this account is formally an experimental mix of travel narrative, autobiography, the interpenetration of cultural- and self-analysis. It is deeply inflected by Wordsworthian modes of perception (the passage preceding the section quoted above echoes 'Tintern Abbey' quite explicitly, in images of 'haunting', a 'secondary music' and a 'cataract' which 'seems to seize its own rhythm and sing it over again, so that the ear and soul are roused by a double vibration'). So the 'great expression' seems to be as much Wordsworth's as Niagara: in fact, as this section opens, 'Nature and Wordsworth' are, as it were, 'the same'. The seeming inevitability of a descriptive collocation pulled by the power of the poetic forebear recedes, however, before a spectacle so toweringly self-authenticating that it furnishes 'its own standard' of appreciation. The observer has to find a different rhetorical vantage point from which to view the 'full wonder of the scene' at its 'proper' distance.

This is a conventional enough – indeed, in relation to Niagara, perhaps an obligatory – gesture in the aesthetics of sublimity, with due attention to point of view; its antecedents include Thomas Jefferson's description of the Shenandoah river driving a cleft through the Allegheny mountains.[3] But it also, here, seems to offer itself as a study in the anxiety of influence. Its haunting is not the benign voice of Nature exercising her pedagogic guardianship over the 'heart that loves her', a 'presence' whose disturbance is joy and elevation, but an undefined 'dread' of an ancient, inimical uncanny which takes hold of the imagination. A violent image of collective cultural guilt disrupts the fiction of presence. In this respect, the passage is much more like another Wordsworthian episode, composed around the same time as 'Tintern Abbey', but which Fuller could not have known:

an act of stealth
And troubled pleasure, nor without the voice
Of mountain-echoes did my boat move on ...
I dipped my oars into the silent lake,
And, as I rose upon the stroke, my boat
Went heaving through the water like a swan;
When, from behind that craggy steep till then
The horizon's bound, a peak, black and huge,
As if with voluntary power instinct
Upreared its head. I struck and struck again,
And, growing still in stature the grim shape
Towered up between me and the stars, and still,
For so it seemed, with purpose of its own
And measured motion like a living thing,
Strode after me ...
after I had seen
That spectacle, for many days, my brain
Work'd with a dim and undetermin'd sense
Of unknown modes of being; in my thoughts
There was a darkness, call it solitude
Or blank desertion ...

huge and mighty Forms that do not live
Like living men moved slowly through the mind
By day and were the trouble of my dreams. (*TP*, 1850, I, 361–426)

Comparison of the 'Tintern Abbey' passage with Fuller's might fairly confidently be pursued a lot further than my few initial gestures, within an enabling story of 'Wordsworth in America' based on priority, influence, the cultural authority of the great Romantic impressed on the fledgling literature of the 'new nation'. I am not going to pursue it further because my purpose is to point out something about what *kind* of exercise it is, to bring out its implicit assumptions. The second pairing, with the passage from the 1798–99 *Prelude* – at least as interesting in the continuities of mood and vocabulary – immediately brings the whole exercise into question with the knowledge that it was not published until 1850.

The juxtaposition of these passages is undeniably suggestive, but none of the moves I have made so far appears to make much impact on the confluences and disturbances that particularize the comparison. In the same vein, it is hard to imagine Nathaniel Hawthorne's very 'American' (whatever one might mean by that) masterpiece, *The Scarlet Letter*, having been written in England or Scotland by an English or a Scottish writer: but both its plot and omnipresent ethos of Victorian cultural and sexual mores are strikingly similar to George Eliot's *Adam Bede* or J.G. Lockhart's *Adam Blair*. In each case the *embodiment* ('style') puts their reader in a frame of reference at once similar, and disconcerting, discordant. Written in the same language, the novels clearly emerge from different cultural and discursive worlds. Oscar Wilde described the Americans and the British as separated by their common language; negotiation between them has involved the treasonable as well as the deferential possibilities of translation.[4] By the 1840s 'English' used 'Americanly' was a sufficiently different idiom for textual comparison necessarily to involve acknowledgement of difference-in-similarity. The national identity politics enshrined in such foundational works as F.O. Matthiessen's *American Renaissance* (1941) offer exceptionalist readings of American Romanticism that were part of the intellectual foundation for American Studies. These assumptions are now being challenged by the pluralities of 'Transatlantic Studies': multicultural, multi-focused, multi-centred.[5] Taking the example of 'Wordsworth's' presence in the prose of Emerson and Margaret Fuller, in this chapter I argue for the place of stylistic analysis in a contemporary account of what Harry Levin some years ago called the 'grounds for comparison' between British and American Romanticisms.[6]

'Comp. Lit'. used to be based in 'influence studies' of the very empirical kind that was residually at work in my rudimentary analysis of 'Tintern Abbey' and *Summer on the Lakes*. The presuppositions, models and expectations of the discipline were initially drawn from the Romantic cultural nationalism of northern Europe; the reflections on literature and nationhood of Goethe, Herder and de Staël assumed pre-eminence.[7] According to George Steiner, institutional location within Modern Languages departments fostered a base in philology and translation studies, and assumptions about the relationship between language-use and 'national expression'. It was also highly idealistic: in the nineteenth century, Comparative Literature characteristically focused on identification of universal themes (usually based on classical cultural models), to demonstrate the parochialism of national boundaries. Indeed, there are interesting readings of Fuller as translator of Goethe, acolyte of Beethoven and commentator on Italian politics, to be made in this context. A preoccupation with transience and exile derived from its early proponents' scholarly marginality: often refugees, often Jews (and in Fuller's case, as a woman), they were outsiders in academic contexts which questioned the standing of their work.[8] In such a frame, certain 'facts' of literary history would assume enormous importance, notably the work of translators, travellers, cultural ambassadors between 'national traditions'. Influence was, more often than not, taken to be demonstrable, and self-evident, on the basis of library borrowings, citations, reviews, or other empirical forms of 'literary relation'. Despite its greater theoretical complexity, Harold Bloom's idea of 'poetic misprision' subsequently continued these suppositions in its acceptance of the generative importance of priority.[9]

The 'influence' story assumes hierarchical or incorporative forms of connection that answer to the political and cultural assumptions of imperialism, in which a dominant (prior) position exerts power and imposes uniformity on a subdued other – a very 'Wordsworthian' story, in some respects.[10] The ground has since been re-colonized in the name of 'intertextuality', which at its loosest becomes a kind of licence to print connections: abandoning causality without reimagining the grounds for comparison, it may amount to little more than 'influence' in the absence of documentary proof. Its rejection of hierarchical, causally based relationships which privilege one pole of the comparison over another (temporally, structurally, politically or otherwise) in favour of a literary history of 'meshing systems' does, however, offer some promise.[11] It is the nearest thing we currently have to a model that allows these transatlantic relations to be held in parallel rather than enforcing a subordinating hierarchy of precedence or master-narrative on them – but it has not, so far, effectively explored the possibilities for specificity offered by stylistic analysis.

On the contrary, loss of confidence in the adequacy of the 'influence' story of comparativism has tended to foster mistrust of detailed textual work across the board. Most recent transatlantic studies have conformed to the generic conventions of cultural history, where texts are analysed in terms of context and situation, or deconstructed to 'reveal' (the term is itself revealing) the ideological predeterminations of form. One can point immediately to three difficulties with treating style as exclusively the *product* of ideology: firstly, it neglects or undervalues the technical aspects of expression which characterize what we understand by 'the literary'; secondly, it locates 'meaning' in the superior heuristic capacities of the interpreter: choices in language, form, genre, intention all become fodder for commentary (whose presuppositions may themselves remain unexamined) which takes to itself the prerogative of 'uncovering' the presence of context within text; thirdly (and to my mind this is perhaps the most fundamental objection) it fails to take account of the provisionality of all judgement in relation to the playfulness, the excess of affect over extractable content that makes literature: the way readers generate meanings *across* words, not inside them, as though they were nuts to be cracked in order to give up their goodness. The literariness of literary texts is precisely the aspect of them that resists grand narratives, big comparisons, abstractable ideas; it is expressed beautifully in a moment in Toni Morrison's *Beloved* where the coming together of Sethe and Paul D. is registered as a confluence of narratives: no big symbolic meanings, no promises for the future; just 'He laid his story next to hers'.[12] This offers the possibility of meaning as transitive, embodied in utterance, particular to context.

Transatlantic studies have not, perhaps, hitherto been very good at acknowledging this compoundedness. They tend to obscure both distinctions between 'literary' and 'non-literary' texts and – more importantly – the constantly renegotiated relation between language and extra-linguistic realities: 'truth', 'the real', 'thought', 'meaning'. This is not simply the proper stamping-ground of philosophy and linguistics; those who map and theorize the complexities of cultural confluence are also – of necessity – readers, whose judgements are, consciously or otherwise, formed in response to the inter-subjective effects of style. Transatlantic studies offer an opportunity to revive and extend the study of *écriture*, the interaction between the rhetorical artifices of style and the historically specific possibilities of language use in time and across space that Roland Barthes called 'form considered as a human intention and thus linked to the great crises of History'.[13]

The idea that style has a central place in transatlantic comparison need not, then, entail an atavistic return to Formalism or New Criticism or any other expression of the convenient belief that the aesthetic is a separate category impervious to the cultural and political pressures that bear on other kinds of writing. There is no reason why a particularized attention to style could not incorporate the general and theoretical insights of cultural analysis – gender, class, race, education and so on – and, indeed, acknowledge that the study of style is itself a historically and culturally bound practice, that descriptive and interpretative acts are effectively inseparable.[14]

Returning to the question of what makes *Summer on the Lakes* 'like' 'Tintern Abbey' or *The Prelude*'s boating episode, and yet manifestly working in different ways, we find it to be an issue with a long genealogy. From 1776 onwards (and arguably even before) American, and indeed British, polemicists discussed what could possibly constitute distinctively 'American' writing: topography, language, democratic institutions, modern urban life and commerce, the Puritan inheritance, were only some of the possibilities canvassed. At one level, style and form did not really become an issue in this debate until the Democratic period of the late 1830s and 1840s when large-scale immigration and a new kind of consciousness of regional differences began to replace a programmatic Republicanism. In literary-historical terms, it coincides with the belated advent of American Romanticism. At another, style was implicit in all versions of the discussion: the 'national accent' was an elusive but vital element to track down. 'Much has been said', wrote Poe in the *Broadway Journal* in 1845, 'about the necessity of maintaining a proper *nationality* in American Letters; but what this nationality *is* ... has never been distinctly understood. That an American should confine himself to American themes, or even prefer them, is rather a political than a literary idea – and at best is a questionable point'.[15] For Poe, the only terrain of writing is the a-location of what Steiner has more recently called 'Extraterritoriality'.[16]

What, then, can be said about the meaning of 'a literary idea' in a transatlantic context? 'Idea', as Lionel Trilling pointed out, 'in one of its early significations exactly means form'.[17] A 'literary idea' as the confluence of two emotions is necessarily the product of style, as much as of ideology. If style is ideology, ideology is also style. But there is no need to take refuge in tautology: a powerful pragmatic argument for returning to the study of style at least in nineteenth-century transatlantic studies is the evidence that for anglophone Americans, reading and writing were inescapably transnational and transatlantic phenomena and that both British and American writers themselves attempted to account for the way in which language translated into new contexts generated new effects primarily in stylistic terms. American literary Romanticism, like the foundational phase of Comparative Literature, was predicated on the condition articulated by Julia Kristeva's 'foreigner', who 'feels strengthened by the distance that detaches him from the others as it does from himself and gives him the lofty sense not so much of holding the truth but of making it and himself relative while others fall victim to the ruts of monovalency', and imbricated with desire to develop a national voice in relation to and distinction from British-ness.[18] English writers were described, admiringly or ironically, for what Hawthorne called their 'beef-and-ale' solidity.[19] 'The Custom House' preface to *The Scarlet Letter* is pervaded by displaced echoes of Dickens and Trollope; how could it *not* be, in the work of one struggling to make a living as a professional author in America in the absence of international copyright, and against competition from established English novelists whose already successful works could be bought cheaply in pirated editions by American readers?

On the other side of the Atlantic, Thomas Carlyle registered the strangeness of Emerson's style in his descriptions of it as, variously, redolent of the thin atmosphere on a mountain-top and as '*a bag of duck-shot* held together by canvas'.[20] The *Edinburgh Review*, in its turn, identified in American writing a 'curious intermixture ... of extreme homeliness and flatness, with a sort of turbulent and bombastic elevation'; variants on the indictment of indecorum reappear in reviews of American poetic epics, and attempts to come to terms with the stylistic extravagances of *Moby-Dick*.[21] 'English', by contrast, was characterized by its stylistic *normality*: Robert Southey declared magisterially in the *Quarterly Review* in 1809 that 'Dwight has failed because he imitated bad models, and Barlow because he formed a bad style for himself'.[22] Culture wars are also style wars. In mid-nineteenth-century transatlantic comparisons, cultural politics and discussions of style developed a compounded vocabulary of relations and departures. The interaction of the transatlantic and Transcendental perspectives offers not only (as Paul Giles has recently suggested) a way of re-assessing 'the prevailing erasure of a British cultural matrix', but also the possibility of reading 'influence' itself as a relational rather than as a hierarchical or prioritizing event based on temporal antecedence (Giles, 3).

At least as far back as the early seventeenth-century Puritan conversion narratives, the physical crossing of the Atlantic itself was the overwhelming, compounded, agent and image of defamiliarization – that endlessly re-invented and metaphorized sea-change, translation reified. The crossing itself is the important bit, and some dictionary definitions help to clarify it: '*Transeo, transire*: to go over, cross, pass over'; '*Transitio* (from *transeo*): A going across, passing over'; and, particularly, *Translatio*: a transferring, handing over – passing the baton, as in culture.[23] In 1782, the outcome of the Revolutionary war which would establish the separate existence of America still uncertain, Thomas Jefferson suggested some 'doubt ... whether nature has enlisted herself as a cis- or trans-Atlantic partisan'.[24] 'Nature' here does not yet – would it ever, quite, in America? – carry the full Wordsworthian prosopopeia unchanging of value ('Nature never did betray the heart that loved her'); 'she' is not a politically neutral, but a movable, transitive force, whose endorsement will be decisive in the conflict. Process, not state, is at issue. Jefferson's 'doubt' embeds the political and moral questions surrounding the patriot case within a much older rhetorical formula: the classical trope of *translatio studii et imperii*, which decreed that virtues flee a decadent civilization for a simpler, regenerate one. The Latin phrase encapsulates a rationale for temporal or spatial translation of cultural and political legitimacy: Norman kings, for example, invoked the *translatio imperii* trope to authorize the transfer of power from the Classical civilizations to the French, and thence to England. They devised the foundational myth of King Brutus of Troy, who instituted the kingdom of 'Britain' (Jefferson became very interested in this story when he sought an appropriate name and official Seal for the new nation which, in a new phase of the *translatio*, was to inherit British imperial grandeur).[25] The trope cross-linked originality – newness – and authority; it encompassed linguistic translation, too, understood as skilful weaving of recognized (authoritative) patterns and elements into a new web of relationships, a carpet with a fresh *figura*.[26]

Eighteenth-century observers of shifting relationships between Europe and her transatlantic colonies renewed the assumption of the *translatio* that civilization consistently migrates from east to west. Its most famous eighteenth-century expression is George Berkeley's poem 'On the Prospect of Planting Arts and Learning in America', which transposes time and space, mapping the rise and fall of empires onto the movement of European migration:

> There shall be sung another golden age,
> The rise of empire and of arts,
> The good and great inspiring epic rage,
> The wisest heads and noblest hearts.
>
> Not such as Europe breeds in her decay; ...
>
> Westward the course of empire takes its way;
> The four first acts already past,
> A fifth shall close the drama with the day;
> Time's noblest offspring is the last.[27]

This is the thinking behind Jefferson's revolutionary 'doubt': *has* 'Nature' made the transatlantic crossing, to seal the victory for America and smooth the transport of empire and cultural authority? The crossing here clearly implies the furtherance of imperial hierarchy and subordinative relation.

An outcome necessarily in question in 1782 could be presented as an inevitability by 1837, when Ralph Waldo Emerson delivered his Phi Beta Kappa Address 'The American Scholar', which opens with a sweeping transitive panorama from Ancient Greece to the medieval troubadours, and from modern Europe to the here-and-now of America. The most striking feature of this address, though, is its transformation of the question of influence ('Nature' is its source, Wordsworth is acknowledged in the expression), which privileges origin and priority, into a spatialized envisioning of relationships:

> The first in time and the first in importance of the influences upon the mind is that of nature ... [the American Scholar] must settle its value in

> his mind. What is nature to him? There is never a beginning, there is never an end, to the inexplicable continuity of this web of God, but always circular power returning into itself.[28]

'The American Scholar' initiates a stylistics of comparison conceptualized laterally, horizontally, anticipating by 150 years Julia Kristeva's term 'transposition', which 'specifies that the passage from one signifying system to another demands a new articulation ... of enunciative and denotative positionality'.[29] 'Transatlantic' and 'Transcendental' are semantically imbricated through the common crossing root 'trans-'; in Emerson's writing a much older tradition of rhetorical analysis acquired new associations: the stylistic ramifications of a single trope pervade American Romanticism. It has implications not only for the particular comparison of American and British Romanticism instantiated in the extracts from Fuller and Wordsworth, but perhaps – given the undeniably post-Romantic cast of all American (if not of all modern) writing – some potential for a wider stylistics of comparison based in 'thinking across'.

In order to understand what is at once 'Romantic' and 'American' about Emerson's prose, we might look to some frequently quoted lines from Wordsworth's early play, *The Borderers* (1797):

> Action is transitory, a step, a blow –
> The motion of a muscle – this way or that –
> 'Tis done – and in the after vacancy
> We wonder at ourselves like men betray'd.
> Suffering is permanent, obscure and dark,
> And has the nature of infinity.[30]

Two things stand out: the defining significance of the transitional 'moment', the hinge of before and after in which consciousness shifts from one 'state' to another; and the definitive solidity of the insight's embodiment: the heavy iamb ''Tis done', set apart by line-break and advanced caesura, the Miltonic stresses which *The Prelude* would later lighten and vary; the end-stopping of thought and sentence with that intransigent 'infinity'. It is a simplification, but perhaps not a distortion, to suggest that transitoriness is held firmly in place not only by form, but by idea. Given the underlying Idealism of Wordsworth's thought, it can hardly be fortuitous to find Emerson re-working the transitive function of language in his later essay on Plato (published the year of Wordsworth's death, 1850). 'Poetic creativeness', he writes, 'is not found in staying at home, nor yet in travelling, but in transitions from one to the other, which must therefore be managed to present as much transitional surface as possible'. This 'transitional surface' is a 'command of two elements', a fluid movement between things and thought, accomplished by 'an object or a symbol'. For

Emerson, Plato's 'things used as language' is the very medium of creativity (*Collected Works*, IV, 32).

The Latin *translatio* is, in Greek, *metaphora* (*meta*: over, *phereia*: to carry). In Rhetoric, the figure of metaphor traditionally embodied the 'handing across or over' of meaning. George Puttenham's *Art of English Poesie* (1589), for example, defined it as 'an inuersion of sence by transport'.[31] According to Puttenham, poets employ 'the figure of transport' either through need – a lack in our descriptive range – or for pleasure, the 'transport of delight'; he regards it as a particularly treacherous trope, a stealthy insinuator of covert meaning, whose *jouissance* is achieved in the tension between formal constraint and semantic possibility (Puttenham, 148–9).[32] Metaphor's peculiar double status is an expression, and an embodiment, of 'things used as thought'; it is a constitutive linking structure which moves away from the centrifugal or hierarchical towards the relational, from position to transition.

Metaphors are tools for thinking with: the transference between things and thought they accomplish (the *translatio*) is available for nation self-articulation that maps the temporal axis of historical destiny (the verticality of influence) onto spatial form, what Emerson in the Plato essay calls 'transitional surface'. For Dugald Stewart, the Scottish Enlightenment professor whose work Emerson studied at Harvard, metaphors are 'necessarily ... *transitive* expressions', embodying contingency of connection in their very articulation.[33] 'Transference' is Stewart's term for what he calls the 'perception of relations' that metaphor embodies; his philosophical distinction between 'responsible' and 'capricious' transference addresses the problem of random relatedness in the absence of demonstrable causation, and restates for a secular context Puritan anxieties about the relationship of manifestation to meaning.[34] In the Romantic writing of New England particularly, metaphor and metonymy exploit contiguity to 'cross' from one verbal context to another and embody the 'trans-gressive' feature, the oxymoron which is involved in recognizing otherness.[35] In the Romantic period these forms of distanced contiguity defined transatlantic and transitive relations. Emerson's essays, for example, are illuminated by an idea of metaphor as both a socially and historically dependent trope, *and* an idealized image of the transformative effect of Atlantic crossing on language. In *Nature*, not only the poet's (as in Shelley's *Defence*) but *all* language is 'vitally metaphorical': metaphor has become not so much an act of comparison, as a means of apprehension embodying the transitive nature of all perception.[36]

At this point a rather puzzling sentence in the passage from Fuller's *Summer on the Lakes* may spring into a new kind of focus: 'I realized the identity of that mood of nature in which these waters were poured down with such absorbing force, with that in which the Indian was shaped on the same soil'. The haunting of Wordsworth's 'sounding cataract' lies in some sense behind this, but at a remove of translation which is embodied in a particular use of metaphor. Let's look again at that Indian, who seems initially to stand as a figure of self-alienation. But that otherness also comprehends – and transcends – the unnamed 'object of dread' ('Tintern Abbey') from which the young Wordsworth fled, the power of nature 'to chasten or subdue', and also the 'dear, dear Sister' Dorothy whose familiar co-presence at the scene stabilizes and sanctifies the relation between past and present. The first, uncanny, encounter with the Indian is progressively rethought in the course of the ensuing narrative as Fuller visits the Plains Indians, incorporates their tales in her text, and naturalizes them as co-creators of 'the mood of [American] nature'. So her use of the 'Indian' as a trope in the text enacts both types of metaphor/*translatio*: the haunting hierarchies of influence and the horizontal relations of association. There is *no* 'ground', here, outwith the relation of tenor and vehicle.

Stewart's notion of the 'transitive' allows for contingency of connection, not organic or intrinsic relationship. It offers a distinction between the hierarchical form of linking preferred by what we might broadly call the 'English' ('Wordsworthian') Romanticism imaged in the vertical emphasis of the 'tall' rock, 'deep' rivers and 'elevated' thoughts of the 'Tintern Abbey' passage, and the American version embodied in Transcendentalism: the 'going beyond', over, which transforms as it translates, as the towering proportions of Niagara are reimagined spatially into the mental landscape in Fuller's *Summer*. Whereas Wordsworth's poetry saw the sublime in nature as woven intricately into the role of the poet, Fuller (like Poe) seems to challenge America's ideological attachment to the vastness of territory and its capacity to be colonized by the mind. As Emerson put it in *Nature*, 'Parts of speech are metaphors, because the whole of nature is a metaphor of the human mind' (*Collected Works*, I, 21). The typological, analogical frame of mind which governed early Congregationalists' self-expression in the spiritual autobiographies of Puritan Massachusetts has here been transmogrified completely into an argument about style. Knowledge and style may be mutually constitutive at the most irreducible level; in both *Nature* and Fuller's Niagara passage the mind-changing properties of language meet the world-changing properties of mind. It helps to read both as manifestos of transatlantic Romanticism, a kind of delayed response to Jefferson's question: (Wordsworthian) 'Nature' *has* traversed the seas and the 'figure of transport' redefines it as a relation (in several senses) of language.

Where the *translatio* was essentially a binary conception, only adequate within a very narrow construction of transatlantic cross-currents and deriving from an essentially imperialistic world view that has little adequate vocabulary for the pluralities of language, race, gender or genre, the transitivity of Romantic metaphor acknowledges the multiplicity of 'weak implicatures' (the phrase is Sperber and Wilson's) in any reader's reception, alongside the 'core' meanings (Weber, 'Towards Contextualized Stylistics', 6). 'America' itself was ideologically construed in the nineteenth century as an emigrant, polyglot nation founded on transitivity and transference, in sympathetic relations – and their violation. In this context, too, the lateral stylistic trope of metaphor, with its cognate implications of 'translation' and 'transfer', offers a more appropriate model for the plural connectednesses of transatlantic literary relations than the vertical prioritizing model of influence which drove earlier 'Comparative Literature' studies.

In 'The Poet', style transports the authority ('Nature') of its origins into new spaces:

> As the limestone of the continent consists of infinite masses of the shells of animalcules, so language is made up of images, or tropes, which ... have long since ceased to remind us of their poetic origin ... [A]ll language is vehicular and transitive, and is good, as ferries and horses are, for conveyance, not as farms and houses are, for homestead'. (*Collected Works*, III, 13 and 20)

Emerson's progression of comparisons is an excellent example of Donald Freeman's contention that 'the metaphoric impulse is grounded not in intellectual abstractions but in the body that is in the mind' ('"According to my Bond": King Lear and Re-cognition', Weber, 292). The embodied imagination is necessarily and inevitably transitive, metaphorizing: verbs in particular, *move across* the conceptual space between subject and object, effecting the traffic of Transcendentalism.[37] The 'succession of moods or objects' which is as much a feature of Emerson's style as of his thought, is a 'necessity' in a world where constant motion is the only way to stay afloat: 'We live amid surfaces, and the true art of life is to skate well upon them' ('Experience', *Collected Works*, III, 32 and 35). The image is continuous with – and seems to recall – both Coleridge's long-legged crane skating on the surface of thought (From Chapter 7 of *Biographia Literaria*), and the exultant, spinning transitive motion of the skating child in *The Prelude*, Book I. Emerson's language, however, embodies the transitivity of thought in detachable sentences paratactically assembled rather than embedded in hypotaxis. Where Wordsworth's poet, employing a discourse of authenticity, 'purified' the diction of low life, Emerson and Fuller experimented with contamination, the generation of possibilities at idiomatic margins which mimicked as they explored the boundary between perception and world. Transcendental philosophy, style, and what we call 'American ideology' are compounded in Fuller's Niagara passage, which Poe quoted as an instance of the 'graphicality' by which the mind paints its contours on a scene.[38] In Emerson's lexicon, all language is transitive because (paradoxically) all perception is reflexive: 'Every word which is used to express a moral or intellectual fact, if traced to its root, is found to be borrowed from some material appearance. *Right* originally means *straight* ... *transgression*, the crossing of a *line*' ('Nature', *Collected Works*, I, 18). His memorialist Cabot described 'the transcendental' as 'whatever *lay beyond* the stock notions and traditional beliefs to which adherence was expected because they were generally accepted by sensible persons'.[39] There's a suggestive trace of the bombast, the 'excess', of metaphor here. To the German *übersetzen* – crossing or jumping over, is added *übertragen* – transference or negotiation. Both senses are there in transatlantic Romanticism, as well as the more literal English 'translation', as it encompasses (in Eve Bannet's words) 'the wandering, the erring of metaphors, the resistance to metaphor', which register cultural disruption.[40]

To return to where I began, Fuller's *Summer on the Lakes* is a Romantic travel journey of self-recovery and therapy through encounter with the forces of nature. In that sense it is a highly Wordsworthian piece of writing, with intriguing anticipations of the poet's autobiographical poem *The Prelude*. But – and here we may locate both its stylistic Americanness and its relationship with an alternative, rhetorical and literary tradition – its structure is precisely identified in that metaphor for 'thinking across' the metaphor of metaphor: 'I wish I had a thread long enough to string on it all these beads that take my fancy', she writes in explanatory mock-apology for the serendipitous inclusiveness of her approach. Like Emerson, in fact, the same year: 'Life is a train of moods, like a string of beads, and as we pass through them they prove to be many-colored lenses which paint the world their own hue ('Experience', *Collected Works*, III, 53–4). In the absence of specifically acknowledged indebtedness, it is impossible to say whether this is influence or confluence; at this point, I would suggest, we are looking at a Romantic metaphor for America, and a consciously transatlantic style: transitional surfaces, arbitrary segments of process. 'This World is not Conclusion –' as Emily Dickinson did not end a poem.[41] It is one that has been generated in the stylistic consequences of 'thinking across'.

We can check this by referring back to the textual afterlife of Wordsworth, the great exponent of 'English' Romantic nature. There is plenty of evidence in Fuller's writing that the poet represented a kind of triangulation point in relation to which her experimental prose measured its unmoorings. From articles on 'Lives of the Great Composers' to autobiographical fragments, Wordsworth is a touchstone for integrity, the quiddity of a great spirit, intransitive singleness. 'One should have climbed to as high a point as Wordsworth to be able to review Milton, or even to view in part his high places. From the hill-top we still strain our eyes looking up to the mountain-peak'.[42] Her essay on 'Modern British Poets' for the Transcendental periodical *The Dial* identifies him as 'Beloved friend and venerated teacher', neatly intercalating horizontal and hierarchical relations. The stylistic traces of 'Wordsworth' (as the proponent and embodiment of 'Nature') occupy a foundational niche in the pantheon of American Romantic writing rather similar to that of King Brutus in the *translatio*.[43] His 'greater power of continuous self-impulse' is evoked in

Fuller's metaphor of transmission, one that gestures towards the already institutionalized figure of 'Wordsworth' in America: 'There is a suggestive and stimulating power in original thought which cannot be gauged by the first sensation or temporary effect it produces. The circles grow wider and wider as the impulse is propagated through the deep waters of eternity'.[44] Wordsworth's metaphor of the stone dropped into the water is transformed by appropriation: vertical plummet, to transverse ripples. 'Throw a stone into the stream', as Emerson had put it, 'and the circles that propagate themselves are the beautiful type of all influence' ('Nature', *Collected Works*, I. 18). This both is, and is not quite, what Fuller means, and begins to suggest some distinctions between the Transcendental transitive they both inhabit. Reviewing Elizabeth Barrett Browning's Poems, Fuller makes it clear that poetic 'depth' is inseparable from the transitive thinking of 'sympathy': 'Wordsworth moves us when he writes "Ode to Duty", or "Dion," because he could also write "Ruth," and the exquisitely tender poems on Mathew' (Bean and Myerson, 21).

Fuller's metaphor for the *translatio* emphasizes not exchange, but transmission; it is multi-directional and it is characteristic of how her writing transposes a cluster which includes penetration, power, depth, in relation to the poet himself, into a spatial matrix of relationships that further analogizes 'The American Scholar's 'circular power'.[45] Westward the spreading ripples take *their* way, their impulse perceived far distant from the originating Word of Wordsworth. (We might compare the conceptual syntax here with Wordsworth's 'spots of time': points of intensification, vertical seeings-into the essence of things, not transitional movements; the 'transport' of 'Surprised by Joy' turns out to be intransitive: it stays with the poetic voice, uncommunicable, in the ante-chamber of the sonnet.[46]) Logocentric patriarchy (the egotistical sublime) elicited admiration, and resistance, in Fuller's literary response, as in many other writers; it accrues a particular stylistic resonance in the transatlantic context as 'child' pays 'father' the equivocal, disarming compliment of imitation/mimicry.[47] Where Emerson (and after him, Whitman) confidently proclaimed the *translatio* as *fait accompli*, Fuller's essay called 'American Literature: Its Position in the Present Time, and Prospects for the Future' held on to the troubling possibilities of a transitive grammar: American writers influenced by Europe are 'colonists and useful schoolmasters to our people in a transition state; which lasts rather longer than is occupied in passing, bodily, the ocean which separates the new from the old world' (*Papers on Literature and Art*, II, 122). Her writing develops Fourier's idea of 'transitions or ambiguous types' – boundary-states like somnambulism, mesmeric trances, 'ambiguous gender' – as areas of crossing, in which metaphor reclaims its earlier sense as the figure of transport that supplies the relation between subject and object and refuses anew the essentialism of the egotistical sublime.[48]

The resistance in Fuller's response invokes our recognition that despite the optative assertions of Emerson's youth, not every verb *is* transitive; the intransitive verb with no direct object stands in the way of metaphoric exchange. 'Transitive' theory entertains, too, the alternative possibility that transatlantic romanticism entails, in Henry James's phrase, a 'sacrifice of relation'. The obverse side of transigence, to 'act across', its necessary self-defining 'other', is intransigence – to fail to come across, or to reach an understanding, or accommodate. This itself becomes a metaphor for Fuller's uncertainty about audience, a failure of confidence that self-alienates voice and end-stops her succession of aphoristic 'beads' in *The Dial* into a curiously tight circularity, so that instead of skating like Emerson's from point to point of a fluid canvas, they turn back redundantly on themselves:

> The man of genius feels that literature has become too much of a craft by itself. No man should live by or for his pen. Writing is worthless except as the record of life; and no man ever was satisfied thus to express all his being. His book should be only an indication of himself. The obelisk should point to a scene of conquest.[49]

But scenes of conquest were notably antipathetic both to her sensibility and to America's ideology of freedom.[50] The principles of exchange that characterized the mutual saturation of economic and cultural values in the transatlantic commerce of the mid-eighteenth century were in the Romantic period perceived as multiply blocked, hindered or thwarted: by events like the Anglo-American war of 1812–14 whose commercial ramifications haunt Washington Irving's *Sketch-Book*; by the pressure of inadequate copyright protection (articulated, for example, in the work of Melville and Dickens); by the cultural misprision fomented by travellers' accounts like those of Harriet Martineau or Frances Trollope. A new grammar of transatlantic Romanticism needs to take account of the disruptive as well as the circulatory possibilities of metaphor, that feature deplored in Samuel Johnson's notorious dismissal of 'heterogeneous ideas ... yoked by violence together'.[51] It is American critics, notably, who have counselled that appropriation and influence are also misappropriation and misprision: one thinks of T.S. Eliot's 'Tradition and the Individual Talent', Walter Jackson Bate's *The Burden of the Past on the English Poet*, Bloom's *Anxiety of Influence and Map of Misreading*. Celebrating the horizontal, transferential relations of the metaphorical chain, we should bear in mind that 'America' has also been the product, and the perpetrator, of the kinds of oppressive, hierarchical thinking implied in imperialism, colonial subordination and the battles for national supremacy that are encapsulated stylistically in Comparative Literature's earlier models of 'influence studies'. As a word, 'influence' (as

Susan Stanford Friedman puts it) 'is implicated in the rationalizing ideology of the conqueror, the colonizer, who envisions his influence as a hegemonic penetration'.[52] Though we may no longer wish to structure our own thinking by it, it too needs to be kept in the grammar of possibilities, in the study of nineteenth-century transnational Atlantic discourse.

No one was more aware of this than Margaret Fuller, finding her audience, and a flexible voice, at last in the transatlantic letters from Europe to the New York *Tribune*. Her description of Carlyle's conversation, too little known, embodies resistance in flow, an exuberant metaphorical chain that assimilates the egotistical sublime and passes through stylistic influence in a manner her writing never achieves with the 'Wordsworth' obelisk:

> He does not converse, – only harangues. It is the usual misfortune of such marked men ... that they cannot allow other minds room to breathe and show themselves in their atmosphere, and thus miss the refreshment and instruction which the greatest never cease to need from the experience of the humblest. Carlyle allows no one a chance, but bears down all opposition, not only by his wit and onset of words, resistless in their sharpness as so many bayonets, but by actual physical superiority, raising his voice and rushing on his opponent with a torrent of sound ... Carlyle, indeed, is arrogant and overbearing, but ... it is the heroic arrogance of some old Scandinavian conqueror, – it is his nature and the untamable impulse that has given him power to crush the dragons. You ... like to see him the powerful smith, the Siegfried, melting all the old iron in his furnace till it glows to a sunset red, and burns you if you senselessly go too near. He seemed to me quite isolated, lonely as the desert ... He pours upon you a kind of satirical, heroical, critical poem, with regular cadences, and generally catching up near the beginning some singular epithet, which serves as a *refrain* when his song is full, or with which as with a knitting-needle he catches up the stitches.[53]

The different 'grammars' of Romanticism in British and American writing begin, then, to define the transitivity or transference between them. Here is a possibility for comparative study based not on temporal priority (the vertical, hierarchizing perspectives of influence), but on a rhizomatic transitive organicism which maps a lateral undergrowth of connection.[54] The transatlantic perspective inevitably involves reflexiveness in the issue of self-definition, as the transaction of metaphor transforms both tenor and vehicle. The principle of semantic *exchange* is intrinsic to the 'figure of transport' which relates percept and object; discovery and invention turn out to be interchangeable tropes in this lateral movement of mutual recognition that, over time, would work itself in both directions across the

Atlantic. Cultural translation becomes a semantic tool. More broadly, as Eve Bannet has suggested, thinking across was both the vehicle and the constitutive structure of the Enlightenment which itself generated the environment of possibility for American independence.[55] Behind – prior to – the cultural nationalism of nineteenth-century Comparative Literature (foundational in Steiner's account) lie other assumptions – expressed, for example, in Goethe's '*Weltliteratur*' – of cultural movement characteristically described in dynamic metaphors of flow: 'stream', 'cross-currents', 'confluences'.

II

At this point it is perhaps necessary to reiterate that this grammar of metaphor is offered here not as a fixed methodology or approach, but as an example of how attention to style might illuminate comparison in a historically specific context. As I have indicated in the reference to Emerson's reading of Stewart at Harvard, this argument might equally be traced through the pedagogical history of tropology from Scottish Enlightenment rhetoric to American College education. Comparison between 'Tintern Abbey' and *Summer on the Lakes* suggests quite different terms of relevance from what might be implied in considering, say, the effect of emigration on Huxley's or Auden's or Thom Gunn's writing; different again from asking about the shared characteristics that might define or identify a 'transatlantic style' in the work of Sylvia Plath (what Paul Giles has recently referred to as her 'Double Exposure') or Martin Amis or Nabokov.[56] Is it possible to identify, in these latter cases, a 'transatlantic style' common to writing which has as it were a foot in both camps? One thing that attending to style in transatlantic literary criticism might enable us to address is the point (if such there be) at which American writing and English swap places, as it were, in their stylistic habitation of the linguistic world they embody: 'at homeness' versus 'departures' – we could construe it in different ways, always bearing in mind that the vantage points are relative and multiply determined. For modernist texts a useful starting point might be Volosinov's idea of the semantic openness of the 'multi-accentual', while the polyglot globalized conditions of ethnic, economic and political transference in contemporary writing would need to be theorized in different terms again, something perhaps closer to the internationalizing sensibility understood in '*Weltliteratur*'.

Has the postmodern condition that Lyotard called 'eclecticism' – the endlessly transferable features of global culture – in fact rendered 'transatlantic comparison' redundant? Is 'style' not now simply another facet of undifferentiated internationalism? The stylistics of transatlantic comparison cannot now draw on monolithic assumptions about national character and authorial identity, or the transparency of 'influence'. But the very fact that neither the integrity of nation nor of self can now be safely taken for granted in criticism makes the turn to style imperative, I would argue, although it complicates the assumptions on which this can be based. I end, therefore, by returning to the *translatio*, to suggest, very sketchily, that the sense of space and the process of crossing it that informs American Romantic style does offer at least some continuing possibilities for transatlantic comparison. Wallace Stevens's poetry embodies a further episode in the transitive story of 'Wordsworth in America', with transatlantic currents flowing in a counter direction: Stevens' blackbird 'whirl[ing] in the Autumn winds' sidesteps to Shelley, as it plays a 'small part' in the repertoire of 'pantomime' which, perhaps, represents the mimicking enactment of 'Romanticism' in America. Following the stylistic shifts precipitated by Symbolism, the image takes on a compressive more than a transitive function: Stevens's blackbird is not a metaphor or – quite – a 'way between', but something more like an empty ground bursting with possible significances, its song of excess pointing reciprocally to an existential absence and a heart of abundance. It takes over from Emily Dickinson's 'Robin' the function of grounding poetic vision in locale, but offering a pluralism to set against her singularity:

II

> I was of three minds,
> Like a tree
> In which there are three blackbirds.[57]

In Stevens's aphorism, metaphor 'creates a new reality from which the original appears to be unreal'.[58]

'Thirteen Ways of Looking at a Blackbird' has recently recrossed the Atlantic to rest/roost as an epigraph to John Burnside's collection *The Light-Trap*, where it re-combines with the less travelled story of Wordsworth in British poetry.[59] American blackbirds are bigger, more variegated, different from British ones; they are, and mean, otherly. They sing differently, but they are also spoken about differently. The 'residue of the untranslatable' survives in the inevitable treason committed in transatlantic passing.

> When the blackbird flew out of sight,
> It marked the edge
> Of one of many circles. (*Collected Works*, 93)

The circle inscribed by the blackbird's evanishment is an Emersonian space created between the eye and the horizon. The space of looking and speculating is defined by the edges of the poetic structure, as Wordsworth defined it, too, in 'Tintern Abbey', but with Stevens's critically important deflection of singer into song – song not as tenor but as vehicle. *The Light-Trap* is a collection preoccupied with relations, the connectedness of things and thoughts, the interpenetration of the unconscious and the landscape, the namer and the named, the past and the future. There are priorities but not hierarchies; links are cross-wise and in process, through space and thinking, not the downwards archaeology of causes. And, in a move very reminiscent of Emily Dickinson, William James and Wallace Stevens, the voice that speaks across the void, supplying it with song, is that of the bird:

> It's not the space
> between the cherry trees,
>
> the angle of our smoke-house
> or the sense
> of something to be filled
> above the lawn;
>
> it's not the gaps
> in matter, or the fear
>
> of losing ground
> that prompts him into song.

It's the mapping of relationships between; the 'thinking across' the spaces. Burnside's version, re-inflected by Stevens, is preoccupied with these spaces created by the singing:

> the blackbird makes
> a territory of light
>
> and fills it with a sound.[60]

Projecting personal memory onto nature, the poetic voice of 'Tintern Abbey' learned to feel the 'presence ... / Of elevated *thoughts*'. When the high thoughts of man give metaphorical place to the journey of 'Man [or woman] think*ing*', something different (as Dickinson, like Fuller, suggests) begins to happen:

> And Place was where the Presence was
> Circumference between –

It is this kind of 'thinking across' about which Transatlantic Studies still has much to learn.[61]

Notes

1. An early version of this chapter was delivered at the Inaugural Conference of *Transatlantic Studies*, in Dundee, July 2002. I am grateful to Peter Rawlings, David Duff, Colleen Glenney Boggs and Eve Tavor Bannet for their helpful comments in the course of its revision.
2. Margaret Fuller, *Summer on the Lakes in 1843*, intro. Susan Belasco Smith (Urbana and Chicago, IL: University of Illinois Press, 1991), 4.
3. See *Notes on the State of Virginia* (1787) in *Thomas Jefferson: Writings*, ed. Merrill D. Peterson (Cambridge: Cambridge UP, 1984), 142–3.
4. To put it in the more technical if less witty frame of linguistics, the '"real world" is to a large extent built up on the language habits of the group. No two languages are ever sufficiently similar to be considered as representing the same social reality'. Edward Sapir, 'The Status of Linguistics as a Science' in *Culture, Language and Personality: Selected Essays*, ed. David G. Mandelbaum (Berkeley and Los Angeles, CA: University of California Press, 1956), 68–9.
5. Paul Giles notes that 'the idiom of comparatist defamiliarization generally finds itself at odds with the more mimetic strategies endorsed by ... American studies': *Transatlantic Insurrections: British Culture and the Formation of American Literature, 1730–1860* (Philadelphia, PA: University of Pennsylvania Press, 2001), 12. A. Owen Aldridge has pointed out that 'American Literature' and 'Comparative Literature' as subjects of academic study were born at almost the same moment in the 1920s: *Early American Literature: A Comparatist Approach* (Princeton, NJ: Princeton UP, 1982), ix. My title alludes to Richard Poirier's study of 1966, *A World Elsewhere: The Place of Style in American Literature*, which identifies a national literary tradition characterized by 'stylistic struggle' between visionary aspiration and conventional diction.
6. Harry Levin, *Grounds for Comparison* (Cambridge, MA: Harvard UP, 1972).
7. Fredric Jameson finds that 'it is from "Romanticism" itself in the most general sense ... that the concept of Comparative Literature springs in the first place': 'The State of the Subject (III)', *Critical Quarterly* 29, no. 4 (Winter 1987): 16.
8. See George Steiner, *What is Comparative Literature?* (Oxford: Clarendon, 1995), 7.
9. Harold Bloom, *The Anxiety of Influence: A Theory of Poetry* (New York, NY: Oxford UP, 1973), 7.
10. For a fuller discussion of these terms, see Susan Manning, *Fragments of Union: Making Connections in Scottish and American Writing* (London: Palgrave, 2002), Introduction.
11. Jay Clayton and Eric Rothstein, 'Figures in the Carpet: Theories of Influence and Intertextuality' in J. Clayton and E. Rothstein (eds), *Influence and Intertextuality in Literary History* (Madison, WI: University of Wisconsin Press, 1991), 17.
12. *Beloved* (1987) (rpt. London: Picador, 1988), 165.
13. *Writing Degree Zero* in Roland Barthes, '*Writing Degree Zero*' and '*Elements of Semiology*', trans. Annette Lavers and Colin Smith (London: Jonathan Cape, 1984), 15.
14. 'The assumption is not that reality itself is relative, but that it is differently punctuated and categorized, by participants of different cultures, or that different aspects of it are noticed by, or presented to, them': Dorothy Lee, 'Lineal and Nonlineal Codifications of Reality' in *Explorations in Communications: An Anthology* ed. Edmund Carpenter and Marshall McLuhan (London: Jonathan Cape, 1970), 136. Mary-Louise Pratt's insistence that we recognize the ideologically determined component of stylistic, as of any form of literary analysis is

salutary: 'Ideology and Speech-Act Theory', in *The Stylistics Reader from Roman Jakobson to the Present*, ed. Weber (London: Arnold, 1996), 181 and 184. Hereafter all essays from this volume will be cited by the editor's last name followed by the page number.

15. Edgar Allan Poe, *Essays and Reviews*, ed. G.R. Thompson (New York, NY: Library of America, 1984), 1076. Emphasis in original.
16. *Extra-Territorial: Papers on Literature and the Language Revolution* (London: Faber and Faber, 1972).
17. *The Liberal Imagination: Essays on Literature and Society* (1940; rpt. New York, NY: Charles Scribner, 1976), 284.
18. Julia Kristeva, *Strangers to Ourselves*, trans. Leon S. Roudiez (Hemel Hempstead: Harvester Wheatsheaf, 1991), 7.
19. Nathaniel Hawthorne, *Letters 1857–1864*, Centenary Edition (Columbus, OH: Ohio State UP 1962–97), XVIII, 229.
20. *The Correspondence of Emerson and Carlyle*, ed. Joseph Slater (New York, NY and London: Columbia UP, 1964), 371. Emphasis in original.
21. Francis Jeffrey, 'Review of Barlow's *Columbiad*', *Edinburgh Review* 15 (October 1809), 24–40 (p. 25).
22. 'Review of *American Annals; or, a Chronological History of America* ... By Abiel Holmes', *Quarterly Review*, 2 (1809), 310.
23. Definitions drawn from Cassell's Latin Dictionary. I read Eric Cheyfitz's *The Poetics of Imperialism: Translation and Colonization from The Tempest to Tarzan*, expanded ed. (Philadelphia: University of Pennsylvania Press, 1997) at a late stage in revising this chapter. His reading of the *translatio*/metaphor motif as an imperialist tool in the imposition of power emphasizes ideology over style. It is an important argument, though in my view flawed by its failure to historicize ideas of translation. On the historical specificity of translation, see Douglas Robinson, *The Translator's Turn* (Baltimore, MD: Johns Hopkins UP, 1991).
24. Jefferson, cited in *Oxford English Dictionary* definition.
25. See Jefferson, *Literary Commonplace Book*, ed. Douglas L. Wilson (Princeton, NJ: Princeton UP, 1989).
26. Information in this paragraph is drawn from http://cla.calpoly.edu/~ dschwart/engl513/courtly/translat.htm, copyright Debora B. Schwartz.
27. Text taken from *The New Oxford Book of Eighteenth-Century Verse*, ed. Roger Lonsdale (Oxford: Oxford UP, 1984), 175.
28. 'The American Scholar' in *The Collected Works of Ralph Waldo Emerson* (Cambridge, MA: Harvard UP, 1971), I, 54 (hereafter referred to as *Collected Works*). A few paragraphs earlier in the essay, Emerson directly echoes Wordsworth's (1802) 'Preface' to the *Lyrical Ballads*: 'Man is not a farmer, or a professor, or an engineer, but he is all. Man is priest, and scholar, and statesman, and producer, and soldier' (84). See William Wordsworth and Samuel Taylor Coleridge, *Lyrical Ballads*: 'The Poet writes under one restriction only, namely, that of the necessity of giving immediate pleasure to a human Being possessed of that information which may be expected from him, not as a lawyer, a physician, a mariner, an astronomer or a natural philospher, but as a Man' (752). Tony Tanner has commented on the 'web' in his 'Notes towards a Comparison of British and American Romanticism' in *Scenes of Nature, Signs of Man* (Cambridge: Cambridge UP, 1987).
29. *Revolution in Poetic Language*, trans. Margaret Waller (New York, NY: Columbia UP, 1984), 59–60.

30. *The Borderers* (1797–99 version), ed. Robert Osborn (Ithaca, NY: Cornell UP, 1982), III. v. 60–5, p. 214.
31. George Puttenham, *The Arte of English Poesie* ([1589]; Menston: Scolar Press, 1968), 128 ('Of Figures and figuratiue speaches').
32. http://www.library.utoronto.ca/utel/rp/criticism/artofp_all.html. The popular phrase 'transport of delight' recurs in poetry of the Romantic period. See also Richard Bradford, *Stylistics* (London: Routledge, 1997), 10; and Beverly Maeder, *Wallace Stevens' Experimental Language: The Lion in the Lute* (New York, NY: St Martin's Press, 1999), 45–74.
33. 'On the Beautiful. Part First', in *Philosophical Essays, The Collected Works of Dugald Stewart*, ed. Sir William Hamilton (Edinburgh: Thomas Constable, 1855), v, 197.
34. Compare Dan Sperber and Deidre Wilson's more recent 'principle of relevance' in Jean Jacques Weber, 'Towards Contextualized Stylistics: An Overview', in Weber, *The Stylistics Reader*, 5.
35. Homi Bhabha has also noted that etymologically metaphor 'transfers the meaning of home and belonging ... across those distances, and cultural differences, that span the imagined community of the nation-people'. 'DissemiNation: Time, Narrative, and the Margins of the Modern Nation' *Nation and Narration* ed. H. Bhabha (London and New York, NY: Routledge, [1990] 1999), 291.
36. *A Defense of Poetry*, in Percy Bysshe Shelley, *Selected Poetry and Prose*, ed. Alasdair D.F. Macroe (London and New York, NY: Routledge, 1991), 206. See also J. Middleton Murry, *The Problem of Style* ([1922] Oxford: Oxford UP, 1976), 11.
37. See Stanley Hussey, *The English Language: Structure and Development* (London and New York, NY: Longman, 1995), 51.
38. Poe, *Essays and Reviews*, 1173. In 1803 The *Edinburgh Review* explained 'Philosophy ... is transcendental, when ... it investigates the subjective elements, which ... modify the qualities or elements of the object as perceived' (Jan. 1803, 258). In Peacock's satire *Melincourt* (1817), Mr Mystic 'explained' how a cylindrical mirror, 'reflecting very deeply on the degree in which the manner of his construction might influence the forms of his perception, ... discovered the difference between *objective* and *subjective reality*: and this point of view is *transcendentalism*' (Ch. 31 of *Melincourt*, ed. Richard Garnett [London: J.M. Dent, 1891], II, 100–1). The object of Peacock's satire here was Kant, but it would not be long before English writers adapted the joke at the expense of American writers (as in the 'two Literary Ladies' of Dickens' *Martin Chuzzlewit*).
39. James Elliot Cabot, *A Memoir of Ralph Waldo Emerson* (2 vols, London: Macmillan, 1887), I, 249. Emphasis added.
40. See her illuminating discussion in 'The Scene of Translation: After Jakobson, Benjamin, de Man, and Derrida', *New Literary History* 24 (1993): 577–95; quotation from p. 584.
41. *Complete Poems of Emily Dickinson*, ed. Thomas H. Johnson (Boston, MA: Little, Brown, 1960), Poem 501.
42. Judith Mattson Bean and Joel Myerson (eds), *Margaret Fuller Critic: Writings from the New-York Tribune, 1844–1846* (New York, NY: Columbia UP, 2000), 245. Hereafter cited parenthetically by the editors' surnames.
43. On the evidence of his extensive edition of nineteenth-century American writers on fiction, Peter Rawlings tells me that Wordsworth, Milton and Shakespeare, in that order, are the writers most frequently alluded to.
44. *Papers on Literature and Art* (2 vols, London: Wiley & Putnam, 1846), I, 89, 61.

45. See, for example, *Letters of Margaret Fuller*, ed. Robert N. Hudspeth (Ithaca, NY: Cornell UP, 1983), II, 242.
46. 'Miscellaneous Sonnets', XXVII, William Wordsworth, *Poetical Works*, ed. Ernest de Selincourt and Helen Darbishire (Oxford: Oxford UP, 1954), 33 (second edition). (At the time of going to press, the Cornell edition of the Sonnets is unavailable.)
47. Which was how Wordsworth's poetry was largely read by his contemporaries, though recent criticism has investigated the presence of plural and feminine voices in the poems. Jeffrey Steele has described how in Fuller's writing 'influence' functions as an allegorical formation for the 'father', and 'intertextuality' for the 'mother'. See 'The Call of Eurydice: Mourning and Intertextuality in Margaret Fuller's Writing', in *Influence and Intertextuality*, Clayton and Rothstein, eds, pp. 271–97.
48. Fourier himself adapted the idea from Mesmer, as Christina Zwarg points out, 'Footnoting the Sublime: Margaret Fuller on Black Hawk's Trail', *American Literary History*, 5:, no. 4 (Winter 1993): 632. In Bhabha's account, these are the ontological boundaries straddled by metaphor, *Nation and Narration*, 296, 302.
49. 'Goethe', *The Dial* II, July 1841 (New York, NY: Russell & Russell, 1961), 4.
50. See, for example, her piece on '1st August, 1845' for the *New York Daily Tribune*, (Bean and Myerson, 183–4).
51. 'Life of Cowley', *Johnson's Lives of the Poets: A Selection*, ed. J.P. Hardy (Oxford: Clarendon, 1971), 12.
52. 'Weavings: Intertextuality and the (Re)Birth of the Author', in *Influence and Intertextuality*, eds Clayton and Rothstein, 152.
53. 'Letter IX' to *The Tribune*, Paris, Nov. 1846, in *Home and Abroad*, ed. Arthur B. Fuller ([1856] Port Washington, NY: Kennikat Press, 1971), 184.
54. Gilles Deleuze and Félix Guattari, *A Thousand Plateaus: Capitalism and Schizophrenia*, trans. Brian Massumi (London: Athlone, 1988), 505–6. Add this to Jameson's point that 'when we move from [a] model of an individual "cultural system", or an individual cultural or literary "text", to a more comparatist perspective ... the emphasis on form can only increase', and it becomes apparent that Tanner's identification of the metaphor/symbol of the web was unerringly central to the issue (Jameson, 'The State of the Subject (III)'; 20).
55. 'Criticism and Intertranslation: The End of Critique in a Democratic Society', *Argumentation* 11 (1997): 23–33.
56. *Symbiosis*, 5, no. 2 (October 2001): 103–20.
57. 'Thirteen Ways of Looking at a Blackbird', *Collected Poems of Wallace Stevens* (London: Faber and Faber, [1955] 1987), 93.
58. 'Adagia', *Opus Posthumous* (New York, NY: Vintage, 1990), 195.
59. 'A man and a woman / Are one. / A man and a woman and a blackbird / Are one'. 'Thirteen Ways of Looking at a Blackbird', (*Collected Poems*, 3).
60. *The Light-Trap* (London: Jonathan Cape, 2002), 37.
61. References are to Wordsworth, 'Tintern Abbey', ll.94–5 ; Emerson, 'The American Scholar' (*Complete Works*, I, 53), Dickinson, *Complete Poems*, Poem 1084, 491).

2
The Wordsworthian Metamorphosis of Natty Bumppo

Richard Gravil

In his most English novel, *The Pioneers* (1823), James Fenimore Cooper created a character who would not let him go: his Natty Bumppo, alias Leatherstocking, alias Hawkeye, alias Deerslayer, alias Pathfinder. Natty was first conceived as an uncouth, archaic, sansculotte hangover in the nascent democracy of upstate New York, a realm where the values of Edmund Burke were, by and large – and especially in the eyes of such landed gentry as Cooper's father, Judge Cooper of Cooperstown – considerably more prevalent than those of Thomas Jefferson or Tom Paine. But Natty did more than prove 'that men who do not wear fine cloaths may feel deeply' (*WL*,I. 315). Despite or because of Natty's uncouth ways, his unfitness for drawing rooms, and his opposition to almost everything Cooper's father stood for, he ran away with the book. Indeed Natty commanded Cooper to explore him backwards and forwards in four further novels.

The Last of the Mohicans (1826), therefore, imagines him in his prime. *The Prairie* (1827) narrates the Ossianic death of the old trapper. At the height of his European involvements in 1829, Cooper wrote what is in some ways the finest of his 'borderer' novels, *The Wept of Wish-ton-Wish* (1829), dealing with the foundations of Anglo-America and conflicts between Puritans and American Indians long before the birth of the Leatherstocking. Much later, and long after his disillusioning return to America, Cooper resuscitated his hero in *The Pathfinder* (1840), a novel redeemed only by the fullest flowering of Cooper's sense of the Romantic sublime. Finally came *The Deerslayer* (1843), the most Edenic of the novels. Here Cooper presents the youthful amity of Natty and Chingachgook as they practise heroic exploits on Lake Glimmerglass (Lake Otsego as it was before Judge Cooper got to work) amid a cardboard cut-out human world made up of two women (one over-sexed, the other simple-minded), and an assortment of blood-curdling savages, white and red, whose sole function is to allow the Adamic virtues of Leatherstocking to shine. In most of these novels, Cooper betrays a fascination with the politics and the aesthetics of Edmund Burke, but a cumulative shift from a Burkean to a Wordsworthian grasp of nature.

Cooper's use of *A Vindication of Natural Society* and of *Reflections on the Revolution in France* is extensive throughout the saga, but his reliance on *A Philosophical Enquiry into the Origin of our Ideas of the Sublime and Beautiful* is absolute. 'Excessive loudness alone', says Burke,

> is sufficient to overpower the soul, to suspend its action, and to fill it with terror. The noise of vast cataracts, raging storms, thunder, or artillery, awakes a great and aweful sensation in the mind. ... A sudden beginning, or sudden cessation of sound of any considerable force, has the same power; ... it may be observed that a single sound of some strength, though but of short duration, if repeated after intervals, has a grand effect. Few things are more aweful than the striking of a great clock, whence the silence of the night prevents the attention from being too much dissipated.[1]

Thus, towards midnight, in *The Wept of Wish-ton-Wish,* heralding the Indian onset upon Mark Heathcote's fortress home, two blasts arise from the conch hung at the fortified gateway so that benighted travellers may seek admission:

> In this momentary but death-like quiet, there arose a blast from the conch at the gate, that might have seemed an echo of that which had lately startled the already excited inmates of the dwelling. At the repetition of sounds so unwonted all sprang to their feet, but no one spoke. ... "The sound is like that which one little used to earthly instruments might raise!" muttered one of those who minds had been prepared by the narrative of Dudley to believe anything marvellous ... . The borderer ... was about to open the door ... when another blast arose on the silence without. The second touch of the shell was firmer, longer, louder, and more true, than that by which it had just been preceded.[2]

The effect is repeated, again and again, without visible cause, until 'the full tones of the shell thrilled on the nerves of the listeners as though they proclaimed the coming of some great and fearful judgement' (*The Wept*, 27).

By the time of *The Wept*, Cooper was a practised artist in such effects of sublimity, having used the noise of Glenn's Falls, and the scream of a horse, to similar effect in *Mohicans*, along with innumerable war-whoops to curdle the blood and unsettle the mind. Less gothically, the landscape descriptions of *The Last of the Mohicans* are permeated, as Steven Blakemore has conclusively illustrated, not merely with a general sense of what constitutes sublimity, which might have been absorbed from the general aesthetic of the late eighteenth century, but with the precise language and effects of Burke's treatise.[3] Moreover, as Daniel Peck has suggested, the descriptive terms of the daughters' journey towards their father in the first part of the narrative, and of the father's journey towards his daughters in the second part, are polarized in terms of the roughness and harshness of the sublime, and the softness of the beautiful.[4]

Ambushed by the treachery of Magua, Leatherstocking and his hapless charges in *Last of the Mohicans* take refuge with the redoubtable Chingachgook and Uncas at the foot of Glenn's Falls, journeying through 'high and cragged rocks', 'tall trees, which appeared to totter on the brow of the precipice', a 'deep and narrow dell', characterized by 'shadowed obscurity' and 'romantic, though not unappalling beauties'.[5] Thomas Gray, recording the terrors of Borrowdale, comes surprisingly to mind. Once his charges are safely encaved, Natty has time to reflect on the passage of time which has changed a 'regular and handsome' sheet of water into the ruinous falls before him:

> 'If you had daylight, it would be worth the trouble to step up on the height of this rock and look at the perversity of the water! It falls by no rule at all; sometimes it leaps, sometimes it tumbles; there it skips; here it shoots; in one place 'tis white as snow, and in another 'tis green as grass ... First it runs angles about and faces the shores; nor are there places wanting, where it looks backward, as if unwilling to leave the wilderness, to mingle with the salt! ... And yet what does it amount to! After the water has been suffered to have its will for a time, like a headstrong man, it is gathered together by the hand that made it, and a few rods below you may see it all, flowing on steadily towards the sea, as was foreordained from the first foundations of the 'arth!' While his auditors received a cheering assurance of the security of their place of concealment from this untutored description of Glenn's, they were much inclined to judge differently from Hawk-eye of its wild beauties. (*Mohicans*, 64–5)

It is never easy to judge of Cooper's ironies. Cooper's reader is clearly meant to derive some pleasure from Leatherstocking's 'untutored' response. At the same time, of course, the very notion of 'tutored spectators' evokes the fact that by the time of writing, the concept of landscape sublimity as defined by John Baillie, developed by Burke and refined by Kant has already become standard fare in Cowper and Collins (the eighteenth-century poets most cited by Cooper), been disseminated in the immensely popular writings of Hugh Blair (whose *Lectures* went through some 52 American editions in Cooper's lifetime), declined into the fatuousness of Gilpin's writing on the picturesque, been reborn in 1798 as Romantic nature feeling, and finally popularized in 1816 by Byron (whose cut-price Wordsworthian rhapsodies provide Cooper with several epigraphs in later novels).

The scene now occupied by Natty and his associates, an ancient Mohican sanctuary, will have two possible fates, either as a source of power and materials (as the author's note indicates), or as a place of scenic resort. The novel was in fact conceived on an excursion to this spot while Cooper was showing Edward Stanley the sights, and it refers later to 'the tourist, the valetudinarian, or the amateur of the beauties of nature ... in the train of his four-in-hand' (*Last of the Mohicans*, 167). For Natty to be thought less capable than his charges of an appropriate response to nature (which is the way most critics have taken it) merely compounds the irony. It is by no means impossible that a man who himself symbolizes sublime resistance to the smooth course of society might recognize some symbol of himself in the scene which makes him so bizarrely eloquent. Despite his general lack of guile, taking silent fun at the expense of his innocent associates is a marked characteristic of the older Natty in *The Prairie*. It is altogether consistent with his conception, both in *The Pioneers* and in the subsequent novels, to see Natty, as the Romantic child of Nature, quietly scandalizing his party of tutored and fashionable but thoroughly (and appropriately) mid-eighteenth-century tourists. However one reads it, the scene is so impregnated with the discourses of the picturesque, and the terms of Natty's description are so redolent of brush marks, that one expects Rowlandson's 'Dr Syntax' to set up his easel – or Cooper's friends Cole and Bryant to take up their poses for that most famous of American paintings, Asher Durand's 'Kindred Spirits' (1849).[6]

It is unlikely that the Leatherstocking of *Mohicans* had read Burke on the sublime and beautiful, if only because the action of the novel is set in the year of that essay's publication, 1757. By the time of *The Pathfinder*, however, though the action is set only a year or two later, the novelist has had some fourteen years to absorb more fully the Romantic development of Burke's somewhat crude theories, and the character of Leatherstocking has been developed so as to embody a consciously Wordsworthian or Bryantesque stance towards nature. Such a development, from an eighteenth-century landscape aesthetic based upon the properties of objects, to a Romantic, post-Kantian view of the interaction of the healthy mind with sublime and beautiful forms, is suggested, also, in the increasing representation of the Romantics in Cooper's epigraphs.

It is as a child of nature that the Leatherstocking develops most consistently throughout the saga, a matter which should occasion little surprise in that the one aspect of Cooper's art that has always seemed beyond criticism is his own descriptions of landscapes, of every kind, in every season. The Leatherstocking of *The Pioneers* was already quite capable of mesmerizing description of remembered landscapes, visited 'more like a man / Flying from something that he dreads than one / Who sought the thing he loved' (*LB*, 'Tintern Abbey' 71–3), that is, as one who climbs the heights to take a distant view of civilization and its encroaching discontents:

> 'The river was in sight for seventy miles, looking like a curled shaving at my feet, though it was eight miles to its banks. I saw the hills in the Hampshire grants, the high land of the river, and all that God had done

> or man could do, far as eye could reach ... When I first come into the woods, I used to have weak spells, when I felt lonesome; and then I would go into the Cattskills and spend a few days on that hill, to look at the ways of man; but now it's many a year since I felt such longings.'[7]

And after describing the beauties of a double fall, with shielded caverns, in what seems a deliberate challenge to the great landscape artists of the Hudson River School to do it better – a fall which his companion says is not 'mentioned in the books' – Natty replies:

> 'I never read a book in my life, and how should a man who has lived in towns and schools know anything about the wonders of the woods! No, no lad; there has that little stream of water been playing among them hills, since He made the world, and not more than a dozen white men have ever laid eyes on it. ...
>
> To my judgement, lad, it's the best piece of work that I've met with in the woods; and none know how often the hand of God is seen in the wilderness, but them that rove it for a man's life ... It's a spot to make a man solemnise.' (*The Pioneers*, 294)

The elderly Leatherstocking of *The Prairie* is so habituated to solemnizing, and so constantly associated with preference for nature over the settlements and 'the wasteful temper of my people', 'their wickedness and their pride, and chiefly their waste', 'the waste and wickedness of the settlements',[8] that he enters the novel as a figure apotheosized by the setting sun, a human form divine, somewhere between Blake's Albion and a sort of Wordsworthian shepherd as transfigured in the as yet unpublished Book VIII of *The Prelude*:

> The sun had fallen below the crest of the nearest wave of the prairie, leaving the usual rich and glowing train in his track. In the centre of this flood of fiery light a human form appeared, drawn against the gilded background ... The figure was colossal, the attitude musing and melancholy, and the situation directly in the route of travellers. But embedded, as it was, in its setting of garish light, it was impossible to distinguish its just proportions or its true character. (*The Prairie*, 14)[9]

The effect on the travelling family of Ishmael Bush is 'instantaneous and powerful', and it is a page or so before Nature allows the outline of her Emissary to appear less exaggerated and more distinct. When it does so Natty greets this travelling family of pioneers in a gloomy tone as 'a sight I had never thought to behold again'. Ishmael, in reply, announces himself as a rival and more naturalistically revised edition of Daniel Boone – the land east of the Mississippi is getting 'a little crowdy' he explains (17) – and

Natty guides him and his unwelcome cattle to a place of foliage and verdure, where 'in a space of time, and with a neatness of execution that would have astonished an ignorant spectator, they stripped a small but suitable spot of its burden of forest, as effectually, and almost as promptly, as if a whirlwind had passed along the place' (19). Ishmael's family is an ominously mobile reincarnation of Billy Kirby, the jovial tree-feller of *The Pioneers*, whose innocent ambition it was to deforest New York State. As Natty pointedly observes to the 'emigrant', who seems oblivious to the nudge, 'the wind seldom blows from the east, but I conceit the sounds of axes, and the crash of falling trees in my ears' (24).

It would not surprise me, though I make no serious claim for its likelihood, if this despairing hunt for a place free of social corruptions had a textual prototype in *The Excursion*. Despairing of social renovation in Europe, Wordsworth's 'Solitary' emigrates in search of that purer humanity promised by Paine and envisaged by the Imlay-inspired Pantisocrats. Disappointed by the colonies he then enacts the westward drive of Leatherstocking

> Let us, then, I said,
> Leave this unknit Republic to the scourge
> Of her own passions; and to regions haste,
> Whose shades have never felt the encroaching axe,
> Or soil endured a transfer in the mart
> Of dire rapacity. There, Man abides,
> Primeval Nature's child. (*Excursion*, III, 913–19)

Unfortunately he fails to find 'that pure archetype of human greatness' (951). Rather, the wilds appear to be populated by 'A creature, squalid, vengeful, and impure; / Remorseless, and submissive to no law / But superstitious fear, and abject sloth' (953–5). One would like to read this passage, Wordsworth's sole unfriendly depiction of American Indians, as auguring the sons of Ishmael Bush.

Insofar as *The Prairie* has a thesis, it is concerned with the extension of America as a result of the Louisiana Purchase in 1803, the masterstroke of Thomas Jefferson's Presidency. The purchase rid the United States of a potential rival, so that 'if ever time or necessity shall require a peaceful division of this vast empire, it assures us of a neighbour that will possess our language, our religion, our institutions, and it is also to be hoped, our sense of political justice' (9). The novel, however, gives little reassurance that 'our' sense of political justice, whatever that may be, will prevail. Rather, it offers a wavering balance between the kinds of justice represented by Leatherstocking, Ishmael Bush, and the government of the Union as represented by Captain Duncan Uncas Middleton. Only one of these authorities seems wholly at home with what Natty calls the rightful owners of the country – the Sioux and Pawnee – and he, of course dies at the end of the book and the saga. In any case, Leatherstocking, as usual, swamps Cooper's conscious theme. This Leatherstocking, reduced by age but freighted with all the insight his 82 years have given him into the forces of nature and the ways of the Pawnee and the Sioux, seems to move about *The Prairie* and the prairies as a sort of tutelary presence, immune to the fresh sufferings of his younger companions, on speaking terms with the cosmos and at home in the universe. When he counsels his youngest companion on the plains, who is destined to become a Kentucky legislator, to 'forget anything you may have heard from me, which is nevertheless true, and turn your mind on the ways of the inner country' (373) the effect, as is generally the case in Cooper's romances, is merely to confirm that there are the ways of truth, and the ways of political society.

The 82-year-old is consistent in this sense with the Leatherstocking of *The Pathfinder*, who in 1759 or so, somewhat anachronistically, has already graduated to a Wordsworthian sense of the speaking face of nature. As a novel, *The Pathfinder is* quite the worst in the series, though it fitted Russian taste like a glove:

> here he shows himself to be, like Shakespeare, a profound interpreter of the human heart ... he has uttered the inexpressible, has reconciled and fused into one the external and the internal, and his *The Pathfinder* is Shakespearean drama in form of the novel – the only creation in this genre, entirely without equal, a triumph of modern art in the sphere of epic poetry'.[10]

There is an excellent opening pursuit scene, constructed on the usual principle of a gentle maiden and a 'comic' character – in this case an *unspeakably* tedious old salt – being guided through hostile territory by the wise and fearless Pathfinder. There is also a brilliant inland lake storm scene, in which the handsome young suitor proves his mettle, and an exciting siege. There is, however, no treatment whatever of Chingachgook, who is engaged in perilous solo sorties most of the time, so we learn nothing whatever of what might have been the book's deepest topos, how it feels to be the last of one's race, after losing one's only son at the end of *Mohicans*. Even Natty is less in evidence *as an agent* than usual except in the preposterous shooting competition (in this justly famous exploit, Natty observes *at a hundred yards* not only that his ball has followed his opponent's into the target, but that it has done so *without touching the wood on either side of the bullet hole*)[11] and in the final desperate shoot-out. In plot terms the novel is a dress rehearsal for *The Deerslayer*. It exhibits a sharp decline from Cooper's *Lord of the Rings* mode to his *Swallows and Amazons* mode.

What saves *The Pathfinder* is that, despite its plot, it represents Cooper's strongest swerve from Burke to Wordsworth in the representation of nature. The shift is seen in the choice of a title-page epigraph from Cowper at his most Wordsworthian in *The Task* – 'Here the heart / May give a useful lesson to the head, / And learning wiser grow without his books' (*The Task,* VI, 86–8) – and underlined by the new prevalence of the Romantics in the epigraphs throughout. Alongside *As You Like It* (a source very proper to pastoral) and *The Task,* these come predictably from Moore, Campbell, Byron and Bryant, and less predictably from Spenser, Milton and Wordsworth. One epigraph from Wordsworth, the first four lines of 'Resolution and Independence' – 'There was a roaring in the wind all night' – strikes the right note for the imaginative quality of Leatherstocking, who at his best, which is not in this novel, has a genuinely Leech-Gatherish quality of belonging to the landscape.

The novel opens with a particularly fine encapsulation of the Romantic application of Burke, with even a hint of Kant:

> The sublimity connected with vastness, is familiar to every eye. The most abstruse, the most far-reaching, perhaps the most chastened of the poet's thoughts, crowd on the imagination as he gazes into the depths of the illimitable void; the expanse of the ocean is seldom seen by the novice, with indifference, and the mind, even in the obscurity of night, finds a parallel to that grandeur, which seems inseparable from images that the senses cannot compass. (*The Pathfinder*, 7)

The scene, specifically, is an American forest, similar to that of *The Wept of Wish-ton-Wish* in its Burkean combination of aesthetic and political qualities.[12] Here and there is an occasional opening among the giant trees for an inferior tree 'to lift its modest head', and for the aspen and birch to enter 'the presence of the stately and great'. The scene combines the sublime and the beautiful with all of Cooper's practised expertise: 'It was the vastness of the view, the nearly unbroken surface of verdure, that contained the principle of grandeur. The beauty was to be traced in the delicate tints, relieved by gradations of light and shadow, while the solemn repose induced a feeling allied to awe'. This is the cue for Mabel, who does not feel at all at home, to comment on the likeness of the scene to the ocean. Much later, she confesses that she is coming to love 'this grand silence of the woods'. But to the Pathfinder this comment shows how little she yet understands:

> The woods are never silent, Mabel, to such as understand their meanings. Days at a time, have I travelled them alone, without feeling the want of company, and, as for conversation, for such as can comprehend their language, there is no want of rational and instructive discourse. (266)

By the time of writing, of course, the influence of Bryant's enthusiastic Wordsworthianism, already evident in the early Cooper, may have been reinforced and theorized by Emerson's *Nature*, though Thoreau's dialogues with the speaking face of nature are yet to come.[13]

In Leatherstocking's final manifestation, in *The Deerslayer*, the plot has to do, as much as anything, with the development of Natty from a young man who can be arrested by a view, but can unthinkingly shoot a mating eagle, into one who feels his relationship with every living thing. Again the novel's epigraphs indicate the increasing Romanticism of the author, drawn for the first time as much from the Romantic tradition as from Shakespeare: epigraphs from Percy's *Reliques*, Chatterton, Joanna Baillie, Felicia Hemans, Scott, Wordsworth, Coleridge, Southey, Byron, Moore and Bryant set a tone far removed from the *Swallows and Amazons* plot.

Viewing Glimmerglass for the first time (Glimmerglass is Cooper's childhood Lake Otsego as it was in its virginity, long before the arrival of the pioneering William Cooper, who fathered both James Fenimore and Cooperstown), the Deerslayer stands entranced, not unlike the young Keats (if we except the [surely anachronistic?] rifle) taking his first view of Windermere:

> Deerslayer made no answer, but he stood leaning on his rifle, gazing at the view which so much delighted him. The reader is not to suppose, however, that it was the picturesque alone, which so strongly attracted his attention. The spot was very lovely, of a truth, and it was then seen in one of its most favourable moments, the surface of the lake being as smooth as glass, and limpid as pure air, throwing back the mountains, clothed in dark pines, along the whole of its Eastern boundary, the points thrusting forward their trees even near horizontal lines, while the bays were seen glittering through an occasional *arch* beneath, left by a *vault* fretted with branches and leaves. It was the air of deep repose, the solitudes that spoke of scenes and forests untouched by the hands of man, the reign of nature, in a word, that gave so much pure delight to one of his habits and turn of mind. Still, he felt, though it was unconsciously, like a poet also. He found a pleasure in studying this large, and, to him, unusual opening into the mysteries and forms of the woods, as one is gratified in getting broader views of any subject that has long occupied his thoughts. He was not insensible to the innate loveliness of such a landscape, either, but felt a portion of that soothing of the spirit which is a common attendant of a scene so thoroughly pervaded by the holy calm of nature.[14]

The arch and vault speak of a Bryantesque treatment of the forest,[15] while the passage insists that the pleasure Deerslayer takes in the scene runs deeper than the picturesque. While the scenic effect, as the narrator observes a little later, in a deliciously Gilpinesque fancy, is 'precisely that at which the lover of the picturesque would have aimed, had the ordering of this glorious setting of forest been submitted to his control' (51), Deerslayer is aware of the scene more Wordsworthianly as 'the anchor of his purest thoughts'. He has habitually, as a wanderer should, found time to impress such scenes upon his mind, and to attach to them his deepest feelings. His sweetheart, as he romantically puts it to the enamoured Judith, is in the forest, 'hanging from the boughs of the trees in a soft rain – in the dew on the open grass' (139) and more Romantically:

> He loved the woods for their freshness, their sublime solitudes, their vastness, and the impress that they everywhere bore of the divine hand of their creator. He rarely moved through them, without pausing to dwell on some peculiar beauty that gave him pleasure ... never did a day pass without his communing ... with the infinite source of all he saw, felt and beheld.

He was, in short, in a now overtly Wordsworthian education by nature, 'thus constituted in a moral sense, and of a steadiness that no danger could appal'.

If the book, the Edenic culmination of the series, has a moral argument, it is quite clearly that of 'Tintern Abbey' reinforced by *Peter Bell*. Numerous passages in the novel are redolent, as Donald Davie points out, of Wordsworthian perceptions in Wordsworthian diction, including the creation of Hutter's simple-minded child, one whose life, as the Indians recognize, is hidden with God.[16] And the point of the novel is to contrast the moral lives of Hetty and the Deerslayer with their savage white associates. Hurry Harry and Thomas Hutter go about their business in a purely self-interested fashion, and in consequence of this mental condition, it is suggested, turn the lake into a battlefield. To these characters, in the mould of Peter Bell, 'a primrose by a river's brim / A yellow primrose was to [them], / And it was nothing more' (259–60). It is *because of* that indifference, the novel argues, that the terrified scream of a child nocturnally scalped, or a young woman shot, generally indicates the presence of one or the other:

> If any earthly scene could be presented to the senses of man that might soothe his passions and temper his ferocity, it was that which grew upon the eyes of Hutter and Hurry, as the hours advanced, changing night to morning ... nevertheless the whole was lost on the observers, who knew no feeling of poetry, had lost their sense of natural devotion in lives of obdurate and narrow selfishness, and had little other sympathy with nature, than that which originated in her lowest wants'. (324)

The plot, in so far as it has one, is driven by one simple economic item. An Indian scalp – now that the colonial government has raised their price – has become a marketable commodity.

Of course Deerslayer, too, while contemplating Glimmerglass in the passage quoted earlier, leans upon his rifle, and the stance, as Tony Tanner has observed in one of the most brilliant of all appraisals of Cooper,[17] presages the development and despoliation of the scene. But we already know, as readers of this late novel, that Natty will resist as far as can be done, over the next sixty years, the corrosive effects of that despoliation. While war threatens, and even briefly invades this fragile Eden, it will still be, when Leatherstocking returns to it fifteen years after the action, an unspoiled place, with Hutter's roofless ark in a state of decay, a fluttering ribbon as a reminder of its beautiful inhabitant, and the abandoned canoes untouched. Such details are reminiscent of 'The Ruined Cottage'. If not quite as poignant as 'The useless fragment of a wooden bowl', the decay of the ark illustrates 'the calm oblivious tendencies' of nature quite as well. But *The Deerslayer* as a whole functions rather like Shelley's unravelling of evil in *Prometheus Unbound*. Cooper's last act, as an increasingly nostalgic historian of the foundations of his culture, was an act of erasure, an attempt to combat the signs of cultural decline with a symbolic potential, for good or evil. 'What good man', Andrew Jackson famously asked in his 1830 inaugural address, 'would prefer a country covered with forests and ranged by a few thousand savages, to our extensive republic, studded with cities, towns, and prosperous farms, embellished with all the improvements which art can devise or industry execute?'[18] One answer, of course, is the Leatherstocking; another – perhaps – his creator.

Technically and historiographically the American Scott, James Fenimore Cooper, as pastoral moralist, is in some respect more obviously the American Cowper. His early fictional strategies have properly been compared to those of Maria Edgeworth and Amelia Opie, and his mature ones to those of Fielding and Smollett. As political philosopher, as analyst of man in a state of nature, as proponent of a contractual view of constitutional theory, and as aesthetician of the sublime, he might be termed the American Burke. Central to his long journey from Federalist, through patriot-at-large, through liberal historian of America, to prophet of Tory values, is his affinity with the similarly paradoxical career of Edmund Burke. His constant travelling companion – and source of the great preponderance of his chapter epigraphs – was Shakespeare. Yet his contemporaries recognized in the creation of the Leatherstocking the values of Romanticism. So the American writer who most pugnaciously and pertinaciously asserted the cultural independence of America is, ironically, the one whose work encompasses with the greatest catholicity the cultural baggage of the old home.

Of Cooper's early readers the one who valued the Romantic Leatherstocking most fully is George Sand. In the creation of this character, more than in any other development, Sand felt, Cooper achieved his major differentiation from Scott.

> This well-loved figure who, in the novels, first goes by the name of the Spy, then the Bravo, and finally the Hunter of the plains, is the complete revelation of Cooper's deepest thought ... There is the superiority of the individual over the society of his time, and perhaps over Scott himself as poet.

Natty raises Cooper above himself and enables a new 'depth of feeling'. 'It is he, who without actually describing anything, depicts the true sublimity of nature: his calm ecstasy seizes us almost unawares and communicates itself to us in order to show us, as if in an enchanted glass, the magnificent scenes his excited eye reflects'. Moreover, 'Nathaniel' is a way of writing about the iniquities involved in creating America without stigmatizing those iniquities; pleading the cause of the Indians without affronting the pride of his country (Dekker and McWilliams 263–7).

This Wordsworthian conception of 'the silent poet' is shared by the reviewer of the *British Critic,* July 1826, who also praised Cooper for heroes who 'are imbued with that intuitive sense of the sublimities of nature and religion which often exists in the minds of men too illiterate to give utterance'(Dekker and McWilliams 73). Sand, who clearly sees Natty as a sort of Western Michael, makes no explicit comparison with Wordsworth, and may have none in mind – France was not notoriously receptive to Wordsworth's stature – but *Colburn's New Monthly Magazine* is twice driven to use quotations from Wordsworth to make its point about Cooper's handling of landscape. Compared with Scott, again, 'his pictures of scenery are more vast, more vivid, more true. His works are the effusions of a man accustomed to study the mighty forms of nature ... To him her colours and images "have no need of a remoter charm, by thought supplied or any interest unborrowed from the eye"' (Dekker and McWilliams 121). Whether or not *Colburn's* reviewer meant this slight on Cooper's imagination, he does accord with George Sand in estimating the importance of Natty in energizing it. Focusing on Natty, he echoes Hazlitt's famous comment on Wordsworth's personal interest in the universe, in *The Spirit of the Age* (1825), remarking that 'the needless slaughter of birds, or the felling of trees, pains him like an affront to himself (quoted in Dekker and McWilliams, 123)'.

That contemporary critics should be found employing Wordsworthian terms in talking of Cooper's aesthetic is not altogether surprising. The year 1824 was an *annus mirabilis* for Wordsworth in America, the year of his first legitimate American collected poems, and of the first really enthusiastic encomiums in both the *North American Review* and New York's *Atlantic*

Monthly.[19] Even before that, however, in the most important aesthetic document Cooper himself produced, a review of Catherine Sedgwick's *A New-England Tale* for the *Literary and Scientific Repository* (May 1822), Cooper gives concrete evidence of some familiarity with the poetics of the 'Preface' to *Lyrical Ballads* and (judging from his unattributed quotation from 'The Old Cumberland Beggar') with the poetry itself.

> The writer carries us out of the world of our self-love ... enjoying our imagination agreeably, by presenting to it such views of the human heart with its affections, and of human life in its appearances, its modes of enjoyment and improvement, of suffering and degeneracy, as interest curiosity, increase our knowledge, correct our false opinions, and what is more powerful than all, appeal to our sympathies. We love an interesting fiction, because, however paradoxical the assertion may appear, it addresses our love of truth – not the mere love of facts expressed by true names and dates, but the love of that higher truth, the truth of nature and principles, which is a primitive law of the human mind ... A good novel addresses itself very powerfully to our moral nature and conscience, and to those good feelings, and good principles, which providence has planted within us, constantly to remind us that 'we have, all of us, one human heart'.[20]

Ironically, despite this passage, Wordsworth's kind of naturalism is usually well beyond Cooper's range. His early work contains no Simon Lee, or Goody Blake, or Margaret, or even 'Crazy Bet', the Edgeworthian or Wordsworthian character he praises in Sedgwick's tale, though there are hints of an interest in idiocy in both *The Wept of Wish-ton-Wish* and *Deerslayer*, both of which works belong to his most Wordsworthian phase.[21] But the *Lyrical Ballads* model may well have pushed Cooper towards another aspect of his fiction which his contemporaries admired, and which George Eliot appears to have learned from: his homely dialogue, and sympathetic pictures of frontier and community life. At his social realistic best, the historian of eighteenth-century Templeton and of seventeenth-century Wish-ton-Wish comes very close indeed to the historian of Raveloe and St Ogg's. And despite the predilection for distinctly un-Wordsworthian 'moving accident' as the staple of his fiction, he introduces the simple character of the old trapper in the 1827 preface to *The Prairie* with a most Wordsworthian note, in which the pressure of Hazlitt's great essay is once again felt: 'It is quite probable that the narrator of these simple events has deceived himself as to the importance they may have in the eyes of other people. But he has seen or thought he has seen, something sufficiently instructive and touching in the life of a veteran of the forest ... to induce him to hazard the experiment of publication' (2).

Moved 'to solemnise' by a waterfall in *The Pioneers,* yet untouched, it seems, by a similar, if less orderly, masterpiece of nature in the next novel, *Last of the Mohicans,* Natty Bumppo requires two decades of reconfiguration to complete the transition from unconscious 'inmate of this active universe' to one of the 'Prophets of Nature' (*TP*, II, 254; XIV, 446). Those two decades – from 1823 to 1843 – were of course the ones in which Wordsworth's American reputation gradually attained ascendancy over Byron's. If Natty's final configuration in *The Deerslayer* and *The Pathfinder,* as a figure who embodies the values of 'Tintern Abbey', owes something to Emerson's *Nature,* the unacknowledged borrowing is fair exchange. After all, Emerson in 'The American Scholar' had usurped quite shamelessly Cooper's prior role as advocate of literary and cultural independence. In both writers, in any case, paradoxically and perhaps inevitably, the mantle of independence cloaks a figural dependence on *the* poet of 'National Independence and Liberty'.[22]

Notes

1. Edmund Burke, *A Philosophical Enquiry into the Origin of Our Ideas of the Sublime and Beautiful,* ed. Adam Phillips (Oxford: Oxford UP, 1990), 76.
2. *The Wept of Wish-ton-Wish* in *Lionel Lincoln and The Wept of Wish-ton-Wish* (Chicago, IL, New York, NY and San Francisco, CA: Belford, Clark, n.d.), 115–25. Subsequent reference are to page numbers in this edition.
3. Steven Blakemore, ' "Without a Cross": The Cultural Significance of the Sublime and Beautiful in Cooper's *The Last of the Mohicans*', *Nineteenth-Century Literature* (1997): 27–57.
4. H. Daniel Peck, *A World by Itself: The Pastoral Moment in Cooper's Fiction* (New Haven, CT: Yale UP, 1977), 127.
5. *The Last of the Mohicans,* ed. John McWilliams (Oxford UP, 1994), 57. Subsequent references are to page numbers in this edition.
6. Famous, because it appears on the dust jackets of the Everyman *William Wordsworth: Selected Poems,* ed. Walford Davies (London: Dent, 1975) and the *Norton Anthology of American Literature,* volume 1, eds Nina Baym, *et al.*, 5th edition (New York and London: W.W. Norton, 1998).
7. *The Pioneers,* ed. James D. Wallace (Oxford: Oxford UP, 1992), 293. Subsequent references are to page numbers in this edition.
8. *The Prairie,* ed. Donald A. Ringe (Oxford: Oxford UP, 1992), 213, 240, 370. Subsequent references are to page numbers in this edition.
9. Compare *The Prelude* (1805), Book VIII, lines 400–16, with their image of the shepherd 'in size a giant' and 'glorified / By the deep radiance of the setting sun', 'A solitary object and sublime'. The perception grounds Wordsworth's sense of 'the human form' as an index of 'power and worthiness'.
10. V. G. Belinsky, cited in George Dekker and John P. McWilliams (eds), *James Fenimore Cooper: The Critical Heritage* (London and Boston, MA: Routledge & Kegan Paul, 1973).
11. *The Pathfinder, or The Inland Sea,* ed. Richard Dilworth Rust (Albany, NY: State University of New York Press, 1981), 161. (Subsequent references are to page numbers in this edition.) This particular feat earned Mark Twain's hilarious derision.

12. According to the narrator of *The Wept of Wish-ton-Wish,* the forest through which Submission and Conanchet are travelling, towards Conanchet's death, is in a continual state of renovation and decay: 'By this provision of nature, the wilderness, in the midst of so many successive changes, is always maintained at the point nearest to perfection, since the accessions are so few and gradual as to preserve its character. The American forest exhibits in the highest degree the grandeur of repose' (323–4). In Burke's famous figure, a stable polity is 'a permanent body of transitory parts [...] the whole is never old, or middle aged, or young, but in a condition of unchangeable constancy, moves on through the varied tenour or perpetual decay, fall, renovation and progression': *Reflections on the Revolution in France* (Harmondsworth: Penguin, 1968), 120.
13. Richard Henry Dana recorded Bryant's enthusiasm on discovering Wordsworth's ballads: 'he said that upon opening the book, a thousand springs seemed to gush up at once in his heart, and the face of nature, of a sudden, to change into a strange freshness and life. He had felt the sympathetic touch from an according mind'. *Poems and Prose Writings* (Boston, MA: Russell, Odiorne, 1833), 148.
14. *The Deerslayer,* ed. H. Daniel Peck (Oxford: Oxford UP, 1993), 46–7, my emphases.
15. 'The groves were God's first temples. Ere man learned/ To hew the shaft and lay the architrave' (William Cullen Bryant, 'A Forest Hymn', 1–2).
16. *The Heyday of Sir Walter Scott* (London: Routledge & Kegan Paul, 1961), 123.
17. *Scenes of Nature, Signs of Men,* (Cambridge: Cambridge UP, 1987), 1–10.
18. *A Compilation of the Messages and Papers of the Presidents,* ed. J. D. Richardson (10 vols. Washington DC, 1896–99), II, 521; cited from Roderick Nash, *Wilderness and the American Mind* (New Haven, CT and London: Yale UP, 1982), 41.
19. Greenwood, writing in the *North American Review,* was perhaps the most encomiastic and apologetic regarding the slowness of Wordsworthian reception in America: '[H]e who has done more than any living writer to restore to poetry the language of feeling, nature and truth, remains unread, unsought for, and almost unknown' yet 'the great distinction and glory of Mr Wordsworth's poetry is the intimate converse which it holds with Nature. He sees her face to face ... [and unravels] those secret influences which we had always felt, but hardly understood'. Not merely describing objects, Wordsworth 'causes them to live, breath, feel'. The alert reader, Greenwood concludes, 'knows that many of the poets, with whose writings this country is so familiar [Byron? Bryant?], have borrowed some of their sweetest minstrelsy from strains which have reached us but rarely and faintly from the mountains of Westmoreland [*sic*]; and he is continually detecting plagiarisms, both in spirit and in letter, made from the volumes of Wordsworth, by those who have joined to depress him'. *North American Review* 18 (1824): 356–71. For wider evidence see William Charvat, *The Origins of American Critical Thought 1810–1835* (Philadelphia, PA: University of Pennsylvania Press, 1936).
20. *Literary and Scientific Repository* 4, no. 8 (1822): 337–8, my emphases. Cooper's unattributed closing quotation is from Wordsworth's poem 'The Old Cumberland Beggar'.
21. As late as 1836 Wordsworth's affection for the simple hindered his acceptance: the editor of the 1836 Philadelphia edition of *The Poetical Works of Coleridge, Shelley and Keats,* while disparaging Coleridge's impenetrable philosophy, praises Shelley because 'his theme is the high one of intellectual nature and lofty feelings, not of waggoners or idiot children', 245.

22. Cooper and Wordsworth represented the poles of opinion on Anglo-American relations in 1826–28. In 1828 Cooper welcomed the role of the anti-American *Quarterly* in 'alienating the feelings of America from England', both in *Notions of the Americans*, and in the 1828 draft of *Gleanings*, as helpful to true 'mental emancipation' (*Gleanings from Europe: England* [1837], ed. Robert E. Spiller [New York, NY: Oxford UP, 1930], 364). In 1826, however, Wordsworth inscribed a long memorandum in the travel album of Elliott Cresson, a visiting Philadelphia Quaker, which concluded: 'It is my earnest wish that animosity may cease between us; that we may think of each other not for the purpose of inflicting reciprocal injuries, but with kindness and good will; and that Emulation may act only to make the two Nations, so closely connected by consanguinity, by institutions, customs and language, every day more and more worthy of each other's esteem. Policy requires this, Justice would infallibly produce it, and Nature sanctions it (11 Sept 1826)'. MS Berg Collection of the New York Public Library, cited from Stephen Gill, *William Wordsworth: A Life* (Oxford: Clarendon, 1969), 349.

3

Discord at Pennacook: Whittier and the Problem of American Picturesque

Bruce Graver

At the end of the introductory section of 'The Bridal at Pennacook', published in 1845,[1] John Greenleaf Whittier writes:

> Yet I trust
> That some, who sigh, while wandering in thought,
> Pilgrims of Romance o'er the olden world,
> That our broad land, – our sea-like lakes, and mountains
> Piled to the clouds, – our rivers overhung
> By forests which have known no other change
> For ages, than the budding and the fall
> Of leaves, – our valleys lovelier than those
> Which the old poets sang of, – should but figure
> On the apocryphal chart of speculation
> As pastures, wood-lots, mill-sites, with the privileges,
> Rights, and appurtenances, which make up
> A Yankee Paradise, – unsung, unknown,
> To beautiful tradition; even their names,
> Whose melody yet lingers like the last
> Vibration of the red-man's requiem,
> Exchanged for syllables significant
> Of cotton-mill and rail-car, will look kindly
> On this effort to call up the ghost
> Of our dim Past, and listen with pleased ear
> To the responses of the questioned Shade.
>
> (*Poems*, 13–14)

Here, Whittier outlines his programme for an American picturesque. The American landscape, he asserts, possesses natural beauties that surpass those of Europe; consequently, poets who celebrate it must discover a different and more impressive poetic style. Moreover, writers of the American picturesque must be preservationists: they must invest places of natural beauty, which unlike Europe's are nearly pristine, with a cultural value that will strengthen them against the destructive pressures of greedy industrialists, speculators, and farmers. Part of this act of preservation is the preservation of American Indian place-names: Kearsarge, Merrimack, Uncanoonuc, Pennacook. When fitted to English metre, these names will help provide poets with the distinctive new melodies they need. But the names also evoke the history of brutal conflict between indigenous and European cultures in which all Americans are implicated. Whittier's aim, then, is more than celebratory and conservative: it is also profoundly moral. He wants to alter the ways in which picturesque tourists perceive natural beauty by forcing them to recognize and lament the genocide that made their wealth and leisure possible.

For more than a decade before composing 'The Bridal at Pennacook', Whittier had been experimenting with ways to map the conventions of the British picturesque on to the American landscape. As he explained in the preface to *Legends of New England* (1831), his first book-length publication, this meant integrating the 'green hills' and 'pleasant rivers' of New England with legendary tales 'of superstition and manly daring and romantic adventure', mostly depicting conflicts between white settlers and Native Americans.[2] The works in this volume, consisting of narrative poems and prose sketches, are almost all in this vein, as was *Mogg Megone* (1836), his Scott-like romance about the death of a seventeenth-century Saco chieftain. Yet, as Whittier himself acknowledged, in his early works the relationship between story and setting is often merely tangential: 'The story of Mogg Megone', he wrote in his headnote, is 'only ... a frame-work for sketches of the scenery of New England' (*Poems*, 33). And he was defensive about the subject matter itself, afraid of being reproached for exposing 'the bigotry of our ancestors' (*Legends*, iv). Towards the end of his life, he sought to have most of these works suppressed.[3]

In 1840, after resigning his editorship of the abolitionist paper, *The Pennsylvania Freeman*, and returning home from Philadelphia to his native Merrimack valley, Whittier again took up the New England landscape and its historical past as his primary poetic subject, with much greater success. Several of these efforts were grouped together and published in 1843 as *Lays of my Home*, a volume which, according to John B. Pickard, 'heralded the birth of a mature poet' (*Letters*, I, 479). Whittier's success can be attributed, in part, to his turning to Wordsworth, especially the Wordsworth of the *Lyrical Ballads*, as a poetic model.[4] Two of the *Lays* are especially important in this regard: 'The Merrimack' and 'The Funeral Tree of the Sokokis'. In these poems, Whittier, like Wordsworth, acts as a tour guide for his readers, first pointing out views for our notice, and offering what seem to be conventionally picturesque descriptions of them. He then inscribes these views with narratives that historicize our perception of them and invest the landscape with a moral significance that transcends the kinds of sensual pleasure usually associated with picturesque beauty. In these respects he is also following Wordsworth's poems such as 'Michael', 'Hart-Leap Well' and 'Tintern Abbey'. But Whittier does so with an important American twist: in the two *Lays*, he focuses on moments of colonial conquest, calling to our attention historical conflicts between European and indigenous peoples. In 'The Bridal of Pennacook', he sets a legendary American Indian tale into the framework of a picturesque tour, to emphasize the cultural loss that has made contemporary tourism possible. In this chapter, I will briefly consider 'The Merrimack' and 'The Funeral Tree of the Sokokis', before turning to a more extended analysis of 'The Bridal at Pennacook'.

I 'The Merrimack'

'The Merrimack' opens as a conventional loco-descriptive poem, employing one of its standard metres, the octosyllabic couplet, and much of its stock diction. 'Stream of my fathers!' Whittier begins:

> sweetly still
> The sunset rays thy valley fill;
> Poured slantwise down the long defile,
> Wave, wood, and spire beneath them smile.

Figure 1 Plate of the Merrimack valley and river to accompany Whittier's 'The Merrimack'. Reproduced from *Poems* (1849). Reproduced from *The Poets of America. Illustrated by One of Her Painters*, ed. John Leese, New York, 1842.

I see the winding Powow fold
The green hill in its belt of gold,
And following down its wavy line,
Its sparkling waters blend with thine.
(*Poems*, 75)

The scene is an idealized Claudian prospect, the light falling obliquely across the hills, farms and winding river, gilding the landscape.[5] But halfway through the poem, Whittier turns from description to history: he attempts to recreate the moment of the first English encounter with the Merrimack valley, in 1614, when Captain John Smith and his crew sailed up the river mouth and claimed the territory for England.[6] Stripped of 'spire', 'wall', and 'farm-house', the landscape is again pristine, and the sight of it brings joy to 'Britain's hearts of oak', who are 'Weary of forest, sea, and sky' (*Lays of my Home*, 1–3). Their response accords with their colonialist enterprise: they plant 'Saint George's crimson cross' 'Midst the tangled vine and dwarfish wood', with 'roll of drum and trumpet blare'. Then, in an oddly erotic twist, Smith names the 'lone promontory' for his Turkish mistress, Tragabizanda,

The sweetest name in all his story; ...
Who, when the chance of war had bound
The Moslem chain his limbs around,
Wreathed o'er with silk that iron chain,
Soothed with her smiles his hours of pain,
And fondly to her youthful slave
A dearer gift than freedom gave.
(*Lays of my Home*, 3)

His staking a colonial claim thus is figured as both a martial conquest and an explicitly sexual act with a beautiful, yet alien, other.

On the face of things, Whittier is celebrating the English as founders of the farms and pastoral towns described in his opening lines. But he has deliberately left something out: the indigenous peoples whom the European colonists have dispossessed. Or rather, Whittier has almost omitted them, for Native American place names are aggressively present from the outset of the poem. 'The Indians', reads the headnote, 'speak of a beautiful river, far to the South, which they call Merrimack' (*Lays of my Home*, 1). Later, as the sailors first view the valley, Whittier writes:

Breaking the dull continous wood,
The Merrimack rolled down his flood;
Mingling that clear pellucid brook,
Which channels vast Agiochook ...

> And more abundant waters given
> From that pure lake, "The Smile of Heaven"
> (*Lays of my Home*, 2–3)

'The Smile of Heaven' is an English translation of Winnipiseogee (Whittier's preferred spelling of Winnipesaukee), one of the sources of the Merrimack. This name, denoting a divinely blessed harmony of nature and humanity, contrasts starkly with the military pomp and implicit sexual violation of the English explorers. Their armour and fanfare prefigure the violence that will make possible the picturesque farming community which Whittier so loves and admires. Ironically, the 'Smile of Heaven' no longer shines for the people who named it.[7] Only their melodious place names 'linger' in the New England countryside, to remind us that European conquest was also 'the red-man's requiem'.

It would be a mistake, however, to read 'The Merrimack' as a critique of English colonialism: it is a poem of praise, both of the spirit of the early explorers, and of the white settlers who cultivated the Merrimack valley. By their labours the 'tangled vine and dwarfish wood' have become tilled fields, 'green hills' and 'poplar colonnades', the 'sparkling waters' are touched with 'busy oars' and dotted with sails, and a 'lonely coast-light' keeps mariners from shipwreck. This is a specifically georgic ethic: the culture Whittier celebrates springs from the soil the colonial settlers have cultivated. But not without cost, tremendous cost, to indigenous peoples, a cost that Whittier explores in another of the *Lays of my Home*, 'The Funeral Tree of the Sokokis'.

II 'The Funeral Tree of the Sokokis'

'The Funeral Tree of the Sokokis' was written and published at the same time as 'The Merrimack', and was intended as a companion poem to it.[8] As in 'The Merrimack', Whittier begins by describing a carefully composed view, and then inscribes it with a narrative that historicizes our understanding of what we see. But this time he has shifted the scene from a cultivated river valley to a favourite New England tourist destination, Lake Sebago in Maine, and rather than a tale about the joy of European explorers, Whittier focuses on a moment of grief and dispossession, told from the point of view of the Sokokis tribe. 'The Funeral Tree of the Sokokis' thus focuses on the darker side of the colonialist enterprise, exposing the violence and slaughter that made it possible for European settlers to enjoy the produce of cultivated valleys, or experience the pleasure of beautiful views. Buried in the picturesque beauty of the New England landscape, Whittier reminds us, are the brutal sins of our ancestors.

Whittier wrote the poem to be illustrated in the picturesque mode. His close friend and fellow poet, Elizabeth Lloyd, had 'an embossed sheet of Bristol Board' on which she wanted draw a frontispiece to a manuscript

Figure 2 Elizabeth Lloyd's frontispiece for 'The Funeral Tree of the Sokokis'. The text reads, from top to bottom, 'Whittier Leaves', 'not left to glide, / Unnoted down oblivion's tide'; 'The Funeral Tree of the Sokokis', '—One lone Beech, unfolding there / Its light leaves in the April air'; '1841'. Reproduced by permission of the Quaker Collection, Haverford College Library.

volume of his poems, transcribed by their mutual friend, Elizabeth Nicholson (see Figure 2). 'Now Greenleaf', she wrote,

> could thee not write something from which I could devise a picture ... ? Is there not some cherished spot of N England scenery yet unsung – which could be painted and poetized – something grand – bold – and characteristic.[9]

And thus Whittier opens the poem with a descriptive passage well-suited to Lloyd's picturesque taste:

> Around Sebago's lonely lake
> There lingers not a breeze to break
> The mirror which its waters make.
> The solemn pines along its shore,
> The first which hang its gray rocks o'er,
> Are painted on its glassy floor.
> The sun looks o'er, with hazy eye,
> The snowy mountain-tops which lie
> Piled coldly up against the sky ... .
> Yet green are Saco's banks below,
> And belts of spruce and cedar show,
> Dark fringing round those cones of snow ... .
> Her tokens of renewing care
> Hath Nature scattered everywhere,
> In bud and flower, and warmer air.
> (*Lays of my Home*, 22–3)

To this point, the poem would seem picturesque travel-writing and its speaker a tour guide, were it not for its title and Whittier's opening footnote, derived almost word for word from a decidedly unpicturesque source: William Williamson's *History of the State of Maine*.

> Polan, a chief of the Sokokis Indians, the original inhabitants of the country lying between Agamenticus and Casco bay, was killed in a skirmish at Windham, on the Sebago lake, in the spring of 1756. He claimed all of the lands on both sides of the Presumscot river to its mouth at Casco, as his own. He was shrewd, noble, and brave. After the white men had retired, the surviving Indians 'swayed', or bent down a young tree until its roots were turned up, placed the body of their chief beneath them, and then released the tree to spring back to its former position. (*Lays of my Home*, 22)[10]

Thus, like the 'straggling heap of unhewn stones' in Wordsworth's 'Michael', the view Whittier has described needs the mediation of a poet to be properly read. In fact, he has described a grave, not simply a pleasurable prospect, and the dominant genre of the poem is elegy, not description. And the elegy is carefully historicized: Whittier calls his readers to witness a specific historical event, the burial of a powerful Sokokis leader, killed by white colonists who claimed his territory.[11]

In the poem, Whittier moves from description to elegy by focusing on the foreground of the picturesque scene. There, in the shadow of a tree, the Sokokis bury their chief according to their traditional ceremony.

> The turf's red stain is yet undried –
> Scarce have the death-shot echoes died
> Along Sebago's wooded side :
> And silent now the hunter's stand,
> Grouped darkly, where a swell of land
> Slopes upward from the lake's white sand.
> (*Lays of my Home*, 24–5)

'With grave, cold looks' they partially uproot a young beech, under it their 'fallen chief is laid', and then 'the roots are backward sent, / The beechen tree stands up unbent – / The Indian's fitting monument!' Whittier continues:

> There shall his fitting requiem be,
> In northern winds, that, cold and free,
> Howl nightly in that funeral tree.
> To their wild wail the waves which break
> Forever round that lonely lake
> A solemn under-tone shall make!
> (*Lays of my Home*, 25–6)

The chief's body thus is absorbed back into nature, his monument neither quarried stone nor cut wood, but a living thing that shows no sign of human presence. For Whittier, the Indian lives and dies in the landscape without disrupting or transforming it, preserving a primal harmony with nature that European colonists often destroy.

The burial scene also engages itself with colonial history in a more deeply problematic way. The year 1756 dates the poem to the time of the French and Indian War, a year after the expulsion of French Acadians from British colonies, including Maine. The Sokokis were allied with the French, and Polan, in attempting to maintain ancestral territory, became a victim of the crossfire between two competing colonial empires. Even the usual excuse, that American Indians were just savage heathens anyway, could not apply in this case: 'The Sokokis', we are told in a footnote, 'were early converts to the Catholic faith', converted by French Jesuit missionaries, and in the poem, Polan is buried with 'The silver cross he loved ... pressed / Beneath the heavy arms' (*Lays of my Home*, 25). Whittier then notes of his murderer:

> The brutal and unchristian spirit of the early settlers of New England toward the red man, is strikingly illustrated in the conduct of the man who shot down the Sokokis chief. He used to say he always noticed the anniversary of that exploit, as 'the day on which he sent the devil a present'. (*Lays of my Home*, 27)

At this point, it is necessary to look more closely at Whittier's source for the poem, Williamson's *History*, in order to have a fuller sense of poet's procedures. Williamson is cited at the end of the note just quoted, but his attitude and Whittier's could scarcely be more different. For Williamson, Polan was 'an inveterate enemy of the settlers', 'resolutely determined never to make a lasting peace with the English', until his ancestral lands were restored; just before his death, he and twenty warriors had ambushed and shot two settlers as they went to work their farm. In retribution for this ambush, another farmer, Stephen Manchester, hunted him down and killed him (Williamson, II, 321). These details are omitted in Whittier's poem, who reduces it all to 'a skirmish', thereby making Polan's death seem an unprovoked murder. Williamson also clearly admires Manchester, calling him 'a man of great courage, – perfectly acquainted with the woods and with the Indian manner of fighting', and describing with approval both his stratagem for killing the chief, and his grim anniversary celebration. (Williamson, II, 322). For Whittier, however, Manchester was 'brutal and unchristian'. Even Polan's conversion to Christianity is downplayed: Williamson merely remarks, with apparent disgust, that at his burial, Polan's arm was cut off 'to be deposited in some holy catholic burying-ground' (Williamson, II, 232). The silver crucifix is apparently Whittier's invention, and only he suggests that the American Indian may be capable of genuine Christian faith. In short, Whittier's judgement is not just on the 'brutal and unchristian' spirit of Manchester and the 'early settlers': it is also on historians like Williamson. In 'The Funeral Tree of the Sokokis', Whittier is not just revising the picturesque: he is rewriting history.

In the *Lays of my Home*, then, Whittier's experiments with the picturesque show a number of tendencies. First, he is interested in reminding his readers of how the landscape looked before Europeans arrived, and in so doing compares the ways in which colonialism has altered a state of nature that Native Americans had left largely pristine. In many ways, the changes have been good: a wilderness has been transformed, by georgic labour, into a prosperous countryside. But Whittier also insists on showing the price we have paid for our prosperity. The views we enjoy as picturesque tourists, or simply as townspeople who climb a neighbouring hill, have been made possible by systematic genocide; thus the pleasure we take in scenic beauty, natural or cultivated, needs to be tempered and complicated by a sense of moral guilt that cannot be explained away with slogans about progress or religion or racial superiority. And Whittier is aware of the need to preserve places of natural beauty, an awareness that grows from the joy such places can produce, and from his sense, especially in 'The Funeral Tree of the Sokokis', that without active preservation, we lose a state of nature that our predecessors in this land knew how to maintain. The 'red man's requiem' may turn out to be a prelude to America's own.

III 'The Bridal at Pennacook'

Figure 3 Plate, engraved by A.C. Warren, illustrating the following lines of 'The Bridal at Pennacook': 'On that strong turbid water, a small boat / Guided by one weak hand was seen to float'. Reproduced from *Poems*, 1849. This illustration by H. Billings.

'The Bridal at Pennacook' is Whittier's most ambitious early poem in the picturesque mode, composed within two years of *Lays of my Home*, and loosely based on historical material that he had begun to collect more than a decade earlier.[12] The poem consists of over 800 lines, divided into nine sections, each with its own distinctive verse form, ranging from blank verse to ballad stanzas to ottava rima. His model is Wordsworth of the *Lyrical Ballads*, especially 'Michael'. Like 'Michael', 'The Bridal of Pennacook' is a frame narrative addressed to picturesque tourists. A group of New Englanders, including the poet, has been touring the New Hampshire mountains, and his account of their travels is a veritable catalogue of American Indian place names.

> And we had rested underneath the oaks
> Shadowing the bank ...
> Of the wild Ammonoosuc. We had tracked
> The winding Pemigewasset, overhung
> By beechen shadows ... We had seen the moon
> Rising behind Umbagog's eastern pines,
> Like a great Indian camp-fire ; and its beams
> At midnight spanning with a bridge of silver
> The Merrimack by Uncanoonuc's falls. (*Poems*, 10)

On their journey, one of the travellers, the daughter of a merchant speculator, grows ill, forcing them to lay up in an inn in Conway. To entertain her in her illness, they recast in verse a legend of the Merrimack valley about the great Pennacook Sachem, Passaconaway. The name 'Pennacook' is important, for besides being the name of Passaconaway's tribe, it also is the name of his settlement and the future site of Concord, New Hampshire. Here we can see how Whittier is revising his Wordsworthian model. In 'Michael', Wordsworth leads conventional tourists off the main road and into a hidden valley, where he inscribes a decidedly un-picturesque pile of stones with a tale of profound moral significance. Similarly, Whittier's tale is not about a conventionally picturesque site: it is about a manufacturing town whose natural beauty has been altered and almost destroyed, and whose indigenous name has been all but forgotten. But unlike Wordsworth, he cannot simply lead his audience off the main road: Concord *is* the main road. Instead, he must rename it, force his audience to erase the city they and their ancestors have built, and reimagine the civilization they destroyed to build it.

Like 'Michael', Whittier's narrative is an elegiac tale of suffering and loss. It tells of the marriage of Passaconaway's daughter to Winnepurkit, Sachem of the Saugus, a tribe which inhabited lands further down the Merrimack. The story is derived from Thomas Morton's *New Canaan*, an early seventeenth-century account of New England, and in Morton the tale is used to exemplify the importance of reputation and honour among the native tribes. In a headnote to the poem, Whittier summarizes Morton's version of the story:

> Winnepurkit ... Sachem of Saugus, married a daughter of Passaconaway, the great Pennacook chieftain ... and the ceremonies concluded with a great feast ... . According to the usages of the chiefs, Passaconaway ordered a select number of his men to accompany the newly married couple to the dwelling of the husband, where in turn there was another great feast. Some time after, the wife of Winnepurkit expressing a desire to visit her father's house was permitted to go, accompanied by a brave escort of her husband's chief men. But when she wished to return, her father sent a messenger to Saugus, informing her husband, and asking him to come and take her away. He returned for an answer that he had escorted his wife to her father's house in a style that became a chief, and that now if she wished to return, her father must send her back, in the same way. This Passaconaway refused to do. (*Poems*, 9)

Morton's original account concludes:

> So much these two Sachems stood upon tearmes of reputation with each other, the one would not send her, & the other would not send for her, least it should be any diminishing of honour on his part, that should seeme to comply, that the Lady (when I came out of the Country) remained still with her father; which is a thinge worth noting, that Salvage people should seeke to maintaine their reputation so much as they doe.[13]

Whittier retains the outline of Morton's narrative, but makes additions which transform its moral significance: rather than emphasizing the pride and honour of the Sachems, Whittier stresses the ambiguous social status of American Indian women, and their suffering at the hands of Native American men.

He does so, first, by an act of naming: Passaconaway's daughter, anonymous in Morton's *New Canaan*, is called Weetamoo.[14] The story itself is told primarily from her point of view. We learn that Weetamoo's mother died in childbirth, and that, in raising her, stern Passaconaway 'from his child ... drew / A life of Love and Hope', a clear echo of Michael's love for Luke (*Poems*, 19). Weetamoo, partly because she lacks a mother, grows up to have a peculiarly close reciprocal relationship with nature: she is called 'Child of the forest', and 'the child of nature'; and in lines that recall the

Wordsworth of the ' Ode: Intimations of Immortality' (and also 'Three Years She Grew'), Whittier writes:

> It is enough for such to be
> Of common, natural things a part,
> To feel, with bird and stream and tree
> The pulses of the same great heart;
> But we, from Nature long exiled,
> In our cold homes of Art and Thought
> Grieve like the stranger-tended child,
> Which seeks its mother's arms, and sees but feels them not.
> (*Poems*, 20–1)

Weetamoo's love for Winnepurkit is also described with surprising sensitivity and intimacy. He shows her no tenderness, 'No fond and playful dalliance', but her love remains strong:

> As o'er some granite wall
> Soft vine-leaves open to the moistening dew
> And warm bright sun, the love of that young wife
> Found on a hard cold breast the dew and warmth of life … .
> For she had learned the maxims of her race,
> Which teach the woman to become a slave,
> And feel herself the pardonless disgrace
> Of love's fond weakness in the wise and brave, –
> (*Poems*, 25)

Though a slave, Weetamoo is figured as a living vine, a vital part of vegetative nature, and as such stands in contrast to her husband, the strong but inanimate granite wall. The vine, Whittier implies, if allowed its foothold, will eventually break the stone to dust.

Whittier's most important addition to the tale is its ending, in which Weetamoo makes a desperate and fatal attempt to return to her husband, alone in a canoe on a Merrimack swollen with the March thaw.[15]

> Down the vexed centre of that rushing tide,
> The thick, huge ice-blocks threatening either side,
> The foam-white rocks of Amoskeag in view,
> With arrowy swiftness sped that light canoe.
> The trapper, moistening his moose's meat
> On the wet bank by Uncanoonuc's feet,
> Saw the swift boat flash down the troubled stream;
> Slept he, or waked he? was it truth or dream?

Sick and aweary of her lonely life,
Heedless of peril, the still faithful wife
Had left her mother's grave, her father's door,
To seek the wigwam of her chief once more.

Down the white rapids like a sear leaf whirled,
On the sharp rocks and piled-up ices hurled,
Empty and broken, circled the canoe
In the vexed pool below – but where was Weetamoo?
(*Poems*, 29–30)

Before discussing this passage, I need to say a little more about the dramatic situation in the Conway inn, where the story is being told. The merchant's daughter is being wooed in her illness by a young clergyman, who sings to her and reads her poetry, specifically 'the sweet songs ... Of him whose whitened locks on Rydal Mount / Are lifted yet by morning breezes' (*Poems*, 12). Thus the tale of Weetamoo is being told against the backdrop of Wordsworth's poetry, and Wordsworthian narrative provides an interpretive key to Whittier's own. For if we are tempted to think that this kind of indifference to women is specific to American Indian culture, we need only recall 'Ruth', 'The Thorn', or 'The Mad Mother', poems which Whittier echoes in phrasing, verse form and plot. These echoes suggest that Whittier sees Native American culture not so much as an alien other, but as consistent, at least in moral terms, with his own. Thus there is a clear moral to be drawn by the father and young lovers who help to tell Weetamoo's tale. And it is important to note that Whittier makes them authors, not just auditors, of the poem. He seems to suggest that the act of writing such stories and shaping them into verse has a transformative power that mere reading does not.

The poem ends with a requiem for Weetamoo sung at the site of her death by the women of the Pennacook tribe. This was the most famous section of the poem, often excerpted, and set to music in 1847 as a solo for tenor or soprano voice, which became a staple of nineteenth-century drawing rooms.[16]

The Dark eye has left us,
  The Spring-bird has flown;
On the pathway of spirits
  She wanders alone.
The song of the wood-dove has died on our shore:
Mat wonck kunna-monee![17] We hear it no more!

O dark water Spirit!
  We cast on thy wave

These furs which may never
Hang over her grave;
Bear down to the lost one the robes that she wore:
Mat wonck kunna mone! We see her no more!

The path she is treading
Shall soon be our own;
Each gliding in shadow
Unseen and alone!
In vain shall we call on the souls gone before:
Mat wonck kunna monee! They hear us no more!

O mighty Sowanna![18]
Thy gateways unfold,
From thy wigwam of sunset
Lift curtains of gold!
Take home the poor Spirit whose journey is o'er:
Mat wonck kunna-mone! We see her no more!
(*Poems*, 30)

With their voices join 'Nature's wild music, – sounds of wind-swept trees, / The scream of birds, the wailing of the breeze, / The roar of waters, steady, deep, and strong', so that in death, as in life, Weetamoo enjoys a peculiar oneness with the rhythms of the natural world (*Poems*, 31). But, standing as it does at the end of the poem, this requiem is not merely for her: it also is a requiem for her people, displaced and destroyed by waves of immigrant Europeans. For the refrain in the Pennacook tongue, Whittier tells us in a footnote, can mean both 'we see her no more' or the less definite 'we see thee no more' (*Poems*, 30). And that's not all. For song is sung at the falls of Amoskeag, the falls whose water power drove the mills of Manchester, New Hampshire,[19] and in our own century would drive as well the turbines of electrical generators. Whittier's 'Song of the Indian Women' is also a requiem for a state of Nature we will never see again, and where we do find it, we must work to preserve it. *Mat wonck kunna-monee* can also be rendered 'We see it no more'.

Notes

1. The first half of the poem was published in the *United States Magazine and Democratic Review* 15 (September 1844): 233, and the entire poem appeared less than a year later in the same periodical, 16 (June 1845): 537. Whittier then republished it in his *Poems* (Boston, MA: Benjamin Mussey, 1849); 'The Bridal at Pennacook' is the first poem in that volume. Throughout, I quote the text from the 1849 edition. Because that edition lacks line numeration, my references will be to page numbers only.

2. John Greenleaf Whittier, *Legends of New England* (Hartford, CT: Hanmer and Phelps, 1831), iii.
3. Whittier later referred to *Mogg Megone* as 'a poem I wish was in the Red Sea'. 'That "big Injun", strutting around in Walter Scott's plaid, has no friends and deserves none'. 'I see no use in setting all the literary ghouls to digging for something I have written in my first attempts at rhyme', he wrote to his first biographer. 'I detest the whole of it'. John Greenleaf Whittier, *The Letters of John Greenleaf Whittier*, ed. John B. Pickard (3 vols, Cambridge, MA: Harvard UP, 1975), III 469–70, 476.
4. Henry Reed's one-volume edition of Wordsworth's complete poetical works (Philadelphia, PA: James Kay, 1837) appeared while Whittier was working in Philadelphia, and it is likely that this publication helped to spark Whittier's interest in Wordsworth's verse, for his letters make clear that Wordsworth's poetry was very much a matter of discussion among the circle of Philadelphia Quakers that he knew. Whittier's plan in 1840 for a poetical history of the Quaker tradition is specifically modelled on Wordsworth's *Ecclesiastical Sonnets*; and from 1837 on his poem to Toussaint L'Ouverture included, in a footnote, Wordsworth's sonnet 'Toussaint, thou most unhappy man of men'.
5. Whittier regularly associated views of the Merrimack valley with paintings by Claude, as, for example, in the early prose sketch, 'Passaconaway' (1833): 'It was like some vivid picture of Claude Lorraine, crowded with his sunsets and rainbows, a natural kaleidoscope of a thousand colors'. John Greenleaf Whittier, *The Works of John Greenleaf Whittier*, ed. Horace Scudder (7 vols, Boston, MA: Houghton Mifflin, 1892), V, 259.
6. Whittier tells us in a footnote that 'The celebrated Captain Smith, after resigning the government of the colony in Virginia, in his capacity of "Admiral of New-England", made a careful survey of the coast from Penobscot to Cape Cod, in the summer of 1614'. John Greenleaf Whittier, *Lays of My Home* (Boston, MA: William D. Ticknor, 1843), 2.
7. In yet another ironic twist, Smith's own name for the 'lone promontory' was itself displaced by the Puritan settlers who followed him: they renamed it 'Cape Ann', the name it still bears. See Whittier's footnote in *Lays of my Home*, 3.
8. 'The Merrimack' initially appeared in the February 1841 issue of *The Knickerbocker*, 104–5; 'The Funeral Tree of the Sokokis' appeared in the March 1841 issue of the same magazine, pp. 192–4. John B. Pickard, *A Descriptive Catalogue of the John Greenleaf Whittier Collection. The Parkman Dexter Howe Library, Part V*, ed. Sidney Ives (Gainsville, FL: University of Florida Press, 1987), 39.
9. Thomas Franklin Currier, *Elizabeth Lloyd and the Whittiers: A Budget of Letters* (Cambridge, MA: Harvard UP, 1939), 56.
10. Williamson's text reads, in part: 'Polan claimed all the lands on both sides of the Presumpscot river from its sources to its mouth; and was resolutely determined never to make a lasting peace with the English, till what he claimed as a right should be restored. He was shrewd, subtle and brave, – and reputed to be a chief. Mr. Bolton, a redeemed captive, stated, after his return from Canada, that when he asked some of the party, what had become of Polan, they said, "he had gone to Mississippi with an hundred men". But after peace, his comrades told, how they bent a stadle, till its roots on one side were turned up, then taking off one arm to be deposited in some holy catholic burying-ground, they placed his body beneath the roots, and let the tree spring to its former position'. William D. Williamson, *The History of the State of Maine from its First Discovery, AD 1602, to*

the Separation, AD 1820, Inclusive (2 vols, Hallowell, ME: Glazier, Masters, 1832), II, 321–2.

11. Lloyd's drawing, reproduced as Figure 2, captures the elegiac character of the poem in her depiction of the beech tree: it is partially blasted, to signify Polan's (and his tribe's) demise.
12. Whittier had published a prose sketch, 'Passaconaway', in *New England Magazine* 4 (February 1833): 121, which recounts an event from the latter part of Passaconaway's life.
13. Thomas Morton, *New English Canaan, or NEW CANAAN. Containing an Abstract of New England* (London, 1632), 40.
14. In fact, Whittier has invented both the names 'Weetamoo' and 'Winnepurkit'. According to Nathaniel Bouton, whose history of Concord appeared in 1856, 'the poet Whittier has made ... a beautiful poem, called the "Bridal of Penacook", in which he names the bride, "Weetamoo"; and the Sagamore-groom he calls "Winnipurkett". The real name of the bride was *Wenuchus*, or *Wanunchus*, and of her husband, *Montowampate*. His English name was *James*, brother of John, of Lynn'. In Nathaniel Bouton *The History of Concord, from its First Grant in 1725, to the Organization of the City Government in 1853, with a History of the Ancient Penacooks*. (Concord, MA: Benning W. Sanborn, 1856), 32.
15. Bouton, *The History of Concord*, 32–4, comments: 'How long his bride was absent, or how she got back, is a matter of conjecture. Whittier, with poetic license, represents her as leaving her father's home at Penacook in the spring, alone, in a canoe. She was seen going over the Falls of Amoskeag, where her frail bark was dashed in pieces, and the bride seen no more [he then quotes the 'Dirge of the Indian Women']. This is indeed beautiful *poetry*; but the *fact* is, that "Weetamoo", *alias Wanuchus*, found means to get back alive to her sagamore lord. But what finally became of Wanuchus, the "Bride of Penacook?" It is unknown; but possibly, after the death of Monowampate, in 1633, she returned to her aged father; for that she had two granddaughters living at Penacook, in 1686, appears from the following testimony: "September 17, 1686. Thomas Guakusses, *alias*, Capt. Tom, now living at Wamesit, neare Pawtucket Falls, aged about seventy-five years, testifieth and saith – 'I know two squaws were living about Pennicooke, one named Pahpocksit, and the other's name I do not know; and I knew that the grandmother of these squaws, named *Wanunchus*. She was a principal proprietor of those lands about Naumkeage, now Salem'."'
16. The song 'The Dark Eye Has Left Us' was written by the Scottish singer, William R. Dempster. Dempster first published the song in a collection of his own vocal music, *Dempster's Original Ballad Soirees* (Boston, MA: 1847); a year later, it was issued as sheet music by the Boston firm of Oliver Ditson (Whittier, *Letters*, II, 8). A musically more interesting version was composed by Samuel Coleridge-Taylor, and published in 1903 (Currier, *Bibliography*, 572–3).
17. This phrase is taken directly from Roger Williams, *A Key into the Language of America, or an Help to the Language of the Natives in that Part of America Called New-England; together with briefe observations of the customes, manners, and worships, &c. of the aforesaid Natives, in peace and warre, in life and death. On all which are added, spirituall observations generall and particular, by the authour, of chiefe and speciall use (upon all occasions) to all the English Inhabiting those parts; yet pleasant and profitable to the view of all men. Collections of the Rhode-Island Historical Society* (Providence, RI: John Miller, 1827), vol. 1, 160. Williams transliterates and translates the phrase thus: 'Mat wònck kunnawmòne, You shall never see him more'. It is important to note that Williams's study is only of the Narragansett language, not

of the language of the Pennacooks, although he believes that the other tribes will be able to understand the Narragansett dialect (Williams 25).

18. Williams writes thus of Sowanna: 'it is famous that the Sowwest (Sowaniu) is the great subject of their discourse. From thence their Traditions. There they say (at the South west) is the Court of their Great God Cautántouwit : at the South-west are their forefoathers soules: to the South west they goe themselves when they dye; From the South west came their Corne, and Beanes out of their great God Cautántouwits field: and indeed the further Northward and Westward from us their Corne will not grow, but to the Southward better and better' (Williams, 21).
19. In the 1856 gazetteer, *New Hampshire As It Is*, pp. 280–1, it is noted that 'The Amoskeag Falls ... are the largest on the Merrimack. In the ordinary stage of the water, the fall to the foot of the locks is 47 feet, and the whole fall in the space of a mile is 54 feet, furnishing power sufficient to run several hundred thousand spindles. This almost incalculable force is the nurse of the vigorous city'. In John Conron, *American Picturesque* (State College, PA: Pennsylvania State UP, 2000), 130–1, Conron reproduces an oil painting, *c.* 1850, entitled *Amoskeag Millyards*, in which 'the river ... remains tree-lined and reflective, as it should be in a Claudean vista, but the stretch adjacent to the mill is a square-diked, bridge-laced drainage canal, troubled and stained by effluents, and dirty smoke stains the sky'.

4

Transatlantic Gothic and Race: Wordsworth, Hawthorne, Poe, Chopin, Cable and Chesnutt

Joel Pace

> I am not a spook like those who haunted Edgar Allan Poe.
>
> Ralph Ellison, *The Invisible Man*

I Gothic's compass: north, south, east and west

In *Gothic America*, Teresa Goddu argues for reading race into Poe's writing by placing it in a national, rather than solely Southern, context.[1] I would like to modify Goddu's approach by looking at gothic's engagement with discourse about race not only on both sides of the Mason-Dixon line, but also on both sides of the Atlantic. The writing that buttressed the slave trade was, like the trade itself, transatlantic: America's complicity was evinced by its participating in the slave as well as book trade – by not only buying and selling humans, but also by importing and (re)printing books that defined and/or were informed by notions of racial otherness. This essay also takes its cue from Betsy Erkkila who argues for positioning blackness and Africanism in a 'whole complex of personal and cultural phobias and fetishes around the body, nature, women, race, the Orient, and the democratic masses that haunt and spook the American imaginary', as well as 'the complicated network of religious, cultural, historical, economic, and ultimately transnational relations in which they were involved'.[2]

Transnational literary relations, as this essay will demonstrate, formed an integral part of this 'complicated network'. Any study that considers transatlantic gothic must consider the extent to which this genre is predicated upon European(-American)s' haunting guilt (of complicity in slavery and its literary, religious, pseudo-scientific, and philosophical constructs of racial otherness). Studies of the transatlantic gothic must also consider instances in which African American writing of this time period 'haunts back', to use Goddu's phrase, by subverting and calling into question gothic's racial constructs. In examining Wordsworth's influence on

American gothic, I position nineteenth-century gothic in the thick of transatlantic debates about race, and show how authors drew upon racist pseudo-science to create an aesthetics of horror and sublimity.[3] This essay also provides a brief overview of the reception of Wordsworth among Northern and Southern practitioners of the gothic.

The South/North divide between anti- and pro-slavery poetics was in many instances as divergent as that of politics. America's Wordsworths are created by many different communities of interpreters; oftentimes one community's persona seems mutually exclusive to another's, as is the case with the predominantly Northern personas of Wordsworth and the widely held Southern one, mainly (de)constructed by Poe. Wordsworth was more than likely unaware that many Southern pro-slavery advocates were using his poems as a basis for their gothic writing, such as William Gilmore Simms and his friend Paul Hamilton Hayne, whose themes of death and love of nature owe much to Wordsworth, Hawthorne and Poe. Likewise Henry Timrod, the 'American Wordsworth', composed 'Ethnogenesis' 'during the meeting of the first Southern Congress in 1861 [and] asserted that nature itself shall serve this "nation among nations" as if it were a knight doing lady-service'.[4] Timrod's poem is written in the chivalric terms of Wordsworth's 1802 Preface, which – as Elizabeth Fay's essay in this volume (Chapter 9) points out – contains the same gender politics, language of romance and honour, and contract between reader and author. Timrod's poem seeks to enlist Wordsworth's Nature that 'never betrayed the heart that loved her' into the service of defining white ties to land in the South.

The Northern reception of Wordsworth was different in many ways. Wordsworth became aware of American anti-slavery appropriations of his poetry when William P. Atkinson wrote to the aged, seemingly conservative poet laureate to request an unpublished composition for inclusion in an American abolitionist anthology. In response to this request, Wordsworth sent a poem to Professor Henry Reed, his American editor, only to be made aware of appropriations of his poetry by more conservative Americans: Reed, a Philadelphia Episcopalian and advocate of gradual emancipation, informed Wordsworth that he would not forward the poem to Atkinson because Wordsworth would not want his name associated with the Boston radicals, the Transcendentalists. As Adam Potkay's essay in this volume makes clear (Chapter 5), one of the strongest and most well-developed American personas of Wordsworth was that constructed by Episcopalians, and this Wordsworth was often defined in contradistinction to the Transcendentalists' Wordsworth.

The beginnings of Wordsworth's reception in America and Philadelphia, however, saw a radically different persona of Wordsworth. The first lyrical ballad of Wordsworth's to be reprinted in America was 'Goody Blake and Harry Gill', in the New Hampshire *Farmer's Museum* of 1799. The editor,

Joseph Dennie, introduced the piece by alluding to Darwin's *Zoonomia*, thus linking Wordsworth's poetry to scientific enquiry regarding the processes through which the human mind perceives external reality and how this perception affects the mind and body. Shortly after reprinting this ballad, Dennie moved to Pennsylvania, where he began reprinting poetry from the *Ballads* in the Philadelphia *Port Folio*. His headnotes to the poems emphasized Wordsworth's focus on the mind's perception and associative qualities, and these editorial notes drew the attention of the publisher and former medical student James Humphreys, who printed an American edition of the poems as part of a series of medical texts meant to examine the effects of external nature and internal emotions on the mind. Humphreys also enlisted the poems in the war he was fighting with type – rather than bullets – against Jeffersonian America, specifically against the policies and customs that denied equal rights to American Indians, African Americans, and women. Humphreys reprinted the *Ballads* alongside Jane Marcet's writings on science, Phillis Wheatley's poetry, and abolitionist material by various authors. In this distinctly American context, then, the stories of Poe and Hawthorne are not simply literary responses to Wordsworth, but can be seen as quasi-scientific documents that enter into the transatlantic discourse on race and the qualities of the human mind by both buttressing as well as critiquing Wordsworthian notions of the ascendancy of the imagination. Through examination of how the mind (in a state of excitement) associates ideas, Poe's and Hawthorne's writings expounded upon the subtleties of Wordsworthian 'inner nature', and in doing so participated in a transatlantic dialogue that was formative for American gothic.

II Gothic narrative: interpretive communities and ruined structures

This essay examines gothic depictions of mental states and race in Wordsworth's, Poe's, and Hawthorne's works as well as the works of the American South, including the short stories of George Washington Cable, Kate Chopin and Charles Chesnutt. It does not seek to demonstrate that there is no American gothic, nor does it seek to show American gothic to be merely derivative. This essay does, however, set out to problematize the commonly held and rigorously defended position that American literature was created *ex nihilo*. Therefore, it attempts to place American literature in the context of an Anglo-American dialogue that was formative for both nations' literary traditions.[5] This essay critiques the Bloomian model of influence that views two, and only two, authors duelling in a vacuum and that removes these authors from their (trans)national socio-political contexts by focusing on a duet rather than the many choirs of voices engaged in a transatlantic literary and cultural antiphony. The choirs, so to speak,

Figure 4 Tintern Abbey (looking east). Lithograph engraved by F. Dangerfield, and published by Robert Taylor, Chepstow.

are American communities of interpreters who develop readings of Wordsworth's poetry.

The notion of a community of interpreters is of course indebted to Stanley Fish and reader-response theory. This notion helps us to understand how Americans formed multiple, and oftentimes mutually contradictory, readings of Wordsworth – interpretations that were often in reaction to (but distinct from) readings of the poet developed by British communities of interpreters. Communal interpretation was a concept the British Romantics were very familiar with: Wordsworth and his circle, for instance, formed one such community themselves. Additionally, Lake School literature, especially the *Ballads*, examines communal interpretation as one of the primary mediums through which humans perceive their environment. Hawthorne and Poe also utilized Wordsworthian and Coleridgean communities of interpreters who re-signify an object so many times that it come to be emotionally and superstitiously perceived: Usher's interpretation of the 'Mad Trist'; the Boston community's interpretation of the scarlet letter as 'Adulteress', 'Angel', and 'Able' as well as the parishioners' interpretations of the minister's black veil; the Lake District village's interpretation of the thorn and its hill of moss as the grave of Martha Ray's child; the mariner's crewmates' interpretation of the albatross as a bird of ill and then good omen (or Bracy and Leoline's interpretations of Christabel's dream), and so on. By retelling tales through communities of interpreters, these authors show how literary structures (and the constructs of taste and meaning they house) can disintegrate and fall into disrepair. In showing how one object can mean so many contradictory things, these authors anticipate the postmodern symbol and twentieth-century psychology. In Poe's and Hawthorne's short stories as well as in Wordsworth's and Coleridge's ballads, the communities of interpreters mirror the readership's interpretive act of reading and destabilize or redefine the meaning of words as well as events.[6]

Like Stanley Fish, Harold Bloom provides a model for thinking about reception and influence. The applicability of Bloomian influence theory to Anglo-American literary relations, particularly as a way of understanding the relationship of the developing American author to his or her British precursors, has been indisputably demonstrated by Robert Weisbuch's *Atlantic Double-Cross* (Chicago, 1986). Although my argument questions, examines and rejects certain of Bloom's tenets, other aspects of Bloomian analysis are incorporated. American authors' anxiety of writing in the shadow of British predecessors emerges in tropes of haunting; rather than banishing the ghosts of Britain's poetical and political legacy, American gothic oftentimes 'haunts back', to use Teresa Goddu's phrase. Admittedly, Wordsworth and Coleridge seem unlikely candidates for influencing American *gothic* when compared to the likes of authorial spectres that loom larger in the American gothic imaginary – such as Walpole, Radcliffe, Lewis and Godwin. It is, however, Wordsworth's and Coleridge's subversion and inversion of their predecessors' and contemporaries' gothic tropes that make them likely models to American Romantic authors who sought to inaugurate an American tradition of supernatural writing separate from (and yet not entirely unrelated to) British gothic and the early American gothic of Charles Brockden Brown. In seeking to dispel the magic of haunted literary structures, these American authors conjured as many ghosts as they banished.

The haunted literary structures are works of literature, which themselves contain haunted houses and that represent the ruin of characters' minds as well as the fragmented and haunted state of the literary work. In Edgar Allan Poe's 'The Fall of the House of Usher', for instance, Usher's mouldering mansion becomes representative of his mind. Poe invokes the mental state of the mad mother and the ancient mariner over ballads that exemplify the redemptive power of imagination.[7] 'Tintern Abbey' ends the 1798 *Lyrical Ballads* with a tone of ascendancy, with the notion that the redeeming qualities of the mind have triumphed. 'The Fall of the House of Usher' leaves the reader with no such consolation. Usher's decaying mind is also represented in 'The Haunted Palace', a poem in which Poe meant 'to imply a mind haunted by phantoms – a disordered brain'. Insofar as the poem and the larger narrative structure of which it is a part can be read as an interpretation or response to 'Tintern Abbey', they seem to read

Wordsworth's poem against its grain by reminding readers that the abbey the speaker's mind comes to represent is in fact a ruined structure (see Figure 4).

In 'Tintern Abbey', there is of course a strong connection between the speaker and the poet. Equally, there are autobiographical elements to Poe's and Hawthorne's works. It is the spectre of British writers – such as Wordsworth and Coleridge, whom Poe and Hawthorne viewed as both models and rivals – that haunts these authors' minds. As will be explored in more detail below, the mind and abbey of the narrator of 'Ligeia' are haunted by the woman for whom the story is named, who holds Wordsworthian views about the spiritual nature of Nature. Likewise, 'The Custom-House' and its narrator are haunted by the Anglo-American legacy represented by Hawthorne's and Salem's British and Puritanical roots.[8] Hester and Hawthorne are haunted by ancestry and ruined structures: 'she saw again her native village, in Old England, and her paternal home; a decayed house of gray stone ... retaining a half-obliterated shield of arms over the portal' (Hawthorne, 61). Like 'The Thorn' and *The Prelude, The Scarlet Letter* also shows how the landscape is haunted, as it is endowed with supernatural significance by individuals and communities of interpreters.[9] *The Letter* is a narrative of the spiritual teleology of emotional ties to landscape, of 'the force of doom, which almost invariably compels human beings to linger around and haunt, ghostlike, the spot [of time] where some great and marked event has given color to their lifetime' (Hawthorne, 75).

A more obvious structural metaphor for the mind can be found in 'Michael', the poem that closes volume two of the 1802 Philadelphia *Ballads*. The ruined sheepfold where Michael retreats and does not lift a single stone symbolizes his despair, is the equivalent of the house where Roderick Usher finds companionship among the 'crumbling condition of the individual stones', and calls to mind the ruined cottage.[10] Michael is bound to his sheepfold as Roderick Usher is to (his mansion and) to 'an anomalous species of terror', 'a bounden slave' (Poe, 100). Poe's narratives are only partially built up (word by word) to form a plot structure that resembles Michael's sheepfold (stone by stone) in its incompleteness and surrounding despair. Poe's leaving the minds of his characters in a perpetually pathological state is a critique of Transcendentalist appropriations of Wordsworth's beliefs about the perfectibility of the human mind. Poe anticipates the Wordsworth of *The Prelude* by showing how flaws, grief and sin shape (and sometimes renovate) the mind.[11]

Each of these authors' works contains gothic structures that mirror mental states: Usher's house, the abbey inhabited by the narrator of 'Ligeia'; the house of seven gables and moss-overgrown old manse; Tintern Abbey, the Grande Chartreuse, Furness Abbey, the ruined cottage; Leoline's castle, Kubla Khan's pleasure dome, the mariner's ship, to list only a handful of structures in each author's works. Poe and Hawthorne, like Wordsworth and Coleridge, show not only how external landscape becomes internal landscape, but also how seemingly trivial objects are endowed with the heaviest emotional significance, whether the object in question is the thorn, an albatross, a black cat, a scarlet letter, a heap of clothes by the side of Esthwaite Water, or the thumping heart of one who has committed a grave sin or that of a murdered man. Drawing a parallel between external landscape and landscape of the mind and endowing seemingly insignificant objects with spiritual and emotional meaning are identifiably Wordsworthian traits that assume a prominence and wield great power in the gothic of Poe and Hawthorne. For Poe and Hawthorne, the mind and the works of literature that reflect it are ruined structures, as dreary and mouldering as the gothic architecture these stories contain.

III Transatlantic Transcendentalism and race: *The Prelude*, *The Scarlet Letter* and 'Ligeia'

Poe's and Hawthorne's stories as well as Wordsworth's and Coleridge's poetry drew upon and contributed to a transatlantic dialogue about the workings of the human mind. From James Cowles Prichard's 1826 London publication of *Researches into the Physical History of Mankind* to Samuel George Morton's 1839 *Crania Americana*, Anglo-American discourse on the workings of the human psyche and its states of degeneration and ruin was inextricably linked to notions of race, and elements of these racist ideas manifest in the gothic works of the time. American and British authors alike were informed by the following transatlantic pseudo-scientific writings and debate about race and the human mind: J.F. Blumenbach, *Decas Tertia Collectionis Suae Craniorum Diversarum Gentium Illustrata* (Göttingen, 1795); Pieter Camper, *The Works of the Late Professor Camper* (London, 1794); Robert Knox, *The Races of Men: A Fragment* (Philadelphia, 1850); Josiah Priest, *American Antiquities* (New York, 1833); Charles White, *An Account of the Regular Gradation in Man* (London, 1799).[12] Through measuring skulls from various regions of the world and attempting to draw a correlation among skull size and shape and certain psychological traits, these studies buttressed imperialism by seeking to associate all traits deemed desirable with Europeans and all traits deemed degenerate with non-Europeans. The authors of these works were informed by transatlantic debates about American degeneracy: for instance, in response to Comte de Buffon's claim that the indigenous flora, fauna and people of America were degenerate versions of European originals, Jefferson held up the American Indians as noble savages (following Rousseauvian primitivism) and attempted to show that African Americans were degenerate.

British and American Romantics combined these racist understandings of the mind with Erasmus Darwin's and David Hartley's theories of the manner in which the mind perceives external stimuli and how it is affected by (and affects) perception of the external world. It is, then, no coincidence that in Wordsworth's poem 'Ruth', the speaker is sure to mention the deleterious effects on the mind that America's indigenous flora, fauna *and culture* cause.[13] Wordsworth, Coleridge, Poe, Hawthorne and others entered into this debate by attempting to probe the inner recesses of the psyche in their gothic writing. The voyages they take into the human mind are not without racial implications. Coleridge's and Poe's nautical journeys to uncharted regions of the mind and poles are not without their allusions to the slave trade and the East India trade as well.[14] Wordsworth picks up this metaphor in a description of the statue of Newton in St John's College, Cambridge, as a 'marble index of a mind forever / Voyaging on *strange seas* of thought, alone', an apt description of *The Prelude* as well (*TP*, 1850, III, 62–3, emphasis added).

Wordsworth's poetics is predicated upon evoking wonder in readers, as Matthew Scott's essay in this volume (Chapter 11) shows. Transatlantic gothic evokes this wonder through tropes of racial otherness and hybridity. It locates the reader in a community of interpreters governed by racist fears about national identity, a xenophobia that includes a fear of miscegenation. Racially motivated tropes that English writers use to describe the Irish, for instance, are used by American authors to describe American Indians, African Americans, and Asian Americans. Wordsworth also equates the mind with racial otherness when he upbraids gothic writing as a contributing factor to the mind's being reduced to a state of 'almost *savage* torpor' (*LB*, 746, italics mine).[15] In 'The Complaint of the Forsaken Indian Woman', an American Indian, like Coleridge's Kubla Khan and De Quincey's Malay, is associated with a dream-like state of the imagination.[16] Wordsworth is attempting to trace the mind's processes of association (its 'fluxes and refluxes') 'by accompanying the last struggles of a human being at the approach of death, cleaving in solitude to life and society, as in the Poem of the FORSAKEN INDIAN' (*LB*, 745).

One example of the transatlantic connection between Wordsworth, the pseudo-scientific discourse on the mind and race can be found in the July 1816 issue of *The Quarterly Review*, which was reprinted in New York and distributed on both sides of the Mason-Dixon line. In this issue's unsigned article on 'Insanity and Madhouses', Wordsworth and Erasmus Darwin are cited against the 'spiritual origin of visionary ... "conceptions" and "apparitions"', which are merely the effects of the 'influence which the fancy is found to possess over the feelings and functions of the physical frame'. Following the lead of the Preface to the *Ballads*, the article's author blames the 'artificial state of civilized society' for mental ailments, noting that 'savages ... are neither nervous or mad'.[17] The supernatural foundations of gothic horror are debunked and replaced with theories of the imagination that hinge upon Rousseauvian constructs of the noble savage.

In the 1850 *Prelude*, Wordsworth describes himself in a moment of solitary imaginative visitation as a 'naked savage, in the thunder shower'(I,

300). Not long after reading the New York edition of Wordsworth's verse autobiography, Hawthorne published *The Scarlet Letter*, a work that links Hester (as the solitary reaper of sown sin) with African Americans, American Indians and the wilderness. The 'American eagle', writes Hawthorne in 'The Custom-House', 'is apt to fling off her nestlings with a ... rangling wound from her barbed arrows' (24). This statement about the American government's harming of those under its power has special significance in the context of Jacksonian policy towards Native Americans. Here, the arrows – usually depicted by the colonizer as representative of American Indian violence towards settlers – are those of the government, connoting Jackson's use of force to remove American Indians from their ancestral lands (likened to an eagle flinging its young out of the nest).

Hawthorne locates the image of the arrow more specifically in relation to American Indians, when he mentions that it is a matter of regret to him that he does not have a means of tracing the pre-Revolutionary history of the 'Protectorate', a way of locating early custom-house papers and their references to 'forgotten or remembered men, and to antique *customs*, which would have affected me with the same pleasure as when I used to pick up *Indian arrow-heads* in the field near the Old Manse' (41, emphasis added). In this work and the novel that follows, Hawthorne shows how nature is inextricably linked to personal and cultural memory, and how America's colonial history of genocide has become grounds for 'pleasure'. The Massachusetts nature of 'The Custom-House' is different from that of Emerson's *Nature*, in which nature is a text of spiritual insights, a bible; Hawthorne's nature is an historical text, layered with cultural memory and meaning. In this respect, it is closer to that of Thoreau; indeed, as Hawthorne tells us in 'The Custom-House', he set about writing *The Scarlet Letter* 'after talking with Thoreau about pine trees and Indian relics, in his hermitage at Walden' (38). The text of Hawthorne's novel contains many scarlet letters, from the 'A' on Hester's clothing to the one that appears in the sky; the more subtle manifestations of the letter 'A' are the American Indian arrowheads in Hawthorne's text and the Massachusetts wilderness.[18]

When the narrator of 'The Custom-House' places the scarlet letter on his chest, he feels pangs of guilt associated with the European settlers' duplicity toward the 'Indian [who] was to be driven with stripes into the shadow of the forest' (54):

> While thus perplexed, – and cogitating, among other hypotheses, whether the letter might not have been one of those decorations which the white men used to contrive, in order to take the eyes of Indians, – I happened to place it on my breast. It seemed to me ... that I experienced a sensation not altogether physical, yet almost so, as of burning heat ... I shuddered, and involuntarily let it fall upon the floor. (43)

In the novel, Nature is its own custom-house with its own hidden stories or texts: its syntax questions America's fulfilment of its duty, places a moral tax on sin, and charges America with injuring those it should have protected by not fulfilling its promise of equality and independence. Nature's (as well as Hawthorne's) text calls into question America's and the Puritans' *customs*, particularly their 'errand into the wilderness', which the scarlet letter is interpreted as buttressing, as it is 'believed by many ... that an Indian had drawn his arrow against the badge, and that the missile struck it, and fell harmless to the ground' (132).[19]

In Thoreau's *Walking*, he celebrates the wild(er)ness of American writing, which he praises as superior to the tameness of British poetry, especially the Lake Poets. Hawthorne does something similar when he associates Pearl's wildness with American literature;[20] Pearl is the letter 'A' made flesh, America's alpha.[21] Pearl is the living text that defies the customs the Puritans brought across the Atlantic, customs that sought to control (human) nature. The other physical manifestation of *The Scarlet Letter* is the novel itself, which also seeks to perform Pearl's function and (through the nature of its 'wild' or unconventional writing and syntax) rethink British customs and conventions and be the American 'A', or beginning of American letters.[22] As Susan Manning notes in Chapter 1, 'it is hard to imagine Hawthorne's very "American" (whatever one may mean by that) masterpiece, *The Scarlet Letter*, having been written in England or Scotland by an English or a Scottish writer: but both its plot and omnipresent ethos of Victorian culture and sexual mores are strikingly similar to George Eliot's *Adam Bede*', and, as Richard Gravil points out in *Romantic Dialogues*, Wordsworth's 'The Thorn' (117–22).

The similarities between Pearl and the novel, then, do not end with their both being the material manifestation of the scarlet letter, but extend to their mixed parentage:[23] if the novel and Pearl have their roots in Anglo-American predecessors, then the symbol of American literature is also a cipher for hybridity. Hawthorne draws the connection to race by implying that Pearl is the daughter of the 'Black Man' and by describing her as wilder than America's indigenous peoples: 'She [Pearl] ran and looked the wild Indian in the face; and he grew conscious of a nature wilder than his own' (188). National anxieties about miscegenation also extend to literature of mixed parentage; hence, the purely 'American' voice, as Karen Karbiener's essay (Chapter 7) shows, that Whitman went to such painstaking lengths to create by covering the Wordsworthian tracks in his work. By characterizing Hester as the Romantic solitary treading the margins of thought and society, Hawthorne equates her with the Wordsworth of the 1790s, fresh in readers' minds from the publication of the 1850 American *Prelude* only two years before *The Scarlet Letter*: Hester 'assumed a freedom of speculation, then common enough on the other side of the Atlantic, but which our forefathers, had they known of it, would have held to be a deadlier crime than that stigmatized by the scarlet letter' (133).[24]

Hester's Wordsworthian characterization is perpetuated by her spiritual connection to nature; she is able to shed the norms of society when she enters the forest. Hester's rejection of the Puritan's views of the good and the evils of (human) nature is indebted to similar statements by her British and American Romantic predecessors and to antinomians such as Anne Hutchinson. Hester's connection to nature is also a connection to racial otherness, as evinced by her dialogue with Pearl:

> '[T]his ugly Black Man offers his book and an iron pen to every body that meets him here among the trees ... Didst thou ever meet the Black Man, mother?' ...
>
> 'Once in my life I met the Black Man! ... This scarlet letter is his mark!' (148)[25]

What is interesting here is that, through Hester, Hawthorne equates Wordsworthian Romanticism with racial otherness. Like 'Young Goodman Brown', *The Scarlet Letter* satirizes and undercuts the Wordsworthian/Transcendentalist notion of nature as a place of beatific ecstasy and shows it to be, instead, a place of literal and metaphorical darkness, as the meaning of Dimmesdale's name implies. Hawthorne's view of nature's darkness has transatlantic roots in his (anti)Wordsworthianism as well as his Puritanism.

Hawthorne's effort to re-inscribe nature as a different text from that of the British and German-influenced Transcendentalists is, in part, an attempt to reclaim Massachusetts wilderness as an American text. The transatlantic debate over whether or not America has its own literature informs Hawthorne's novel. Numerous British critics described American literature as degenerate, as an inferior version of the Anglo-European models. This debate linked American writing to American nature and to race, most notably in Comte de Buffon's claim that the flora, fauna and indigenous peoples of America are degenerate. Through Hawthorne's reply to Wordsworthian expostulations about nature, the tables are turned on European and British critics of America and its literature by Hawthorne's associating the writing of England's late Laureate with degeneracy, a move that seeks to marginalize Wordsworth at the expense of African Americans and Native Americans.[26]

Like Hawthorne, Poe also associates Wordsworthian characters with racial otherness: Ligeia, who elucidates 'the many mysteries of ... transcendentalism', has eyes that are different from 'the ordinary eyes of our race' and fuller than the 'eyes of the tribe of the valley of Nourjahad' (85, 82). Her eyes fill the narrator with the feeling of something far more deeply interfused, that 'God is but a great will pervading all things by nature of its intentness', which is similiar to the Wordsworthian notion of 'a motion and a spirit, that ... rolls through all things'(83–4). 'Ligeia' is spurred along by the narrator's fear that he as well as his second wife are transforming into her, that the text is resurrecting Romanticism from its grave, as she 'haunts the narrator like a passion'; Poe's writing, as Erkkila points out, contains points in which 'Orientalism intersects with Africanism and a whole complex of white cultural fears about mixture with and violation by the dark other, whether black, red, or Mohammedan' ('The Poetics of Whiteness', 47). As with Pearl, there is the fear of textual and sexual miscegenation as 'the fair-haired and blue-eyed Lady Rowena Trevanion, of Tremaine' (88) becomes Ligeia with her 'dishevelled hair ... *blacker than the raven wings of midnight*' and her 'black' and 'wild eyes'.

IV Wordsworth and the Southern gothic short story

> The object of my writings would be not so much the elevation of colored people as the elevation of the whites – for I consider the unjust spirit of the caste which is so insidious as to pervade a whole nation, and so powerful as to subject a whole race and all connected with it to scorn and social ostracism – I consider this a barrier to the moral progress of the American people; and I would be one of the first to head a determined, organized crusade against it.
>
> (Charles W. Chesnutt, *Journals*)

Those interpreting literature from a theological perspective – whether it was James Marsh and the Vermont Transcendentalists, Emerson and the Boston Transcendentalists, Andrews Norton and the Harvard Unitarians, the Princeton Calvinists, or Noah Porter and Yale scholars – were the arbiters of taste in the Northeast.[27] They held fast to critical and aesthetic criteria that associated Wordsworth's poetry with a form of social amelioration predicated upon élitist pity coupled with the ability of literature and education to enact social change. This blending of American moral, religious and aesthetic constructs led to Wordsworth's gaining in popularity and Poe, Byron, and Shelley's becoming marginalized. In Poe's fiction and criticism for the *Southern Literary Messenger*, he further defines a Southern gothic (drawing on the elegies of the 'Poet's Corner' section of eighteenth-century gazettes) and adds significantly to a Southern school of criticism (dating back to the *Maryland Gazette* of 1726) that provided a counter-aesthetic to Northern journals such as the *North American Review* and the *Dial*. Poe and many other writers and readers of Southern gothic praised Shelley as well as Byron, who was, for example, Jefferson Davis's favourite poet.

Although many Southern gothic writers contributed to the creation of a regional persona of Wordsworth, there were also others who engaged with, imitated, and redefined Northern Wordsworthian didacticism and moral inculcation. 'Ligeia', 'Annabel Lee', and 'The Raven' are all haunted by the

Lucy poems, and they contain a narrator who is possessed by/obsessed with an (imagined) (un)dead female presence:

> She died and left to me
> This heath, this calm and quiet scene,
> The memory of what has been
> And *never more* will be
> (*LB*, 'Three Years She Grew in Sun and Shower', ll. 39–42, my emphasis)

Poe's poems are also connected to Wordsworth's 'To a Sexton', itself haunted by Donne's 'The Relic'. 'What is "Annabel Lee"', writes Richard Gravil, 'but a kitsch and anapestic Lucy?' (*Romantic Dialogues*, 128). Thomas Holley Chivers is a good example of a Southern writer who subscribed more to the Transcendentalists' persona of Wordsworth than that of his good friend Poe. Chivers's Wordsworthian/Swedenborgian theology is most prominent in *Eonchs of Ruby* (1850). His theology of immortality attempted to reverse Poe's reversals of Wordsworth's ascendancy of the imagination: Chivers's lost love replies 'Yes! Forevermore'.[28] Like Caruthers, Chivers adopts Wordsworth's poetic common language by mimicking and appropriating the language of African American spirituals – especially in his response to the Lucy poems, 'The Lusiad' (Bain and Flora, *Fifty Southern Writers* 127).

Kate Chopin draws on the Lucy poems in 'Désirée's Baby', a short story titled after the main character whose baby, to her husband's surprise, is bi-racial, a nod to Hawthorne's depiction of Pearl as being of mixed parentage. The husband, Armand, banishes Désirée and the baby, and they both, like Lucy, disappear into nature never to be seen again. Chopin uses the genre to show male tyranny in the domestic sphere, as Armand's behaviour towards her and the slaves is monstrous. Chopin draws on conventions of gothic of the mind to paint 'a grim psychological portrait of a woman who has never dared to think independently' (Bain and Flora 137). Désirée's wandering the fields with the child connects her to Hetty of *Adam Bede*, as well as Martha of 'The Thorn', and resonates with 'The Mad Mother' and 'The Female Vagrant'. Her death and downward spiral into despair, like Margaret's in 'The Ruined Cottage', is mirrored and prefigured by images of architecture and nature; Chopin describes the house as having a roof that 'came down steep and black like a cowl ... Big solemn oaks grew close to it, and their thick-leaved, far-reaching branches shadowed it like a pall'.[29] The pall prefigures Désirée's death in nature and her becoming a *genius loci*, as is the fate of Lucy who is rolled in earth's diurnal round with rocks and stones and trees. The story ends with Armand's realization that his mother, not Désirée, 'belongs to the race that is cursed with the brand of slavery' (342).

Just as Hawthorne's engagement with racial gothic indicates that literature which buttressed pro-slavery arguments was written by Wordsworth-influenced writers on both sides of the Mason-Dixon line, the writing of George Washington Cable indicates that abolitionist writing was also penned by Northern as well as Southern Wordsworthians. His *Madame Delphine* depicts a mother who, like Hester Prynne, defies the moral status quo: she helps her daughter to marry a Creole man thereby disobeying and denouncing laws against interracial marriage. In order to criticize the New South movement's exploitation of African Americans and the environment, Cable draws on Wordsworth's poems against slavery ('To Thomas Clarkson, on the Final Passing of the Bill for the Abolition of the Slave Trade', 'The Banish'd Negroes' and his sonnet to Toussaint L'Ouverture) as well as the Lake Poet's works advocating environmental conservationism.

Cable's gothic stories have many Wordsworthian elements; his 'Jean-Ah Poquelin' (from *Old Creole Days*, 1879) is a post-Louisiana Purchase twice-told tale in which the once opulent Jean Marie Poquelin attempts to care for his leprosy-stricken brother and keep his property from being the site of the road the new 'Anglo-American' government would like to build. Like Wordsworth's and Hawthorne's narratives, the tale hinges on a superstitious community of interpreters, who believe Poquelin has killed his brother and that the pasty-white likeness they often spy Poquelin walking with is the brother's spirit. Cable reverses the racially signed gothic of certain of Poe's and Hawthorne's works in which anything black is an object of horror (whether it is a cat, a tarn, or a minister's veil) and makes Poquelin's brother's 'ghostly white[ness]' (367) the revolting signifier of fear, despair, and blankness (*à la* Poe's vision at the end of *Pym*,[30] Wordsworth's Mont Blanc, Lafcadio Hearn's 'The Ghostly Kiss', and Melville's whale). Poe and Coleridge describe both whiteness as well as blackness as the cause of fear. *Pym* describes the non-white peoples as cannibals, and Coleridge's 'Rime' describes the undead crew as having 'black lips' and, in lines attributed to Wordsworth, the mariner as being as 'brown / As is the ribb'd Sea-sand' (*LB*, 228–9). The horror-inducing whiteness of the Poquelin's brother is similar to that of Life-In-Death whose 'skin is as white as leprosy' (198). The subversion of Burke's racial constructs of associating whiteness with the beautiful and non-whiteness with the sublime has an antecedent in *The Interesting Narrative of the Life of Olaudah Equiano*: 'I asked them', writes Equiano referring to a query put to his fellow prisoners about the slave-ship's crew, 'if we were not to be eaten by those white men with horrible looks, red faces, and long hair'.[31]

Cable's use of a ruined structure, Poquelin's mansion, to symbolize the mental condition of his character harkens back to Poe's 'The Fall of the House of Usher', Wordsworth's 'Michael' and 'The Ruined Cottage' as well as earlier Gothic structures, such as Walpole's *Castle Otranto*. The state of natural decay mirrors the moral despair and disrepair; Poquelin's marsh with its 'dead cypresses' and 'coarse and spiritless flowers' (360) owes as much to the 'rank sedges' and 'trunks of decayed trees' (95) near Usher's mansion as it does to Margaret's garden, which mirrors her mental state, in 'The Ruined Cottage'. Poquelin's 'plantation-house half in ruin' (360) is as symbolic of the corrupt system of slavery that supports the house and its plantation (as well as the post-Civil War South's state of disrepair) as Michael's sheepfold is of England's laws that do not protect the field labourers of the Lake District. The house is a testimony to civil law's violation of people's property rights as well as the violation of civil rights of making people into property: the plantation-house's 'pillars, grim, solid, and spiritless [and] its massive build [were] ... strong reminder of days still earlier, when ... the insurrection of the blacks [was] a daily contingency' (360). Cable attempts to diversify perspective by portraying a community of interpreters that is not just white, for among 'both blacks and whites the house was an object of a thousand superstitions', but the attempt is undercut by a narrative that refers to the haunted marsh as being 'as wild as Africa' (362). The end of the story attempts to show harmony when both Poquelin's white leper brother and mute black slave walk away from the marsh and into the 'jungle' together; however, the vision of racial harmony is undermined by the slave's being described in this final scene as having 'the strength of an ape' (372).

Cable's story is one of many literary nods to 'The Murders in the Rue Morgue' and the racist pseudo-science of Pieter Camper. The racialized infrastructure of the gothic conventions is not called into question until Charles Chesnutt (a writer with connections to the Midwest and the South) supercedes and subverts the genre in stories such as 'Po' Sandy' (*The Conjure Woman*, 1899). Chesnutt gives African Americans a voice in gothic narratives; the former slave Julius McAdoo, unlike the mute slave in the story of Chesnutt's friend Cable, is the master of narrative whose storytelling capabilities far exceed those of his white employer, John, who frames and repeats Julius's tale. Julius tells the story of why the old schoolhouse on John's property is haunted. The lumber from which the schoolhouse was made, Julius explains, did not come from an ordinary tree, but a slave, Sandy, who had been turned into a tree by the conjure magic of his love, so he could elude the cruel plantation owner. The twice-told tale carries an ecological moral, as it criticizes the New South movement's industrialization at the expense of natural resources. The story also subverts the gothic convention of having a house haunted by villainous non-white racial otherness by showing 'the darker side of slavery', a white power structure (344). It shows how the perpetrator of the murder was the white master whose house, like other plantations, is built from the blood, sweat and tears of slaves, and the ways in which America's villainy haunts the house of state, making it a house divided by segregation; the Jim Crow Laws are slavery's ghost, never fully banished by the Civil War.

After hearing Julius' story, John's wife Annie, the careful interpreter of the community of interpreters formed by herself and her husband, reflects on slavery: '"What a system it was", she exclaimed when Julius had finished, "under which such things were possible!"' (349). John, who has not understood the tale's meaning, responds '"What things? ... Are you seriously considering the possibility of a man's being turned into a tree?"' (349). John's denial represents his unwillingness to be haunted by slavery's ghost, to believe in the dehumanization that slavery involved, as it has been whitewashed out of his cultural memory, reconstructed into a structure of complicit guilt masked by denial.

Chesnutt's having Sandy be turned into a tree also transforms the pastoral convention of humanized nature/naturalized humans – exemplified by Wordsworth's boy of Winander, a pan-like figure who is part human/part nature – by showing how slavery dehumanizes its victims. The (super)natural human – a stock convention of eighteenth-century neo-classical pastoral with its images of wood nymphs, centaurs and satyrs – is shown to be a genre not as easily adapted to American landscape, for the world of pastoral in which labourers in the field have only to think about making sweet the noontide hour with song does not correspond to a landscape where fields of cotton were places of suffering, where labourers in the field were humans treated worse than beasts. The beast or monster in Chesnutt's tale is the slaveholder who was 'monst'us mad' for supporting a monstrous institution (348).

After hearing the story, Annie changes her plans and decides that she does not wish to use the wood of the schoolhouse for her kitchen, and tells John that she would like to give the old schoolhouse to Julius, who has requested to use it to accommodate him and his fellow worshippers who have split from the 'Sandy Run Colored Baptist Church'. The result of the narrative is that the plot structure turns the power structure on its head, as Julius supplants John as master of the frame house and the frame narrative; the twice-told tale becomes a means of subversion. The ruined structures of plot and architecture are rebuilt and re-signified by Chesnutt from places of despair and ruin to places of hope and renewal. John becomes the equivalent of the Romantic authors who wish to equate racial otherness with states of mind; in commenting on and introducing Julius's narrative, John says that his stories are 'wildly extravagant, revealing the Oriental cast of his imagination' (344).

'What rose up out of collective needs to allay internal fears and to rationalize external exploitation', Toni Morrison writes, 'was an American Africanism – a fabricated brew of darkness, otherness, alarm, and desire' (38). Chesnutt's stories seek to call into question such constructs in gothic literature and their corresponding social and pseudo-scientific constructs of race upon which they draw and depend; Chesnutt holds that the

> subtle almost indefinable repulsion towards the Negro, which is common to most Americans ... cannot be stormed and taken by assault

> ... The negro's part is to prepare himself for social recognition and equality; and it is the province of literature to open the way for him to get it – to accustom the *public mind* to the idea; and while amusing them to lead them on imperceptibly, unconsciously step by step to the desired state of feeling.[32]

Unlike Poe's stories in which reading produces no beneficial effects, Chesnutt's narratives are similar to Wordsworth's *Ballads* in their mission of changing readers' poetics, politics, aesthetics and notions of literary diction and heroes, through calling into question prejudicial notions about a group of people whom society is marginalizing and exploiting. Like the Romantics, Chesnutt uses the community of interpreters to call institutions and customs into question.

The lack of demonstrable Wordsworthian influence in Chesnutt's tale would perhaps be a deterrent to scholars seeking solely to show the call and response of textual allusion and reference. It would also be questionable to attempt to subsume African American literature into the British gothic tradition of Wordsworth, or the British-influenced gothic of Poe and Hawthorne. And yet to shut down dialogue among all of these texts would also be to misrepresent their complex intertextuality. According to Julia Farwell, *The Conjure Woman* 'is a book that operates in dual rhetorics, speaking across the boundary between oral and written voices, African and European literary traditions ... Such oppositions meet at the divisive line of race, a line that polices racial distinctions in favor of white hegemony, thereby reinforcing the authority of "race" itself'.[33] Teresa Goddu's description of African American texts as 'haunting back' provides a useful model, as it implies a dialogue between traditions, but resists conflating and assimilating through an oversimplified model of influence. Chesnutt's subversions of racial conventions of gothic that have roots in Wordsworth, Poe, Hawthorne and other Anglo-American authors does not mean that he is writing under their influence, but precisely the opposite – that he is writing over (beyond) their influence. It is necessary to push the too-neat narrative of Wordsworth's seemingly omnipresent influence on American literature and culture to the point where it breaks down, to the point where the presence is no longer identifiably Wordsworthian and/or no longer able to be categorized as 'influence'. And just as Hawthorne and Poe provide instances in which Wordsworth's influence is, to a degree, demonstrable, Chesnutt provides the counter-example where the poet's individual influence is not able to be proved.

Although it is demonstrable that Poe and Hawthorne read the *Lyrical Ballads*, it would be inaccurate to argue, in a Bloomian fashion, that Wordsworth is the sole predecessor to whom they are responding.[34] Contextualizing a study of the call and response between Wordsworth and Poe as well as that of Wordsworth and Hawthorne attempts to place dialogue among these authors in the context of the (many) (trans)national conversation(s) in which their writing participated. It does not seem accurate to ignore the influence of other authors, as the approach of two monolithic authors duelling in a Bloomian vacuum might, but it is also difficult to identify single yarns connecting authors without losing sight of the complex web of intertextuality linking works. As Wordsworth's conventions are taken up by a transatlantic conversation that redefines them with every repetition, there comes a point when they are, arguably, no longer identifiably Wordsworthian. Such a point of saturation may very well speak to the extent to which the Wordsworthian aesthetic has been subsumed into the habitus of American culture, even as it is mimicked, modified, superceded and completely redefined by gothic's communities of writers and interpreters.

Notes

1. Teresa A. Goddu, *Gothic America: Narrative, History, and Nation* (New York, NY: Columbia UP, 1997).
2. Betsy Erkkila, 'The Poetics of Whiteness: Poe and the Racial Imaginary' in *Romancing the Shadow*, eds J. Gerald Kennedy and Liliane Weissberg (Oxford: Oxford UP, 2001), 44. Jack G. Voller also places gothic in a transnational perspective: *The Supernatural Sublime: The Metaphysics of Terror in Anglo-American Romanticism* (De Kalb, IL: Northern Illinois UP, 1994). See also Paul Gilroy, *The Black Atlantic* (Cambridge, MA: Harvard UP, 1993).
3. This essay is also indebted to Cornel West's 'A Genealogy of Modern Racism' and his examination of 'the way in which the very structure of modern discourse *at its inception* produced forms of rationality, scientificity, and objectivity as well as aesthetic and cultural ideals which require the constitution of the idea of white supremacy': *Prophesy Deliverance! An Afro-American Revolutionary Christianity* (Philadelphia, PA: Westminster, 1982), 47. West indicates the transatlantic roots and routes of racist nineteenth-century pseudo-science and the ways in which the radical environmentalists of the period made connections between race and landscape.
4. Jack Debellis, 'Henry Timrod' in *Fifty Southern Writers Before 1900*, eds Robert Bain and Joseph M. Flora (New York, NY: Greenwood, 1987), 469. Hereafter, this volume is cited parenthetically by the surnames of the editors.
5. My purpose in this essay is not to identify and analyse the gothic elements in Wordsworth's work, as has been done excellently by many scholars already, but to build on this scholarship by indicating points of departure and connection for a transatlantic assessment of his influence. The best source on Wordsworth's (and Romanticism's) engagement with the gothic is Michael Gamer's *Romanticism and the Gothic* (Cambridge: Cambridge UP, 2000), to which this essay is indebted for the definition of gothic 'neither as a mode nor as a kind of fiction (the "gothic novel") but as an aesthetic ... that must be defined in part by its ability to transplant itself *across* forms and media' and, as this essay argues, the Atlantic (4).
6. Writing about the function of Wordsworth's and Hawthorne's use of superstitious narrators and interpreters within their works, Richard Gravil notes in *Romantic Dialogues* (Basingstoke and New York, NY: Palgrave Macmillan, 2000) that 'the reader is decoyed into judgement – on Martha and the community in

Wordsworth's case; on Dimmesdale and the community in Hawthorne's. To believe Young Goodman Brown, *or to grant substance to the promptings of the scarlet letter*, is to accuse a community of witchcraft. No doubt Hawthorne felt guilt at his ancestors' complicity in the imputation of evil, but his response is not the obvious one, of distancing himself from their imputed "hypocrisy". Rather, he illustrates the ease with which his contemporaries and ours can be led into the same spirit of accusation while congratulating themselves on our immunity to superstition.' (121)

The architecture of Wordsworth's and Hawthorne's plot structures contains traps for the readers who attempt to make their way through them. In *The Scarlet Letter* and 'The Thorn', as soon as a reader has judged one of the characters as guilty, he or she has committed the same 'sin' ['Judge not, lest ye be judged'] as the townsfolk by condemning someone based on hearsay and subscribing to the customs as well as beliefs of the works' communities of interpreters. These works become, during sympathetic reading of them, mental autobiographies, the (scarlet) letters stitched to the psyches of their writers and readers. The behavioural patterns of Hester Prynne and Martha Ray, as well as the villagers' stories about them, are the burdens of minds in a state of distress. Individuals' feelings are projected onto objects, persons and narratives, and it is implicit that the reader will repeat the thought processes exemplified by the works' characters, subjects, or speakers, so that 'the manner in which we associate ideas in a state of excitement' (Preface, *LB*, 743) is explained by example. The function of Wordsworth's and Hawthorne's use of this narrative technique is also to critique the gothic's as well as the reader's own notions of poetics, politics and morals, to 'maneuver the reader into significant encounter with what Wordsworth [in the Preface] called "his pre-established code of decision"' (Gravil, 122). The works place the readers as surveyors in their own custom-houses, in which all their customs and ideas that are imported are weighed in the balance, examined in the sense of the word's Latin roots. See also note 13.

7. For more on Poe's ruins and fragments in a transatlantic context, see Susan Manning, *Fragments of Union* (Basingstoke: Palgrave, 2002).
8. '[T]hat first ancestor ... was present to my ... imagination as far back as I can remember ... It still haunts me': Nathniel Hawthorne, *The Scarlet Letter*, ed. Ross C. Murfin (Boston, MA: Bedford, 1991), 26. Subsequent parentetical citations are to page numbers in this edition.
9. Wordsworth, Hawthorne and Poe draw upon the spectre of regional history – on that of poor farmers and British landed gentry, the Salem Witch Trials as well as the displacement of Native Americans, respectively – as implicit or explicit backdrops to intensify the horror of their tales. These tales and poems, like the characters and structures they portray, contain hidden compartments, subtexts of guilt and anxiety.
10. *Selected Writings of Edgar Allan Poe*, ed. Edward H. Davidson (Boston, MA: Houghton Mifflin, 1956). Unless otherwise noted, all Poe citations correspond to this edition.
11. Although Hester is able to rise from her ruins, Dimmesdale's inability to overcome his vexed mind aligns him with Usher and Margaret of 'The Ruined Cottage': '[B]e the stern and sad truth spoken, that the breach which guilt has once made into the human soul is never, in this mortal state, repaired. It may be watched and guarded ... [b]ut there is still the ruined wall, and, near it, the stealthy tread of the foe that would win over again his unforgotten triumph' (Hawthorne, 158). In Hester and Dimmesdale's conversation in the forest, she

attempts to restore him to his former self, but unlike Dorothy's and Nature's effect on Wordsworth of 'Tintern Abbey', neither Hester, nor Nature, shows Dimmesdale anything enduringly redemptive in the still sad music of humanity. In contrast to 'the ruined wall' of Dimmesdale's mind is Dorothy's mind as described in 'Tintern Abbey', 'thy mind / Shall be a mansion for all lovely forms' (*LB*, 140–1).

12. See Peter J. Kitson, 'Coleridge and "the Ouran Utang Hypothesis": Romantic Theories of Race' and Tim Fulford, 'Theorizing Golgotha: Coleridge, Race Theory, and The Skull Beneath the Skin', both in *Samuel Taylor Coleridge and the Sciences of Life*, ed. Nicholas Roe (Oxford: Oxford UP, 2001).
13. The 1802 version of 'Ruth' contains the following lines:

    Whatever in those Climes I found
    Irregular in sight or sound
    Did to my mind impart
    A kindred impulse, seem'd allied
    To my own powers, and justified
    The workings of my heart.

    Nor less to feed unhallow'd thought
    The beauteous forms of nature wrought. (*LB*, 72–9)

14. The Orientalism of the British Romantics is discussed in Saree Makdisi's *Romantic Imperialism* (Cambridge and New York, NY: Cambridge UP, 1998).
15. Like *The Scarlet Letter*, the 'Advertisement' to the 1798 *Lyrical Ballads* calls into question the 'most dreadful enemy to our pleasures, our own pre-established codes of decision' (739). Preconceived notions (not wholly uninfluenced by the gothic, especially with regards to a reader's aesthetics) replace the supernatural spectres of the gothic, insofar as these notions are, to Wordsworth, truly 'dreadful' and 'the enemy'. The Preface to the *Ballads* seeks to proselytize its new aesthetic by converting readers, who previously subscribed to neo-classical and/or gothic aesthetics, by shaping their poetic sensibilities, so that Wordsworth and Coleridge can create the taste by which their work is to be appreciated. The endeavour of the Preface is to create a new community of interpreters for whom the common diction, characters and imagery that neo-classical poets would consider beneath their contempt is re-signified as the *ne plus ultra* of poetics. The ministry of these authors' works is clear: they are an alternative and antidote to gothic literature, to what the Preface calls 'frantic novels ... and idol and extravagant stories in verse' which 'blunt the discriminating powers of the mind' by satisfying a 'craving for extraordinary incident' (*LB*, 747). By utilizing and transforming gothic conventions (ruined architecture of the mind and others), Wordsworth's poems as well as Poe's and Hawthorne's stories harness the power of gothic to elicit strong emotional reactions in readers. These authors tap into gothic's readership to sharpen the discriminating powers of the mind. Wordsworth's aversion to the gothic is part and parcel of his subversion of its conventions, his critique from within its tradition. His ironic and problematic stance towards the gothic of his British predecessors (Horace Walpole, Ann Radcliffe, William Godwin, Monk Lewis) is one that influences his British and American successors and contemporaries (Coleridge, Poe, Hawthorne, the Shelleys). Michael Gamer notes that Wordsworth and Coleridge 'attempt to separate gothic writing's penchant for shock and sensation from its interest in extreme states of consciousness in order to reject the former and renegotiate the

value of the latter' (*Romanticism and the Gothic*, 114). Like Wordsworth and Coleridge, Hawthorne distanced himself from the gothic, critiquing romances from within the tradition. In the preface to *Tales of the Grotesque and Arabesque*, Poe only aligns 'Metzengerstein' with that 'species of pseudo-horror which we are taught to call Germanic': *Edgar Allan Poe: Poetry and Tales* (New York, NY: Library of America, 1984), 129.

16. See Timothy Fulford, 'Primitive Poets and Dying Indians' in *1800: The New Lyrical Ballads*, eds Nicola Trott and Seamus Perry (Basingstoke and New York, NY: Palgrave, 2001), 44–73.
17. 'Insanity and Madhouses', *Quarterly Review* 15 (July 1816), 398–9, reprinted in New York for Thos. Kirk and Thos. R. Mercein, at the Office of the *Edinburgh* and *Quarterly Reviews*, No. 19 Wall-Street. As a cure the author recommends not the gothic, but 'literary pursuits' and the 'delightful recollections and associations which they inspire', and steering clear of American politics by hinting 'that the present habits of society have rather too strong a tincture of democratical freedom for the well-being of individuals' (399–400).
18. The arrows appear not only as symbols in the earth, but also the sky. After the 'A' appears in the night sky, Hawthorne comments, 'Nothing was more common, in those days, than to interpret all meteoric appearances, and other natural phenomena, that occurred with less regularity than the rise and set of the sun and moon, as so many revelations from a supernatural source. Thus, a blazing spear, a sword of flame, a bow, or a sheaf of arrows, seen in the midnight sky, prefigured Indian warfare ... The belief was a favorite one with our forefathers, as betokening that their infant commonwealth was under a celestial guardianship of peculiar intimacy and strictness. But what should we say, when an individual [Dimmesdale, Wordsworth?] discovers a revelation, addressed to himself alone, on the same vast sheet of record! In such a case, it could only be the symptom of a highly disordered mental state, when a man, rendered morbidly self-contemplative by long, intense, and secret pain, had extended his egotism over the whole expanse of nature' (127).

    Hawthorne buttresses neither the Puritan notion of the forest as the evil dwelling place of Native Americans (as in Mary Rowlandson's narrative) nor the Lake School/Transcendentalist conception of the forest as a place of divine revelation. Both of these interpretations hinge upon a one-to-one correspondence between signifier and signified; Hawthorne shows how a sign (such as the seemingly portentous 'A' that appears in the sky after Governor Winthrop's death) can take on many, oftentimes mutually contradictory, meanings. As Richard Gravil notes, 'Hawthorne's forte ... is the scrutiny of Emerson's faith in the translucence of symbol' (*Romantic Dialogues*, 123).
19. Hester is taxed by her sin, and the Puritans make it her duty to be a walking commandment to enforce their customs: 'Thus she will be a living sermon against sin, until the ignominious letter be engraved upon her tombstone' (64).
20. Hawthorne points out the difficulties of duplicating the British landscape in America: 'the proprietor already appeared to relinquish, as hopeless, the effort to perpetuate on this side of the Atlantic, in a hard soil ... the native English taste for ornamental gardening' (93). According to Pearl, she had 'not been made at all, but had been plucked by her mother off the bush of wild roses, that grew by the prison door' (97).
21. Pearl's obstinate replies during her conversation with Mr Wilson about her parentage (95) recall the conversation between the speaker and the child in 'We Are Seven', and show yet another American response (in addition to Whitman's

as examined by Karen Karbiener's essay in this volume (Chapter 7) to the poem, which was pirated and reprinted in America as a chapbook. Pearl also becomes the antithesis of the child in the 'Ode. Intimations of Immortality', as (rather than 'trailing clouds of glory' from heaven) she is thought of as the devil's daughter. She is the letter, not the word, made flesh, and (as opposed to being closed in by shades of the prison house as she grows older) emerges as a babe from the prison turning her head away from the light of the sun (56–7). Instead of perceiving nature and children as blessed, as does the 'Ode', for Pearl, the 'ugliest weeds of the garden were their [the Puritans'] children' (85). Pearl's relationship with Hester contrasts with that of Wordsworth's to his mother in the 'Blest the infant babe' passage of *The Prelude*'s second book: whereas Wordsworth holds mute dialogues with his mother's heart, the first thing which Pearl noticed about Hester was 'not the mother's smile, responding to it, as other babies do, by that faint, embryo smile of the little mouth', but the scarlet letter (86). Pearl's inheritance is neither 'clouds of glory' nor 'intercourse of sense', but only 'enmity and passion had Pearl inherited, by inalienable right, out of Hester's heart' (84). This description resounds with the language of the Declaration of Independence. As Sohui Lee has pointed out to me in an email of 1 December 2003: Pearl is the meta-text of Hester's scarlet letter as well as well as Hawthorne's *Scarlet Letter*: Pearl is 'the scarlet letter in another form; the scarlet letter endowed with life' (90). Pearl represents the novel's attempt to refashion British customs and conventions, to custom tailor the novel into an American 'A', a declaration of American literary independence as well as inheritance from the British. The comparison between the 'Ode' and the *Letter* was initially made by Richard Harter Fogle, *Hawthorne's Imagery* (Norman, OK: University Press of Oklahoma, 1969), 27–8, 34.

22. Henry James refers to the novel as 'the finest piece of imaginative writing yet put forth in this country', as a work that could be 'sent to Europe as exquisite in quality as anything that had been received'; *Hawthorne* (New York, NY: AMS, 1968), 110–11.
23. Hawthorne informs the reader of his connection to the wilderness and of his own Anglo-American heritage, of (in his words) the 'deep and aged roots my family has struck into the soil. It is now nearly two centuries and a quarter since the original Briton, the earliest emigrant of my name, made his appearance in the wild and forest-bordered settlement, which has since become a city [Salem]' (26). Tellingly, Pearl also becomes heir to 'a very considerable amount of property, both here and in England' (199), and once Hester returns to America, she and Pearl quite literally participate in a transatlantic exchange of letters, Pearl's arriving in America with 'armorial seals upon them, though of bearings unknown to English heraldry' (200).
24. My argument is indebted to Darrel Abel, *The Moral Picturesque: Studies in Hawthorne's Fiction* (West Lafayette, IN: Purdue UP, 1988), 180, 207. Hester's radicalism and eventual apostasy follow the same arc as Wordsworth's: initially, Hawthorne portrays her as radical, but by the end of the novel she is more sceptical of her role in a revolution for equality, coming to doubt her own prophetic vocation (201). In this sense, however, the ending of the *Letter* is precisely opposite the ascendant ending of *The Prelude*, which confirms Wordsworth's calling as a prophet.
25. Hawthorne further connects Hester to racial otherness as well as Romantic solitude and radicalism by describing her as having 'wandered, without rule or guidance, in a moral wilderness; as vast, as intricate and shadowy, as the untamed

forest ... Her intellect and heart had their home, as it were, in desert places, where she had roamed as freely as the wild Indian in his woods. For years past she had looked from this estranged point of view at human institutions ... criticizing all with hardly more reverence than the Indian would feel for the clerical band ... The tendency of her fame and fortunes has been to set her free. The scarlet letter was her passport into regions where other women dare not tread. Shame, Despair, Solitude! These had been her teachers, – stern and wild ones, – and they had made her strong, but taught her much amiss' (157).

26. See Lawrence Buell, 'Postcolonial Anxiety in Classic US Literature' in *Postcolonial Theory in the United States: Race, Ethnicity, and Literature*, eds Amritjit Singh and Peter Schmidt (Jackson, MS: University Press of Mississippi, 2000), 196–219, and Sohui Lee, '"[O]ur American kinsman": British Nationalism and Book Reviews of American Literature in the 1840s', *Romanticism on the Net* (forthcoming, 2004). Chillingworth is also parallel to the Wordsworth of *The Prelude*, as he, like the poet, attempts to delve into (dissect) the human mind to understand its development and the ways in which it is formed by, and copes with, sharp emotional experience, such as developing an internal theology to reckon with guilt and loss. Like Hester's letter and Wordsworth's *Prelude*, the *Letter* is Hawthorne's text; 'The Custom-House' functions as the minister's black veil: 'We may prate of the circumstances that lie around us, and even of our self, but still keep the inmost Me behind its veil'(23). Hawthorne, though, inveighs against Wordsworth's project of seeking to read and transcribe the text of his innermost self. It is Chillingworth who, like Wordsworth, seeks to read the innermost writing: 'He [Dimmesdale] bears no letter of infamy wrought into his garment ... but I shall read it on his heart' (73).

    According to Wordsworth 'We murder to dissect'; for Hawthorne, however, we dissect to murder. Chillingworth's sin is greater than Dimmesdale's or Hester's, for he 'has violated, in cold blood, the sanctity of a human heart' (154). Chillingworth operates, so to speak, on Dimmesdale's mind and heart by scrutinizing and dissecting his honour from his guilt: he scientifically separates Dimmesdale the innocent minister from Dimmesdale the guilty sinner, thereby pushing him inexorably to his death: 'He now dug into the poor clergyman's heart, like a miner searching for gold; or, rather like a sexton delving into a grave possibly in search of a jewel that had been buried on the dead man's bosom' (109). It is evident that Chillingworth's link to the poet whose surname shares the last syllable of his own is more than phonetic; in addition to being associated with Wordsworth, he is also connected to racial otherness: 'By the Indian's side, and evidently sustaining a companionship with him, stood a white man [Chillingworth], clad in a strange disarray of civilized and savage costume' (62). One possible source for aspects of Chillingworth's background and return is Leonard from 'The Brothers', who returns to his former village after a long absence and questions a priest to interpret the misery that has befallen his family, all the while keeping his identity anonymous.

27. By listing these groups together, I do not mean to imply that their theological interpretations are interchangeable or even parallel. These divergent notions of theology led to equally divergent interpretations of Wordsworth's works, yet each group perceived literature's worth as being inextricably linked to its morality.

28. Thomas Holley Chivers, *Eonchs of Ruby: A Gift of Love* (New York, NY: Spalding and Shepard, 1851), 14.

29. Kate Chopin, 'Désirée's Baby', *American Gothic: An Anthology, 1787–1916*, ed. Charles L. Crow (Oxford: Blackwell, 1999), 340. Citations to works of Cable and

Chesnutt are also from this volume and will be cited parenthetically with the page number.

30. Toni Morrison, *Playing in the Dark: Whiteness and the Literary Imagination* (Cambridge, MA: Harvard UP, 1992), 58.
31. Olaudah Equiano, *The Interesting Narrative of the Life of Olaudah Equiano*, ed. Robert J. Allison (New York, NY: Bedford, 1995), 54.
32. *The Journals of Charles W. Chesnutt*, ed. Richard Brodhead (Durham, NC: Duke UP, 1993), 140.
33. 'Goophering Around: Authority and the Trick of Storytelling in Charles W. Chesnutt's *The Conjure Woman*' in *Tricksterism in Turn-of-the-Century American Literature: A Multicultural Perspective*, eds Elizabeth Ammons and Annette White Parks (Hanover, NH: University Press of New England, 1994), 79. My essay is also indebted, here, to Paul Gilroy's *The Black Atlantic* (1993) and his notion of a transnational and trans-cultural interplay of European and African influences in the creation of (post)modernity.
34. Elizabeth Palmer Peabody, writing to Wordsworth about Hawthorne, 1838, is quick to distance him from the morbid genre of the gothic and to align him with Wordsworth: '[Hawthorne] said he was from sunrise to sunset quarrelling with sea captains & owners – about measuring out their cargoes of salt & coal & potatoes – according to the laws – and then he went home to his room & read Wordsworth ... I send you also this little volume of Tales – as you will agree that the popular story tellers are the ballad makers of the nation; and I should like to show you – what I think is best in this line. Some of the tales evince a morbid direction of the fancy – yet I think they are redeemed by the glimpses of the inner nature which he gives us in the Reflection with which he closes each.'

    Poe's quotation from and reaction to the *Ballads'* Preface in *Letter to B*—takes up the same adversarial stance to Wordsworth and Coleridge's new aesthetic as these poets take towards to the gothic in their critique of the tradition from within by using its own words (and conventions) against it: 'Those who have been accustomed to the phraseology of modern writers, if they persist in reading this book to a conclusion (impossible!) will, no doubt, have to struggle with feelings of awkwardness; (ha! ha! ha!) they will look round for poetry (ha! ha! ha! ha!) and will be induced to inquire by what species of courtesy these attempts have been permitted to assume that title.'

5

Wordsworth, Henry Reed and Bishop Doane: High-Church Romanticism on the Delaware

Adam Potkay

On 6 June 1851 Theodore Parker wrote of Christopher Wordsworth's *Memoirs of William Wordsworth* in a familiar letter to Miss Hannah Stevenson, a cultured spinster who usually lived in Parker's Boston household and whom he addressed in correspondence as 'dear old ladye':

> I have just finished the Life of Wordsworth ... Wordsworth was a dear old granny, with a most hearty love of mankind, especially of the least attractive portions of it, – *beggars* and *fools*, and Bishop Doane, who he thinks was a great and good man. Wordsworth heard him preach once at London; saw him at his (Wordsworth's) house, and liked him much. If Wordsworth had lived a little in London, and felt the presence of some one who was manly and differed from him, it would have done him service. He runs in a narrow round of objects, ideas, and sentiments; is humane (and means to be so in his penal sonnets), devout, self-denying, and genial; but he lived too much in solitude, was too much with his worshippers, and limited himself in his reading ... But I love the dear old poetical Betty more after reading his Life than before. You will rejoice in the book, which will wait for you when you return.[1]

That Parker here banters affectionately with a 44-year-old woman in his care takes some of the sting out of his references to the older Wordsworth as a 'dear old granny' and a 'dear old poetical *Betty*' – a name, as the *Oxford English Dictionary* tells us, 'given in contempt to a man who occupies himself with a woman's household duties' (the related 'to betty about' is illustrated by a quotation from Parker). Parker's complaint that this feminized Wordsworth was too fond of 'the least attractive portions' of mankind is not in itself remarkable – the vulgarity of Wordsworth's subjects was bemoaned since Southey's review of *Lyrical Ballads* and his 'namby-pamby' manner since Jeffrey's review of the 1807 *Poems in Two Volumes*.[2] What is apt to give pause is Parker's singling out from the unattractive mankind that Wordsworth loved 'Bishop Doane'. Who *was* Bishop Doane, and what was it about him that won Wordsworth's esteem? Correspondingly, what was it about Doane and about Wordsworth's ability to love him that elicited Parker's disdain? (Let us for the sake of argument assume that Doane's bishopric *per se* would not be quite a sufficient goad.)

My aim in this essay is to answer these questions in a broadly contextual way, and in doing so to develop a thesis about conflicting appropriations of Wordsworth in antebellum America: while Parker and his Boston circle saw in the older (indeed, post-1807) Wordsworth effeminacy and decline, Wordsworth's career was viewed as perfectly integrated, and integrally High Church, by Bishop Doane and his Delaware valley friend – and Wordsworth's American editor – Henry Reed.

First, some basic identification is in order. George Washington Doane (1799–1859), the second Episcopalian Bishop of New Jersey (consecrated 1832), was the chief American proponent of Tractarianism or the Oxford Movement, and the editor of the first American edition of John Keble's *Christian Year*.[3] Doane was the first American bishop – perhaps even the first American clergyman – to preach in the Church of England (in Coventry on 1 August 1841), Parliament having just repealed an act prohibiting American clergy from preaching in English churches. Doane first met Wordsworth through the Tory baronet Sir Robert Inglis, at a Literary Society dinner in London on 11 July 1841.[4] Doane later visited Wordsworth at Rydal Mount on 5 August and published a detailed account of their day together in his journal, *The Missionary*, recalling with particular fondness his pansy-hunting with the poet, in commemoration of the 'Ode: Intimations of Immortality' (*WP*, 'The Pansy at my feet / Doth the same tale repeat: / Whither is fled the visionary gleam?' [54–6]).[5] Doane was a man of letters in the broadest sense: in addition to his hundreds of sermons and addresses, and his editorial duties on several Church journals, he was a lyric poet and hymn-writer, routinely included in American anthologies of 'best-loved verse' through the middle-twentieth century. He was also a professor of rhetoric and English literature for most of his adult life, teaching first at Washington (later renamed Trinity) College in Hartford, Connecticut (1824–28) and later at the two educational institutions he founded in Burlington, New Jersey, eighteen miles up the Delaware river from Philadelphia: the innovative female seminary, St Mary's Hall, founded in 1837 (the same year that Mary Lyons established Mount Holyoke), and Burlington College, founded 1846.[6]

Figure 5 Bishop George Washington Doane by Henry Inman, circa 1840. Courtesy of Reverend J. Connor Haynes, St Mary's Church, Burlington, NJ.

The one deed that has preserved Doane's name among Wordsworth scholars is recorded in a note to *Ecclesiastical Sonnets* 3.13–15, on 'Aspects of Christianity in America'. Wordsworth's 1845 note reads,

> American episcopacy, in union with the Church in England, strictly belongs to the general subject; and I here make acknowledgement to my American friends, Bishop Doane, and Mr. Henry Reed of Philadelphia, for having suggested the propriety of adverting to it, and pointed out the virtues and intellectual qualities of Bishop White, which so eminently fitted him for the great work he undertook. Bishop White was consecrated at Lambeth, Feb. 4, 1787, by Archbishop Moore; and before his long life was closed, twenty-six bishops had been consecrated in America, by himself. For his character and opinions see his own numerous Works, and a *Sermon in Commemoration* of him, by George Washington Doane, Bishop of New Jersey.

William White, the first Bishop of Pennsylvania and the chief architect of the Protestant Episcopal Church in America, is the subject of Wordsworth's sonnet 3.15: the 'patient energy' that Wordsworth attributes to him is a direct quotation from Doane's 1836 commemorative sermon.[7]

Wordsworth's other 'American friend', Henry Reed (1808–55), was Professor of Rhetoric and English Literature at the University of Pennsylvania, Wordsworth's American editor and, after 1837, his regular correspondent.[8] Reed was also an ardent Churchman, a close friend of Doane's, and since 1834 proudly married to the granddaughter of Bishop White. Reed received his BA at the University of Pennsylvania in 1825 and, after a brief stint in the law, returned to teach at the University in 1831. In 1837 he published his edition of Wordsworth's poetry, which adds Wordsworth's *Yarrow Revisited and Other Poems* (1835) to the fourth collected London edition of 1832, and includes supplementary notes by Reed.[9] Reed then published a 70–page critical essay on Wordsworth's poetry in the *New York Review*.[10] His university lectures on literature and literary history, most of them originally delivered in the 1840s and early 1850s, were posthumously collated and introduced by his brother, William B. Reed, and published by Parry and McMillan of Philadelphia in three instalments: *Lectures on English Literature from Chaucer to Tennyson* (1855); *Lectures on English History as Illustrated by Shakespeare's Chronicle Plays* (1856); and *Lectures on the British Poets*, 2 volumes (1857).

The last book Reed published during his lifetime was the American version of Christopher Wordsworth's *Memoirs of William Wordsworth*, the work we found Theodore Parker reading at the outset of this essay. This American edition of the *Memoirs* is markedly different from the English version, as Reed incorporated into it all of his letters from Wordsworth, including one that apparently solves the riddle of why Parker should find

Figure 6 Henry Reed, engraving by A.B. Walter. Courtesy of the Library Company of Philadelphia.

Bishop Doane and Wordsworth's attitude towards him so provoking. On 16 August 1841, Wordsworth wrote Reed a letter that begins with effusive praise of Doane – 'a man of no ordinary powers of mind and attainments, of warm feelings and sincere piety' – and concludes with a blanket denigration of the Boston intellectual scene – 'Where is the thing which now passes for philosophy at Boston to stop?' (*Memoirs*, II, 389–90).[11]

This essay will examine two localized and competing ways of reading, teaching and generally promulgating Wordsworth in the 1830s through 1850s. Examinations of Wordsworth in America most often boil down to Wordsworth in Boston or, more specifically, Wordsworth among the Transcendentalists – chiefly Emerson, Thoreau and Hawthorne, with glances at the addresses and classroom practices of Theodore Parker,

Bronson Alcott and Elizabeth Palmer Peabody[12] – American intellectual history having until very recently been a phenomenology of the Massachusetts spirit as it evolves from Puritanism to the Great Society. I will here chiefly be concerned, by contrast, with Wordsworth's reception among an Episcopalian circle in the Delaware river ports of Philadelphia and Burlington, New Jersey – at a time when the Episcopalian Church was rapidly expanding in the mid-Atlantic region.[13] My focus will be on the lectures, sermons, essays and letters of Henry Reed and Bishop Doane, authors who were anti-Unitarian, anti-Transcendentalist, and opposed to the contemporary literary productions of Boston (excepting Longfellow) from the *North American Review* to Emerson. Doane preached and Reed nodded to the one catholic and apostolic church that spanned from England to America,[14] and both promulgated an ethical creed of domesticity, placing a particular emphasis on the exemplary spirituality of little children and (only mildly idealized) women.

Reed and Doane shared as a central tenet that Wordsworth was the greatest poet of the age. While Reed ranked him as 'native to the same region of poetic inspiration' as Chaucer, Spenser, Shakespeare and Milton (*New York Review*, 2–3), Doane 'canonized' him in a stronger sense, calling him in 1845 'the solace and the glory of our dry and dusty age' and, on 4 July 1850, 'the Sage and Poet of our times; saintly, in all his life, now sainted, in his death' (*Life and Writings*, IV, 87, 251). Between them, Reed and Doane fashioned a Wordsworth who expressed their core values of a corporate Christian faith and companionate marriage, and who in their view *had always done so*, in verse that grew only deeper in wisdom and craft as his career advanced. Although some Bostonians were already complaining of Wordsworth's poetic decline after his alleged Tory conversion, for Reed and Doane Wordsworth's poetic corpus and political character are both perfectly integral and consistent: as Reed writes, excepting a few months in which he was deluded by the disguised 'licentiousness' of the French Revolution, Wordsworth has always been a lover of 'liberty' in its British and Christian senses, and 'may foster a lover of freedom and of country, the wide world over' (*New York Review*, 61). Wordsworth in his later years approved of this literary image of himself and of those who purveyed it, to the consternation of progressive Boston intellectuals such as Parker.

Yet Reed and Doane's strong reading (or misprision) of Wordsworth's canon may contain some insights for today's progressive literary critics, as its retrospective corporatism contests the individualist excesses of Transcendentalism and indeed of 'Romanticism' as that term developed in later nineteenth- and early twentieth-century literary criticism.[15] Moreover, Reed and Doane's goal of gender equity affords some counterweight to Victorian anxieties about the fate of masculine hegemony, anxieties glimpsed in Parker's view that what Wordsworth needed was a 'manly' man who might have stopped him from bettying about.[16] Reed and Doane's readings of Wordsworth attempt to harmonize not only the successive parts of Wordsworth's canon, but also the gendered interpretive roles of the readers of that canon. Reed and Doane envisioned, with utopian élan and with Wordsworth's blessing, a *corpus* both of Wordsworth's writings and of his readers; it is, I would suggest, a corporate vision we might salvage without necessarily equating it, as they did, with a corporate Church.

Wordsworth's own objection to the Boston philosophy was that it would sever the bonds that hold a people, a Church, and a language together. Wordsworth charges Emerson and his British counterpart, Carlyle, 'our two present Philosophes', with having 'taken a language which they suppose to be English for their vehicle' and arriving at 'mutual admiration' and general unintelligibility (*Memoirs*, II, 390). This stylistic eccentricity is matched by spiritual singularity. In the radical Christology of Emerson's Harvard Divinity School Address of 1838 – which reappears in Parker's 1841 sermon, 'The Transient and Permanent in Christianity' – Jesus became God through intuiting the moral law, or God, rolling through all things; he then tried to show others how they could do the same, until his trope of divine incarnation was misunderstood as a literal truth that became the foundation of 'this eastern monarchy of a Christianity, which indolence and fear have built'. Emerson proceeds to a stunning assertion of what is a man's by 'manly right' – no less than the unmediated legislation of the world:

> Accept the injurious impositions of our early catechistical instruction, and even honesty and self-denial were but splendid sins, if they did not wear the Christian name. One would rather be 'A pagan, suckled in a creed outworn', than to be defrauded of his manly right in coming into nature, and finding not names and places, not land and professions, but even virtue and truth foreclosed and monopolized. You shall not be a man even. You shall not own the world; you shall not dare, and live in the infinite Law that is in you ... but you must subordinate your nature to Christ's nature; you must accept our interpretations; and take his portrait as the vulgar draw it.[17]

If Wordsworth read these lines – the Divinity School 'Address' may have been included in the Emerson writings sent to him by Elizabeth Palmer Peabody – we can well imagine his dismay. Emerson's passage may be read as a gloss on the whole of the Wordsworth sonnet from which it quotes, 'The world is too much with us'. Wordsworth had there lamented, 'Little we see in Nature that is ours', perhaps referring – if we recall 'Tintern Abbey' – to the mind's failure to half-create the world it should only half perceive. The line could also refer, however, to the mind's fundamental alienation from the processes and pleasures of the natural world, the tragic theme of 'Lines written in Early Spring'. Emerson turns the delicate ambiguity of Wordsworth's line into a clearly implied injunction: 'Be a man. Own the world'. Wordsworth, confronting the Christian or post-Christian impediments to owning or even inhabiting nature, concludes in 'The world is too much with us' that better than an inanimate or dispossessed modern world would be the mythopoeic imagination of ancient religion:

> – Great God! I'd rather be
> A Pagan suckled in a creed outworn;
> So might I, standing on this pleasant lea,
> Have glimpses that would make me less forlorn;
> Have sight of Proteus rising from the sea;
> Or hear old Triton blow his wreathed horn. (9–14)

In Emerson's appropriation, Wordsworth's isolated line – 'A Pagan suckled in a creed outworn' – conjures a preference for a polytheistic sense of nature over a Christian one, and a properly Transcendentalist sense of nature over a polytheist one. Wordsworth was rarely so programmatic, and was certainly not so here.

Neither 'The world is too much with us' nor the pagan nostalgia and/or Transcendentalist aspiration that gave the poem a pride of place in Massachusetts circles[18] translated into the altogether different Wordsworthian idiom concurrently cultivated along the Delaware river. Reed responded to Wordsworth's dismay at Emerson's essays: 'You ask where is the thing they now call philosophy at Boston to stop? It has assumed all the various phases of Socinianism, and with the restlessness of that heresy, it seems to be traveling to infidelity and pantheism' (*Wordsworth and Reed* 60). In Reed and in Doane, by contrast, we find a robustly Christian Wordsworth, a poet of social ethics, eleemosynary gospel injunctions, and the three theological virtues of faith, hope, and charity. Reed's fullest critical engagement with Wordsworth, his *New York Review* essay of 1839, concludes with a paragraph summarizing his – and anticipating Doane's – views of the poet:

> It is the highest and holiest purpose of nature to minister to the sorrows inherent in human nature. To this have Wordsworth's genius and his life been consecrated, and when we behold him sending the soul into itself, to be admonished of its weakness, or made conscious of its power – taking thought for the poor and humble – elevating the sense of humanity by the imaginative idea of childhood – in a word, forever cherishing in the heart of man, Faith, and Hope, and Love – then in the sublimity and beauty of his Muse, we can trace – in the sweet phrase of Spenser – 'The lineaments of Gospell bookes'. (70)

Of Reed's claims here, one particularly requires explication: what does it mean to 'elevate the sense of humanity by the imaginative idea of childhood'? Reed here alludes back to his Christianizing of Wordsworth's ideal of childhood, especially as it appears in the 'Ode: Intimations of Immortality'. Reed, whether consciously or not, opposes the poem's treatment by the educator Bronson Alcott, as recorded in Elizabeth Palmer Peabody's *Record of a School* (1835). In her 1836 preface, Peabody explains that in their Boston grammar school Bronson Alcott teaches that the individual soul pre-exists, shapes, and ought not be eclipsed by its body, 'and that is all the preexistence that is meant in Wordsworth's ode on Immortality, or that Plato himself meant to teach'.[19] Through classroom discussion of Wordsworth's 'Ode', Alcott taught, if not metempsychosis, at least a type of Gnostic lore that accords with what Harold Bloom calls 'the American Religion' but opposes orthodox Christianity.[20] Alcott engages with the poem's ostensible concern with prenatal existence over the promise of personal immortality; Reed, by contrast, does his best to reverse the apparent proportions of Wordsworth's poem. He begins with the Wanderer's lines from *The Excursion*, IX, 23–44, themselves a re-writing of the 'Ode: Intimations of Immortality', on 'why in age / Do we revert so fondly to the walks / Of Childhood'? Reed reads these lines as showing 'how holy a thing, even with all its frailty, the heart is, before worldly passions throng to take possession of it'; recognizing this holiness is 'persuasive to aspirations after a renewed innocence' (*New York Review*, 35). Reed proceeds to examine the 'Ode', quoting extensively from the poem's 'antistrophe' or counter-turn (*TP*, stanzas 5–6, beginning 'Our birth is but a sleep and a forgetting') and its 'epode' or stand (stanza 9, beginning 'The thought of our past years in me doth breed / Perpetual benedictions'). He argues, 'In the image of childhood the heart recognizes its own imperishable nature, and in the innocence of those days it discovers faintly shadowed forth promises of the soul redeemed and happy' (37). Reed then ushers the 'Ode' into a fully Christian arena: childhood, for Wordsworth, is 'a foretokening and assurance of heaven'. Wordsworth hearkens to:

> that narrative which tells us that Jesus bade his busy disciples suffer the little children to come unto him – and proclaiming that "of such is the kingdom of God", "took them up in his arms, put his hands upon them, and blessed them". The Saviour announces in one short sentence that "of such (the little children) is the kingdom of heaven" ... Thus, when Wordsworth sends his spirit to explore the heart of childhood and bring to light the beauty of its innocence, the beauty of his chastened poetic instinct is in accordance with the teachings of childlike simplicity which distinguish Christianity, and the deepest of his musings is consecrated to the truth of revelation. (37–8)

Reed concludes this discussion with quoting the pendant poem of the 'Ode', 'My heart leaps up', which for him not only encapsulates Wordsworth's Christian commitment to childhood and childlike innocence but also symbolizes the articulated continuity, the integrity and consistency, of Wordsworth's life and poetic career – and, indeed, of any properly lived life or career:

> My heart leaps up when I behold
>   A Rainbow in the sky:
> So was it when my life began;
> So is it now I am a Man;
> So be it when I shall grow old,
>   Or let me die!
> The Child is Father of the Man;
> And I could wish my days to be
> Bound each to each by natural piety.

In his introductory letter to Wordsworth, 25 April 1836, Reed professes that through his own repeated recitation of this poem he has managed to preserve not only his soul but his companionate marriage: by reciting Wordsworth's poems aloud 'again and again ... to my *one* listener', his wife, 'we have felt that you were aiding us in "binding our days together by natural piety"' (*Wordsworth and Reed*, 3). In his edition of Wordsworth's poems, Reed provides a discursive note to 'My Heart leaps up' from *The Friend*, in which Coleridge argues that while hard-hearted men 'exist in fragments', the tender-hearted know with Wordsworth to keep the past and future ever present to the mind (*Complete Poetical Works*, 36). Finally, in his *Lectures on the British Poets*, Reed attributes Wordsworth's 'undiminished vigour' of imagination in his 70s to the poet's ongoing practice of what he had preached in 'My Heart leaps up': by always recalling his childhood self, Wordsworth ever builds upon the power of a past that has never really passed (II, 204–6). Repeating the repetitions inscribed in 'My heart leaps up' becomes, as it were, a sacramental escape from *chronos* into *kairos*.

'My heart leaps up' was, in turn, a touchstone for Bishop Doane. In his third commencement address at St Mary's Hall (1846), Doane urged his graduating women, 'Seek ... to be the comfort and the charm of life, to be your fitness for eternity, and foretaste of its joy, THE SPIRIT OF LITTLE CHILDREN' – for children are confident, humble, and hopeful, – but here his text had been the first part of Thomas Gray's 'Eton Ode' (*Life and Writings*, IV, 96–102). In addressing the graduates of Burlington College in 1855, however, it is Wordsworth's 'Ode' and in particular its tag 'The child is father of the man' that provides a lesson – not about retaining a childlike innocence, but in the importance of church-school discipline. Wordsworth's 'is the lesson of the Holy Ghost, by Solomon,

"Train up a child, in the way he should go; and, when he is old, he will not depart from it"'. Doane proceeds to divide this lesson into a number of injunctions, the first of which is:

> If 'the child is the father of the man', *we should be watchful of him.* He has a fallen nature. He was born in sin. The flesh wars, in him, with the Spirit ... .We have need, in such a case, of utmost watchfulness. To secure his earliest entrance into the heavenly kingdom, by the new birth, of water and the Spirit ... . To teach him, as he can receive it, the path of present duty, and the way of everlasting happiness. (*Life and Writings*, IV, 59–61)

According to Doane's reading of 'My heart leaps up', the adult speaker who rejoices in seeing the rainbow does so because he recalls not the intuitive responses, but rather the Bible lessons, of his childhood. Indeed, Doane links the child's instincts, in an Augustinian (and decidedly pre-Romantic) way, to original sin. According to Doane, the continuity of self that Wordsworth's poem proclaims, and that his poetry as a whole evinces, stems from a self properly disciplined in the Church; there is, in Doane's mind, no difference at all between 'My heart leaps up' and the 'Ode' and Wordsworth's poems on Baptism from *Ecclesiastical Sonnets*, which Doane quotes in a sermon of 1847,

> Blest be the Church, that, watching o'er the needs
> Of Infancy, provides a timely shower,
> Whose virtue changes to a Christian Flower
> The sinful product of a bed of weeds.
> (*Life and Writings*, IV, 187)

To the contemporary critical sensibility reared on accounts of Wordsworth's so-called 'great decade' (1797–1807) and the subsequent 'anti-climax' of his last forty-odd years, there is something audacious if not scandalous in Reed and Doane's depiction of Wordsworth as a perfectly consistent and consistently Christian poet. Yet as William Galperin has observed, 'Prior to Matthew Arnold ... many Victorians, including Ruskin, were reluctant to segregate the earlier and later Wordsworth'.[21] To any such list of reluctant Victorians we clearly need to add Reed and Doane. Perhaps their fashioning of Wordsworth may be further illuminated by Galperin's deconstructive question about what it is that Ruskin sought to accomplish in hyperbolic statements such as 'Wordsworth may be trusted as a guide in everything': Galperin asks, 'does the writer actually believe what he is claiming for Wordsworth, or is it more that Ruskin wants to believe such things precisely because they are unbelievable?' (18). There is in Ruskin's argument a 'determined wrongness', an 'irony' (18) that Galperin proceeds to describe, in a finely evocative phrase, as 'a certain *charitable irony* that makes ... [Wordsworth's] poetry less "determined" in the end than it sometimes appears' (21; emphasis mine). The 'charitable irony' that Galperin detects in Ruskin may be found as well in Reed or, *a fortiori*, in Doane, where it serves not only as a tribute to the indeterminacies of Wordsworth's verse (such as we have seen above in 'The world is too much with us') but also as adherence to Augustine's exegetical 'law of charity' which holds that scripture (or, in this case, Wordsworth's inspired verse) always and everywhere supports the dual injunction to love God and neighbour, and where a given text does not literally support that injunction, it must be interpreted allegorically to produce such a reading.[22] With the same spirit in which Augustine imposed integrity on the scriptures, Reed and Doane impose integrity on Wordsworth's canon – making it, in effect, the first truly *canonical* body of modern literature.

Reed and Doane's practices of reading Wordsworth need to be understood in relation to those Victorians before Arnold who, sometimes following Percy Shelley, broke Wordsworth in two, segregating the earlier from the later Wordsworth. In at least Reed's purview, censure of the later Wordsworth could seem another erroneous aspect of the Boston philosophy. Reed wrote to Wordsworth in October 1844:

> The last No. of the North American Review [the Boston literary journal] contains a reviewal of your poetical works – I do not know by whom – probably by the Editor. It may be sent to you from Boston or come under your eye in some way ... . I should have expected in that quarter (vitiated unfortunately by Socinianism) nothing but confusion and error respecting all in your Poems that relates to the Church, but surely there might have been much better apprehension of the political poems. (*Wordsworth and Reed*, 132–3)

The article Reed glances at here is a 32-page *North American Review* essay on Wordsworth's career (framed as a review essay of Reed's 1837 edition of Wordsworth's poems) by Edwin Percy Whipple (1819–86), Boston author and Lyceum lecturer, later ranked with Poe and Lowell as an authoritative literary critic.[23] In Whipples's estimation, Wordsworth is merely one of the four great poets of the age, alongside Scott, Byron, and the poet who appears to have Whipple's highest regard, Shelley (352). The two great influences on this group of poets, according to Whipple, were 'the French Revolution, and that tendency in the highest minds towards spiritualism, which was expressed in the revival of what is now vaguely called "the transcendental philosophy"' (355). Wordsworth began his career alongside Coleridge and Southey as one of 'the true democrats of poetry', full of Revolutionary zeal; as a facet of the Revolutionary promise of 'the reconstruction of the world', Wordsworth's 'intense spiritualism' fully displayed itself in 'Tintern Abbey' (*LB*, 359–64). But with Wordsworth's Tory conversion or descent into the mundane affairs of church and state, evident at least since *The Excursion*, his poetic powers clearly declined:

> when Wordsworth deals with virtue, freedom, justice, and truth in the abstract ... no poet can be more grand and impressive [thus, we are later told, Wordsworth's best work marks him with Shelley as a utopian 'poet of the future']; but when he connects these [virtues] with the acts and policy of English Tory politicians, or with the state and church of England, we are conscious that the analogy is false, if not ludicrous (381).

Whipple's judgement would become standard Romanticist fare in the twentieth century, but athwart the critical genealogy that connects Whipple to M.H. Abrams's *Natural Supernaturalism* (1971) we find a vector from Henry Reed to James Chandler's *Wordsworth's Second Nature* (1984), highlighting Wordsworth's abiding Burkean commitments to custom and place, church and state. As though anticipating charges of anticlimax and apostasy, Reed proclaims in his *New York Review* 'there is a symmetry in the productions of Wordsworth's youth, his manhood, and more advanced years ... his imagination strengthening with his years' (25). In his *Lectures on the British Poets*, Reed explained to his University of Pennsylvania students that Wordsworth's brief sympathies with the French Revolution 'were only with the pure elements of the cause', namely, 'the miseries of the peasantry'. But the Revolution was soon 'stricken with the worst of Egypt's plagues; benighted in moral darkness, it was visited with the pestilence of blood throughout the land'; Wordsworth rightly sought 'the homeward road to England' (II, 211). Addressing 'Tintern Abbey', Reed's confusion about where Wordsworth spent his five years' absence from the banks of the Wye leads to this thrillingly Burkean account of the Revolution:

> the beauteous forms of the external world revisited his memory and his feelings even in unpropitious circumstances – doubtless amid the tumultuous agitations of the Parisian mobs, the frenzy of the factions, the waves of a ruthless multitude beating against the ancient palace of their kings, the convulsion of every resting-place of society, the unnatural ferocity of revolutionary women, and the boundless vengeance of the metropolis, with the sympathetic restlessness of the provinces. (II, 214)

(Reed had earlier assured his students that the French Revolution was the very antithesis of the glorious American Revolution, in which 'the struggle was to vindicate and secure old principles; to guard the [English] Constitution; not to manufacture new schemes of government; to save the good old cause, as it was styled' (II, 91–2.) Wordsworth's poetry, its Englishness annealed in the fires of the French inferno, has the power to shed 'benignant light ... on your domestic hearth, upon all your intercourse with your fellow-men, upon your civic responsibilities to your country, and the sublimer [religious] relations in which man is placed' (II, 219).

A sentence such as the last reminds us that in his lectures Reed was attempting to educate an audience of young men, and that the educational aims of the age were for the most part unabashedly moral and political. Reed's broad-ranging *Lectures on English Literature* begin with 1850 a lecture on literature's place in the 'higher education', 'which is akin to religion, for it is a ministry of the soul, and deals not so much with what we know as with what we are, what we can do and what we can suffer, and what we may become here and hereafter' (39). This imperative of higher education leads Reed into a fascinating discussion of what we would now call gender and gender relations: 'Literature, according to this conception of it, is to be employed for culture of character – manly character and womanly character' (41). But these two characters, reluctantly distinguished by Reed 'because attention has lately been drawn to the social position of woman', ideally ought to exist in a gender synergy: 'the divinely-instituted principle of *companionship* ... having nothing to do with equality or superiority or inferiority on one side or the other' (42). Reed takes off from Tennyson's conclusions in *The Princess* – 'Yet in the long years liker they must grow, / The man be more of woman, she of man' – to argue for an androgynous practice of reading, in which his male students have much to learn from cultured women:

> The man's mind reacts more on the book, sets himself more in judgement upon it, and trusts less to his feelings ... That pervading error of drawing a broad line between our moral and intellectual nature, instead of recognizing the intimate interdependence of thought and feeling, is a fallacy that scarce affects the working of a woman's spirit. If a gifted and cultivated woman takes a thoughtful interest in a book, she brings her whole being to bear on it, and hence there will often be a better assurance of truth in her conclusions than in man's more logical deductions. (48–9)

Argue with Reed's gender politics as one will, we must none the less allow them to be far advanced of Parker's coeval remark that what the old granny Wordsworth needed was a 'manly' character to set him straight. To the contrary, Reed attributes the poetic greatness of both Wordsworth and Cowper to the 'reciprocal influences' of their respective female friends and advisers, Dorothy and Mrs Unwin; he concludes, in a Wordsworth allusion, that the woman's mind leads 'the man's to a wiser passiveness' (50). A later lecture in this series, on 'Contemporary Literature', segues associatively from Wordsworth to 'the genius of women' in 'the literature of our times', foregrounding for their 'genuine womanly power' Frances Anne Kemble and Elizabeth Barrett Browning (306–8).[24] In his *Lectures on the British Poets*, Reed elaborates in successive lectures on Byron (Lecture 14) and Wordsworth (Lecture 15) a sustained contrast between their characters that turns, fundamentally, on their opposed attitude towards women (II, 163–231). Byron had 'a man's most unmanly and pitiful habit, – *quarrelling with the women*' (II, 180), and this misogyny served as cause and sign of his selfish, licentious, and atheistical character (Reed colorfully calls Byron's poetry 'the blackest monument of intellectual depravity in the annals of our language' (II, 197). Wordsworth, by contrast, had a reverence for 'the daily household worth of woman', void of 'romantic exaggeration or vapid sentimentality', that contributed to and reflected his love of God and neighbour (II, 226–8).

Reed's image of Wordsworth as the poet of 'homely life and household affections' (*New York Review*, 24) has a lineage that extends back at least to Felicia Hemans's 1828 poem, 'To Wordsworth'; both this image of Wordsworth, and the poetry of Hemans, were particularly dear to Bishop Doane. Hemans's 'Evening Prayer, in a Girl's School' provides an apt centrepiece to Doane's tenth Commencement Address at his own girl's school, St Mary's Hall (*Life and Writings*, IV, 133). Doane's favourite poem to read with his female students, however – it is the only poem that he employs at two commencement addresses, his very first (1845) and his thirteenth (1857) – is 'She was a phantom of delight', which Wordsworth professedly wrote of his wife, Mary, 'When first she gleamed upon my sight', 'Her household motions light and free, / And steps of virgin-liberty'.[25] I will quote the poem's final stanza and Doane's subsequent remarks from the text of his first Address, titled 'A Perfect Woman Nobly Planned':

> And now I see with eye serene
> The very pulse of the machine;
> A Being breathing thoughtful breath,
> A Traveller between life and death;
> The reason firm, the temperate will,
> Endurance, foresight, strength, and skill;
> A perfect woman, nobly plann'd,
> To warn, to comfort, and command;
> And yet a Spirit, still, and bright
> With something of an angel-light. (21–30)

> Hang this sweet picture, from your necks, my daughters. Imprint it on your hearts. Live yourselves into it ... Let home content you, as your empire. Home duties occupy your minds. Home pleasures satisfy your hearts. (*Life and Writings*, IV, 88–9)

(In the seventh Commencement Address, 'God Speed', Doane expands the proleptic sphere of his graduates' future activities to include nursing, teaching, and missionary work, IV, 119, cf. IV, 156.) To further emphasize, in a Wordsworthian way, the normative value of homely pleasures, Doane assigned the St Mary's women weekly literary exercises on topics such as 'Flowers by the Wayside', 'A Dream', or more 'matter-of-fact' items including 'A Pencil', 'A Needle', 'Chalk', 'A Blackboard' (I, 63–4). With perfect gender equity (if rather more quixotic expectation), Doane made the appreciation of home-life his goal for Saint Mary's neighbouring male students as well. In an Address on 'The Ends and Objects of Burlington College', Doane announced:

> The single word, which best expresses all our ways and all our wishes, is the sacred monosyllable, HOME. To be *domestic*, first, and, then, *religious*; blending the two ideas, which God never meant should be disjoined, since He first knit the family bond, in Eden ... comprises all we count on, for good influence, and hope for, as good result, from Burlington College. The Poet of our times has made the sky-lark the best emblem of our aims and prayers

Doane then quotes the second stanza of Wordsworth's 1827 'To a Skylark', laying special emphasis on its final lines, 'Type of the wise, who soar, but never roam, / True to the kindred points of Heaven and Home!' (IV, 200–1).[26]

The sermons and graduation addresses which Doane gave to his students – at least his St Mary's students – were held in a gothic-revival chapel, the earliest in America, which Doane had built for St Mary's Hall in 1845 by the Edinburgh-trained architect John Notman. This 'Chapel of the Holy Innocents' was, as one architectural historian avers, 'the first building in the United States designed in at least partial accord with the tenets of the Cambridge Camden Society', a group that spearheaded the movement to revive the architecture and ritual of the medieval English Church.[27] Declaiming 'Phantom of delight' in a gothic chapel by dim candle-light – a space full of Oxford and *Il Penseroso* associations – before, as the Cambridge Camden Society's *Ecclesiologist* noted, the first '*exclusively* ... female community sitting in choir to be found in the communion of Canterbury for the last three centuries' – represents a further and dramatic aspect of Wordsworth's churching, the American realization of the Society's ideal of Wordsworth as, in Stephen Gill's words, 'a founding father'.[28] The final churching of Wordsworth, as it were, came with the Ambleside church memorial window dedicated to the poet, and financed with the contributions of Americans including Reed and Bishop Doane.[29]

Doane's reading from Wordsworth's corpus in a gothic-revival chapel founds its counterpart in Reed's reading *of* Wordsworth's corpus *as* a gothic cathedral – whole and holy – in a rhapsody building upon the poet's famous remark in his preface to *The Excursion* that his projected opus on 'Man, Nature, and Society' would be 'a Gothic church', and providing a fitting ending to the High Church image of Wordsworth that I have sought here to recollect as an important aspect of what nineteenth-century Anglo-American continuities could mean outside Massachusetts:

> We know of no fitter type of the complete structure of Wordsworth's poetry than some illustrious model of Gothic architecture ... Proud thoughts must bow down at the very threshold. Passing into the inner region the student may feel, that, in the poet's solemn musings on the mind of man – his lofty contemplations of nature, with a fidelity to her smallest forms – the stories of saints and good men, glowing with the tints of his imagination – the tributes of private grief – the memorials of deeds famed in his country's annals ... there is no capricious likeness to the high embowed roof – the dim aisles – all that is vast with a prodigality of delicate forms – the monumental effigies – the colored rays from the 'storied windows' – and the awful perspective of the nave, leading up to the light that breaks in at the East above the altar. Not only at the entrance and in the interior is this similitude; – but when the visitant comes forth in the open air, still feeling that his spirit, at first humbled, has been expanded into a sense of infinitude, he may look back from the thronged street and amid the intrusion of trivial cares, and behold the edifice in its outward glory – pinnacle and spire high reaching to the sky. (*New York Review*, 31)

Notes

1. Christopher Wordsworth, *Memoirs of William Wordsworth*, ed. Henry Reed (2 vols, Boston, MA: Ticknor, Reed and Fields, 1851), which is the American edition of the London version (Moxon 1851). Parker's letter appears in Octavius Brooks Frothingham, *Theodore Parker: A Biography* (Boston, MA: James R. Osgood, 1874), 297–8. Thanks to Sandra Burr for first bringing this letter to my attention. On Hannah Elizabeth Stevenson (1807–87), see Burr's biographical entry in *The Louisa May Alcott Encyclopedia*, ed. Gregory Eiselein and Anne K. Philips (Westport, CT: Greenwood, 2001), 317–18.
2. The early responses to Wordsworth's poems are conveniently summarized in John L. Mahoney, *Wordsworth and the Critics: The Development of a Critical Reputation* (Rochester, NY: Camden House, 2001), 1–30. Francis Jeffrey's *Edinburgh Review* attack on Wordsworth's *Poems in Two Volumes* (1807) inaugurated the complaint that Wordsworth descended to still more vulgar topics – daisies and daffodils – in a feminine, 'namby-pamby' manner: see Judith W. Page, *Wordsworth and the Cultivation of Women* (Berkeley, CA: University of California Press, 1994), 38.
3. John Keble, *Christian Year*, ed. George Washington Doane (Philadelphia, PA: Carey, 1834). For Doane's correspondence with Newman and his relation to the Oxford movement, see Lawrence N. Crumb, 'American Reflections on the

Oxford Movement: Two Unpublished Letters', *Anglican and Episcopalian History* 59, no. 1 (1990): 99–107.

4. F.B. Pinion in *A Wordsworth Chronology* (Boston, MA: G.K. Hall, 1988) has Wordsworth arriving in London on 10 July to dine with Henry Crabb Robinson, and leaving London on the 13th (195). Bishop Doane records in a letter dated 12 July having dined with Wordsworth on the preceding night (*Life and Writings*, ed. William Croswell Doane, 4 vols (New York, NY: D. Appleton and Co., 1860–61), vol. 1:353. I can find no record of Wordsworth's having 'heard him preach once in London', as Theodore Parker – perhaps erroneously – claims in his letter to Miss Stevenson.
5. Doane's fullest account of his visit to Rydal Mount, originally published in *The Missionary* 7, nos. 7–8 (July–August 1850): 30, is reproduced with commentary in Kenneth Walter Cameron, 'Wordsworth, Bishop Doane, and the Sonnets on the American Church', *Historical Magazine of the Protestant Episcopal Church* 11 (1942): 83–91. A somewhat abbreviated (and less candid) account appears in the biography of Doane written by his son, William Croswell Doane, that comprises the first volume of G.W. Doane's four-volume *Life and Writings*; see vol. 1:354–5. For the extant correspondence of Doane and Wordsworth, with commentary, see Kenneth Walter Cameron, 'Wordsworth and Bishop Doane: New Evidence', *Emerson Society Quarterly* 25 (2nd Quarter 1961): 6–12; 'Wordsworth and Bishop Doane: More Evidence', *Emerson Society Quarterly* 29 (4th Quarter 1962): 20–1.
6. St Mary's Hall made the transition in the 1960s to St Mary's Hall/Doane Academy, a co-educational college preparatory day school, in which form it continues to flourish to the present day. Burlington College officially closed in 1875. For a history of both institutions, see Adam Potkay, *An Education on the Delaware: St Mary's Hall and Doane Academy 1837–1999* (Burlington, NJ: Burlington County Historical Society, 2000).
7. As Abbie Findlay Potts shows in her critical edition of *The Ecclesiastical Sonnets of William Wordsworth* (New Haven, CT: Yale UP, 1922), all three of Wordsworth's sonnets on the American church generously allude to Doane's sermon (notes, 288–90); see also Potts's textual history of these sonnets (50–3). For an overview of White's importance to the Church, as well as Doane's, see Raymond W. Albright, *A History of the Protestant Episcopal Church* (New York, NY: Macmillan, 1964).
8. See *Wordsworth and Reed: The Poet's Correspondence with His American Editor, 1836–1850, and Henry Reed's Account of His Reception at Rydal Mount and Elsewhere in 1854*, ed. Leslie Nathan Broughton (Ithaca, NY: Cornell UP, 1933). Aside from Broughton's introductory biographical essay, the only twentieth-century assessment of Reed I have been able to find is Dennis Barone, 'The Tragedy of Henry Reed: A Note on Power, Rhetoric, and Virtue in Nineteenth-Century America', *Pennsylvania History* 59, no. 4 (October 1992): 327–40, which was kindly sent me by the author.
9. William Wordsworth, *The Complete Poetical Works of William Wordsworth*, ed. Henry Reed (Philadelphia, PA: James Kay, 1837).
10. Henry Reed, 'Wordsworth's Poetry', *New York Review*, 4, no. 7 (January 1839): 1–70.
11. In printing Wordsworth's letter, Reed's *Memoirs* substitutes dashes for the particular Boston names Wordsworth mentions, Elizabeth Palmer Peabody and Emerson; the names are supplied in *Wordsworth and Reed*, 57. I am indebted to Joel Pace for helping me to solve the riddle of Parker's ire.

12. See Leon Chai, *The Romantic Foundations of the American Renaissance* (Ithaca, NY: Cornell UP, 1987) and Richard Gravil, *Romantic Dialogues: Anglo-American Continuities, 1776–1852* (New York, NY: St Martin's Press, 2000).
13. For example, the growth of the Episcopalian Church in New Jersey during Doane's episcopate (1832–59) was substantial, increasing from 900 to 5,000 communicants. The population of New Jersey doubled during this period, but the ratio of population to each communicant in the diocese shrank by roughly two-thirds. See George Morgan Hills, *History of the Church in Burlington, New Jersey*, 2nd edn (Trenton, NJ: W.S. Sharp, 1885), 812–14; Nelson R. Burr, *The Anglican Church in New Jersey* (Philadelphia, PA: Church Historical Society, 1954), 463.
14. My essay may thus contribute to the fuller study of Wordsworth and the Oxford Movement that Stephen Gill calls for, and helps to sketch, in *William Wordsworth: A Life* (Oxford: Oxford UP, 1900), 397–8, and *Wordsworth and the Victorians* (Oxford: Clarendon, 1998), 63–80.
15. For a prime example, see Irving Babbitt's influential *Rousseau and Romanticism* (Boston, MA: Houghton Mifflin, 1919), an attack on 'Romanticism' conceived as a socially irresponsible individualism radiating outwards from Rousseau to Wordsworth, Byron, Chateaubriand and Schiller.
16. On 'the condition of manliness question', see Herbert Sussman, *Victorian Masculinities: Manhood and Masculine Poetics in Early Victorian Literature and Art* (Cambridge: Cambridge UP, 1995), 44–51.
17. Ralph Waldo Emerson, *Essays and Lectures*, ed. Joel Porte (New York, NY: Library of America, 1983), 81.
18. In a history of Wordsworth's reception in antebellum New England, Wordsworth's 'The world is too much with us' – whether or not mediated through Emerson – would play a major role. Thoreau claims to have 'exulted like "a pagan suckled in a creed" that had never been worn at all' with his Indian guide during his third excursion in *The Maine Woods* (*A Week on the Concord and Merrimack Rivers; Walden; The Maine Woods; Cape Cod*, ed. Robert F. Sayre (New York: Library of America, 1985) 371. Mrs. Sarah P. Green, head of the short-lived Rydal Mount Ladies' Boarding School (1845–50/52?) of Charlestown (now a part of Boston), quotes from Wordsworth's poem in her lecture, 'Poetry of Nature', that she sent the sage of Rydal Mount in 1846; see John L. Mahoney, 'The Rydal Mount Ladies' Boarding School: A Wordsworthian Episode in America' in *Cultural Interactions in the Romantic Age: Critical Essays in Comparative Literature*, ed. Gregory Maertz (Albany, NY: State University of New York Press, 1998), 105–22. A summary of Mrs Green's lecture, with its Wordsworth quotation, appears on page 110.
19. Peabody, *Record of a School: Exemplifying the General Principles of Spiritual Culture*, 2nd edn (Boston: Russell, Shattuck, 1836), xi–xii. On Alcott's Socratic teaching of Wordsworth's 'Ode', see 107–11. Peabody offers in conclusion general reflections on teaching children (nondenominational) spiritual happiness, 168–74. In the centrality given to Wordsworth's 'Ode' by Alcott and Peabody, if not necessarily in their reading of it, one finds anticipated Emerson's later judgement, in *English Traits*, chap. 17: 'The Ode on Immortality is the high water-mark which the intellect has reached in this age' (*Essays and Lectures*, 928).
20. For Bloom, professedly writing in the line of Emerson and William James, the 'American religion' is wholly experiential, centred on the individual in solitude, and fundamentally Gnostic in character; see *The American Religion: The*

Emergence of the Post-Christian Nation (New York, NY: Simon & Schuster, 1992), 21–44.

21. William H. Galperin, *Revision and Authority in Wordsworth: The Interpretation of a Career* (Philadelphia, PA: University of Pennsylvania Press, 1989), 5.
22. Augustine expounds the law of charity in *De Doctrina Christiana*, Book 3, paragraphs 14–16; see *On Christian Doctrine*, trans. D.W. Robertson (Indianapolis, IN: Bobbs-Merrill, 1958), 87–9. The law of charity subsequently becomes fundamental to medieval exegesis and composition, as D.W. Robertson has famously argued in *Preface to Chaucer: Studies in Medieval Perspectives* (Princeton, NJ: Princeton UP, 1962), and applies to much eighteenth-century practice as well, as Martin Battestin suggests in *The Providence of Wit: Aspects of Form in Augustan Literature and the Arts* (Oxford: Oxford UP, 1974). For my knowledge of Augustine, as for so much else, I am grateful to Monica Brzezinski Potkay.
23. *North American Review* 59, no. 125 (October 1844): 352–84. For the identification of Whipple's authorship, see William Cushing, *Index to the North American Review* (Cambridge, MA: John Wilson, 1878), reprinted in *Research Keys to the American Renaissance*, ed. Kenneth Walter Cameron (Hartford, CT: Transcendental, 1967).
24. Honourable mentions go as well to Joanna Baillie, Maria Edgeworth, Anna Jameson and Caroline Norton.
25. Reed quotes the poem in its entirety as well in his *New York Review* 58.
26. 'To a Skylark' is quoted again in Doane's funeral sermon on his friend the Rev. Dr. Croswell, IV, 584.
27. Constance M. Greiff, *John Notman, Architect 1810–1865* (Philadelphia, PA: Athenaeum, 1979), 25; a full architectural description of the chapel appears on 102–3, but the chapel's ceiling has been restored to its nineteenth-century appearance since Grieff's 1970s photograph. See also Potkay, *An Education on the Delaware*, 18–32.
28. *The Ecclesiologist* is quoted by Greiff, 102–3. I quote Gill from *Wordsworth and the Victorians*, 63.
29. In *Wordsworth and Reed*, 189, Broughton transcribes Mary Wordsworth's list of the eighteen Americans, in addition to the organizing Reed, who contributed to the memorial.

6
Henry David Thoreau as Wordsworthian Poet

Lance Newman

> To live to a good old age such as the ancients reached – serene and contented – dignifying the life of man – in these days of confusion and turmoil – That is what Wordsworth has done – Retaining the tastes and the innocence of his youth – There is more wonderful talent – but nothing so cheering and world famous as this.[1]

During the post-Revolutionary decades, as the northern United States changed from an agrarian ex-colony into the heartland of an industrial capitalist nation, nature, as accessed in rural and wild landscapes, became a central reference point in the evolving self-definition of the region's ruling class. Members of the increasingly urban-based bourgeoisie adopted the paradoxical role of benevolent, country patriarchs in relation to a growing and increasingly turbulent working class.[2] At the same time, bourgeois radicals, especially those associated with the Transcendentalist movement centred on Concord, Massachusetts, faced a crucial problem: how to invent a self-definition suited to 'days of confusion and turmoil', one that would allow them to mount a compelling critique of the deepening class divisions in the new cities. They too based their image of themselves on claims of a close relationship to nature. In this context, William Wordsworth, the 'Poet of Nature', came to stand as the foremost example of the appropriate functions and demeanour of the cultural critic. It was in relation to this touchstone that the young Henry David Thoreau built his initial sense of himself as a poet. For ten years, he worked with and against a distinctly Wordsworthian persona and poetics. More, the habits of thought that he acquired during these formative years strongly shaped his great prose narrative, *Walden*.

I Wordsworth in America

An 1824 reviewer of the first American edition of Wordsworth's poems had been able to claim that:

> If we have unworthily neglected this original and admirable poet, we have but followed the example of our countrymen ... With the exception of the Lyrical Ballads, which were printed many years ago, if we remember rightly at Philadelphia ... not a single work of Wordsworth has been republished in this country.[3]

The small edition under review sold more steadily than its predecessors.[4] The poet received his warmest welcome at Harvard where young Unitarian intellectuals, including centrally Ralph Waldo Emerson, had begun looking for an alternative to their parents' materialism (of both the epistemological and the more mundane varieties). After a decade of growing interest, in 1835, James Munroe – the Boston publisher who would bring out Emerson's *Nature* the following year – published *Yarrow Revisited and Other Poems*. The book met with a small storm of praise from reviewers for American magazines.[5] Two years later, James Kay of Philadelphia published the complete works in an edition that was widely reprinted throughout the century. The text – among the first American critical editions of any poet – was edited by Henry Reed, Professor of English at the University of Pennsylvania, and it was greeted as a national triumph:

> It is, what it professes to be, a complete edition of his poetical works, such as might be sought for in vain in his own country ... The publishers may challenge for themselves a full portion of praise, for having sent forth a book which confers credit on the American press.[6]

By 1840, Emerson was able to declare that 'the fame of Wordsworth is a leading fact in modern literature'.[7]

Emerson went on, though, to say that, 'more than any other poet his success has not been his own, but that of the idea which he shared with his coevals, and which he has rarely succeeded in adequately expressing' (150). For Emerson, the idea responsible for this surge of interest in Wordsworth was democracy, the leading principle of the incoming age. Christopher Pearse Cranch, a young member of the Transcendentalist Club, provided a somewhat different emphasis in a late retrospective piece on Wordsworth's career:

> One of his deepest beliefs was in the beneficent ministry of nature to the soul of man ... Nature is for him never dully and densely material, but radiant and glowing with spiritual meanings ... What an antidote was

> his sanative poetry to the morbid Byronism and Werterism that enervated the youths and maidens of the early years of this nineteenth century! Honor to the seer ... whose laborious hands gave such help in draining off the stagnant scum of the malarial waters which infected those days![8]

That Cranch's rhetoric should remain so elevated half a century later gives some indication of the fervour with which the Transcendentalists consumed Wordsworth's works in the 1830s as, with his help, they transformed early national America's fields of enlightened political experimentation into meadows of Romantic self-discovery. Now it may seem that Emerson and Cranch appreciate Wordsworth in very different, even contradictory, terms. For since Percy Bysshe Shelley so forcefully claimed that in becoming the Poet of Nature, Wordsworth abandoned his duties as the Prophet of Democracy, it has been difficult to see that many of his readers felt that these two roles were cognate. In fact, many of New England's bourgeois radicals in the 1830s felt that the turn to nature was a turn to the people. For these readers Wordsworth's rustic persona seemed to embody an especially 'sanative' version of the democratic impulse.

II A conservative utopia

Yarrow Revisited and Other Poems consists of a diverse mix of 'evening voluntaries', romances like 'The Egyptian Maid' and 'The Russian Fugitive', and occasional poems. The most unified sections are two sequences of sonnets bound together by implied travel narratives. The first of these, 'Poems Composed during a Tour in Scotland, and on the English Border, in the Autumn of 1831', opens with the ballad, 'Yarrow Revisited'. Wordsworth remarks that the title 'will stand in no need of explanation, for Readers acquainted with the Author's previous poems suggested by that celebrated stream'.[9] This is the third of three separately published poems commemorating visits to the river of that name. The other two are 'Yarrow Unvisited', composed in 1803, and 'Yarrow Visited, September, 1814'. Read together, the three form a parable of maturation: 'the Morn of youth/With freaks of graceful folly' gives way to 'Life's temperate Noon', and 'her sober Eve' (4). This intertextual parable introduces the Yarrow sequence as a whole, serving notice that the poems contain the utterances of achieved eminence, experience and wisdom. Making sure no one misses this point, Wordsworth explains that 'the following stanzas are a memorial of a day passed with Sir Walter Scott, and other Friends visiting the Banks of the Yarrow under his guidance, immediately before his departure from Abbotsford, for Naples' (3). Indeed, we soon find that 'grave thoughts ruled wide on that sweet day / Their dignity installing / In gentle bosoms, while sere leaves / Were on the bough, or falling' (4).

Given such portentous beginnings, what follows seems oddly slight. 'Yarrow Revisited' is a gracious leave-taking, making Scott's imminent departure for the Mediterranean to restore his failing health into an occasion for conventional sentiments on the redeeming eternity of Nature and the Muse. The poem makes a virtue of the claim that 'No public and no private care / The freeborn mind enthralling, / We made a day of happy hours, / Our happy days recalling' (4). Likewise, the rest of the sequence is singularly bare of Wordsworth's characteristic gravid public pronouncements. Instead, we read a loosely connected series of solemn effusions on rural scenes, ruined mansions, highland huts, ancient trees, Roman antiquities, worn monuments and brownies. The poems seem to aspire no higher than Cranch's placid assertion 'that all is somehow and somewhere for the best' (251).

One way to give context to the sequence is to point out that while Wordsworth was pacing Yarrow's banks with Scott in 'the autumn of 1831', the House of Lords was rejecting the Reform Law. Widespread unrest surrounding this decision culminated in the Bristol Riots on 29–31 October. Supporters of wider franchise wrecked Mansion House and set the Bishop's Palace on fire. Troops and cavalry attacked demonstrators, killing many, and in the following weeks four dissidents were executed and 22 deported. A possible reading based on these facts would emphasize Wordsworth's observation in the concluding 'Apology', that 'every day brought with it tidings new / Of rash change, ominous for the public weal' (32). And it would argue that this sequence of poems represents another example of the Wordsworthian strategy of displacement, that characteristic way of evading deeply significant political events and social realities, taking refuge instead in the cheap comforts of the romantic ideology of natural supernaturalism. But Wordsworth would not have alluded to these events unless he felt that there was something to be gained from meditating on the coincidence. And he would not have earned reviews as deeply respectful as those published by Cranch, Emerson and Greenwood unless they felt that he offered valuable answers to deeply important questions.

In other words, the Yarrow sequence both asks for, and received, serious consideration as political argument. Does Wordsworth, then, offer an alternative to the levelling of Mansion House and to the Tory thuggery that followed? A hint comes in the concluding 'Apology', which begins, 'No more: the end is sudden and abrupt, / Abrupt – as without preconceived design / Was the beginning' (31). These are not, then, a sequence structured around a narrative or argument:

> The several Lays,
> Have moved in order, to each other bound
> By a continuous and acknowledged tie,
> Though unapparent, like those shapes distinct

That yet survive ensculptured on the walls
Of Palace, or of Temple, 'mid the wreck
Of famed Persepolis; each following each,
As might beseem a stately embassy,
In set array; these bearing in their hands
Ensign of civil power, weapon of war,
Or gift, to be presented to the Throne
Of the Great King; and others as they go
In priestly vest, with holy offerings charged,
Or leading victim's drest for sacrifice. (31)

These lines guide our experience of a heterogeneous cast of characters. In 'At Tyndrum', we meet Scotland's 'hardy Mountaineer', who unlike the garlanded shepherds of polite Arcadian pastoral, 'will cross a brook / Swoln with chill rains, nor ever cast a look / This way or that, or give it even a thought' (18). 'The Brownie' tells of an old clansman whose independence was so fierce and proud that he retired to a hut to live out his last years 'with no one near save the omnipresent God' (22). In 'On the sight of a manse in the south of Scotland', the good gardening priest

who faithful through all hours
To his high charge, and truly serving God,
Has yet a heart and hand for flowers,
Enjoys the walks his Predecessors trod,
Nor covets lineal rights in lands and towers. (11)

'Countess's Pillar', memorializes Anne Countess Dowager of Pembroke, who in 1656, erected a monument to her mother and left an annuity of four pounds 'to be distributed to the poor of the parish of Brougham, every 2d day of April for ever'. 'While the poor gather round, till the end of time / May this bright flower of Charity display / Its bloom, unfolding at the appointed day' (29). Like the figures of the ancient Persian officers, functionaries, priests and sacrificial victims on the wall at Persepolis, these figures are defined not by their individuality, but by their representativeness, by their exemplary performance of the functions that define the positions they hold in a definite social hierarchy. The Yarrow sequence, then, does not spin a tale nor does it expound an explicit argument; rather, it displays emblematic portraits of the various stations in life that together form a coherent social order. These figures compose an 'embassy' of subjects to a 'King', carrying out the rituals of mutual indebtedness and obeisance that maintain peace and stability. That romanticized feudal order, the residuum of which Wordsworth claims to have found in the Border country, is the proper subject of the Yarrow sequence.

Wordsworth goes further to make nature itself embody the character of this idealized social estate. The reader is invited to see the Border country through the eyes of its inhabitants, who learn from it the simple virtues on which they pride themselves, and who memorialize their simultaneously economic and pedagogic relationship with the land by naming 'yon towering peaks, "The Shepherds of Glen Etive"' (17). Likewise, 'The Avon', emblematizes modesty, 'contented, though unknown to Fame' (26). The planet Venus is a sign of aristocratic benevolence:

> Holy as princely, who that looks on thee
> Touching, as now, in thy humility
> The mountain borders of this seat of care,
> Can question that thy countenance is bright,
> Celestial Power, as much with love as light? (23)

A rest station for weary travellers 'at the Head of Glencroe' allegorizes the 'absolute stillness' that 'faith bestows', allowing the soul to 'win rest, and ease, and peace' (20). The just peace of this social order depends on the piety and humanity which the mountainous country itself breeds in the people. It bids them, even, to 'love, as Nature loves, the lonely Poor ... meek, patient, kind, and, were [their] trials fewer, / Belike less happy. – Stand no more aloof!' (21). In Wordsworth's naturalized utopia, the oppressions and privations of feudal society have been erased by an abstract parallelism of duties, trials, and rewards, and by an emphasis on the moral and spiritual richness of the exchanges that occur within its networks of social power.

These poems, though, are distinctly elegiac, for the reader is being asked, like a tourist at Persepolis, to contemplate the beauties of a decidedly past order. That pastness is most obviously marked by such monuments as 'The Earl of Breadalbane's Ruined Mansion and Family Burial-Place, Near Killin' (19). The countryside is haunted now by 'the holy Abbot's gliding Shade'. The spirits that wander the countryside do not mourn for merely personal tragedies, but for the loss of the social hierarchies within which their identities were meaningful:

> The Warrior-chief, a ghost unlaid,
> Haunts still his Castle, though a Skeleton,
> That he may watch by night, and lessons con
> Of Power that perishes, and Rights that fade. (27)

Even the landscape itself has descended from its former glory: 'The forest huge of ancient Caledon / Is but a name, nor more is Inglewood, / That swept from hill to hill, from flood to flood' (27). This spectacle of impermanence, this knowledge that 'life is but a tale of morning grass, / Withered at eve' (13), serves simultaneously to 'chasten fancies that presume / Too high', and to reinforce the lesson on the value of lost virtues. Contemplating 'Roman Antiquities', the rural poet realizes that if 'of the world's flatteries the brain be full, / To have no seat for thought were better doom' (30). In other words, overly ambitious dreams of personal triumph or social perfection can lead only to disappointment or disaster. A more just and humane social estate will come not through conscious striving, but when people, rich and poor, learn from nature, when the nation reads the rural landscape of the Border country and cultivates the sense of modesty, decency and fairness recorded there. The poet's duty, then, is to rediscover the virtues of the rural utopia that once graced these mountains and then model them for the modern nation. This was Wordsworth's answer to both the working-class radicalism and the Tory repression that industrialization had brought to England – and that had appeared on the horizon of modernizing New England. He sent forth an embassy of sonnets, appealing to his readers to learn from the example of an imagined feudal society whose fairness and stability depended on its people's hardiness, independence, generosity, devoutness, and, above all, on their pious dedication to the duties of their station. *Yarrow Revisited* maps that idealized past, offering it as a schematic diagram of the benign social order that will result should the pedagogy of nature take wide hold.

III The nature of democracy

For New England's bourgeoisie, the 1820s and early 1830s were a period of rapid ideological transformation in response to spectacular economic expansion.[10] Emerson, the high priest of the radical wing of the class, saw the period this way:

> A selfish commerce and government have caught the eye and usurped the hand of the masses. It is not to be contested that selfishness and the senses write the laws under which we live, and that the street seems to be built, and the men and women in it moving not in reference to pure and grand ends, but rather to very short and sordid ones. ('Thoughts' 148)

What seemed sordid and ominous was not only the open profiteering of *nouveaux riches*, but also the growing demands of newly organized workers. Class conflict, sometimes violent, had become an inescapable new reality.[11] Boston's ruling class interpreted emergent social divisions according to republican ideology's implied narrative of crisis and decline, seeing strikes and demonstrations as harbingers of an imminent social collapse.[12] Adding to their anxiety was the fact that Andrew Jackson's Democrats had appropriated the rhetoric of agrarianism, representing themselves as true yeomen at war with a usurping 'money power'.[13] When Jackson was elected to a second term in 1832, many read the period typologically according to their notions of the French Revolution's decline into radicalism and violence:

> Men gazed upon the spectacle [of the French Revolution] with trembling awe, yet sanguine expectations ... Alas! the sun which had risen with such splendor upon the moral universe, was destined to undergo a dark and bloody eclipse. The philosophers and philanthropists, who had given the first impulse to the movement, were soon rudely pushed aside by unprincipled demagogues and sanguinary fanatics, who turned their fair land into a vast slaughter-house; one revolting scene of hideous saturnalia.[14]

It was not that liberty had led to licence, rather, centuries of monarchic despotism had degraded the people, rendering these 'emancipated slaves unfit for those blessings to which man is as much entitled as to the air he breathes' (708). Such weakened people were easily swayed by ambitious demagogues, like 'King Jackson', who regarded them as no more than tools, and who would likely lead them to destroy the hard-won republic.

In this context, Wordsworth's poetry of utopian conservatism began to matter urgently. Interestingly though, his biography provided the primary interpretive context for most readers.[15] For instance, the poems themselves did not form the central focus of most reviews in New England in the 1830s and 40s, instead reviewers dwelt urgently and at length on the story of his retreat to the Lake Country. However, most told the tale of Wordsworth's retirement rather differently than has been usual lately. For instance, Henry Theodore Tuckerman argued that:

> In an intellectual history of our age, the bard of Rydal Mount must occupy a prominent place ... The mere facts of his life will preserve his memory. It will not be forgotten that one among the men of acknowledged genius in England, during a period of great political excitement should voluntarily remain secluded amid the mountains ... from time to time sending forth his effusions, as uncolored by the poetic taste of the time, as statues from a quarry.[16]

This is not the now familiar story of malfeasance, of neglecting the duties of revolutionary struggle. Rather, Wordsworth is represented as working for the same end by different means:

> A hermit among the mountains, attaching himself to no party, and asking no favors from power ... he has never deserted the cause of freedom and of man. On the contrary, everything that he has written ... expresses that high and enduring sense of the innate and essential

> dignity of man, which must ever be the chief foundation and support of republican institutions. (Anonymous, 709)

This Wordsworth, the poet of natural democracy, embodied an important ideological innovation that allowed New England's bourgeois radicals to represent themselves as leading the way forward towards further social progress. As personified in the poems, Wordsworth demonstrated an apparently democratic, because sympathetic, mechanism of directing the lawless 'passions' of the mob. He showed how to lead without resorting to demagoguery:

> He is emphatically a poet of liberty, not by passionate invocations to popular enthusiasm, but by calm and beautiful appeals to those manly qualities, those chastening virtues and noble sentiments, which are perhaps more often found in the cottage than in the halls of opulence. (709)

Emulating such democratic sentiments allowed the New England's radical bourgeoisie to represent itself as wearing the mantle of non-violent evolutionary progress during a period of intensifying class conflict.

In New Haven's *Quarterly Christian Spectator* for August 1836, Noah Porter explains that Wordsworth is so revered by 'the young' of New England as a 'guide and teacher' because he embraces 'his appropriate duties as a poet' with such high seriousness.[17] What were these duties? To use nature to teach sympathy:

> Man has been clothed with sympathies such as were fitted to bind him to his fellow-man in bonds of love ... But the tendency of man is to degrade himself by sensuality and cunning; to harden himself against all gentleness by a false and foolish pride, or the lying and hollow vanities of social life ... In all ages, the true poet awakens man from his brutishness, and excites his kindlier and nobler feelings. (130–1)

The poet's most reliable method for redeeming people who have become lost in material pursuits is to direct 'our eye and our heart to all that is lovely upon earth'. He teaches the hardened materialist 'to draw forth from his bosom his most cherished feelings, and to associate them with those objects in nature with which they seem to correspond, thus making those feelings more distinct and permanent' (131). This role is critically important, for people have been imbruted by modernization to such a degree that learning to see correspondences between feelings and nature requires a kind of cultivation only the poet can now provide:

> From his own mind he will spread over all nature associations more various and exciting than any which we could originate; and he will

> teach us to look on her with feelings like his own. The lofty mountain-top, which awakens in him grander and more elevating emotions than it excites in the minds of the great mass of mankind, he should cause, by the magic of his verse, to become to us all that it is to himself. (131)

Directed observation of nature becomes, then, 'a course of self-inspection' (135) wherein the subject recovers 'those feelings, those unchanging realities, which the given object is fitted to awaken in the bosom of every one who calls himself a man' (137). This restorative contact with the eternities reflected in nature makes possible 'a noble and a true generosity' towards 'humanity' (140), teaches us to sympathize, and therefore to be democratic.

Wordsworth, who opposed parliamentary reform and poor laws in the 1830s, may seem a strange hero for American bourgeois radicals. But he was felt to offer a viable road to social redemption. Emerson provides an answer to this puzzle in his 'Man the Reformer':

> Let our affection flow out to our fellows; it would operate in a day the greatest of all revolutions. It is better to work on institutions by the sun than by the wind. The state must consider the poor man, and all voices must speak for him. Every child that is born must have a just chance for bread. Let the amelioration of our laws of property proceed from the concession of the rich, not from the grasping of the poor.[18]

In the manner of an idealized country aristocrat, Wordsworth was seen as combining sincere concern for the poor (what was once called, approvingly, condescension) with stern opposition to their self-organized attempts to improve their lot. In other words, he provided a perfect model, authorized by his stature as poetic genius, of the ways of thinking appropriate to a reforming élite during a period of sharp anti-élitism.

What is remarkable about this particular ideological constellation is the firmness of the association between nature and democracy:

> All which is worthy [of] man's attainment, can be and is realized in far higher perfection amid the genial influences of rural life, than in the hot and unquiet atmosphere of the crowded city ... The modes of living, the habits of intellectual activity, the character of the emotions, both in strength and refinement, and the moral and religious worth, which are formed by the one, are not in our opinion to be compared with those that grow up in the other ... Those who are anxious to train their fellow-men to true greatness, did better know wherein true greatness consists, and under what influences it grows up to its true height and just proportions. (Porter 141)

Wordsworth so completely embodied the idea of democratic sympathy specifically because he so effectively deployed the anti-rational pedagogy of nature. New England's bourgeoisie had seen their Enlightenment habits of thought come under withering attack: the idea that rational pursuit of the social good prepared one for political eminence suddenly came to seem embarrassingly élitist. On the other hand, the idea that observation of nature could form properly republican *sentiments* allowed them to begin to reconstruct the grounds of their social and political legitimacy. They did so by representing themselves as *emotionally* engaged in their natural duties to the lower orders.[19]

IV Wordsworth and Thoreau

Henry Thoreau began to train himself seriously as a poet during the year before his 1837 graduation from Harvard.[20] His most ambitious and compelling project was an intensive study of the history of poetry in English. He read two massive collections – including Alexander Chalmers 21-volume anthology of the British poets, which he claims in *Walden* to have read through 'without skipping'.[21] Thoreau's zeal was no doubt redoubled by Emerson's commencement address, 'The American Scholar', which called on the graduates to lead a cultural naissance. During the next ten years, Thoreau wrote hundreds of poems and he filled several commonplace books with extracts of poetry.[22] Indeed, it is not too much to say that for first decade of his adult life, he thought of himself mainly as a practising poet.[23]

During this time, his primary model, the main poet he emulated and against whom he rebelled, was Wordsworth.[24] Wordsworth appears consistently in Thoreau's early essays in literary criticism as a benchmark of poetic excellence. The 'Poet of Nature' is always described, either explicitly or implicitly, as one of the most important of English poets, though Thoreau's praise is always mixed. For instance, in a passage from the early essay, 'Aulus Persius Flaccus', Thoreau simultaneously pays homage to Wordsworth and dismisses him in a gesture of youthful bravado: 'Homer, and Shakspeare [*sic*], and Milton, and Marvell, and Wordsworth, are but the rustling of leaves and crackling of twigs in the forest, and not yet the sound of any bird'.[25]

Of course, the implication is that Thoreau himself will burst into bird-like song at any moment, silencing his rustling, but necessary, forebears.

Like his contemporaries, Thoreau was fascinated by Wordsworth's life and persona, and saw the poems as only one part of the picture:

> Wordsworth with very feeble talent has not so great and admirable as persevering genius
> heroism – heroism – is his word – his thing.

> He would realize a brave & adequate human life. & die hopefully at last. (*Journal*, II, 223)

According to this way of reading, Wordsworth's poetic achievement is inseparable from, only one part of, the complete picture of his historical and cultural importance.[26] In 'Homer Ossian Chaucer', Thoreau specifies the terms of his approval: Wordsworth embodies 'a simple pathos and feminine gentleness' (*Early Essays* 169). This is not, though, a genteel or trivial emotionalism: Thoreau goes on to stress the radicalism of Wordsworth's preference for 'his homely but vigorous Saxon tongue, when it was neglected by the court, and had not yet attained to the dignity of a literature' (165). In other words, he read Wordsworth's emotional openness and linguistic plainness as democratic.

Moreover, Thoreau saw such democratic sentiments as a necessary corollary of a close relationship with nature. In 'Thomas Carlyle and his Works', he describes Carlyle's early moral education in 'Annan, on the shore of Solway Firth':

> From this place, they say, you can see Wordsworth's country. Here first [Carlyle] may have become acquainted with Nature, with woods, such as are there, and rivers and brooks ... and the last lapses of Atlantic billows. (*Early Essays* 219)

The literary persona formed in this decidedly natural place produced books that Thoreau describes this way:

> When we remember how these volumes came over to us ... and what commotion they created in many private breasts, we wonder that the country did not ring from shore to shore ... with its greeting; and the Boones and Crocketts of the West make haste to hail him, whose wide humanity embraces them too. (222)

Carlyle, like Wordsworth, learned his wide humanity from the rugged Border country in which he was raised.

Crucially, Thoreau frequently represents democratic sympathies in terms of sickness and health. For instance, while making a final comparative assessment, Thoreau states that 'Carlyle has not the simple Homeric health of Wordsworth' (248). While Carlyle may not measure up entirely, still, he and Wordsworth occupy one end of a spectrum whose implied other is marked by the hyper-civilized and unnatural personae of 'Coleridge the Morose Scholar', 'Byron the Rake', 'Shelley the Atheist' and others (Weisbuch 137–42). During 'days of confusion and turmoil', when the health of the nation and of the body politic was the object of great concern, Wordsworth's 'sanative poetry', as Cranch put it, seemed to offer an 'antidote' to 'the morbid Byronism and Werterism ... the stagnant scum of the malarial waters which infected those days!' (quoted in Weisbuch, 251).

Thoreau generalized from this understanding of Wordsworth's life and practice to develop his initial sense of the function of poetry and the poet. First poetry is a vehicle for the weightiest and most urgent human truths: 'There is no doubt that the loftiest written wisdom is either rhymed, or in some way musically measured, – is, in form as well as substance, poetry'.[27] The ability to create such music is not the reward of study, not the produce of culture: 'Yet poetry, though the last and finest result, is a natural fruit. As naturally as the oak bears an acorn, and the vine a gourd, man bears a poem, either spoken or done' (91). It is not just that poetry is the natural language of humanity, but more, that when people produce poetry, nature is working directly and immediately through them: 'The poet sings how the blood flows in his veins. He performs the functions, and is so well that he needs such stimulus to sing only as plants to put forth leaves and blossoms ... It is as if nature spoke' (91–2). Just as poetry is the language of nature, it is also definitively wholesome, even hygienic: 'Good poetry seems so simple and natural a thing that when we meet it we wonder that all men are not always poets. Poetry is nothing but healthy speech' (*Journal*, I, 338). Not surprisingly, during diseased times, when most people have lost contact with nature, the poet must protect himself by maintaining a safe distance:

> We are often prompted to speak our thoughts to our neighbors or the single travelers we meet, but poetry is a communication addressed to all mankind, and may therefore as well be written at home and in solitude, as uttered abroad in society. (*Journal*, II, 44)

The poet's solitude should not be mistaken for aloofness though. Instead, detachment from particulars allows a more general engagement, a clear focus on matters that the rest of humanity has lost sight of: 'Though the speech of the poet goes to the heart of things, yet he is that one especially who speaks civilly to Nature as a second person, and in some sense is the patron of the world' (*Journal*, I, 338). This last phrase renders with exquisite accuracy Thoreau's developed sense of the cultural role of the poet in degenerate times – 'patron of the world'. The poet serves as a beacon of natural health and wholesome sentiments to a world diseased by the rising tide of urbanization, industrialization, and class conflict under capitalism.[28]

V Thoreau's poetry and persona

The working understanding of poetry and the role of the poet that Thoreau appropriated from Wordsworth was something with which he struggled actively throughout the years that he wrote. He produced a remarkably various body of poetry, at first writing reverentially imitative works, and later experimenting, searching for ways to embody in verse ideas and stances that conflicted with the tradition he had entered. Perhaps his clearest attempts to emulate his predecessor come in poems that, like Wordsworth's great odes, take 'a fact out of nature into spirit' (*Journal*, I, 69), mounting extravagant sallies of speculative thought in response to common events or conventional scenes.[29] For instance, the deceptively simple poem, 'The Bluebirds', begins with the building of a nest-box 'in the midst of the poplar that stands by our door'. Thoreau lovingly and particularly narrates the arrival of a breeding pair, their mating rituals, nesting and eventual migration. Only once this preparatory work is complete does he describe a moment of self-transcendence triggered by contemplation of this example of the spectacular perfection of the natural world:

> I dreamed that I was an waking thought –
> A something I hardly knew –
> Not a solid piece, nor an empty nought,
> But a drop of morning dew.[30]

In other poems, the stimulus is merely implied; we read only the revelation, stripped of its triggering context, as in the following quatrain that Thoreau composed for *A Week on the Concord and Merrimack*:

> True kindness is a pure divine affinity,
> Not founded on human consanguinity.
> It is a spirit, not a blood relation,
> Superior to family and station. (*Essays and Poems*, 577)

This is a kind of abstract poetry that we are no longer trained to appreciate. However, it has a recoverable coherence, based on the idea that the poet's special ability was to distil the universal from the particular, to harvest the truth from experience and deliver it pure:

> There are two kinds of writing, both great and rare; one that of genius, or the inspired, the other of intellect and taste, in the intervals of inspiration. The former is above criticism, always correct, giving the law to criticism. It vibrates and pulsates with life forever. It is sacred, and to be read with reverence, as the works of nature are studied. (*Week*, 375)

Thoreau, following Wordsworth, approached his duties as a poet with high seriousness and strove in much of his early work for what he thought of as universality rooted in experience.

Thoreau was acutely conscious of his dependency on Wordsworth, and he was anxious to do his part to engender domestic American literary culture. Thus as his poetic decade progressed, he moved increasingly in the direction of particularity, isolating and extending this part of the generative tension in his mentor's work. As he did so, he began to develop his own voice and practice, informed by the idea that the poet should speak directly about his immediate experience to an audience of his actual peers:[31]

I seek the Present Time,
No other clime,
Life in to-day ...
What are deeds done
Away from home?
What the best essay
On the Ruins of Rome? (608)

His initial response to this imperative was to compose loco-descriptive poems. At first, his efforts in this mode were only weakly local: 'On Ponkawtasset' and 'Assabet' use eastern Massachusetts place names but operate in the generic space of highly conventional pastoral. On the other hand, poems like 'The Old Marlborough Road' sustain a high level of detailed engagement with quite particular places:

Where they once dug for money,
But never found any;
Where sometimes Martial Miles
Singly files,
And Elijah Wood,
I fear for no good;
No other man,
Save Elisha Duggan, –
O man of wild habits,
Partridges and rabbits,
Who hast no cares
Only to set snares,
Who liv'st all alone,
Close to the bone,
And where life is sweetest
Constantly eatest. (626)

This was a way of thinking about poetry that contradicted Wordsworth's theory; however, it was at least partially validated by his practice, as manifested in the many pieces of occasional verse, titled simply with dates of composition, as well as in the sketches of common life, like 'Simon Lee' and 'Goody Blake and Harry Gill'.

One of Thoreau's most important and successful poetic innovations was his attempt to repeat and even complete Wordsworth's decision to write in the 'real language of men', in this case, real Yankees. Many of the published poems are marked by a kind of strained, artificial diction:

> Thou dusky spirit of the wood,
> Bird of an ancient brood,
> Flitting thy lonely way,
> A meteor in the summer's day. (579)

But at the same time that he was writing in this vein, he was also experimenting with pithy and local language:

> Conscience is instinct bred in the house,
> Feeling and thinking propagate the sin
> By an unnatural breeding in and in.
> I say, Turn it out doors,
> Into the moors.
> I love a life whose plot is simple,
> And does not thicken with every pimple,
> A soul so sound no sickly conscience binds it,
> That makes the universe no worse than't finds it. (615)

This decision to employ the New England vernacular reaches its peak in verse that never saw print in Thoreau's lifetime, much of which has only quite recently become available. At its best, Thoreau's verse in this mode is vibrantly alive:

> I have seen some frozenfaced connecticut
> Or Down east man in his crack coaster
> With tort sail, with folded arms standing
> Beside his galley with his dog & man
> While his cock crowed aboard, scud thro the surf
> By some fast anchored Staten island farm,
> But just outside the vast and stirring line
> Where the astonished Dutchman digs his clams
> Or but half ploughs his cabbage garden plot
> With unbroken steeds & ropy harness –
> And some squat bantam whom the shore wind drownd
> Feebly responded there for all reply,
> While the triumphant Yankee's farm swept by. (614)

This is something quite new and powerful, and had Thoreau produced a large and consistent body of work in this mode, he might well be ranked with Whitman and Dickinson as one of the first truly American poets.[32]

Thoreau was driven to innovate, not just by cultural nationalism and his consciousness of dependency, but also by the pressure of historical events on the Wordsworthian model of poetry: there was an inherent conflict between the urgency of the period's political debates and the leisurely, genteel speculation to which he felt constrained. Early on, he had attempted to address political questions, but was unable to break free of a kind of contemplative abstraction:

> In the busy streets, domains of trade,
> Man is a surly porter, or a vain and hectoring bully,
> Who can claim no nearer kindredship with me
> Than brotherhood by law. (517)

The depression of 1837–44, the movement to abolish slavery, Polk's invasion of Mexico – these all demanded passionate and particular response. And Thoreau responded, writing several poems that directly address the most urgent questions of the mid-1840s. His earlier efforts are often quite conventional, as in this address to the people of the North, calling on them to take independent action to abolish slavery:

> Wait not till slaves pronounce the word
>   To set the captive free,
> Be free yourselves, be not deferred,
>   And farewell slavery. (577)

Similarly, Thoreau produced a distinctly Wordsworthian meditation on the woman question that embodies the kind of essentialist beliefs that were typical even of the feminists within his milieu:

> Ive seen ye, sisters, on the mountain-side
> When your green mantles fluttered in the wind
> Ive seen your foot-prints on the lakes smooth shore
> Lesser than man's, a more ethereal trace,
> Ive heard of ye as some far-famed race –
> Daughters of god whom I should one day meet –
> Or mothers I might say of all our race. (604)

As with all his poetry, the more that Thoreau deployed the vernacular, the more successful his political verse became. For instance, in his journal for 28 November 1850, he transcribed the following:

> I am the little Irish boy
>   That lives in the shanty
> I am four years old today
>   And shall soon be one and twenty

I shall grow up and be a great man
And shovel all day
As hard as I can[,]

Down in the deep cut
Where the men lived
Who made the Rail road. (631)

The absolute simplicity of Thoreau's language gives real power to this sketch of the stark poverty afflicting hundreds of thousands of Irish immigrants.

There are many explanations for why Thoreau stopped writing poetry in the mid-1840s. The most practical is that once *The Dial* folded in 1844, he was left without a venue for his work. On a more personal level, he offers the following in his journal:

Each more melodious note I hear
Brings this reproach to me,
That I alone afford the ear,
Who would the music be. (530)

This has been the most common explanation, that Thoreau abandoned poetry because he finally admitted that he had a wooden ear. But to accept this requires us to deafen ourselves to the rhythms and melodies of *Walden* and the essays. Another explanation he offers is this: 'My life has been the poem I would have writ, / But I could not both live and utter it' (*Week*, 343). It has been usual to believe that he means here that he was unable simultaneously to maintain the poet's heightened receptivity to nature and the poet's discipline of composition. But he never gave up writing intensively composed material; he just stopped writing verse. Instead, Thoreau may have meant to record the recognition that the stance, the persona, of the poet is more culturally important than metre or rhyme.[33] It is certainly true that the narrative persona Thoreau adopts throughout *Walden* corresponds closely to his exalted notion of the poet. Finally, the overall direction of Thoreau's intellectual development during the 1840s was away from Emersonian idealism, and towards an increasingly particular engagement with the material world.[34] So the larger truth must certainly be that he turned to prose because he felt he was able to engage more directly with the natural and social landscape before him, free of the limits imposed by a way of thinking about poetry that he found himself unable entirely to overcome.

Though he never fully developed the poetic innovations with which he experimented, he was able, at last, to turn his study of Wordsworth to good account. Thoreau acquired a copy of *The Prelude* not long after it was published in 1850. And while we cannot fix the date that he read it absolutely, his journal suggests that he did so sometime in late 1851.[35] In the journal volumes that cover the late 1840s through August 1851, there are few mentions of Wordsworth or even of poets and poetry. Then the volume for August 1851 through April 1852 is littered with references to all three subjects. In other words, after a hiatus of several years, Thoreau was energized by a sustained encounter with his old mentor, and he entered into a period of sustained interest in the subject of poetry and the proper role of the poet in society. And he did so just before he began the most intensive period of rewriting *Walden* (Gravil, 104). From early 1852 to 1854, he amplified the manuscript's account of his retreat into nature, with its central critique of alienation under capitalism, added a much fuller account of the texture of his life at the pond, and finally added the chapter 'Conclusion'.[36] The rewritten book amounts to an aestheticist manifesto, an extravagantly confident paean to the power of the creative, self-reliant individual to inspire organic, wholesale social change.[37] This manifesto begins by laying a foundation of particularity, with the long prose poem about sand flowing out of the bank in the railroad cut:

> As it flows it takes the forms of sappy leaves or vines, making heaps of pulpy sprays a foot or more in depth, and resembling, as you look down on them, the laciniated, lobed, and imbricated thalluses of some lichens; or you are reminded of coral, of leopard's paws or birds' feet, of brains or lungs or bowels, and excrements of all kinds. (*Walden*, 305)

Thoreau builds from this lovingly rendered concrete image of renewal towards the claim that even 'a man [is] but a mass of thawing clay', and from here to the assertion that not only the earth, 'but the institutions upon it are plastic like clay in the hands of the potter' (309). Throughout, Thoreau speaks in the voice of a 'patron of the world', a seer, a poet rooted in nature, who can see 'the character of that morrow which mere lapse of time can never make to dawn', and who can guide a blind world to the truth that 'There is more day to dawn. The sun is but a morning star' (333). *Walden*'s conclusion, in other words, recapitulates the structure of a classic Wordsworthian poem, building from a recollected experience to a crescendo of wisdom. And were it not for Thoreau's apprenticeship, it might well have remained the story of a field of beans.

Notes

1. Henry David Thoreau, *Journal*, eds John C. Broderick *et al.* (4 vols. to date, Princeton, NJ: Princeton UP, 1981–), II, 200–1. Sections I–II of this essay appeared in different form as part of Lance Newman, 'Wordsworth in America and the Nature of Democracy', *New England Quarterly*, 72.4 (Summer 2002): 1–25. Sections IV and V appeared in different form as part of '"Patrons of the World": Henry Thoreau as Wordsworthian Poet', *The Concord Saunterer*, N.S. 11 (Winter 2003): 155–72.

2. As the Federalist bourgeoisie in the early national period enriched themselves by building factories and banks in the new urban centres, it became increasingly necessary to overcome the anti-commercial prejudices of the stalwart Jeffersonians who remained dominant in the countryside. So this new Northern business class set out to occupy the enemy's high ground, by purchasing and settling large agricultural estates. On these model farms, they not only won ribbons for innovative farming techniques, but more importantly, they harvested a rich crop of positive associations with rural life. They made cultural and political hay from the Puritan doctrine of a productive calling, the physiocratic idea that agriculture formed the true foundation of national prosperity, and the agrarian notion of virtuous producers defending the nation against luxury and vice. New England's country-seat Federalists fashioned themselves a benevolent leadership, whose rationality and impartiality were most centrally symbolized by their adopted role as wealthy farmers. (See Ronald P. Formisano, *The Transformation of Political Culture: Massachusetts Parties, 1790s-1840s*. (New York, NY: Oxford UP, 1983); Daniel Walker Howe, *The Political Culture of the American Whigs* (Chicago, IL: University of Chicago Press, 1979); and Tamara Plakins Thornton, *Cultivating Gentlemen: The Meaning of Country Life among the Boston Elite, 1785–1860* (New Haven, CT: Yale UP, 1989).
3. F.W.P. Greenwood, 'The Miscellaneous Poems of William Wordsworth', *North American Review* 18 (1824): 356.
4. Joel Pace observes that Greenwood ignores 'the hundreds of times that passages from *The Excursion* were reprinted in Unitarian anthologies and the thousands of times Wordsworth's verse appeared in magazines, journals, papers and miscellanies. One school reader containing Wordsworth, an American reprint of C.L. Murray's, sold through thousands and thousands of copies in America. Also, an anthology, *The American First Class Book*, edited by the Unitarian John Pierpont was, according to law, issued to every schoolchild in Massachusetts' (personal correspondence). In other words, the American enthusiasm for Wordsworth was actively gestating for at least three decades before it finally reached culmination with the response to *Yarrow* and the *Complete Poems*. Pace documents this history in '"Gems of a soft and permanent luster": The Reception and Influence of the *Lyrical Ballads* in America', *Romanticism on the Net* 9 (February 1998) <http://www.erudit.org/revue/ron/1998/v/n9/005782ar.html>, and 'Wordsworth, the *Lyrical Ballads*, and Literary and Social Reform in Nineteenth-Century America' in *'The Honourable Characteristic of Poetry': Two Hundred Years of* Lyrical Ballads., ed. Marcy Tanter, *Romantic Circles Praxis Series* (November 1999) <http://www.rc.umd.edu/praxis/lyrical/pace/wordsworth.html>.
5. Annabel Newton, *Wordsworth in Early American Criticism* (Chicago, IL: University of Chicago Press, 1928).
6. J. Walker, 'Review of The Complete Poetical Works of William Wordsworth', *Christian Examiner* 22 (1837): 132.
7. Ralph Waldo Emerson, 'Thoughts on Modern Literature', *Dial* 1 (1840): 150.
8. Christopher Pearse Cranch, 'Wordsworth', *Atlantic Monthly* 45 (1880): 251.
9. William Wordsworth, *Yarrow Revisited and Other Poems* (Boston, MA: James Munroe, 1835), 3.
10. Richard D. Brown, *Modernization: The Transformation of American Life, 1600–1865* (New York, NY: Hill and Wang, 1976).
11. In 1831, New York witnessed its first labour demonstrations as stonecutters protested the use of prison-cut stone in the construction of public buildings. The same year the Boston Workingmen formed much the largest contingent in the

Independence Day parade. In 1834, New York City's General Trades Union moved to create a National Trades Union to take in all skilled trades on a national basis, celebrating with a march that stretched a mile and a half. During the same year, the women of Lowell's mills struck against wage reductions. Sailors, shipwrights, riggers, and stevedores struck in New York, and bloody battles broke out between secretly organized Irish workers on the Chesapeake and Ohio Canal and a group of scabs, prompting Jackson to send in federal troops. See Anthony Bimba, *The History of the American Working Class* ([1927] New York, NY: International Publishers, 1968); John Commons *et al. History of Labor in the United States* (New York, NY: Macmillan, 1935); and Joseph G. Rayback, *A History of American Labor* (New York, NY: Macmillan, 1964).

12. Sacvan Bercovitch, *The Rites of Assent: Transformations in the Symbolic Construction of America* (New York, NY: Routledge, 1993), 168–93.
13. Philip Gould, *Covenant and Republic: Historical Romance and the Politics of Persuasion* (New York, NY: Cambridge UP, 1996), 176–84; see also Marvin Meyers, *The Jacksonian Persuasion: Politics and Belief* (Stanford, CA: Stanford UP, 1960).
14. Anonymous, 'William Wordsworth', *Southern Literary Messenger* 3 (1837): 708.
15. James K. Chandler, 'Representative Men, Spirits of the Age, and Other Romantic Types' in *Romantic Revolutions: Criticism and Theory*, eds Kenneth Johnston *et al.* (Bloomington, IN: Indiana UP, 1990), 133–57; William G. Rowland Jr, *Literature and the Marketplace: Romantic Writers and Their Audiences in Great Britain and the United States* (Lincoln, NE: University of Nebraska Press, 1996), 39–62; Willard Spiegelman, *Wordsworth's Heroes* (Berkeley, CA: University of California Press, 1985), 1–23.
16. H.T. Tuckerman, 'Wordsworth', *Southern Literary Messenger* 7 (1841): 105.
17. Noah Porter, 'Wordsworth and his Poetry', *Quarterly Christian Spectator* 8 (1836): 129.
18. Ralph Waldo Emerson, 'Man the Reformer', *Dial* 1 (1840): 537.
19. This can seem like little more than jockeying for political position, but an accurate assessment of the historical progressiveness of New England's second- and third-generation bourgeoisie, requires a two-sided observation. At the same time that they presided over an historic intensification of the exploitation of the Northern working class, they also led the revolutionary overthrow of the slave-owning South. Their appropriation of Wordsworth's poetry of humble country life was, thus, quite politically complex. The poems were used as manuals for self-instruction in democracy, in natural feelings of brotherhood with the common people. Yet, the final goal of such training was to reclaim the social authority necessary to address the double threat of, on one hand, the pro-slavery Jacksonian Democrats and, on the other, the emergent working class, as each adapted the rhetoric of republican virtue and democracy to their own equally complex ends.
20. Thoreau's poetry has been re-edited in a new collected edition by Elizabeth Hall Witherell (New York, NY: Library of America, 2001), superseding Carl Bode's edition (Baltimore, MD: John Hopkins UP, 1964), which had been the standard for several decades. Witherell has also condensed the results of her textual and historical scholarship into two articles, one a survey of his poetic decade, the second a reading of what she regards as Thoreau's crowning poetic achievement, a sequence of five related poems exploring the place of man in nature. Arthur Ford mounts the most extensive close reading of the verse, focusing on Thoreau's desire to capture in poetry the experience of self-transcendence through total immersion in

nature. Ford also provides a very useful annotated bibliography of sources on Thoreau's poetry through 1970. Since then, critical work on the subject has been quite sparse and was mostly produced in a burst of activity during the early 1970s. Betsy Colquitt provides a sensitive and concise survey of Thoreau's theories of poetry ('Thoreau's Poetics', *ATQ*, 11 (1971): 74–81). Robert Evans argues that Thoreau's poems are destroyed when removed from the context of the prose narratives within which many were originally published ('Thoreau's Poetry and Prose Works', *ESQ*, 56 (1969): 40–52). Several articles explore particular tropes or image clusters: Mary Kaiser surveys the symbolism of celestial bodies ('"Conversing with the Sky": The Imagery of Celestial Bodies in Thoreau's Poetry', *Thoreau Journal Quarterly*, 9.3 (1977): 15–28); Kenneth Silverman explores Thoreau's unfulfilled desire for energy and heroic action ('The Sluggard Knight in Thoreau's Poetry', *Thoreau Journal Quarterly*, 5.2 (1973): 6–9); Carla Mazzini describes two poems that centre on epiphanic experiences ('Epiphany in Two Poems by Thoreau', *Thoreau Journal Quarterly*, 5.2 (1973): 23–5); and Paul Williams documents the centrality of the concept of inspiration to Thoreau's poetics ('The Concept of Inspiration in Thoreau's Poetry', *PMLA*, 79 (1964): 466–72).

21. Henry David Thoreau, *Walden, or Life in the Woods* (Princeton, NJ: Princeton UP, 1971), 259.
22. Robert Sattelmeyer, *Thoreau's Reading: A Study in Intellectual History* (Princeton, NJ: Princeton UP, 1988), 3–24.
23. Elizabeth Hall Witherell, 'Thoreau as Poet' in *The Cambridge Companion to Henry David Thoreau* (Cambridge: Cambridge UP, 1995), 57–70.
24. Perry Miller and Lorrie Smith offer valuable overviews of Thoreau's place in the international tradition of Romanticism (Thoreau in the Context of International Romanticism', *New England Quarterly*, 34 (June 1961), and '"Walking" from New England to America: Re-Viewing Thoreau's Romanticism', *New England Quarterly*, 58.2 (June 1985) 221–41, respectively). Frederick Garber describes the importance of Wordsworth as Thoreau's exemplar of both the strengths and weaknesses of Anglo-European Romanticism ('Thoreau and Anglo-European Romanticism', in *Approaches to Teaching Thoreau's Walden and Other Works*, ed. Richard J. Schneider (New York, NY: MLA, 1996): 39–47). Neill Joy first suggests and Robert Moldenhauer exhaustively documents the influence of Wordsworth's *Guide to the District of the Lakes* on Thoreau's general ideas about landscape, as well as specifically on *Walden* ('Two Possible Analogues for "The Ponds" in *Walden*, Jonathan Carver and Wordsworth', *ESQ*, 24 (1978) 197–205, and '*Walden* and Wordsworth's Guide to the English Lake District', *Studies in the American Renaissance*, (1990): 261–92, respectively). Karen Kalinevitch documents *Walden*'s many allusions to the great odes ('"Apparelled in Celestial Light" / "Bathed in So Pure a Light": Verbal Echoes in Wordsworth's and Thoreau's Works', *Thoreau Journal Quarterly*, 12.2 (1980): 27–30). The fact that Wordsworth was a strong influence on Thoreau has never been seriously questioned and the central focus of scholarship has always been on their habits of thought about the relationship between humans and nature. For decades, debate centred on whether Wordsworth saw imagination (or mind or man) as shaping nature or vice versa, and on whether Thoreau maintained the same position. The best summaries of those conversations can be found in the work of Carl Dennis and Laraine Fergenson ('Correspondence in Thoreau's Nature Poetry', *ESQ*, 58 (1970): 101–9, and 'Was Thoreau Re-Reading Wordsworth in 1851', *Thoreau Journal Quarterly*, 5.3 (1973): 20–3, respectively). In the last two decades, the terms of the debate have shifted with the rise of Ecocriticism. Ecocritics ask whether Wordsworth and Thoreau were

homocentric or biocentric, giving an environmental political edge to a question which had previously been quite scholastic. James McKusick provides a culminating statement of this avenue of research, arguing that the English Romantics inaugurated a tradition of organicist, localist, ecocentric writing that the American Transcendentalists cultivated and extended (*Green Writing: Romanticism and Ecology* (New York, St Martin's, 2000)). Greg Garrard sees a more antagonistic relationship, arguing that Thoreau appropriates Wordsworth's tentative early biocentrism and then radicalizes it in an act of Bloomian rejection ('Wordsworth and Thoreau: Two Versions of Pastoral', in *Thoreau's Sense of Place*, ed. Richard J. Schneider (Iowa City, IA University of Iowa Press, 2000)). Also, in the context of increasing interest in Romanticism as a transatlantic phenomenon, the relationship between Wordsworth and Thoreau has become a case study for the investigations of the direction and character of influence between British and American literatures. Robert Weisbuch (following Harold Bloom) argues that Wordsworth's influence was strong and strongly resented, and that Thoreau had to reject it in order to claim his own voice (*Atlantic Double Cross* (Chicago, IL: University of Chicago Press, 1986)). Richard Gravil, on the other hand, maintains that *Walden* manifests an astonishing openness to the living Wordsworth and that Thoreau's attitude towards the poet was one of profound identification (*Romantic Dialogues* (New York, NY: St Martin's, 2000)).

25. Henry David Thoreau, *Early Essays and Miscellanies*, eds Joseph J. Moldenhauer and Edwin Moser (Princeton, NJ: Princeton UP, 1975), 122.
26. Robert Weisbuch, *Atlantic Double-Cross: American Literature and British Influence in the Age of Emerson* (Chicago, IL: University of Chicago Press, 1986), 143.
27. Henry David Thoreau, *A Week on the Concord and Merrimack Rivers*, eds Carl F. Hovde *et al.* (Princeton, NJ: Princeton UP, 1980), 91.
28. Thoreau shared many of his habits of thought about the poet and poetry with the rest of the Transcendentalist circle. Helen Hennesy and Joel Myerson survey these ideas in the context of histories of the central Transcendentalist organ in *The Dial* ('The Dial: Its Poetry', *New England Quarterly*, 31 (1958): 66–87, and *New England Transcendentalism and* The Dial (Rutherford, NJ: Fairleigh Dickinson, 1980)).
29. Richard Gravil, *Romantic Dialogues: Anglo-American Continuities, 1776–1862* (New York, NY: St Martin's Press, 2000), 108.
30. Henry David Thoreau, *Collected Essays and Poems*, ed. Elizabeth Hall Witherell (New York: Library of America, 2001), 514. All remaining quotations from Thoreau's poetry are taken from this source, and page numbers are hereafter cited parenthetically in the essay.
31. Paul O. Williams, 'Thoreau's Growth as a Transcendentalist Poet', *Emerson Society Quarterly (ESQ)* 19 (1973): 189–98.
32. Henry W. Wells, 'An Evaluation of Thoreau's Poetry', *American Literature* 16 (May 1944): 99–114.
33. Paul O. Williams, 'The Concept of Inspiration in Thoreau's Poetry', *Publications of the Modern Language Association* 79 (1964): 466–72.
34. James McIntosh, *Thoreau as Romantic Naturalist: His Shifting Stance Toward Nature* (Ithaca, NY: Cornell UP, 1974), 17–48.
35. Laraine Fergenson, 'Was Thoreau Re-Reading Wordsworth in 1851', *Thoreau Journal Quarterly* 5, no. 3 (1973): 20–3.
36. J. Lyndon Shanley, *The Making of Walden* (Chicago, IL: University of Chicago Press, 1957), 18–33, 55–73.
37. I make this argument at length in 'Thoreau's Natural Community and Utopian Socialism', *American Literature* 75.3 (September 2003): 515–44.

7

Intimations of Imitation: Wordsworth, Whitman and the Emergence of *Leaves of Grass*

Karen Karbiener

The Child at the Tomb

We find this eloquent anecdote in the journal of a traveller in the East:

> (– A little child
> That lightly draws its breath,
> And feels its life in every limb –
> What should it know of death?)

> At Smyrna, the burial ground of the Armenian, like that of the Moslem, is removed a short distance from the town, is sprinkled with green trees, and is a favourite resort not only with the bereaved, but with those whose feelings are not thus darkly overcast. I met there one morning a little girl with a half playful countenance, busy blue eye, and sunny locks, bearing in one hand a small cup of china, in the other a wreath of fresh flowers. Feeling a very natural curiosity to know what she could do with these bright things in a place that seemed to partake so much of sadness, I watched her light motions – Reaching a retired grave, covered with a plain marble slab, she emptied the seed – which it appeared the cup contained – into the slight cavities which had been scooped out into the corners of the level tablet, and laid the wreath on its pure face. 'And why', I inquired, 'my sweet girl, do you put the seed in those little bowls there?' 'It is to bring the birds here', she replied, with a half wonderful look; 'they will light on this tree', pointing to the cypress above, 'when they have eaten the seed, and sing'. 'To whom do they sing?' I asked, 'to you, or to each other?' 'Oh no', she quickly replied, 'to my sister; she sleeps here'. 'But your sister is dead'. 'Oh yes, sir, but she hears all the birds sing'. – 'Well, if she does hear the birds sing, she cannot see

that wreath of flowers'. 'But she knows I put it there; I told her before they took her away from our house, I would come and see her every morning'. 'You must', I continued, 'have loved that sister very much, but you will never talk with her any more, never see her again'. 'Yes, sir', she replied, with a brightened look, 'I shall see her always in heaven'. 'But she has gone there already, I trust'. 'No, she stops under this tree, till they bring me here, and then we are going to heaven together'.

Walt Whitman, *Brooklyn Daily Eagle* (2 September 1846): 2

From Wordsworth's death in 1850 to Whitman's 'birth' in 1855; from *The Prelude* to 'Song'; from the 'splendor' to the *Leaves of Grass*: the progression from Wordsworth to Whitman's Romanticism appears natural and sure. Yet the relationship between the poets is very difficult to determine. Despite Wordsworth's increasing popularity and the wide availability of his works in America throughout the 1840s, Whitman very rarely made public reference to the poet laureate. His silence has often been taken as a sign of Whitman's ambivalence or ignorance concerning Wordsworth's work; however, neither position seems a likely one for an ambitious young journalist who introduced and developed a 'Books Lately Published' column in the *Brooklyn Daily Eagle* in 1847. Indeed, unpublished notes and marginalia that survived Whitman's 'clean-ups' indicate that Wordsworth was very much on Whitman's mind during the seed-time of *Leaves of Grass*. And a single, striking discovery of Whitman's borrowing from Wordsworth provides new ways in which *Leaves of Grass* can be read as a response to (and rebellion against) Wordsworth's poetic legacy:

A Nation announcing itself,
I myself make the only growth by which I can be appreciated,
I reject none, accept all, then reproduce all in my own forms.

Democratic and self-centered, earthy and spiritual, simple and grand, confident and contradictory: the message of these lines can be described as characteristically 'whitmanesque'. First published in 1856, the passage was the original introduction of 'Poem of Many in One', a work that gradually metamorphosed into 'By Blue Ontario's Shore'. 'Poem of Many in One' is considered the thesis poem of the second edition; as Harold Blodgett and Sculley Bradley note, it 'took a position among those poems which support the meaning of *Leaves of Grass* as a whole'.[1] In fact, the lines, like many others from the work, are poetic transcriptions of important statements made in the 1855 'Preface'. Whitman seems to be attempting to establish his own famous 'proof of a poet': 'that his country absorbs him as affectionately as he has absorbed it'.[2] 'The soul of the nation ... rejects none, permits all', Whitman continues in the 'Preface'. 'Only toward *as good* as itself and toward the like of itself will it advance half-way' (*Poetry and Prose*, 26). The fact that this poem was never cut from any of the six editions of *Leaves of Grass*,[3] and that the above passage remained virtually unchanged in a poem that had undergone many revisions, indicates how important these ideas remained to Whitman throughout his career.

Ironically, however, the very line in which Whitman discusses the problems confronted by an 'original' artist – the line that contributes to the understanding of Whitman as a 'visionary' – also betrays his status as a 'revisionary'. For in noting that he himself makes 'the only growth by which I can be appreciated', he was transplanting an idea, rather than cultivating his own. Whitman's own reticence, his destruction of notes, and his extensive revisions make tracing his influences unusually difficult; in this case, he left a significant clue in a promotional extract bound in the second imprint of *Leaves of Grass* (1855). Writing of the need for poetry to become the 'exponent of a new spirit through new forms', Whitman continues:

> The new forms are not to be judged by the old models, but are to be judged by themselves. Wordsworth truly said that every original first-rate poet must himself make the taste through which he is to be fully understood and appreciated.[4]

The original formulation is from 'Essay, Supplementary to the Preface (1815)', though Wordsworth's phrasing is slightly different: 'Every Author, as far as he is great and at the same time *original*, has had the task of *creating* the taste by which he is to be enjoyed' (657–8). Whitman was either familiar with Wordsworth's original essay, or he read extracts and criticism about it in contemporary periodicals; indeed, one such article exists, heavily annotated by Whitman, among his private papers.[5]

This is a rare example of a traceable line of influence between Wordsworth and Whitman. Such relationships were more often sensed than proven or confirmed by Whitman himself, even by people who might have learned of the truth from Whitman himself. In 1867, Whitman's good friend John Burroughs discussed several parallels between the poet and Wordsworth in *Notes on Walt Whitman as Poet and Person*.[6] Burroughs's ideas were confirmed by another one of Whitman's associates, Edward Dowden, who wrote to Burroughs that 'knowing Whitman enables one to discover the place of Wordsworth'.[7] Dowden's comparison of Whitman and Wordsworth's concepts of truth appears in his article 'The Poetry of Democracy: Walt Whitman', which Whitman never commented on but saved among his private papers (Feinberg 32.40). Whitman also clipped out the review of his friend Richard Maurice Bucke's *Walt Whitman* in *The Academy* comparing the progress of both poets' careers (Feinberg 33.291 in NYPL's Berg Collection). Whitman's friend William Douglas O'Connor found similarities between the two writers in his introduction to *The Good*

Gray Poet; Esther Shephard claims in *Walt Whitman's Pose* that Whitman read the introductory piece 'several times, corrected the proof himself, and even supplied passages'.[8] Thomas William Rolleston, a close associate of Whitman's and the German translator of *Leaves of Grass*, delivered a lecture on Whitman in 1883, writing to the poet about another speaker who impressed him because

> He said what I had reported about you reminded him of Wordsworth. Now this was really remarkable, for I had always held that Wordsworth was the true predecessor of the L. of G. and on asking Edward Dowden once about this, he fully confirmed what I thought. (Wordsworth is calculated to lead a courageous, though not a timid, person up to W.W.) (Frenz, 78)

Rolleston continued to explain that he meant to publish his Whitman lecture with another lecture on Wordsworth, to show readers 'in what direction the connection between you and Wordsworth is to be looked for' (78). Whitman noted his receipt of Rolleston's 'lecture pamphlet, "Wordsworth and WW"' on 19 December 1883.[9] But when it appeared in the Camden *Daily Post* on 13 February 1884, the section in which Rolleston compared Whitman and Wordsworth had been removed.[10] Perhaps Whitman did not wish the study to be taken out of the academic context it had in O'Connor's and Rolleston's publications; he may also have been worried that the *Post*'s working-class readers were more likely to associate the authorship of the piece with the local resident Whitman than a German scholar.

Despite Whitman's attempts to disregard or quietly discourage comparisons between himself and Wordsworth, Whitman's obituary mentioned the likenesses between the poets[11] and the commonalities between them have continued to intrigue scholars. 'There is no document more allied to Whitman's prefaces, in the conception of the function of the poet as "a man speaking to men", in the stress on natural emotion ... than Wordsworth's "Preface to *Lyrical Ballads*"', claims F.O. Matthiessen, who goes on to compare and contrast the poets' styles and themes.[12] David Simpson also argues for the viability of comparing Wordsworth's 'Preface' to Whitman's 'Preface' to *Leaves of Grass*.[13] Tony Tanner notes that 'Song of Myself' seems to have much in common with *The Prelude*;[14] Robert Weisbuch thinks it is 'highly likely' that 'Whitman is deliberating Wordsworth and *The Prelude* in "Song of Myself"'.[15] In *Walt Whitman and the American Reader*, Ezra Greenspan describes 'Out of the Cradle Endlessly Rocking' as 'Whitman's equivalent to a Wordsworthian study of the growth of the poet's mind'.[16]

If suggestions for the comparative study of Whitman and Wordsworth have been made, follow-ups have remained rather tentative, and often superficial; for example, two of the three articles on the two poets listed in

Wordsworthian Scholarship and Criticism are described as 'frequently oversimplified' and 'overly general'.[17] Even critics known for their thoroughness and insight, such as those cited above, have not gone on to analyse the comparison in detail. Despite Matthiessen's claims of Wordsworth's powerful influence on Whitman, he spends less than four pages discussing the two in conjunction; ironically, most of his points concern the poets' differences. Tanner turns away from the idea of comparing them after the 'first glance', and Simpson is quick to note that Whitman was not 'in any thorough or conscious way a disciple of Wordsworth, or of Wordsworthianism' (289). Greenspan, after noting that Wordsworth was 'the English Romantic closest in sensibility and theory of poetry' to Whitman, quickly concludes that Whitman exhibited no more than a 'primary (and occasionally rather gossipy) interest in the poet as a man' (75). The longest and best study, found in *Atlantic Double-Cross*, is very cautiously set forth; Robert Weisbuch begins by admitting 'in linking Whitman and Wordsworth, I must confess speculation' (178).

What most inhibits comparative studies of these two poets is Whitman's silence regarding Wordsworth, often understood as a sign of his lack of interest in or knowledge of the poet. 'There is no extra-textual evidence whatsoever to support a claim of direct influence nor are there any obviously telling allusions in "Song of Myself" to *The Prelude* or any of Wordsworth's poems', admits Weisbuch (178). There are no records of Whitman's responses to his friends' comparisons of Wordsworth and himself; in fact, Whitman rarely mentioned Wordsworth at all in his published writings after *Leaves of Grass* was published, though he did put his guard down to acknowledge his debts to Scott (*Specimen Days; Poetry and Prose* 699), Byron,[18] and Burns ('November Boughs', *Poetry and Prose*, 1152–61). Much as he wrote about Bryant, he never mentioned Wordsworth's influence on the poet – something he had noted to himself more than once, in private jottings.[19] In his essays on Emerson, Whitman demonstrated his familiarity with books such as *English Traits*, and Emerson's admiration for literary men as obscure as Lovelace and Waller, though Wordsworth again received no mention. Despite the fact that Wordsworth often appears on Whitman's private lists of writers and thinkers, he is not among the figures who received consistent and public praise from the poet: in his notes on Elias Hicks in 'November Boughs', Whitman supplies a long list of 'loudest reverberating names' from 1740 to 1830 that includes Scott, Burns and Byron but leaves out Wordsworth (*Poetry and Prose*, 1222–3); in 'Notes Left Over', he names Shakespeare, Burns and Tennyson among the 'great undying songs' (1069); in the late poem 'Old Chants' Shakespeare, Scott and Tennyson are amongst those 'preluding' America with song (646). In 1881, Whitman likened the British spirit of the last 50 years to an army led by Carlyle, Byron, Scott, and Tennyson (912).

Ignorance of Wordsworth's poetry simply cannot be considered an explanation for Whitman's silence regarding the poet laureate. Annabel Newton notes that Wordsworth's popularity in America was on a remarkable upswing from 1824 to 1850 – 'seed time' for the future author of *Leaves of Grass*.[20] When Whitman began attending public school in 1824, Wordsworthian criticism consumed an 'increasing amount of space in the best periodicals' and included 'evidence of the strength and religious appeal in Wordsworth's poetry' (Newton, 119). The moral tone of *The Excursion* made it an easy favourite with American middle-class readers and an obvious choice for inclusion in school texts, including *The American Class Book* of 1823 (Newton, 118–19) and others Whitman may have used. When he became a teacher in the next decade, Whitman may well have employed a popular grammar book containing Wordsworth's poetry: Jonathan Barber's *Grammar of Elocution* (1830) included 'Lucy Gray', accompanied by 'graphs to indicate pauses and emphasis, as a sample for reading practices'.[21]

When Wordsworth's stateside popularity was boosted by his induction as England's poet laureate in 1843, Whitman was in the first years of his journalistic career. Though he never wrote a review of a new edition of Wordsworth's poems or included one in the *Eagle*, Whitman – as an attentive measurer of trends and tastes – must have known about the publication of at least a few of the new collections of Wordsworth's poems.[22] David Simpson notes that Wordsworth's popularity in America first went on the increase in the 1830s, when the first American edition of Henry Reed's *Complete Works of William Wordsworth* appeared in 1837. Reprinted in 1839, 1844, 1846, 1848, and so on, Reed's American edition brought high praise for Wordsworth from the *North American Review* and the *New York Review*, in which Wordsworth was ranked with Shakespeare and Milton (Simpson, 282). More American editions of Wordsworth's poetry appeared, including republications of Edward Moxon's *Poetical Works of William Wordsworth*. The New York publishing house of Wiley and Putnam published Moxon's six-volume edition in 1841, a revised and enlarged seven-volume edition in 1846, and another revised edition in 1849.[23] Additionally, the most popular poems were issued separately in cheap, unauthorized chapbooks.[24] By the time *Leaves of Grass* was published, Wordsworth's canon had become available to Americans through many pirated British collections and at least fifteen American editions (Hanley, 1–8). Indeed, American conventional wisdom so favoured Wordsworth by mid-century that the historian George Bancroft could claim Wordsworth 'as much a possession of America as England'.[25]

Reaching out to the American public through textbooks, penny dailies and prestigious literary periodicals, in sermons and speeches, poems and paintings and political tracts, Wordsworth did indeed seem to 'lie at the heart of the people' of the New World, as Harriet Martineau observed in

1837 (Hill 146). The truth of her observation would grow increasingly more apparent in the next decade, as the concept of *Leaves of Grass* began to take shape in Whitman's mind. By 1850, when Whitman had given up regular employment to concentrate on his writing, Wordsworth's death had boosted his American popularity even higher. 'No country contains a larger number of intelligent admirers of Wordsworth's genius than our own', proudly declared a critic for the *North American Review* in October 1851 (vol. 73, no. 53, p. 494). The *Literary World* of New York, a journal that Whitman expressed his admiration for in the *Eagle*, had published the laudatory 'Visit to the Poet Wordsworth' in 1848 (vol. 3: 879–80); in June 1850, Wordsworth's editor Henry Reed upped the ante in a long article that claimed the 'zealous admiration' and 'grateful and affectionate attachment' felt for the poet by his countrymen 'is shared on this side of the Atlantic'. He included a quotation from a letter written by Wordsworth in 1837, demonstrating that the appreciation between the poet and his American fans was mutual: 'The acknowledgements I receive from the vast continent of America are among the most grateful that reach me'. A few months later, an article by 'A.M.' in the *Southern Literary Messenger* (August 1850, vol. 16: 474–9) relayed the author's conversation with the poet shortly before his death, demonstrating his enduring interest in American affairs. Praising his 'brother bards across the Atlantic', Wordsworth expressed a desire to 'see both countries united more and more strongly in the bonds of brotherhood'. His wish would come true posthumously in 1852, when literary circles in England and America united to purchase a memorial to Wordsworth, placed in a church at Ambleside. 'In the United States the true inspiration of the poetry of Wordsworth and its moral as well as its imaginative influences, were early recognized, perhaps as soon as in Great Britain', read the address issued in connection with the enterprise. 'These influences spreading far and wide have entered into many an American mind' (*Literary World* 13 (1853: 512–13)).

Emerson, Longfellow, Sigourney, and others who had worked towards the establishment of an independent American literature, nevertheless paid their respects to the English poet laureate through contributions to the Ambleside project. Still involved in periodical publishing at this time, Whitman must have read about this well-publicized event, and probably saw contributors' letters that were published in the New York journal *The Literary World* (vol. 13: 512–13). Though his reaction is not recorded,[26] he must have been concerned that much-needed funds were being used to fund projects abroad – even as he slowly gathered the money and materials needed to finish the book that would herald the arrival of 'an American bard at last'.

From his earliest journalism to his late prose commentary, Whitman expressed concern over the American public's fondness for British literature, which he saw as symbolic of America's lingering political and social dependence upon England. Establishing a national literature was not simply a matter of pride with Whitman; he saw an American literature as a crucial cohesive force and expressed his views in insistent, emotional language. Whitman's political editorials for the *Eagle* often depict the British as haughty tyrants, stifling the rights of the Chinese (*Eagle,* 19 July 1847), the Irish and the Scottish (19 March). Indeed, Whitman's sympathy for these countries under British influence may explain why he felt less compromised in his praise of Scottish writers like Scott or Burns, or even expatriates like Byron. While he could not ignore the importance of English books as works of art, and could not resist reviewing and commenting upon many of them, he recognized the American interest in British literature as symbolic of the country's lingering political and social dependence upon their colonists. 'Presumptous and vain it would be for us to decry their glorious merits. But it must not be forgotten that many of the most literary men of England are the advocates of doctrines that in such a land as ours are the rankest and foulest poison', Whitman warned *Eagle* readers on 11 July 1846. English books might be considered classic, but they were also grounded in principles from which America had fought long and hard to gain independence; distributing these bad seeds on fertile American soil might result in an outbreak of smothering weeds. New American seeds must be sown to rival the towering English growths: 'Without any irreverence, we think it not amiss to say that we of America must rival even the literary greatness of the past', he announced on 12 May 1846. Instructing publishers to end the flood of foreign literature in this country, Whitman also warned the public of the consequences of being swept up in it.

Whitman's early unpublished notebooks and scrapbooks indicate that he was indeed concerned about Wordsworth's high status with the American people.[27] What comes forth in these notes is Whitman's particularly acute case of the anxiety of influence regarding Wordsworth. The American poet was unnerved by Wordsworth's popularity on these shores, especially because of Wordsworth's increasing conservatism and 'Englishness'. 'So it seems Wordsworth made a "good thing" from the start, out of his poetry. Legacies! A fat office! Pensions from the crown!' wrote Whitman in response to an article on *The Prelude* in the *American Whig Review* of May 1851.[28] Whitman, who would write in his own 'Preface' that a poet should 'despise riches', would never desire nor receive such politicized financial support himself. As early as 1838, Whitman had voted to abolish capital punishment, much to the dismay of other members of the Smithtown Debating Society;[29] a few years later, Wordsworth's sonnets justifying the practice of capital punishment were published in magazines Whitman habitually read, such as the *United States Magazine and Democratic Review.*[30] If not already infuriated by Wordsworth's conservative tone in the sonnets, Whitman must have been further incensed by the reviewer, who expressed disbelief that the radical young poet of 'The Convict' could become such a turncoat.

While he dialogued with himself regarding Wordsworth's art and politics, Whitman seems to have made a conscious choice not to further Wordsworth's reputation by mentioning him in print. Whitman's complex relationship with the looming presence of Wordsworth – his struggle between awe and envy, attraction and repulsion, emulation and rebellion – was perhaps too personal and too revealing to share with his readers. Following his own directive to 'take no illustrations ... make no allusions' when it came to Wordsworthian matters,[31] he probably hoped to help write Wordsworth out of American literary history – and to ease his own anxieties regarding Wordsworth's influence on his own art. In time, Whitman grew increasingly proud of his ability to elude definition and identification. 'I give you fair warning, before you attempt me further, / I am not what you supposed, but far different', he teased in 1860 ('Whoever You Are Holding Me Now in Hand', *Poetry and Prose*, 270).

One has cause to wonder, then, about a significant slip in Whitman's silent routine in the *Eagle* of 2 September 1846. Perhaps the new editor was under pressure to locate copy that would be a surefire sell to readers; perhaps Whitman was convinced that he had covered his tracks thoroughly enough; maybe he had absorbed Wordsworth to such an extent that he thought the story was his own. Whatever the case, Whitman's retelling of 'We Are Seven' as a story entitled 'The Child at the Tomb' proves that the so-called 'Christopher Columbus of American art',[32] 'the one pioneer' (Woodress, 211) whose 'exceedingly great stench ... *is* America'[33] was reading, absorbing, and being creatively inspired by the work of the British poet laureate.

'–A little child', begins Whitman, thereby misquoting (and not naming) the shortened version of the original first line of the poem: 'A simple child, dear brother Jim'. Since Wordsworth had made the change for the 1815 edition of *Poems*, Whitman's use proves that he consulted this or an even newer edition – perhaps the Moxon edition published under the auspices of Wiley and Putnam. Whitman's substitution of 'little' for 'simple' may have been the result of a bad memory or perhaps an effort to obscure his connection to Wordsworth's poem (as his switch from Wordsworth's poetry to his prose seems to be).[34]

The theme of the tale following the quote is obviously derived from 'We Are Seven'. With her 'busy blue eye and sunny locks', Whitman's heroine resembles the fair beauty of Wordsworth's imagination. Both maids are happy and active, but willing to engage in a frustrated question-and-answer drill with a nosey and didactic observer. Each narrator is curious about the girl's understanding of death, and persists in his efforts to teach the young that death is an end in itself. But both heroines remain unfazed by the ruthless inquiries. The maid of 'We Are Seven' continues to count her dead brother and sister as among the living, and Whitman's child claims that her dead sister waits for her 'under this tree, till they bring me here, and then we are going to heaven together'. Both pieces, then, are debates of six exchanges between intuitive and rational thought in which impassioned youth has the last word.

Whitman does, however, attempt to provide some distance between his version and Wordsworth's by introducing 'The Child at the Tomb' as an anecdote found 'in the journal of a traveller in the East'. The real author of the piece could thus be almost anyone, though the exotic locale of Smyrna (the former name of Izmir, Turkey) draws readers' minds far away from the pastoral scenes of Westmorland. Conscious or no, Whitman's decision to use a blue-eyed blonde child in the Turkish setting reminds us that the move to Smyrna is only a change in the backdrop of the story. She may have been moved to the Middle East, but the maid is still exceedingly western in her demeanour, actions and appearance. In fact, Whitman's heroine possesses the colouring of many of the Whitman children, including Walt himself – bringing to mind another reason why 'We Are Seven' may have been especially significant to him. Though eight Whitman children survived infancy, Walt served less as a sibling and more as a guardian or overseer, thanks to an abusive, possibly alcoholic father and a mentally disturbed older brother. The 1844 sketch by Whitman entitled 'My Boys and Girls' depicts the speaker as the custodian of seven children, many of whom share names with Whitman's real siblings.[35] If 'We Are Seven' did remind Whitman of his own family, one might suppose that his change from two dead children to one may have been purposeful: the unnamed dead sister of 'The Child at the Tomb', replacing Jane and John of 'We Are Seven', may be a tribute to one of Whitman's sisters, who died unnamed in infancy.

Death is indeed the central issue for both 'We Are Seven' and 'The Child at the Tomb'; but as the titles suggest, Wordsworth and Whitman have approached the subject differently. The graves in 'We Are Seven' are but 'twelve steps or more from my mother's door' in the churchyard, while Whitman's protagonist has walked to the burial ground 'a short distance from the town', deliberately outside of everyday goings-on. Wordsworth's cottage girl has no ritual associated with her tribute to the dead; she routinely does her chores or eats meals at graveside. But Whitman's child is not quite that 'simple' – as his change to the first line of 'We Are Seven' suggests. She tells and shows the stranger that she partakes in several rituals, visiting the tomb each morning, bringing offerings such as a wreath of flowers, and seed to attract songbirds. The marble slab over the sister's grave serves as a reminder that there is a separation between the states of life and death; Whitman's protagonist agrees with her questioner that her sister is in fact dead, and that her experiences as such differ from a live person's. Her sister cannot see the wreath of flowers, and cannot be seen until both girls are dead and in heaven. The maid of 'We Are Seven', however, refuses to let death separate her from her sister. Wordsworth's capitalization of 'Are' in the title is significant, since the little girl continues to use the present tense even in reference to her dead siblings. By emphasizing the more worldly and somewhat pagan ways his heroine memorializes the dead, Whitman seems to offer an alternative to Christian-based 'natural piety' of Wordsworth's protagonist. Nevertheless, Whitman has not yet devised the open, original spirituality that would permeate *Leaves of Grass*; in 'The Child at the Tomb', his heroine still delights in conventional objects and rituals, and even believes in a separation between 'heaven' and her own sphere.

The religious conversion between the two works is accompanied by the transformation of Wordsworth's narrative poem to Whitman's poetic narrative. Of course, Whitman may have switched mediums in an effort to disguise his borrowing, or to distinguish his final product from Wordsworth's. But the ease with which he alternates from poetry to prose is an early indication of his desire to break the established boundaries between the two forms. The sweeping, unrhymed, irregular lines of *Leaves of Grass* initiated another American revolution against conformity and tradition, but puzzled and offended many early reviewers. 'The body of the volume is filled with ... lines of rhythmical prose, or a series of utterances (we know not what else to call them), unconnected, curious, and original', writes a reviewer in *Life Illustrated* of 28 July 1855.[36] Whitman must have been pleased by the writer's choice of words, for as he expressed so many times himself, what mattered most to him was capturing the rhythm and music of the human voice on paper. In 'The Child at the Tomb', Whitman converted Wordsworth's dialogue in poetry to one in prose, but he preserved and even emphasized natural patterns of speech, coming even closer than Wordsworth to a language really used by men and women. What has been called the 'orality' of his mature poetry relies on his ability to create a living dialogue, whether it is with his reader or himself. 'He is the answerer', Whitman speaks of his role as poet. 'What can be answered he answers, and what cannot be answered he shows how it cannot be answered' ('Song of the Answerer' in *Textual Variorum*, I, 139). Here, and in many other poems in *Leaves of Grass*, Whitman seems to concur with the answer given by Wordsworth to his own questions in 'Preface to *Lyrical Ballads*': 'what is a Poet? To whom does he address himself? And what language is to be expected from him? He is a man speaking to men'.

And what do such men speak of? In 'We Are Seven' and 'The Child at the Tomb', they seek to reveal simple truths of human existence, such as the importance of trusting one's instinct over rationality, and believing in the natural wisdom of children. In 'We Are Seven', the rhetorical debate is won by the child, who refuses to allow the narrator's language to impose upon her and leaves her questioner frustrated. At the last, the authority of the older and supposedly wiser narrator, established in the first stanza's condescending question, is completely undermined. As

Thomas MacFarland suggests, 'The little girl is at once one who refuses to accept reality and one who serves a higher reality'.[37] She has answers to all of his questions, and she will not be swayed.

Whitman's little girl is just as confident in her opinions and as incredulous at the narrator's questioning, though Whitman's substitution of a 'half wonderful look' for the cottage girl's 'wondering look' is a bit awkward. She, too, has the last word. Additionally, she has an appreciation for ritual, beauty and the power of love that gives her definitive supremacy over him; as she tells her questioner, who reminds her that the dead girl cannot see the flower wreath, 'she knows I put it there'. Like Wordsworth's cottage girl, Whitman's little girl knows that there is something beyond the realm of sensory experience that is not seen, but felt.

Careful to keep up appearances, expert in the art of concealment, Whitman convinced audiences that he travelled far and wide, that he sired illegitimate children, that he did not write those flattering 'anonymous' reviews of *Leaves of Grass*. But in cultivating the image of himself as a 'chanter of Adamic songs, / Through the new garden the West' ('Ages and Ages Returning at Intervals', *Poetry and Prose*, 264), Whitman was unable to cover up everything that fertilized the *Leaves*. Perhaps if he had been called upon to explain his re-working of 'We Are Seven' in the *Eagle*, Whitman might have provided a convincing argument regarding the immense marketability of Wordsworth's poetry[38]; nevertheless, one now has cause to investigate further the remarkably similar themes (and titles) of 'There Was a Child Went Forth' and 'There Was a Boy', the call-and-response relationship of Wordsworth's 'Preface' to *Lyrical Ballads* and Whitman's 1855 'Preface' to *Leaves of Grass*, the celebration of children's experience and regenerative cycles of life in 'Ode: Intimations of Immortality' and 'Out of the Cradle Endlessly Rocking'. Even Whitman eventually recognized the brashness and futility of his earlier claims of originality. 'It must be carefully remember'd that first-class literature doesn't shine by any luminosity of its own; nor do its poems', he cautions in the 1888 essay 'A Backward Glance O'er Travel'd Roads'. 'They grow of circumstances, and are evolutionary. The actual living light is always curiously from elsewhere – follows unaccountable sources, and is lunar and relative at the best' (*Poetry and Prose*, 660).

Yet 'Out of the Cradle', the 'Preface' to *Leaves of Grass*, and 'There Was a Child Went Forth', like his other great works, can best be described as 'Whitmanesque'. Despite any ingredients that flavoured the mix, the final product is nothing but his own. 'The Child at the Tomb' may indicate Wordsworth's presence in Whitman's oeuvre, but the piece also demonstrates how much Whitman developed as a writer in the decade preceding the 1855 publication of *Leaves of Grass*. No passage in any of the twelve poems is so obviously derivative or clumsily imitative, though Wordsworth was undoubtedly part of the final project. Whitman's graceful, original absorption and translation of his influences, his ability to construct a strongly original poetic identity despite his borrowings, stand out as his particular gifts. It is up to the reader to discover just how such characteristically American sentiments heralding new beginnings and democratic relationships could be inspired by English poetry mourning the passing of childhood faith and wisdom:

> A child said, What is the grass? Fetching it to me with full hands;
> How could I answer the child? ... I do not know what it is any more than he. (*Poetry and Prose*, 31)

Notes

1. Walt Whitman, *Leaves of Grass*, eds Harold W. Blodgett and Sculley Bradley (New York, NY: New York UP, 1965), xlvii.
2. Walt Whitman, *Poetry and Prose*, ed. Justin Kaplan (New York, NY: Library of America, 1996), 26.
3. In *Leaves of Grass*: *The Textual Variorum*, Bradley and Blodgett note that 'Whitman ultimately excluded nearly one out of ten poems that had appeared in *Leaves of Grass* from 1855 to 1881. Presumably many were discarded because of their lack of relevance to the developing idea of the "poem"' (xxv). *Leaves of Grass: The Textual Variorum of the Printed Poems*, eds Sculley Bradley, Harold W. Blodgett, Arthur Golden and William White (3 vols, New York, NY: New York UP, 1980).
4. The quotation can be found on the eighth page of the unnumbered addendum to *Leaves of Grass* (1855), second imprint.
5. See Whitman's annotations to 'Egotism. Manifested in the Works and Lives of Great and Small Men', in *Graham's Magazine*, March 1845. The manuscript is number 180 in Duke University's Trent Collection. Unless otherwise specified, all annotated clippings discussed in this study can be found in Duke University's Trent Collection. Smaller collections of marginalia include those in the New York Public Library's Berg Collection, and in the Library of Congress.
6. John Burroughs, *Notes on Walt Whitman as Poet and Person* (New York, NY: American News Company, 1867), 46–7. The remarks in Burroughs's book are of particular interest because Whitman was allegedly involved in its composition. In 'The End of a Literary Mystery' (*American Mercury* 1 (April 1924): 471–6), Frederick Hier attempts to prove that the book is almost completely Whitman's. If this is true, the comparisons between Whitman and Wordsworth in the book support not only the idea that Whitman was responding to Wordsworth, but that he felt the need to be covert in this response.
7. *Whitman and Rolleston: A Correspondence*, ed. Horst Frenz (Dublin: Browne & Nolan, 1952), 78n4.
8. Esther Shephard, *Walt Whitman's Pose* (New York, NY: Harcourt, Brace, 1938), 352. In O'Connor's piece as well as Burroughs's work, Wordsworth is described as possessing a devout and loving yet simple and limited view of nature – a view that Whitman corrects and expands (compare Burroughs's *Notes* on pages 46–7 with O'Connor as found in Richard Maurice Bucke and Edward Dowden's *Walt Whitman* (Philadelphia, PA: David Mckay, 1888), 87. Similarities between the pieces confirm the possibility that Whitman had a hand in the writing of each;

if so, his silence suggests that he was anxious about making such comparisons under his own name.

9. *The Correspondence*, ed. Edwin Haviland Miller (5 vols, New York, NY: New York UP, 1961–69), II, 349.
10. The Camden *Post* version of Rolleston's piece, translated by Horace Traubel's father, can be found in Frenz, *Whitman and Rolleston*, 109–17. On p. 115, Traubel notes 'here follows a long metaphysical examination and statement' where the Whitman–Wordsworth comparison should be. Though the omission may have been the translator's choice, Whitman certainly had the last word on such editorial decisions. Nevertheless, there is no sign of Whitman's reaction regarding the comparison, or its omission.
11. The obituary was published in the Academy on 2 April 1892, and can be found in Frenz, *Whitman and Rolleston*, 127–8.
12. F.O. Matthiessen, *American Renaissance: Art and Expression in the Age of Emerson and Whitman* (Oxford: Oxford UP, 1941), 613–14.
13. David Simpson, 'Wordsworth in America' in *The Age of Wordsworth: Critical Essays on the Romantic Tradition*, eds Kenneth R. Johnston and Gene W. Ruoff (New Brunswick, NJ: Rutgers, 1987), 289.
14. Tony Tanner, 'Notes for a Comparison Between American and European Romanticism', *Journal of American Studies* 1, no. 2: 87.
15. Robert Weisbuch, *Atlantic Double-Cross: American Literature and British Influence in the Age of Emerson* (Chicago, IL: University of Chicago Press, 1986), 178.
16. Ezra Greenspan, *Walt Whitman and the American Reader* (New York, NY: Cambridge UP, 1990), 204.
17. Mark Jones and Karl Kroeber (eds), *Willliam Wordsworth: Scholarship and Criticism: An Annotated Bibliography* (New York, NY: Garland, 1985), 59.
18. Floyd Stovall, *The Foreground of Leaves of Grass* (Charlottesville, VA: University of Virginia Press, 1974), 242–3.
19. 'The same thoughts and themes ... which Wordsworth treats in his 'Intimations of Immortality', Bryant in his 'Thanatopsis' and in 'The Flood of Years', and Whittier in his pieces, W.W. also treats in Leaves of Grass', writes Whitman in an unpublished note (*Notes and Fragments*, ed. Richard Maurice Bucke, ([1899] rpt, Ontario: A. Talbot, n.d.), 60). In another note Bucke recorded that was obviously a commentary on a specific work, Whitman writes, 'Wordsworth, it seems, is the originator of this kind of poem – followed here by Bryant and others' (112).
20. Annabel Newton, *Wordsworth in Early American Criticism* (Chicago, IL: University of Chicago Press, 1928).
21. Raoul Granqvist, *Imitations as Resistance: Appreciations of English Literature in Nineteenth Century America* (Madison, NJ: Farleigh Dickinson UP, 1995), 121.
22. Floyd Stovall suggests that Whitman did not write reviews of Wordsworth's poems 'because no important new poem or collection of poems was published while he was editor' (*The Foreground*, 238), but this is not the case. In 1846, a revised, seven-volume edition of the original six-volume *Poetical Works of William Wordsworth* was published by Wiley and Putnam, whose books were often reviewed by Whitman at this time. While Whitman edited the *Brooklyn Freeman* and wrote for several other papers in 1849, *The Excursion* was first published in America, as was Henry Tuckerman's important collection of Wordsworth poems – complete with an introductory essay on his life and writings. And when *The Prelude* was published the next year, Whitman was still freelancing for several periodicals.

23. Keith Hanley, *An Annotated Critical Bibliography of William Wordsworth* (London: Prentice Hall, 1995), 5.
24. For example, 'We Are Seven' was issued in several American chapbooks, including an 1836 Philadelphia imprint entitled 'The Little Maid and the Gentleman' (Hanley, *Annotated Critical Bibliography*, 7).
25. Alan G. Hill, 'Wordsworth and his American Friends', *Bulletin of Research in the Humanities* 81, no. 2 (Summer 1978): 146.
26. As Joann Krieg notes in *A Whitman Chronology*, very little is known of Whitman at all for the years 1851 through 1854. Joann P. Krieg, *A Whitman Chronology* (Iowa City, IA: University of Iowa Press, 1998), 23.
27. The Trent Collection holds copies of the following articles, all annotated by Whitman and containing detailed discussions of Wordsworth: 'Recollections of Poets Laureate: Wordsworth and Tennyson' (*American Whig Review*, June 1852; Trent manuscript 166); 'The Prelude' (*American Whig Review*, May 1851; Trent manuscript 163), 'Egotism. As Manifested in the Works and Lives of Great and Small Men' (*Graham's Magazine*, March 1845; Trent manuscript 180), 'Dies Borealis. No. 1' (*Blackwood's Edinburgh Magazine*, June 1849; Trent manuscript 179). Several other Trent holdings contain mention of Wordsworth as well. The New York Public Library's Berg Collection holds Whitman's annotated copy of a review entitled 'William Wordsworth', from the *American Whig Review*, July 1851. Considering Whitman's disorganized record keeping and his occasional widespread clean-up attempts, the survival of so many clippings exclusively about Wordsworth is indicative of a keen – and lifelong – interest.
28. Whitman's notes can be found on page 457 of the article, which is manuscript 163 in the Trent Collection.
29. See Katherine Molinoff's monograph, *An Unpublished Whitman Manuscript: The Record Book of the Smithtown Debating Society 1837–1838* (Brooklyn, NY: Comet, 1941), 5.
30. 'Wordsworth's Sonnets on the Punishment of Death', a reprint of and critical commentary upon the poems, was published in March 1842's *United States Magazine and Democratic Review*, 272–88.
31. *Notebooks and Unpublished Prose Manuscripts*, ed. Edward F. Grier (6 vols, New York, NY: New York UP, 1984), I, 101.
32. James Woodress (ed.), *Critical Essays on Walt Whitman* (Boston, MA: G.K. Hall, 1983), 68.
33. Ezra Pound, 'What I Feel About Walt Whitman', *American Literature* 27 (1955): 59.
34. Strangely enough, 'little' was the original word chosen by Coleridge, who wrote the stanza for Wordsworth. But this fact is only supplied by Isabella Fenwick's note, written down in 1843 and available first in Moxon's edition of *Poetical Works* (1857). Since Whitman could not have known of the original wording in 1846, his use of it seems coincidental – though one is given cause to wonder if Fenwick's note was made available to the public in an edition of Wordsworth's work that has escaped notice.
35. 'My Boys and Girls' is published in *Walt Whitman: The Early Poems and the Fiction*, ed. Thomas L. Brasher (New York, NY: New York UP, 1963), 248–50.
36. The review, included in the second issue of 1855's *Leaves of Grass*, can be found in Kenneth Price's *Walt Whitman: The Contemporary Reviews* (Cambridge: Cambridge UP, 1996), 8.
37. Thomas McFarland, 'The Wordsworthian Rigidity' in *William Wordsworth: Modern Critical Views*, ed. Harold Bloom (New York, NY: Chelsea House, 1985), 156.

38. Though the poem was sometimes ridiculed in intellectual circles, 'We Are Seven' appealed to the American public's taste for sentimentality and rustic simplicity. Joseph Dennie, one of America's most influential men of letters, recognized the appeal of 'We Are Seven' and published it in the *Gazette of the United States* in 1800; 'We Are Seven' was thus one of the first of Wordsworth's poems available to American readers, printed in Dennie's journal two years before the appearance of an American edition of *Lyrical Ballads*. See Leon Howard, 'Wordsworth in America', *Modern Language Notes* 48 (1933): 360. The poem was popular enough to be issued in several unauthorized chapbooks, including an 1836 Philadelphia imprint under the name of 'The Little Maid and the Gentleman' (Hanley, *Annotated Critical Bibliography*, 7).

8
The Wordsworthian Cast of Dickinson's Romantic Heritage

Richard E. Brantley

Anglo-American Romanticism runs the gamut from rational empiricism and the scientific method, through theistic, rather than Deistic, natural religion, to immediate, as distinct from traditional, revelation.[1] For example, such an Anglo-American triptych of Late Romantic writers as Carlyle, Tennyson, and Emerson at once emphasizes inductive reasoning – that is, what Wordsworth's most strictly empirical mood calls 'sense, conducting to ideal form' (*TP*, 1850, XIV, 76) – and highlights the spiritual sense. I have previously described the latter as 'passivity at first, activity at last, the physical senses as analogies to spiritual insight, and, most intriguingly perhaps, the physical senses as both harbingers and accompaniments of at once transcendent and immanent truth' (*Anglo-American Antiphony*, 230). Now, my philosophical and religious contextualizings of Anglo-American writers shade over into reading the poetry of Emily Dickinson (1830–86). Her High-to-Late Romantic forebears and peers, without being culpably particular take both their sensationalist epistemology and their testimonial heart-religion *straight*, at least by comparison with the slant truth-telling[2] to be found throughout *her* Late Romanticism. (They even gravitate towards the goal of synthesis, as distinct from remaining true to their best standard of intellectual, spiritual and imaginative receptivity – namely, 'being in uncertainties, Mysteries, doubts, without any irritable reaching after fact & reason'.)[3] Dickinson does not so much simply cultivate '*Negative Capability*' as choose to 'dwell' within the positive 'Possibility –' (Dickinson, 466, 1) of the synthesizing process itself. Still, she is not all that 'anxious' about Wordsworth, I argue[4] – instead, the spiritual as well as natural vision of her chief precursor nurtures her wisest tone, and perhaps even inspires her most optimistic import. Her art is all the more accessible, and perhaps even all the subtler, for this constructive influence.

Dickinson, specifically, 'see[s] into the life of things' (*LB* 'Tintern Abbey' 50) – that is, again to apply the words of Wordsworth to her case, she exercises her spiritual as well as natural vision in 'the world / Of all of us, the place in which, in the end, / We find our happiness, or not at all' (*TP*, 1850,

X, 725–7). The triangle of empirical philosophy, evangelical religion and Romantic literature informs all that the Anglo-American century from 1770 to 1870 found resonant not only in what Wordsworth elegizes as 'the *burden* of the mystery' (*LB* 'Tintern Abbey', 39; emphasis added) but also in what he praises as mystery itself. Carlyle, Tennyson and Emerson, on the one hand, intone their Late Romantic version of what Wordsworth feels as tragedy – that is, as 'the heavy and the weary weight / Of all this unintelligible world' (*LB* 'Tintern Abbey', 40–1). On the other hand, they celebrate their Late Romantic experience of what Wordsworth receives as comedy – that is, as 'another gift, / Of aspect more sublime; that blessed mood, / In which the burden of the mystery, / ... / Is *lighten'd*' (*LB* 'Tintern Abbey', 37–9, 42; emphasis added). Similarly, insofar as Dickinson earns for herself the vocabulary of her 1789 personae, this poet of flesh and blood is as much a lyricist of comedy and of tragicomedy as a maker of satire or a bard of tragedy. Her poetry, modulating from epistemology (narrowly so called) to the twin-experiential realms of philosophy and religion, realizes both natural and spiritual progress towards all manner of other-ness. She does not so much suspect 'false' consciousness, after the manner of Marx, Nietzsche or Freud,[5] as expect truth, grace and joy, like Locke, Wesley and Edwards. Her achievements of truth-seeking, and perhaps even her wisely passive (*LB*, 'Expostulation and Reply', 24) receptivity to the influxes of grace and the surprises of joy, are more than merely modest in that her still-imitable combination of watchfulness with openness enhances the 'high argument', ('Prospectus' to *The Recluse*, 71) the innovative, communitarian sublimity, of her more than merely Miltonic imagination.

As a consequence, just as Dickinson's 'obscurity' can be 'palpable',[6] so too can her mystery be urgent. Her love-producing, as well as simply awe-inspiring, collapsing of nature into spirit, and vice versa, on her pilgrimage of art, if not of life, 'calls us to the things of this world',[7] which, from her Late Romantic perspective, include such 'fruits of the Spirit'[8] as faith, hope, grace and joy. Thus, although 'the lady whom the people call the *Myth*'[9] remains so subjective as to seem solipsistic, and although she can be so reclusive as to seem isolated,[10] the paradox of her solitude is, nevertheless, that she sets herself apart from the world in order to apprehend it. She participates, thereby, in the Anglo-American Romantic colloquy of experience and faith. As I fill in some of the background to her 1789 poems, and as I develop readings, I name or allude to Wordsworth in each one of my paragraphs. It is not so much that Dickinson works with his very words and phrases as that she breathes in the atmosphere to which he gives his expression, and which, for that matter, bears his signature. Building, in particular, on the spiritualized as well as 'naturalized imagination'[11] that I have consistently endeavoured to locate among such High-to-Late Romantic writers of the Anglo-American world as Wordsworth and Emerson, Dickinson absorbs, alters and distils their broadly experiential dialectic. The Anglo-American

Romantic tenet that sense-based reason is not only analogous to spirit but also part of it primes Dickinson's 'soul-competency',[12] which, in turn, underlies her more Late Romantic than premodern art.

I

Harold Bloom, who comments on everything, has pronounced: 'She had the best mind of all our poets, early and late'.[13] But Dickinson had the best heart of all our poets, too. What her first reviewer, Arlo Bates, admires as her *emotional thought* is what Richard B. Sewall, her most thorough biographer, praises as her 'ideas felt on the pulses, in the bloodstream'.[14] Sewall echoes Wordsworth's 'sensations sweet, / Felt in the blood, and felt along the heart, / And passing even into my purer mind, / With tranquil restoration', (*LB*, 'Tintern Abbey', 29–31), thus suggesting that the emphasis on both *mind* and *heart* that defines British Romanticism must also energize Dickinson's 'upheavals of thought'.[15] I would only add that she contributes all her strength of mind, *soul*, and heart to Romantic Anglo-America, as well as simply to what Bloom calls 'the Western canon'.[16] Her fusion finds perhaps its most inclusive antecedent in such *spiritual* phrasings as Wordsworth's 'sensations *sweet*', '*purer* mind', and 'tranquil *restoration*' (*LB*, 'Tintern Abbey', 28, 30, 31; emphasis added).

Wordsworth, specifically, hovers near Dickinson's dramatic as well as lyrical combination of the spirit of sceptical counter-interpretation with a heart-felt sense of traditional presence. Wordsworth's most strictly sceptical mood, on the one hand, actually prefers 'the world / Of all of us' to the blandishments of any transcendental realm. Dickinson, similarly, positively celebrates 'The Fact that Earth is Heaven – / Whether Heaven is Heaven or not' (Dickinson, 1435, 1–2). On the other hand, Wordsworth's most strictly transcendental mood declares that 'trailing clouds of glory do we come / From God, who is our home' ('Ode: Intimations of Immortality', 64–5). Similarly, Dickinson's homebody-ness reflects a certain *contemptus mundi* of her own. Most characteristically, perhaps, just as Wordsworth bares his 'Romantic Religion'[17] on the *tabula rasa* of his poetry, so too does Dickinson quite thoroughly subscribe to the broadly experiential criterion of both truth and value. Thus following Blake to 'cleanse the doors' of her 'perception'[18] of both a world elsewhere and 'the world / Of all of us', she cultivates, without necessarily valuing process over results, Wordsworth's most thoroughly idealistic mood of 'Effort, and expectation, and desire, / And something evermore about to be' (*TP*, 1850, VI, 608–9). Dickinson's personae, accordingly, as though they were so many amateur 'Scientist[s] of Faith' (Dickinson, 1261, 12), put the very doctrine of immortality to the test of their experience, which, somewhat after the manner of Wordsworth's 'intimations' of immortality, offers a muted, yet reasonable, hope-against-hope for the afterlife.

Let me show, as an initial reading harking back to Wordsworth's 'Ode: Intimations of Immortality' (1802–04), just how experience and faith operate in such a signature lyric or miniature poetic manifesto of Dickinson's Late Romantic imagination as Poem 373, which, above all, attests to everlasting life:

This World is not conclusion.
A Species stands beyond –
Invisible, as Music –
But positive, as Sound –
It beckons, and it baffles –
Philosophy, don't know –
And through a Riddle, at the last –
Sagacity, must go –
To guess it, puzzles scholars –
To gain it, Men have borne
Contempt of Generations
And Crucifixion, shown –
Faith slips – and laughs, and rallies –
Blushes, if any see –
Plucks at a twig of Evidence –
And asks a Vane, the way –
Much Gesture from the Pulpit –
Strong Hallelujahs roll –
Narcotics cannot still the Tooth
That nibbles at the soul –

Debate centres on whether the persona's faith *survives* her experience. Cynthia Griffin Wolff observes 'the systematic way [the poem] examines the leakage and finally the loss of faith'.[19] Christopher Benfey suggests that the poem 'could almost be a gloss on Emerson's "Montaigne; or, The Skeptic"' (1846).[20] Jane Donohue Eberwein, with particular pertinence to my interests here, emphasizes how 'the hope of immortality [in these lines] finds insufficient supports in [such] human wisdom' as science, philosophy and theology.[21] Lawrence Buell goes so far as to conclude that the persona of Poem 373 'is just as aware of the precariousness of doctrinal structures as Emerson, but she feels the problems and possibilities of her position more keenly because she sees these structures both as all-important and as bankrupt'.[22] David Porter, similarly, thinks that the poem illustrates 'the absence of a controlling design'.[23] Nevertheless, Ben Kimpel finds that 'this poem in every respect is ... a parallel of Augustine's *Confessions* ... Basic to this poem is a confident affirmation that there is an order of reality which is other than the world, and is transcendent of it in the sense that it is "beyond" it'.[24]

The insight closest to my own view is that of Daniel J. Orsini, who observes, 'Obviously, the poem never proves the narrator's initial thesis, but it does at least spare her religious beliefs, since the evidences of the senses, of science, appear no more conclusive than her lofty spiritual yearnings'.[25] What the poet elsewhere calls 'Sweet skepticism of the Heart' (Dickinson, 1438, 1) equates here to experience that includes both doubt and faith. The persona's *un*systematic questioning is not so much the 'leakage' of faith as the *true sign* thereof. Absence, for her, does not so much signify that God is dead as reveal that the Unknowable *is* God. If it is too much to speak of the persona's 'confident affirmation', then her religious beliefs are surely more than merely 'spared'. 'The evidences of the senses' and of 'her lofty spiritual yearnings', after all, are alike inconclusive and *con*clusive – that is, not so much clouded as enriched by her experience. It is as though, for her, 'the meanest flower that blows' (*WP*, 'Ode: Intimations of Immortality', 202) can give more moment-by-moment than merely momentary 'Intimations of Immortality'.

Thus, despite the faintly satirical, constructively sceptical edge to Poem 373, its outlook stands as guardedly optimistic, if not, for that matter, as relatively robust and untroubled. Although scholarship here is of little avail against enigmas of the spirit, and although philosophy here is of no avail in solving the riddle of immortality, the humble, sense-based reason of inductive, sensationalist epistemology is, nevertheless, of considerable avail here in all matters of experiential faith, including 'intimations' of immortality. 'Faith' that 'Plucks at a twig of Evidence – / And asks a Vane, the way –' is not just analogous to, but even fully employs, the physical senses. 'Faith' that 'slips –' but 'laughs, and rallies –' is schooled in contingencies, as well as simply sustained by grace. The very hope of heaven takes its rise and footing, as well as simply its bearings, from experience, for, just as the 'Species ... beyond –', though 'Invisible', remains 'positive, as Sound –', so too does it beckon, or remain positive, as vision. Therefore, although the persona is not so certain of either truth or value as rationalists are of the mind's lordship, she is, nevertheless, at least as confident of the quasi-Darwinian, as well as simply heavenly, 'Species' as logical positivists are of empirical knowledge. (After all, just as she 'hears' loved ones who have crossed over, so too does her Darwinian language for life after death suggest continuing 'sight' of them, as well.) Accordingly, since not even institutional religion (called the opiate of the masses) can calm her spiritual insistence, the ache of her painful desire for transcendence constitutes not so much her passionate inference of God as her clamorous longing for eternity. She holds both tough- and tender-mindedly, as well as simply nostalgically, not only to the High Romantic 'faith that all which we behold / Is full of blessings' (*LB* 'Tintern Abbey', 134–5) but also to High Romantic 'Intimations of Immortality'.

II

The Wordsworthian cast of Dickinson's Romantic heritage undergirds the *constructive* scepticism whereby her poetic method *gives rise* to the almost more than merely natural apperceptions of her poetic faith. *This* faith, if not the genuine religion in her faith per se, emerges from her Late Romantic imagination as an unscathed prop, and perhaps even as an unattenuated mainstay, of her mind, soul and heart. Although her premodern mode toughens her tone, and although her postmodern intimations undermine her import, her doubt/faith dialectic draws energy from, and perhaps even abides in, the broadly experiential, spiritual as well as natural vision of Anglo-American Romanticism. Her art, in my judgement, centres on a point closer to High Romanticism than to High Modernism, notwithstanding her prescience. Her intimations of *immortality*, after all, are a far cry from both the midnight-worshiping *death*-theme of her premodern mode[26] and the outright nihilism of her *postmodern* intimations.

Dickinson's 'postexperiential perspective',[27] to be sure, is a riddle for her readers to puzzle over, if not exactly to be diverted by. Aftermath, for her, can seem like dissolved sugar, or like a bird either featherless or too fat to fly: 'Too happy Time dissolves itself / And leaves no remnant by– / 'Tis Anguish not a Feather hath / Or too much weight to fly–' (Dickinson, 1182). The poet, moreover, has learned enough from her experience not only to articulate 'Proverbs of Hell'[28] but also to substitute them for the outmoded, greeting-card-like sentimentality of such received wisdom as 'Time heals all wounds':

> They say that "Time assuages" –
> Time never did assuage –
> An actual suffering strengthens
> As Sinews do, with Age –
>
> Time is a Test of Trouble –
> But not a Remedy –
> If such it prove, it prove too
> There was no Malady – (861)

The speaker here, in the middle stages of her postexperience, does not claim to know much, and she conveys ambiguity concerning whether human suffering merely gets worse, or whether we get stronger the worse our suffering becomes. Without a doubt, however, she is sentient enough, if I may apply to her case the words of Shelley, 'to repeal / Large codes of fraud', if not of 'woe'[29] – that is, to defamiliarize cliché by means of 'craft or sullen art'.[30] It is as though she knows, with Hopkins, that her own 'cries' have become 'a chief / Woe, world-sorrow',[31] or that they have matured, like those of Wordsworth, into 'Thoughts that do often lie too deep for tears' (*WP* 'Ode: Intimations of Immortality', 203). It is almost as though she would now no longer even want the merely facile consolation of nostrums about the passage of time. It is as though she would exclaim with Wordsworth, and in a vein of self-correction similar to his, 'Through what power, / Even for the least division of an hour, / Have I been so beguiled as to be blind / To my most grievous loss!'(*WP* 'Surprised by Joy', 6–9).

Within the walls of Dickinson's postexperiential prison, notwithstanding her suffering there, 'moments of escape' (Dickinson, 360, 11) testify to the persisting possibility that love will continue to sustain her, perhaps even after she has apparently lost it. That is why 'A Prison gets to be a friend –', or 'A Geometric Joy –', to the point that 'The Liberty we knew' is 'avoided – like a Dream –' (Dickinson, 456, 16, 29–30). Or, as Wordsworth puts it, 'Nuns fret not at their convent's narrow room' ('Prefatory Sonnet', 1). I have in mind here, moreover, the freedom that exists, paradoxically enough, *because of* the prison walls of Byron's 'Prisoner of Chillon', or of Beethoven's *Fidelio*. This kind of freedom, in the case of Dickinson, is the choice to do something, anything, in defiance of postexperiential despair, and on the assumption that the fact of doing trumps whether action is effectual:

> At leisure is the Soul
> That gets a staggering Blow –
> The Width of Life – before it spreads
> Without a thing to do –
>
> It begs you give it Work –
> But just the placing Pins –
> Or humblest Patchwork – Children do –
> To Help it's [*sic*] Vacant Hands –(683)

These lines concern not so much 'the woman in her dealings with Power'[32] as the woman poised for action, no matter how unspectacular.

Dickinson's broad concept of experience, then, remains crucial to her aesthetic procedures and principles. Regardless of whether any close correlation obtains between her life and her art, her personae are other-directed. Somewhat after the manner of Wordsworth's 'Love of Nature Leading to Love of Man', (*TP*, VIII) one of her speakers confesses, 'I thought that nature was enough / Till Human nature came / And that the other did absorb / As Parallax a Flame –'. Thus the impersonal yields to the personal. The personal, in turn, grows towards the Other: 'Of Human nature just aware / There added the Divine' (Dickinson, 1269, 1–9). This speaker joins nature to God.

Roger Lundin, to be sure, in his account of *Emily Dickinson and the Art of Belief* (1998), contrasts 'the muteness of nature [in Dickinson's poetry] with the talkative role it had long assumed in romantic thought'. Whereas Emerson had taught that 'the ancient, "Know thyself" and the modern precept, "study nature", become at last one maxim', Dickinson, for her part, 'struggled to believe that mind and nature were knit together as Emerson had said they were, but she could not do so'.[33] Such lines as 'We pass, and [nature] abides, / We conjugate Her Skill / While She creates and federates / Without a syllable –' (Dickinson, 798, 5–8) reveal the poet's larger fear that 'nature', as Lundin puts it, 'goes on with her business, saying nothing intelligible to us, even as we labor to interpret her' (153). Nevertheless, as indicated by Dickinson's Prose Fragment 119, the poet entertains alternately, if not at once, the difficulty and the possibility of knowing Nature well:

> We must travel abreast with Nature if we want to know her, but where shall be obtained the Horse –
>
> A something overtakes the mind – we do not hear it coming[34]

The first paragraph implies that we lack the means of satisfying our desire for intimacy with Nature. The second suggests that nature herself, whenever she comes abreast of us in her own good time and way, supplies that very intimacy. The two paragraphs, taken together, suggest that Dickinson not only rises to the challenge of solving Nature's riddle but also cultivates the 'wise passiveness' (*LB* 'Expostulation and Reply', 24) of leaving the riddle unsolved. Her latter strategy, paradoxically enough, is a no less efficacious means of acquiring natural knowledge and of strengthening spiritual belief.

On one occasion, as though Dickinson were announcing the divorce of seeing from knowing, she declares that 'Not seeing, still we know -' (Dickinson, 1566, 1). Thus, in an echo of I Peter 1: 8 ('Whom having not seen, ye love; in whom, though now ye see him not, yet believing, ye rejoice with joy unspeakable and full of glory'), the poet 'is now able to accept belief in an afterlife without proof'.[35] On almost all occasions when she is *not* referring to the afterlife, however, and perhaps even on some occasions when she *is*, she reveals that, as far as she is concerned, there can be no substitute for *seeing* – that is, for being in the presence of the thing one knows. Consider, if you will, the opening lines of Poem 1028, which, arguably enough, operate along a continuum joining nature to spirit: 'Who *saw* no Sunrise cannot say / The Countenance 'twould be – / Who *guess* at seeing, guess at loss / Of the Ability' (emphasis added). (The wistful implication here is that seeing will be believing even in 'that great getting-up morning bye and bye'.) '*Intimations* of Immortality', albeit necessarily at the lowest possible threshold of experience, whether of the natural or of the spiritual kind, or whether of both kinds at once, offer more comfort in the here and now than any merely abstract doctrine of immortality could ever begin to provide. Meanwhile, 'What we see we know somewhat / Be it but a little – / What we don't surmise we do / Though it shows so fickle' (Dickinson, 1272, 1–4). This poem 'discusses the conflict between empiricism and supposition, but supposition's daring, even criminal procedure is the subject'.[36] 'Even criminal' is overstated, perhaps, since Dickinson might well be willing to forgive the all too human tendency to *act* as though we see, whether we see or not.

As soon after *On the Origin of Species* (1859) as 1865, to be sure, Poem 995 takes God to task:

> The missing All, prevented Me
> From missing minor Things.
> If nothing larger than a World's
> Departure from a Hinge
> Or Sun's Extinction, be observed
> 'Twas not so large that I
> Could lift my Forehead from my work
> For Curiosity.

The speaker here, depicting a more *preventing* God of extinctions than any Wesleyan God of *prevenient* grace, suggests that 'The missing All' is Himself extinct, but she only *feigns* indifference to the absence, or to the death, of God. Just as a range of thinkers from Coleridge and Emerson to Max Weber, Paul Ricoeur and Richard Rorty feels deeply the loss of the external world as the language of God, so too does Dickinson attempt, yet fail, to break the silence of Being and of God (Lundin 43–7). Poems as early as numbers 340 and 347, and as late as numbers 610, 778 and 1072, as Lundin points out, lack Wordsworth's confidence in hearing 'this mighty sum / Of things for ever speaking' (*LB* 'Expostulation and Reply', 24). Nature, in Dickinson's time, becomes, if not what Lundin calls an 'endless play of signs without design', then, surely, what he phrases as 'a mere trope of human desire', as distinct from a clear type of God's loving intentions (151–3). Nevertheless, while both Darwin's science and the Civil War were undoubtedly the necessary, if not sufficient, conditions for the force with which Dickinson foretold both modernism and postmodernism, her recognition of the split between science and religion was of long standing. It included the same sort of creative tension, as distinct from antipodal opposition, that produced the rich strangeness of her lifelong 'art of belief'.

Dickinson's 'art of belief', I suggest, comes not so much despite, as because of, her disbelief. As she declares, 'We both believe and disbelieve a hundred times an Hour, which keeps believing nimble – '(*Letters of Emily Dickinson*, III, 728).[37] I maintain, indeed, that her oscillation between, if not her dialectic of, poetic method and poetic faith obtains at any given moment of her career, whether before or after the *Origin of Species*, or whether before, after, or during the Civil War. She never stops 'dwell[ing] in Possibility –' of synthesis, in large measure because she resists all attempts to *disenchant* 'the world / Of all of us'.

Poem 1475, written about 1878, is perhaps the most explicit case in point. Here Dickinson pits all the sweetness of her Late Romantic imagination against her chief postmodern premonition – namely, the overweening proclivity of 'man-unkind' to debunk whatever comes within his ken:

Whoever disenchants
A single Human soul
By failure or irreverence
Is guilty of the whole –

As guileless as a Bird
As graphic as a Star
Till the suggestion sinister
Things are not what they are –

Thus, although I yield to no one in my admiration for the bravery with which Dickinson contemplates nothingness ('"Tis so appalling it exhilarates', 341, 1), I spurn, nevertheless, the temptation to focus too exclusively on poems like no. 1581, which, haunting Lundin, nags at his efforts to establish Dickinson's belief (4, 34, 78, 134, 149):

Those – dying then,
Knew where they went –
They went to God's Right Hand –
That Hand is amputated now
And God cannot be found –

The abdication of Belief
Makes the Behavior small –
Better an ignis fatuus
Than no illume at all –

The insufficiently emphasized final four lines suggest that even the foolish fire of combustible marsh gas might yield to what Wordsworth would call 'light that never was, on sea or land' (*WP* 'Elegaic Stanzas: Suggested by a Picture of Peele Castle', 15) – that is, inward illumination.

Dickinson's persona appears, by corollary, to believe that experience keeps her ideals trustworthy, and perhaps even her goals true. If, towards the end of the poet's career, she does not exactly maintain so positive a view of empirical procedures that they emerge as her necessary and sufficient basis for progress in the world, then her poems, at any rate, never quite renounce her faith in experience. If she comes, at last, to fear that Experiment would not be Faithful, or that natural religion would be unavailing, then her poems hold out hope, none the less, for an experience of faith. Regardless of whether she wants to 'Ring in the Christ that is to be',[38] or to 'forge in the smithy of [her] soul the uncreated conscience of the race',[39] she poises herself, as Wordsworth does, between nature and spirit. Regardless of whether she effects her version of Tennyson's, or of de Chardin's, enterprise of reconciling, however vaguely, and in however anachronistic a fashion, evolution with religion,[40] she stakes out, in any case, her opposing positions, and perhaps even gropes towards synthesis through the spiritual sense.

Mediating, then, between Dickinson's premodern tone and her Late Romantic import, I seek to tilt the balance of critical emphasis in favour of the latter. I cannot help thinking, in this connection, of the last stanza of Frost's 'Neither Out Far Nor In Deep' (1936), which, insofar as it is more post-Romantic than High Modern, applies instinctively to Dickinson's poetry: 'They cannot look out far. / They cannot look in deep. / But when was that ever a bar / To any watch they keep?' Randall Jarrell, in an anti-Romantic mood of reading this stanza, observes that 'it would be hard to find anything more unpleasant to say about people'. Along Romantic lines, however, and against the quasi-postmodern notion of Frost as a curmudgeon, Brad Leithauser queries, in answer to Jarrell, 'Isn't [Frost] saying that, as seekers after the truth, we're to be commended for our immoderate appetites, rather than damned for our modest achievements?'[41] Thus, even the 'Great Old Modern' admits of Romantic interpretation, for 'Neither Out Far Nor In Deep' seems finally consistent with Blake's perception that 'More! More! Is the cry' of Man and that 'less than All cannot satisfy'.[42] For her part, Dickinson the Romantic out-quests other Romantics. Like Wordsworth, who recognizes that, 'As it sometimes chanceth, from the might / Of joy in minds that can no further go, / As high as we have mounted in delight / In our dejection do we sink as low' (*WP* 'Resolution and Independence', 22–5, 114), she grasps the manic-depressive proximity of happiness to sadness. Her 'hope', however, perhaps even stronger than his, is almost never 'unwilling to be fed' (*TP*, 1850, VI, 605–7).

Dickinson's hope in Poem 314, perhaps most notably, not only endures against all odds but also poises itself to soar:

> "Hope" is the thing with feathers –
> That perches in the soul –
> And sings the tune without the words –
> And never stops – at all –
>
> And sweetest – in the Gale – is heard –
> And sore must be the storm –

That could abash the little Bird
That kept so many warm –

I've heard it in the chillest land –
And on the strangest Sea –
Yet – never – in Extremity,
It asked a crumb – of me.

These lines, if they do not exactly speak of the persona's happiness, express nothing more pessimistic than hope-against-hope. They remain sufficiently Romantic at least and, at most, quintessentially so, for 'the thing with feathers –' is 'perhaps ... even every human's potential for music and poetry, brave stays against the brooding dark' (Wolff 478). (Standing 'behind Dickinson's famous poem' is a pictorial emblem 'available to her at the time', which, shades of Coleridge, shows a drowning man clinging to an albatross.)[43] According to my Romantic interpretation, the spiritual sense of Dickinson's 1789 personae blends their knowledge with their faith. Their more moment-by-moment than merely momentary stay against confusion – that is, their natural/spiritual dialectic of experience – helps their unbelief. Indeed, their Wordsworthian hope-against-hope is for spiritual as well as natural *blessing* from 'this mighty sum / Of things for ever speaking'. Dickinson's 'something evermore about to be', therefore, is not primarily in the nature of either an avant-garde or a heavenly reward. Instead, her great, if somewhat vague, 'expectation' is of 'something' both subtly and simply in synchrony with the rich and strange auspices of the here and now.

III

'Lyric poetry', declares Adam Kirsch, should not so much 'cede narrative and drama' to 'an acute ability to consider consciousness' as 'attempt to force the mind's half-tones and shadows out into the bright light of art'. It is as though 'nothing can have any value as art that is not rigorously retrieved and patterned, and thereby brought back into the world' from whence art comes in the first place.[44] Dickinson, notwithstanding her fey sobriquet as 'the lady whom the people call the *Myth*', is by no means so single-minded in her focus on her consciousness as either to neglect the narrative and dramatic aspects of her art or to overemphasize her mind's half-tones and shadows. Indeed, the patterns of her poems are culturally powerful in part because they arise from the well-grounded stuff of her life, whether 'Felt in the blood, and felt along the heart', or whether 'passing even into [her] purer mind / With tranquil restoration'. The naturally experiential 'world / Of all of us' and spiritually experiential 'moments in the being / Of the eternal Silence' (WP 'Ode: Intimations of Immortality' 155–6) inform the synthesizing imagination of the Myth of Amherst.

Dickinson's 'Compound Vision –' (Dickinson, 830, 9) – that is, her coordination of the physical senses with the spiritual sense – 'Distills amazing sense / From Ordinary Meanings –' (Dickinson, 446, 3–4). The reader expects different capitalization here – namely, 'Amazing Sense / From ordinary meanings –'. Dickinson, however, reverses expectations. She suggests that, far from having to transmogrify the ordinary in order to render it amazing, she finds it so. To apply the words of Wordsworth to her case, 'meadow, grove, and stream, / The earth, and every common sight' seem 'Appareled', for her, 'in celestial light', and perhaps even suffused, for her, with 'The glory and the freshness of a dream' (*WP* 'Ode: Intimations of Immortality', 2, 4–5). The supernal seems accessible to her, and, to 'dwell in Possibility -' indeed, the commonplace and the miraculous seem able at any given point on her pilgrimage of art, if not of life, to interpenetrate both deeply and well.

Dickinson's personae, accordingly, 'burn' not so much with the 'hard, gem-like flame' of a decadent, premodern sensibility[45] as with her own Late Romantic desire for the 'obscure', yet 'palpable', consummation of the here and now with the noumenon. She is not so much enamoured of philosophical conundra nor so much given to ideas of sensation as intent on the ideals thereof whereby she emerges, on balance, as both 'impatient ... to share the transport' of everyday grace and 'Surprised by joy' thereof (*WP* 'Surprised by Joy', 1–2). If only by dint of her preternatural effort on grounds of her Spartan, yet intense, existence, and perhaps even of her strenuous, yet abundant, experience, her personae all but reconcile their knowledge with their belief. They are especially self-consistent where they do not so much value destination, whether despaired of, wished for, supposed, hoped for, or finally trusted in, as pilgrimage itself.

Dickinson's 'Compound Vision –', then, is not so much *mazed* by her way of knowing as *a*mazed by her way of believing. Although she tempers the hard drive towards synthesis that such an Anglo-American pairing of Late Romantic writers as Carlyle with Emerson favours, and although she is more apt to keep her epistemological rigor and her spiritual autobiography in play than to harmonize them, her personae compound, nevertheless, method with faith. The poet adds one part sensationalist epistemology and one part theological free will to one part synthesizing imagination. It is as though Keats's faith in life's relevance to art were uppermost in Dickinson's mind: 'I am certain of nothing [writes Keats] but of the holiness of the Heart's affections and the truth of Imagination – '.[46] Dickinson's art, therefore, is in creative tension with Anglo-American Romanticism. Her 'Effort, and expectation, and desire' are aimed not so much at generating mere meaning-after-meaning as at discovering truth, grace and joy.

Modern painter Piet Mondrian, according to Jed Perl, not only entrusts 'the spare language of an ascetic' to his 'unsparing, unsentimental canvases' but also 'shapes his overflowing romantic emotions'. Thus, just as Mondrian exhibits 'stand-alone individuality and emotional complexity' at the same time that he effects his version of Prufrockian withdrawal from experience,[47] so too do the broadly experiential vision of Dickinson's Late Romantic imagination and the postexperiential perspective of her premodern mode coexist. If I am reading her poems aright, they are every bit as deeply rooted in her binational past as justly ascendant in our present. They are ascendant in our present, indeed, *because* they are rooted in her past. Her premodern mode is every bit as demythologizing as F.C. McGrath claims Modernism is.[48] Her Late Romantic imagination, moreover, can be as iconoclastic as Bloom claims High Romanticism is.[49] Nevertheless, her art can be as *tender* as I claim the art of Wordsworth, or of Emerson, can be. And since her poetry flourishes on the British as well as American ground of a *rigorous* as well as hopeful, *empirical* as well as expectant Romantic method, her Late Romantic imagination is no less Romantic for being as *tough* as I claim Anglo-American Romanticism can be.

'Not the fruit of experience, but experience itself', Walter Pater observes, 'is the end of life'.[50] For Dickinson, the point of living is not so much to achieve synthesis as to practise dialectic, with experience as her polestar of both truth and value. It is not so much that she gives due weight to the experience of doubting the validity of experience itself as that she is willing to engage with the actual and 'Surprised by joy' of the ideal. Her poems not only acknowledge 'all the unhealthy and o'erdarkened ways / Made for our searching'[51] but also bear witness to the grace of our becoming.[52] Her personae, perhaps even where they cannot hold on to their experience of faith, never altogether lose their faith in experience. Indeed, if only by corollary with what I have described as 'the empirical/evangelical dialectic of Anglo-American Romanticism', her poetry progresses at once towards more truth than falsehood and towards more joy than sorrow. With the both/and logic of her Late Romantic imagination, she resists the nothing-comes-of-nothing mentality of her premodern mode, and perhaps even trumps the anti-experiential propensity of her postmodern intimations.[53] Her more wise and well-earned than merely foolish optimism wins out in her art, if not exactly in her consciousness moment-by-moment.

Dickinson's more Late Romantic than premodern art, above all, not only still bears 'the burden of the mystery' – that is, 'the heavy and the weary weight / Of all this unintelligible world' – but also still resonates with mystery. She can still inspire, thereby, her readers to declare, as Wordsworth inspires her to believe, 'And I have felt / A presence that disturbs me with the joy / Of elevated thoughts; a sense sublime / Of something far more deeply interfused' (*LB* 'Tintern Abbey', 38–40, 93–6). Thus, although Wordsworth testifies that presence disturbs as well as elevates him, his sublime imagination gravitates, nevertheless, towards mystery. Dickinson's poetry, too, is no less tough for being tender, and vice versa. Just as Wordsworth blends thought and style to construct the High Romantic argument that experience is the last, best hope for knowledge-with-belief, so too does Dickinson's life of writing include her essentially Late Romantic theme of natural and spiritual experience. Her broadly experiential vision, as distinct from the postexperiential pessimism of her premodern mode, re-envisions idealism for us, not as warm, fuzzy feeling, nor even necessarily as deep feeling, and certainly not as sentimentality, but, instead, as a deliberately imprecise, practically messy, yet abidingly un-cynical and fully moral hope-against-hope. Without either oversimplifying intellectual problems or underestimating spiritual dilemmas, and certainly without betraying any merely wishful thinking on her part, she remains sufficiently close to her experiential ground of both knowledge and belief to engage the minds, souls and hearts of her readers. She calls upon us to contemplate whatever problems of epistemology, religious methodology or aesthetics might lie near to our hands.

In sum, 'the fascination of what's difficult'[54] about the historical and critical interdisciplinary study to which I remain committed climaxes in the study of Dickinson's art. I have attempted here to apprehend anew the philosophical, religious and literary triangle that I have previously tried to delineate. I have asked here, above all, just how Dickinson the Romantic stands on the broadly experiential common ground between sensationalist epistemology and testimonial heart-religion. She stands there quietly, yet sturdily, with no rigidity. She stands there resolutely, yet resourcefully, after the manner of wily Odysseus, or of resilient Jeremiah, or of both. And, as though her stance there were far and away the most captivating purport of her entire life of writing, she stands ready to move, albeit with more of 'honest doubt' than of 'creeds',[55] and if only in speech acts, toward truth, grace, and joy. Her 'wise passiveness', to reinforce the Wordsworthian cast of Dickinson's Romantic heritage, makes her as much Wordsworth's prime legatee as Whitman's 'self-reliance' makes him Emerson's.

Notes

1. See Richard E. Brantley, *Coordinates of Anglo-American Romanticism: Wesley, Edwards, Carlyle, and Emerson* (Gainesville, FL: UP of Florida, 1993) and Brantley, *Anglo-American Antiphony: The Late Romanticism of Tennyson and Emerson* (Gainesville: UP of Florida, 1994). See also Brantley, *Wordsworth's 'Natural Methodism'* (New Haven, CT: Yale UP, 1975); and Brantley, *Locke, Wesley, and the Method of English Romanticism* (Gainesville, FL: UP of Florida, 1984).
2. Cf. Emily Dickinson, Poem 1263, line 1. Quotations of Dickinson's poems are reprinted by permission of the publishers and Trustees of Amherst College from *The Poems of Emily Dickinson*, ed. Ralph W. Franklin (Cambridge, MA.: Belknap Press of Harvard UP, 1998), Copyright © 1998 by the President and Fellows of Harvard College. Copyright © 1954, 1955, 1979 by the President and Fellows of Harvard College. Hereafter cited parenthetically in the essay by referring to the number of the poem followed by the line number.
3. John Keats to George and Thomas Keats, 21, 27 December 1817.
4. For a different view, see Joanne Feit Diehl, *Dickinson and the Romantic Imagination* (Princeton, NJ: Princeton UP, 1981). See also Harold Bloom, *The Anxiety of Influence* (New York, NY: Oxford UP, 1973).
5. Paul Ricoeur, *Freud and Philosophy*, trans. Denis Savage (Cambridge: Cambridge UP, 1970), 27.

6. John Milton, *Paradise Lost* (1674), II: 406.
7. Richard Wilbur, 'Love Calls Us to the Things of This World' (1955).
8. Gal. 5: 22; Eph. 5: 9. Quotations of the Bible are from the King James Version.
9. Mabel Loomis Todd as quoted in Emily Dickinson, *The Years and Hours of Emily Dickinson*, ed. Jay Leyda (2 vols, New Haven, CT: Yale UP, 1960), II, 357, 376.
10. I have in mind, in particular, Dickinson, Poem 1696: 'There is a solitude of space / A solitude of sea / A solitude of Death, but these / Society shall be / Compared with that profounder site / That polar privacy / A soul admitted to itself –'.
11. Jack Stillinger, 'Imagination and Reality in the Odes of Keats' in *The Hoodwinking of Madeline, and Other Essays on Keats's Poems* (Urbana, IL: University of Illinois Press, 1971), 99–119.
12. I adapt to my purposes the chief latter-day Protestant doctrine of early twentieth-century Southern Baptist master figure E.Y. Mullins, as discussed in Harold Bloom, *The American Religion: The Emergence of the Post-Christian Nation* (New York, NY: Simon & Schuster, 1992), 164–83.
13. Harold Bloom, *The Western Canon: The Books and School of the Ages* (New York, NY: Harcourt Brace, 1994), 300.
14. See Richard B. Sewall, 'Teaching Dickinson: Testimony of a Veteran' in *Approaches to Teaching Dickinson's Poetry*, eds Robin Riley Fast and Christine Mack Gordon (New York, NY: Modern Language Association, 1989). See also Richard B. Sewall, *The Life of Emily Dickinson*, 2 vols (New York, NY: Farrar, Straus & Giroux, 1980).
15. I allude to Martha C. Nussbaum, *Upheavals of Thought: The Intelligence of Emotion* (Cambridge: Cambridge UP, 2001). I have in mind, as well, the emphasis on *emotional intelligence* in both the philosophy and the fiction of Iris Murdoch.
16. Bloom only half-whimsically includes Dickinson among the 26 most authoritative writers in all of western history. See Bloom, *Western Canon*, 291–311.
17. I conflate the pairing in Stephen Prickett's title, *Romanticism and Religion*. His subtitle is *The Tradition of Coleridge and Wordsworth in the Victorian Church* (New York, NY: Cambridge UP, 1976).
18. William Blake, *The Marriage of Heaven and Hell* (1793), plate 14.
19. Cynthia Griffin Wolff, *Emily Dickinson* (Reading, MA: Addison-Wesley, 1988), 269–70, 440.
20. Christopher Benfey, *Emily Dickinson and the Problem of Others* (Amherst, MA: University of Massachusetts Press, 1984), 14, 16.
21. Jane Donohue Eberwein, *Dickinson: Strategies of Limitation* (Amherst, MA: University of Massachusetts Press), 227–8.
22. Lawrence Buell, *New England Literary Culture: From Revolution through Renaissance* (Cambridge: Cambridge UP, 1986), 133–4.
23. David Porter, *Dickinson: The Modern Idiom* (Cambridge, MA: Harvard UP, 1981), 106–7.
24. Ben Kimpel, *Emily Dickinson as Philosopher* (New York, NY: Mellen, 1981), 228–31, 277.
25. Daniel J. Orsini, 'Emily Dickinson and the Romantic Use of Science', *Massachusetts Studies in English* 7.4–8.1 (1981): 57–69, esp. 63–4.
26. I have in mind, in particular, Bloom's insight, 'Dickinson was no worshiper of Midnight, as Yeats was to be' (*Western Canon*, 299).
27. Vivian R. Pollak, *Dickinson: The Anxiety of Gender* (Ithaca, NY: Cornell UP, 1984), 212.
28. Blake, *The Marriage of Heaven and Hell*, plates 7–10.
29. Percy Bysshe Shelley, 'Mont Blanc' (1817), lines 80–1.
30. Dylan Thomas, 'In My Craft or Sullen Art' (1946), line 1.

31. Gerard Manley Hopkins, 'No Worst, There is None' (1885), lines 5–6.
32. Dorothea Steiner, 'Emily Dickinson: Image Patterns and the Female Imagination', *Arbeiten aus Anglistik und Amerikanistik* 6.1 (1981): 57–71, esp. 65.
33. Roger Lundin, *Emily Dickinson and the Art of Belief* (Grand Rapids, MI: William B. Eerdmans, 1998), 153. Lundin quotes from Ralph Waldo Emerson, 'The American Scholar' (1837).
34. Emily Dickinson, *The Letters of Emily Dickinson*, eds Thomas H. Johnson and Theodora Ward (3 vols, Cambridge, MA: Harvard UP, 1958), III, 929.
35. Virginia H. Oliver, *Apocalypse of Green: A Study of Emily Dickinson's Eschatology* (New York, NY: Lang, 1989), 86–7.
36. Suzanne Juhasz, *The Undiscovered Continent: Emily Dickinson and the Space of the Mind* (Bloomington, IN: Indiana UP, 1983), 136–8, 140–1, esp. 137.
37. *Letters of Emily Dickinson*, III, 728. See also James McIntosh, *Nimble Believing: Dickinson and the Unknown* (Anne Arbor, MI: University of Michigan Press, 2000).
38. Alfred, Lord Tennyson, *In Memoriam* (1850) 106: 32.
39. I adapt to my purposes the presiding idea of Stephen Dedalus in James Joyce, *Portrait of the Artist as a Young Man* (1908).
40. See Graham Hough, 'The Natural Theology of *In Memoriam*', *Review of English Studies* 33 (1947): 244–56. See also Eugene R. August, 'Tennyson and Teilhard: The Faith of *In Memoriam*', *PMLA* 84 (1969): 217–26.
41. Brad Leithauser, 'Great Old Modern', *New York Review of Books* 43 (8 August 1996): 42.
42. Blake, *There Is No Natural Religion* (1788), plate b7.
43. Barton Levi St Armand and George Monteiro, 'Dickinson's "'Hope' is the thing with feathers"', *The Explicator*, 47, no. 4 (Summer 1989): 34–7. See also St Armand and Monteiro, 'The Experienced Emblem: A Study of the Poetry of Emily Dickinson' in *Prospects: The Annual of American Cultural Studies*, ed. Jack Salzman (New York, NY: Burt Franklin, 1981), VI, 187–280.
44. Adam Kirsch, 'The Trouble with Lively', *New Republic* (13 July 1999): 39.
45. Walter Pater, 'Conclusion' to *Leonardo da Vinci* (1873).
46. Keats to Benjamin Bailey, 22 November 1817.
47. Jed Perl, 'Absolutely Mondrian', *New Republic* (31 July 1995): 27–32, esp. 27.
48. F.C. McGrath, *The Sensible Spirit: Walter Pater and the Modernist Paradigm* (Gainesville, FL: UP of Florida, 1986).
49. Harold Bloom, *Ruin the Sacred Truths* (Cambridge, MA: Harvard UP, 1989).
50. Pater, 'Conclusion' to *The Renaissance* (1868).
51. Keats, *Endymion: A Poetic Romance* (1817) 1: 10–11.
52. I have in mind, in particular, Poem 401: 'Dare you see a Soul *at the White Heat?* / Then crouch within the door – / Red – is the Fire's common tint – / But when the vivid Ore / Has vanquished Flame's conditions, / It quivers from the Forge / Without a color, but the light / Of unanointed Blaze. / Least Village has it's Blacksmith / Whose Anvil's even ring / Stands symbol for the finer Forge / That soundless tugs – within – / Refining these impatient Ores / With Hammer, and with Blaze / Until the Designated Light / Repudiate the Forge –'.
53. I have in mind, in particular, Poem 760: 'Pain – has an Element of Blank / It cannot recollect / When it began – Or if there were / A time when it was not – / It has no Future – but itself – / It's Infinite contain / It's Past – enlightened to perceive / New Periods – Of Pain'.
54. William Butler Yeats, 'The Fascination of What's Difficult' (1910).
55. Tennyson, *In Memoriam*, 96: 11–12.

9

Wordsworth, Bostonian Chivalry and the Uses of Art

Elizabeth Fay

Tennyson's *Idylls of the King* (1859) and Mark Twain's *Connecticut Yankee* (1889) were two of the most powerful expressions of Victorian medievalism in the nineteenth-century transatlantic cultural imagination. But Tennyson's reverential treatment of Camelot was perhaps more influential, or so thought Mrs Arthur Bell, who in reviewing Edwin Austin Abbey's 1901 mural cycle for the Book Delivery Room of the Boston Public Library, wrote: 'Mr. Abbey's "Quest of the Holy Grail" is as fine a thing in painting as Tennyson's interpretation of the same theme in verse, and is a proof, if proof be needed, of the close kinship between all great thinkers of the Anglo-Saxon race whatever their nationality'.[1] Tennyson in high seriousness and Twain parodically used the medieval as an allegorical space in which to explore themes of disruption and healing, conflict and loyalty, and above all, the uses of chivalry to mediate social ills. Mid-Victorians found chivalry an admirable and highly serious way to undertake social remedies, their admiration stemming from a not-inconsiderable body of literature that had begun to build in the eighteenth century with the interest in gothic architecture by antiquarians like Horace Walpole and the publication of works that elevated the gothic over Grecian styles, such as Richard Hurd's *Letters on Chivalry and Romance* (1762). But one of the most influential publications supporting the medieval aesthetic and its implicit ethical system, if not gothic novels and tragedies, was another volume of British poetry that preceded Tennyson's *Idylls* and that is not usually associated with American or British Victorian chivalry: Wordsworth's and Coleridge's *Lyrical Ballads*.

Victorian chivalry as a form of social consciousness found public expression in a variety of reformist venues, motivated by landmark works such as John Ruskin's programme for gothic architectural design as a way to install social reform in *The Seven Lamps of Architecture* (1849) and *The Stones of Venice* (1851–53). Late nineteenth-century Boston began to be marked by institutional buildings reflecting Ruskin's interpretation of the gothic as a revival of medieval communal relations. Wordsworth, Tennyson and

Ruskin were all important British contributors to the chivalry of Victorian popular culture, but their own motivation begins from a clearer call to reform than that which moved late-Victorian Bostonians. Wordsworth, among other Romantic writers, was responding to the impetus felt in Britain to transform the civic humanism of the Enlightenment into a renewed interest in the morality of the medieval chivalric code.[2] By the time Edwin Austin Abbey was commissioned to paint his fifteen-panel 'Quest for the Holy Grail' for the Boston Public Library – and by the time that private institutions like Harvard University were using chivalric narratives to decorate their buildings, as in the stained glass of Sanders Theatre – educational spaces in the public sphere were conceived of as places to inspire and produce civic-mindedness as a matter of chivalric honour. Lancelot the king's champion, Perceval the gallant knight, Galahad the spiritual questor are all figures for the viewer to adopt for himself, while the grail provides a metaphor for the transformative. Galahad the Virgin Knight leads the eye through the panels as he learns to subject manly endeavour to a mindful passivity that resists bodily seductions and aggressions. The medieval versions of the grail romance, known as the Vulgate cycle, rehearse the exploits and miracles of the Arthurian tales only in order to refocus attention from derring-do to spiritual endeavours, and Abbey further narrows the Vulgate version by focusing on the last five chapters of the story featuring Galahad. Lancelot himself is reduced to an unworthy one in the face of the beautiful purity of youthful resolve. The importance of the Grail story was its usefulness as a spiritual wake-up call to an increasingly decadent court culture, and the signal achievement of the Vulgate's interpolation of the Lancelot stories through the additions of the sangrael and Galahad was to reassert a vigorous and militant Christianity that could sustain both natural and supernatural attacks on, and seductions of, the mortal body. The gendering of Abbey's thematic material and of the viewer's identity match the masculinity associated with public spaces, and the viewer's interpretation of chivalric figures and their stories was clearly meant to initiate a conversionary experience having to do with individual heroism and the needs of the public.

Public visual narratives of knightly quests were meant to inspire; to translate the viewer's internal drive of individualism into the external drive of civics through a chivalric spiritualization of the self. In doing so, I want to argue, these narratives carry out the high purpose of Wordsworth's 1800 Preface to the *Lyrical Ballads*, already implicit in his 1798 poems. In his 1802 revision of the Preface, Wordsworth describes the character of the poet in knightly terms and, I want further to suggest, challenges the reader to understand his medieval-inspired ballads as manly, public-spirited and spiritually elevating. The contract Wordsworth makes with his reader in the Preface mediates the social contract described by Rousseau with the knight's vows to produce an obligation on the reader's part that raises him to a higher level of civic duty than the private act of reading and its associated detachment of the social contract normally convey. It is a verbal contract replicated in the conversion pact that the viewer of Abbey's library murals also experiences; both presume that the reader or viewer is educable, not just in need of help himself, but capable of helping others by rising above his own self-absorption. The reading practises of nineteenth-century public library and university constituencies, with their primary and grammar or writing school preparation for such practise, were conducted under the auspices of this obligation to read for the higher good. And the chances are good that visitors to the Boston Public Library had already read a good selection of Wordsworth's poetry.[3]

I Wordsworth and chivalry in the *Lyrical Ballads*

In order to conceive of the *Lyrical Ballads* in terms other than, or in addition to, our received ones of the volume as exemplifying a new kind of poetry and a revolution in taste, it is necessary to reconsider what 'new' and 'revolutionary' might also mean. For Wordsworth, the reading public too quickly associated the gothic with 'sickly German tragedies', as he terms it in the Preface (*LB* 747), rather than with chivalry and its ethos. If the renewed interest in the gothic as a style and the medieval aesthetic in the prior century was no longer new and revolutionary by 1798, perhaps Wordsworth's use of it for his ballads – a verse form associated with tales of romance and chivalry as much as with the common folk, and therefore a leveling genre – was. Wordsworth's political and civic interpretation of knightly behaviour in the current age, to push my argument further, was as a revolutionizing force, a way to reform social ills that reflected the lessons in individual morality he had learned in France from the revolutionary activities of Michel Beaupuy, with whom he associated medieval romance and knightly derring-do (*TP*, IX, 328–36). And indeed, Wordsworth relates in the 1805 *Prelude* that he had initially considered writing an epic version of the Arthurian legend instead. It is also in the 1805 version that he describes Beaupuy's influence on him and makes clear his association of Beaupuy with chivalric honour and medieval romance as well as civic and moral duty (IX, 446–68).

Opening the 1798 *Lyrical Ballads* – Wordsworth and Coleridge's collabourative project that Wordsworth began to claim as his own through the additional poems for the 1800 edition – the contemporary reader came upon a volume of the ballad miscellany type, in which one would expect to find folk ballads rubbing up against contemporary imitations, as with Bishop Percy's *Reliques of Ancient English Poetry* (1765). Instead of anachronistic renditions of old songs such as abound in Percy – Dr Grainger's 'Bryan and Pereene. A West Indian Ballad', for instance – one found instead *purposeful* anachronism placed against contemporary idioms. The range of topical subjects in the anonymous *Lyrical Ballads* – from exotic voyages to the pastoral familiar, from the nightingale of romance to the nightmare of melodrama, from madness to introspection – appears disordered. Yet it hides a careful progression from the Ancient Mariner's dream of the initial and initiating poem into the increasing realities of deprivation, desperate states caused by the very carelessness of others that is also the mariner's – and by implication, the reader's – terrible sin.[4] The volume can be read as a cycle, a narrative account of sin and reformation that bears a structural resemblance to the narratives that comprise the Arthurian tales, once Mallory reorganized the miscellany of Arthurian ballads and tales into the *Morte D'Arthur* – an operation Wordsworth somewhat analogously performs in organizing his ballads so carefully, beginning with Christian sin and ending with the holy grail of 'Tintern Abbey'.[5] At the very centre and depths of the volume lies 'The Idiot Boy', a poem whose awkwardness was criticized by reviewers.[6] It is a poem that makes clear the reader's complicit guilt in not caring for others – in unchivalrous behaviour – and after confronting its riddle the reader is allowed to ascend again through poems of retrospection and reflection until rewarded by the transcendence of 'Tintern Abbey'. The social implications prefigured by the Mariner's sin, and the deep passions noted in the Advertisement formulate the sensibility of this volume, one that forces the reader to confront the poems cognitively and emotionally. This readerly role is prefigured by the Lyrical Ballad poet[7] – increasingly Wordsworthian – who places himself in and between the poems, seemingly in the place of the discomfited tourist, but always within the purview of a mariner himself already reformed and transformed into literary knowledge. The poet knows the force of carelessness, and how to make a tale of it so that others can be transformed. This is the lesson the reader must learn and take to heart.

But the lesson is not easy, and is offered as a confrontation between reader and poet – like that of the Mariner and wedding guest – which is promoted in the 1798 Advertisement to the volume and integrated into the poems. The poetic 'I' accomplishes this integration by seemingly asserting a private relation to the text yet also inserting the reader's presence into the text through his speaking persona. In this way the reader is not implied or, as in a dramatic monologue, textualized, but is rather configured by successive poems, and with the reading of each poem that increasingly complicitous reader is layered into the text. With the Mariner as the initial trope for both poet and reader, the first having finished his voyage and the second just beginning it, the reading experience takes on the feel of chivalric romance. It becomes a guided quest in which things animate and inanimate exert a heuristic pressure on the individual. At the same time, contemporary society itself is inserted into the poems such as would normally be elided from the ballad or folk paradigm. But the overriding effect of baladic metre – the unavoidable refrains, tetrametres and trimetres that insist on the romance of balladry in the face of rural disquietude – is to collapse the contemporary into the time of romance, anachronizing present time and the reader's quest experience through the collection. Because the estranging effect is moral rather than supernatural, the poet – and, because of the synecdochal relation between the two, the reader with him – gradually becomes refigured, changing from guilty mariner to romance knight.

Thus the confronted reader stands in charged relation to the poet. This is especially so because in the particular moment of lyric experience the poet does not know what it is he representatively *knows* as the authorial force behind the collection, while in coming to each new poem the reader must balance what he[8] has learned thus far both about his quest and about his poet-guide. The poet's status changes as the reader becomes more knowledgeable, but this is an effect carefully orchestrated through the Advertisement and sequencing of poems, because the reader's status must change as well. The reader must move from passive to active, from careless to protective. The poet determines the reader's position by charging him, indeed challenging him, to read like a man, in the sense of engaging honourably as a gentleman with the volume. This use of courtesy as a heuristic device prepares us for the famous definition of a poet as a man speaking to men of the Preface. But it also furthers the temporal disparity between the romance of the volume's presentation and generic choices and the contemporary social issues that form the *Lyrical Ballads'* thematic base. Chivalry is paradoxically both the anachronistic glue and rupture that disturb the poet's negotiation for the reader's compliance.

The reader's romance quest in the 1798 volume begins with the Advertisement, in which he had to imagine how to interpret poems that were 'experiments', and how to 'not suffer the solitary word Poetry ... to stand in the way of their gratification' (ii). I have suggested how experimental poems whose collective title infers a retrograde relation to poetic tradition, as for a ballad chapbook or antiquarian collection of medieval and contemporary ballads, can be programmematically and formally new. At the same time, the 'experimental' forms of these poems were not all unfamiliar: readers would have recognized the popular magazine descriptive lyric in Wordsworth's 'Lines' poems,[9] as well as the travelogue poems (especially on Native Americans like 'The Complaint of a Forsaken Indian Woman'), and poems deriving from Cowper's 'Crazy Kate' idiom such as 'The Female Vagrant' and 'The Mad Mother'. And if other poems, particularly the first of the volume, present themselves as intentional anachronisms – even the spelling of 'Rime of the Ancyent Marinere' forces the reader to view it as a 'relique' – then it is also true that the reader had literary precedent for such new relics in the poems of Chatterton and Macpherson. Similarly the 'ruins' or fragment form was equally familiar, while the ode as practised by Cowper – as a conversational poem – is recognizable in 'The Nightingale, a Conversation Poem', as well as two of the 'Lines' poems: 'Yew-tree' and 'Tintern Abbey'.

The 1798 volume, then, intentionally disturbs readerly expectation by proposing contemporary idioms as already old, as the stuff of chapbooks.[10] At the same time it fosters this disturbance by the play with formal and thematic expectations: lyrics in ballad form, 'lines' poems in ballad form, love ballads about unexpected maternal love or unexpected parental love loss, the supernatural presented as superstition. To position this disruptive reading practise, the Advertisement predetermines the reading of the poems as experiments: the feeling of incongruity can come from the very old or the very new artefact, a feeling that helps disorient the reader and put him on increasingly estranging and defamiliarizing ground in the conventional manner of romance beginnings. The challenge to the reader is to embrace the strangeness of the artefact as an opportunity to transcend presuppositions about what 'poetry' is, an adventure the Advertisement assures the reader is an engagement of 'honour': 'It is the honourable characteristic of Poetry that its materials are to be found in every subject which can interest the human mind' (738). In honourable engagement the reader will learn to think like the poet, and the reader of 1798 is invited into the mystery of the volume as an adventurer whose world is reconfigured, not as the ancient mariner's nightmare but as the poet's romance, so that he may learn anew. That identification with the poetic quest will move the reader past mere emotion into effective action by aligning passion (by questing through the 'natural delineation of human passions' (*LB* 739), with honour.

Thus is the aesthetic of the lyrical ballad experiment set out for the reader from the beginning, both through the Advertisement, or if one skips that, through the 'Rime' that first meets the reader's eye. That is, the ugliness of everyday life – of social guilt, of deprivation – and the baldness of language, is at once ameliorated by the natural rhythms of that life and by the promise of human redemption. Deep passions inform and purify what we otherwise dismiss out of moral carelessness. The Lyrical Ballad poet contends and hopes that the reader's better nature will conspire with a willingness to engage honourably, and with the inner urge toward the poetic itself. The experience of reading the volume must work upon the reader in a manner figured by the Ancient Mariner's moral and vocational (that is, literary) conversion. The everyday and ugly becomes the romanced and beautiful. The concern of all the prefatory materials is, finally, how to move the reader from being stylistically critical (a '[reader] of superior judgment' for whose taste the poems 'will not exactly suit' (*LB* 739), to recognizing that the compulsion to relate social ills and the passions that endow them with human interest – a compulsion meant to move others to action – is the heart of poetry, and not mere style. Moreover, the reader must feel honour-bound to engage in this conversion.

In response to the need for clearer articulation of this purpose, Wordsworth's relation to the reader becomes increasingly complicated by the 1800 and 1802 prefaces. Like the 1798 Advertisement, these essays target the reader as a political being who is therefore necessarily constructed as male, whose moral and political agency is accessed emotionally in the poems through elements associated with natural rights theory, and reinforced in the prefaces through social contract theory.[11] Significantly, Wordsworth's 1802 Preface retains the introductory posture that marks his 1798 Advertisement and 1800 defence of the *Lyrical Ballads*, a combination of assurance and challenge that targets the reader's readerly merit without preamble. The increasingly emphasized terms of courtesy in the Preface are ones to which Coleridge objected, but can be seen as key to Wordsworth's revisionary poetics.[12] Yet they are not given with a tone of complete assurance, and this lack of absolute certitude has something to do with the lack of absolute time; by straddling romance with present time something is lost, and certainly the posture of the Preface constructs a poet uneasy with his own time. He follows his initial challenge with a show of humility that appears forced and defensive: 'I had formed no very inaccurate estimate of the probable effect of those Poems: I flattered myself that they who should be pleased with them would read them with more than common pleasure', but otherwise, 'with more than common dislike' (741). Moreover, the poems are anticipated by an essay whose length indicates that the common reader has proved inadequate to the task of parsing this complex project. Finally, the initial section of the Preface reveals that the task is complex and distasteful to some because this art resists being read as the outpourings of a natural or inspired poet. It is an art guided by a poetic theory or code, and 'if the views with which they [these Poems] were composed were indeed realized, a class of Poetry would be produced, well adapted to interest mankind permanently' (*LB*, 742). Thus, the Preface serves at once to historicize the poems, making them of their compositional moment, and to medievalize them by insisting on the reader's demand for authorial courtesy, the author's contractual 'engagement' to answer this demand, and a code that both poet and reader must share.

In other words, to bind the reader to the present moment, to the politics at hand, Wordsworth uses a species of contract that appears to maintain its obliging structure, but that actually slides into an ahistorical *oblige*, the taking of a vow of honour. Rousseau's social contract that by 1798 has not proved itself reverts to the feudal one. The reason this slippage functions so well is that contracts are never between equals; the very act of contracting distinguishes contractor from contracted in a balance of power based on the voluntary obligation of one party to another. The 1780s and 90s witnessed the rise of liberalism and liberal politics in Britain, and Wordsworth's concern with negotiating readerly resistance and readerly suasion is in tension with the shift from civic humanism, with its defining civic virtue, to liberal democracy, founded on volunteerism and political obligation.[13] Wordsworth's knightly reader is not so readily determined that he can be wrested from the élitism still implicit in a virtuous readerly behaviour; he must be wooed into a contractual relation of obligation in order that he read, as it were, 'naturally', and thus actively and trans-historically, that is, transcendently. This 'natural' reader reads through the liberality of the Wordsworthian aesthetic just as the citizen under liberal democracy considers his political obligation to be the result of natural feeling. For the citizen to behave responsibly he must not see the contract that obliges him, viewing his duty as self-assumed rather than enforced. For Wordsworth's new reader, the act of reading these poems rather than any others must be a matter of self-assumed desire, a voluntary decision to read more responsibly, without any imposed obligation to do so. Thus the reader's poetic quest must seem self-imposed, his revelation deeply personal and affectively compelled. Wordsworth calls attention to the act of contracting his reader for the very purpose of realigning the reader's responsible courage to the poet's responsible honour, and through this idealized or romanticized version of contractual relations, to bind the reader to him as through a feudal oath (because the feudal oath was voluntarily sworn, it was, in fact if not ideally, contractual).[14]

That oath is nascent even in the 1798 volume, in the sense that the reader feels compelled to quest. The quest romance, radically disguised in Coleridge's 'Rime', nevertheless makes itself known to the 1798 reader as the volume draws that reader into a heroic relationship with it. The nadir of the volume, 'The Idiot Boy', represents for the reader, specifically the male reader, a type of the underworld experience through which he must successfully pass if he is to complete his quest mission in the spiritual grail of 'Tintern Abbey'. To this end, 'The Idiot Boy' is the story of a failed quest; moreover, its poetic guide proves unequal to the task, thus requiring the reader to become more self-reliant as a tale teller and interpreter of romance elements. The idiot himself stands in for the common man, the folk, yet also figures the hero of romance, provoking the question at the heart of revolutionary politics: who can be a hero?

In the poem, Betty Foy has been unable to teach her 'idiot' son the rudiments of chivalric behaviour; he not only cannot save the ill Susan, but must be rescued himself by his mother, the entire poem demonstrating the failure of romance in the modern world. The effect of the poem's drawn-out narrative, trotting rhythm, and the onomatopoeia that idiotically replicates Johnny's mental world, is to irritate the reader into considering the poem to be an extended focus on the unaesthetic, and then the nature of Johnny's quest. The speaker emphasizes this shift by explaining that Betty's frantic search for her son is less interesting ('And how she ran, and how she walked, / And all that to herself she talked / Would surely be a tedious tale' (*LB*, 214–16)) than what the poem is *really* about.

This poetic incompetence makes the reader question what is real, and what might the relation of romance quest to a love for nature be? The reader must read past the speaker's protestations that he is unable to recount Johnny's adventures or musings ('Oh gentle muses! let me tell / But half of what to him befel, / For sure he met with strange adventures' (*LB*, 349–51)), so that he may come to terms with what *is* real in the poem. The romance of the boy's adventures hinges on the word 'strange', which means both errant and erring. The speaker's inability to recount the capacity for romance in the unaesthetic – to decide whether Johnny is knight or idiot, or more strongly, whether romance is a critically sufficient aesthetic – puts the reader in the role of poet. This gesture transforms the reader from mariner to knight by virtue of the poem's formal effect on the reader's sense of honour. The poem specifically denies the reader any opportunity to sympathize with Johnny or distance him as a sentimental object. Johnny must be understood as a tale to be retold, as the thing that is real in the reader's own production of the aesthetic: 'O gentle Reader! You would find / A tale in every thing' (*LB*, 'Simon Lee', 67–8).

This performative reading relies on the reader's participation in the poet's strategy for reassessing the present in terms of the past, particularly through the poet's call to literary action. But the 1800 *Lyrical Ballads* cannot rely in the same way on an incipient oath, since the two-volume organization erases much of the strategic readerly positioning achieved by the 1798 poem order.[15] The Preface must, therefore, emphasize those terms of honour, courtliness and contract no longer conceptually available through the poetic sequence alone. This reversion to courtliness, an intensification that begins to displace timeliness in the Preface's discourse, allows the poet to present himself as knightly defender of a higher truth, challenging the liberal or natural reader's presumed innocence before he begins his reading experience. That position, 'who am I but an innocent reader', is demasked in the Preface by an insistence on the political nature of reading, so that even by the essay's end and before the reader meets the first poem (now the less mystifying but also less confrontational 'Expostulation and Reply'), the reader is transformed: 'I am he who has come to this volume by choice'. Self-chosen, the reader thus places himself, as if before the fact, in a contractual position. The effect of Wordsworth's courtliness, then, as it frames the self-imposed contract, is to recast the volunteerism of that political obligation into an even more natural virtue than that of liberalism or of civic humanism, by reverting to the virtue of knightly vows. In the 'real' poetry that underwrites the quest, 'the metre obeys certain laws, to which the Poet and Reader both willingly submit because they are certain, and because no interference is made by them with the passion but such as the concurring testimony of ages has shown to heighten and improve the pleasure which co-exists with it' (*LB*, 754). The reader engages to attend the poet on a knightly quest, a search aided by attention to passion for something that recent verse and contemporary gothic novels have dispossessed but that can, like the holy grail, be restored. This prepossession of purpose must belong to poet and reader alike if the mission is to be achieved; readerly resistance would only, as for the knights of Camelot, cause the loss of the grail's redemptive appearance and the subsequent downfall of the kingdom.

Thus the poet who was anxious not to '*reaso[n]*' his readers into appreciating his new 'class of Poetry' 'well adapted to interest mankind permanently' (*LB*, 742) has by 1800 scarcely toned down the knightly challenge of the Advertisement.

> And if, in what I am about to say, it shall appear to some that my labour is unnecessary, and that *I am like a man fighting a battle without enemies*, I would remind such persons, that ... a practical faith in the opinions which I am wishing to establish is almost unknown. (*LB*, 750; emphasis mine)

In adding a second volume to the 1798 selection, none of Wordsworth's defensive anxiety about the reception of those experimental poems appears to have abated, while a significant number of poems on medieval topics or personal honour have been added (including 'Hart-leap Well', 'The Fountain' the 'Lucy' poems, 'Nutting', 'A Fragment [The Danish Boy]', 'Ellen Irwin', 'Tis said, that some have died for love', and Coleridge's 'Love'). Again, challenge is mediated by deference to readerly expectations. But if Wordsworth gives in to a readerly desire for romance in 1800 by adding such poems (at the same time lampooning that desire in mock romances like 'The Oak and the Broom'), the politicized romance compelled by courtesy and there from the beginning, overrides and over-interprets it. The reader who does not engage the poetic project of the 1798 volume will not understand the temporal disparity of the 1800 additions, nor Wordsworth's own complicated relation to the present moment as history. The later ballads must be read in terms of the earlier ones.

That even the 1798 ballads may not be read correctly is clearly the concern of the 1800 Preface. The Advertisement fails in its job precisely because it does not contain the readerly contract of the 1800 Preface, with its displacements of obligation for virtue, of politics for courtesy, and of experimentation for recognizable romance:

> It is supposed, that by the act of writing in verse an Author makes a formal engagement that he will gratify certain known habits of association ... but I am certain, it will appear to many persons that I have not fulfilled the terms of an engagement thus voluntarily contracted. (742–3)

Indeed, Wordsworth acknowledges, his very experimentation means that some readers will ask 'by what species of courtesy' these poems can be called such – the very question emphasized by the Advertisement – and his Preface, he assures us, will

> explain some of the chief reasons which have determined in the choice of my purpose ... that I myself may be protected from one of the most dishonourable accusations which can be brought against an Author; namely, that of an indolence which prevents him from endeavouring to ascertain what is his duty, or, when his duty is ascertained, prevents him from performing it. (*LB*, 743)

The terms of this contract – honour, courtesy, duty, virtue – he is only lacking largesse – are the terms of medieval chivalry according to period treatises on the subject, while inaction and not ascertaining his duty was Perceval's downfall in his quest for the Holy Grail, although he ultimately aids Galahad in achieving the Grail. Wordsworth's allusory language weights inaction against duty, extending a kind of promissory note to the reader in a suspension of the Percival–Galahad, questor–champion equation that interpreting action and inaction correctly – not in old-fashioned romance terms but in civic-minded terms – will lead to a proper and redemptive heroism.

The readerly contract as it is set up, which contains this promised experience, is presented as a Rousseau-like social bond that is mediated by being structured like a feudal relation. The social contract can only work when understood by the terms of chivalry and a code of honour. The poet will impart pleasure when his 'style is manly' (*LB*, 755), that is, not a 'slavish and mechanical' imitative style (*LB*, 751), nor one that – like Rousseau's contractual theory – uses 'personifications of abstract ideas' in a 'mechanical' manner (*LB*, 747), nor one that substitutes for the 'real passion' of a poet, thus 'encourag[ing] idleness and unmanly despair' (*LB*, 751), but one that generates 'truth ... general, and operative', a truth 'carried alive into the heart by passion' (*LB*, 751). The poet is, like the knights of Percy's medieval romances, a man 'originally possessed of much sensibility' yet armoured against the 'gross and violent stimulants' promoted by the unmannered abusers of romance, 'frantic novels' and 'sickly' gothics (*LB*, 747). The 'magnitude of the general evil' facing the reader indeed requires a knight's challenge to battle (*LB*, 747). That he gleans his poetry from the 'language of ordinary men', the very men hearing or reading the folk romances available in the countryside, requires both a defence to the reader and a further knightly quality, *homage*:

> Nor let this necessity of producing immediate pleasure be considered as a degradation of the Poet's art ... [I]t is a task light and easy to him who looks at the world in the spirit of love: further, it is a homage paid to the native and naked dignity of man (*LB*, 752).

The homage here is not to an overlord but to human dignity, yet it is couched in the language of chivalric love; honour and the love and protection of the people are the attributes of the medieval model of manly perfection. The poet 'is the rock of defence for human nature; an upholder and preserver, carrying everywhere with him relationship and love' (*LB*, 753). Thus the poet shows himself to have achieved the promise of 'Tintern Abbey', which he holds forth to the reader: through the cycle these ballads construct, the reader will also feel compelled to uphold and preserve, carrying everywhere relationship and love.

II Edwin Austin Abbey and the Boston Public Library Murals

The key terms I have emphasized in my discussion of Wordsworthian chivalry are readerly romance, experimental anachronisms of time and form, and courtesy, all of which work to compel the reader's compliance. The reader becomes a volunteer in the social enterprise of chivalric romance through the conversion experience of his interpretive quest, a conversion that then contracts him for a higher social purpose. These terms need to be added to Ruskin's interpretation of the medieval aesthetic as it was generally adopted for projects that addressed the public weal and seats of learning. Although Wordsworth did indeed turn from the radical politics of 1798 as his critics claimed, his poetry continues the programme set forth in the *Lyrical Ballads* Preface, and throughout his life he only increased his faith in the healing ability of chivalric poethood and a social contract mediated by a code of honour.[16] Ruskin follows, however unconsciously, Wordsworth's sense of medieval chivalry as a form of social consciousness unallied to gothic mystery and its seductively passive role for the reader. For Ruskin, the gothic style represented the active social awareness structured into the communal networks and feudal relations of medieval society.[17] Gothic architecture in particular – the art of communal space, buildings that institute the ethos guiding the community – evinces the honour inherent in proper feudal relations in which each class understands and exercises its duty to the others, and each class is permitted its own dignity. If the Library's new Copley Square building, for which Abbey's murals were commissioned, is not specifically gothic in architecture (it is 'Renaissance Beaux Arts', to complement the Romanesque Trinity Church across from it), its planning was certainly grounded in Ruskinian principles: it was the country's first municipal public library, with only private or association libraries existing prior to its being founded in 1848.[18] Its Boyleston Street inscription announces 'The Commonwealth requires the education of the people as the safeguard of order and liberty', a sentiment that invokes Ruskin's belief that public order stems from a caretaking that is chivalrous in its attention to public safeguards. The paintings decorating the library invoke even more a Wordsworthian chivalric ethos, which Ernest Fenollosa articulated in 1896 as,

> The significance of the mural painting in the Boston Public Library should now be plain. Here we have established the first great centre of a future civic series. Here the principle is first openly, and on a large scale, acknowledged by the public authorities.[19]

Despite his 'new' chivalry and call to honour, Wordsworth appeared uneasy about using romance anachronisms at the same time that he issues the challenge of social honour. But by the late nineteenth century chivalry had so gained an imaginative hold on cultural imperatives that it seemed a natural idiom for institutions of social welfare, reform and learning. Wordsworth's sense of destabilized time had given way to the programmematic assurance of progressivism, a confidence about historical progress built up by the Oxford Movement, the Young England party associated with Disraeli, Tennyson's and Ruskin's medievalism, and tied in indelible ways to the Victorian preference for gothic architecture, Pre-Raphaelite art and literature, and William Morris's decorative arts. If Wordsworth worried that Rousseau's social contract is disaffecting and impersonal and needs to be redressed through courtesy, late nineteenth-century culture on both sides of the Atlantic had no difficulty costuming contemporary issues in medieval dress. Arthurian figures and their analogues could be found in book illustrations, paintings, interior décor, architectural detailing, and the fabric and wallpaper designs of the Arts and Crafts Movement. Edwin Austin Abbey, growing up in Philadelphia and succumbing early in his youth to the Victorian fascination with Arthurian romance, was perfectly situated to put a Wordsworthian ethos into place within the terms propagated by Tennyson, Ruskin and the Pre-Raphaelites. Beginning his career as a book and magazine illustrator, he became used to creating visual narratives but he rarely felt bound to the texts he was working with. Instead, he designed scenes that conveyed the spirit rather than the letter of the text, and substituted accuracy of visual historical details for accuracy of storyline, producing his own vision of the tale to be told. Wordsworth-like, Abbey's substitutions created anachronisms that were compellingly time-straddling. And although Abbey felt more comfortable in romance time than in the modernism of his age, he also found romance time, like Ruskin and other Victorian medievalists, to be constitutionally more moral and politically motivating.

If Abbey was well suited to install a Wordsworthian scheme – and one dependent on literary narrative for its moral message – into his vision of library space, the Boston Public Library was already positioned to receive such a scheme. In 1852 the *Report of the Trustees* of the library specifically refers to the written word as art:

> Of all human arts that of writing ... [is] without exception the most useful and important. It is the great medium of communication between

> mind and mind .... It is principally in the form of books that the art of writing ... has exerted its influence on human progress.[20]

Moreover, it is the function of the public library to continue the 'great system of [public] instruction, administered in schools rising in gradation from the most elementary to those of a highly advanced character, open to the whole population, and supported by a most liberal public expenditure' (4). While the school, college and university are 'but the first stages in education', it is the public library that would allow young adults to 'carry on their education and bring it to practical results by private study' (6–7).

In his murals for the Book Delivery Room of the Boston Public Library, Abbey structures the social-feudal contract revalidated in Wordsworth's public-minded ballads into the story he visually relates. Abbey's choice of scenes emphasizes the association of books with delivery, enlightened understanding and ethical conversion, and the success of his Arthurian decoration for the new building can be measured by that fact that they 'remained the most popular murals in America for decades'.[21] Abbey's historical reconstructions are characterized as both 'literary' painting and the 'grand opera' style, elabourate and highly detailed narratives that sweep the viewer into their romanticized world. He so thoroughly researched the costumes, domestic objects and furnishings, the subject matter and story, and the locales for his paintings that he was 'recognized as the greatest medievalist of his day'.[22] Abbey was invited in 1890 by Augustus Saint-Gaudens (the sculptor for the library) to create the murals for the library's Book Delivery Room, but moved to England the next year and painted them there, sending the panels for 'The Siege Perilous' back to Boston in 1893, and for the rest of the first half of the 'Quest of the Holy Grail' cycle in 1895 and the remaining panels in 1901.

Abbey, a committed anglophile, was elected to the Royal Academy and Royal Water Colour Society, and given the commission to paint Edward VII's coronation portrait. His influences were decidedly British, first Benjamin Robert Haydon's large-scale historical paintings, and then the Pre-Raphaelite school, particularly the work of Dante Gabriel Rossetti, Ford Madox Brown and Edward Burne-Jones. Like the Pre-Raphaelites, Abbey paid careful attention to historical detail and archaeological reconstruction, and to the meaning – both literary and moral – behind the visual story.[23] However, Abbey's conception of the Grail story sacrifices authenticity for a purer storyline in that peculiar Victorian brand of amalgamation and certainty. The first panel consists of the babe Galahad, held up by the nuns who will raise him to an angel holding the Grail, his appearance clearly a condensation of Camelot's highest aspirations. In the second panel Galahad holds his required vigil for knighthood, Lancelot and Sir Bors attaching his spurs with the attendant nuns behind them.

Figure 7 Second panel ('Galahad's Vigil') of Edwin Austin Abbey's 1901 fifteen-panel mural cycle ('Quest for the Holy Grail') for the Book Delivery Room of the Boston Public Library.

Galahad then visits the Round Table and prepares to take the Siege Perilous led by his ancestor Joseph of Arimathea, and in the fourth panel Galahad and Camelot's knights prepare for their quest for the Grail through prayers with the militantly Christian Cistercian monks. Next Galahad visits the mysterious Castle of the Grail alone (panel 5), where the Fisher King lies in a life-in-death spell while the impure courtiers live a death-in-life existence highly resonant with meaning for the intrepid viewer. Galahad, however, fails to ask the imperative question that will release the king from the curse, and for his failure he must undergo countless adventures sinless, including the Castle of the Maidens and forsaking his new bride Blanchefleur, before he can again attempt the Castle of the Grail. Sacrificing his wife to higher principles, Galahad wins the Grail and, in Malory's version, he carries it with Bors and Perceval (the other knights of great purity) in Solomon's Ship to Sarras. Significantly, Galahad then dies in ecstasy, but in the Abbey version, the angel bears the Grail to Sarras where, having followed in Solomon's Ship, Galahad must achieve the Grail and be crowned king. He then builds the beautiful Golden Tree of panel fifteen, where a choir of angels seems to inhabit the tree in echo of Galahad's attendant nuns, while the golden urn in which the tree is rooted echoes and intensifies the gold Grail held aloft by Joseph of Arimathea. The angels, nuns, vision and blessing bring first and last panels full circle.

Abbey's romantic vision contrasted strongly with the visual realism of the modernist aesthetic pursued by his friend, John Singer Sargent, who received the commission for the murals of the Library's 'Sargent Gallery'. Sargent spent longer than Abbey, thirty years in total, creating the murals for his 'Judaism and Christianity', a work he considered his masterpiece (Wick 46). While Abbey focused on the altruism and ethos of medieval romance (using Tennyson's *Idylls* as his main literary source), Sargent used his more allegorical murals in the Boston Public Library to explore a history of religion.[24] Both artists carefully designed their murals to illustrate particular kinds of histories and visions, but more importantly in the context of library space, they designed their works to conform to the moral, spiritual and educative requirements of institutional architecture and the Victorian public. But whereas Sargent's murals were easily comprehensible to a nineteenth-century church-goer – from Moses holding the tablets in the Frieze of the Prophets to 'Our Lady of Sorrows' on the west wall – Abbey's narratives required a more active participation on the part of the viewer. We read in his mural duty before pleasure, but duty appearing as beautiful Pre-

Figure 8 Fifteenth and final panel ('Galahad and the Golden Tree') of Edwin Austin Abbey's 1901 mural cycle ('Quest for the Holy Grail') for the Book Delivery Room of the Boston Public Library.

Raphaelite figures highly allegorized. Indeed, duty appears as seductively – yearningly – charming as pleasure and the reward for achieving the Grail is kingship. Perhaps for this reason, even if the figures' signifying function is clear, their articulation is so insistently literary, so installed in romance time, that the moral – indeed the entire script – is not entirely so legible, and as Kathleen Foster points out, informative titles and accompanying explanations were necessary: 'It took a guide book to interpret Abbey's personal version of Galahad's "Quest" ... Intuitively – without guidebook – the murals impress the viewer with a sense of high ideals and noble sacrifices, brave deeds and mysterious supernatural forces' (15). None other than Henry James wrote the guide, an indication of both the literary density of the visual quest and the import of the Library's allegorically saturated Book Delivery Room. But like Wordsworth, with his 1800 Preface, Abbey's work requires an aid that itself requires work: interpretation is a labour undertaken by the knight-viewer who, in agreeing to stay long enough to interpret the 'Holy Grail' panels encircling the Book Delivery Room, has entered into a contract with Abbey to pursue that grail of educative transformation – reading the text, reading the image, reading himself – a contract Sargent's gallery does not demand or require.

James finds the moral to be drawn in the fifth panel depicting Galahad's first attempt of the Grail Castle. As James's guide explains, Galahad fails on this essay because he thinks he has been so well taught as a child in the knowledge of the world and of chivalry that he can guess for himself the answer:

> gazing at it [the scene] he tries to arrive, in his mind, at an interpretation of what it means. He sees the bearer of the Grail, the damsel with the Golden Dish, ... the two knights with the Seven-branched Candlestick, and the knight holding aloft the Bleeding Spear. The duty resting upon him is to ask what these things denote, but, with the presumption of one who supposes himself to have imbibed all knowledge, he forbears, considering that he is competent to guess. But he pays for his silence.[25]

This moral, situated in the Public Library's Book Delivery Room, cannot be plainer to one who accepts the Wordsworthian challenge of the allegory. Significantly, the Golden Tree that Galahad builds in Sarras is produced out of his recognition of the healing question that must be asked to attain knowledge, and it represents a material version of the Grail as, in James's words, 'that which is the source of all life and knowledge and power'. A potent text indeed.

If Abbey became renowned for his narrative paintings – at one point undergraduates at Yale, Harvard and Princeton found it necessary to acquire framed photographs of one or more sections of the 'Holy Grail' cycle as part of their college education[26] – he had only completed one oil painting during his career as an illustrator before being given the Boston Public Library commission. He was chosen for the Book Delivery Room decoration, then, on the strength of his ability to communicate morally instructive narratives despite his relative lack of accomplishment as a painter. This educative element, with its highly literary imperative, makes sense in terms of a space for public reading. It also makes sense in terms of Wordsworth's interpretation of the chivalric ethos, as a tool for translating individual experience (with the idiot boy as an everyman, a figure for the common reader, but a figure for the heroic reader as well) into a call to civic spiritedness. As for Wordsworth, Abbey emphasizes chivalry's troubled relation to the body by translating a feminized passivity into masculine achievement: witnessing and self-denial, if properly guided, as questing behaviours that lead to the request for knowledge from authoritative and visionary others. Indeed, without a familiarity with Wordsworth's poetic morality – available not just in reading lessons at school, but in the works of Victorian moralists like Mill and Ruskin – the reading public would not have had such a positive response to Abbey's allegory for a civic library.

Notes

1. This quote from Mrs Bell's 1901 review in *The Artist* is one the Boston Public Library prefers for its promotional materials on the Book Delivery Room. I am indebted for my interest in the Abbey murals to my student David Weiher, whose unpublished paper on the murals traces their deviation from the medieval Arthurian tales. Images of murals reproduced by permission of the Boston Public Library.
2. I argue this in chapter 3 of *Romantic Medievalism: History and the Romantic Literary Ideal* (Basingstoke: Palgrave Macmillan, 2002).
3. Boston's public was primarily educated through the public system, all children attending primary school and then a writing school or grammar school, and graduating at the equivalent of our eighth grade. Eligible boys could also complete a college preparatory school such as the Boston Latin School, located near the Public Library. By 1878, girls could attend the Girls' Latin School to prepare for college. See Otis Cauldwell and Stuart Courtis, *Then and Now in Education 1845–1923* (New York: Arno, 1971), and Pauline Holmes, *A Tercentenary History of The Boston Public Latin School 1635–1935* (Cambridge, MA: Harvard UP, 1935). The Latin School curriculum for 1870 included Wordsworth, Coleridge and Keats, in the Fourth Year (age 15), Tennyson and Ruskin in the Fifth Year, and medieval history in both years. By 1880 more emphasis was placed on literature (after interim curricular changes, the 1891 curriculum followed that of 1880): Holmes, *Tercentenary History*, 283–7, 290–4). Those not attending Latin school would have received less intensive instruction in English and literature.
4. For the significance of ordering, see Neil Fraistat, *The Poem and the Book* (Chapel Hill, NC: University of North Carolina Press, 1985), James H. Averill, 'The Shape of *Lyrical Ballads*', *Philological Quarterly* 60 (1981): 387–407, and Alan Boehm, 'The 1798 *Lyrical Ballads* and the Poetics of Late Eighteenth-Century Book Production', *English Literary History* 63 (1996): 453–87. For the *Lyrical Ballads* as experiment,

see Mary Jacobus, *Tradition and Experience in Wordsworth's 'Lyrical Ballads' (1798)*, (Oxford: Oxford UP, 1976), Stephen Parrish, *The Art of the Lyrical Ballads* (Cambridge, MA: Harvard UP, 1973), and Jared R. Curtis, *Wordsworth's Experiments with Tradition: The Lyric Poems of 1802* (Ithaca, NY: Cornell UP, 1971).

5. Boehm notes Wordsworth's and Coleridge's careful attention to details of printing and page appearance of the *Lyrical Ballads*, a care that itself calls attention to the logic of ordering in the poem sequence. It was Wordsworth, however, who took on the task of ordering the poems.
6. Wordsworth specifically defends this poem in his Preface against hostile criticism. In describing the poem's awkwardness, which I am reading as intentional, I will use the 'unaesthetic', which I want to distinguish from the Burkean 'ugly'. For the implications of aesthetic categories, see Terry Eagleton's *The Ideology of the Aesthetic* (Oxford: Basil Blackwell, 1990).
7. I will use this term to distinguish the 1798 'poet' from the Wordsworth of 1800 and 1802.
8. I interpret the reader's gender as weighted towards the male, whose journey through the romance quest of the ballads is what I am arguing is installed into the volume.
9. Robert Mayo, 'The Contemporaneity of the "Lyrical Ballads"', *Publications of the Modern Language Association* (*PMLA*) 69 (1954): 486–522.
10. For a repositioning of the relation between the *Lyrical Ballads* and chapbooks or broadsides, see Linda Venis, 'The Problem of Broadside Balladry's Influence on the *Lyrical Ballads' Studies in England Literature* 24 (1984): 617–32.
11. This reading of the Preface significantly differs from the Coleridgean view of it as degraded or incompetent theory. For an analysis of how the standard view of the Preface is informed by Coleridge's rewriting of it, see Don H. Bialostosky, 'Coleridge's Interpretation of Wordsworth's Preface to *Lyrical Ballads*', *PMLA* 93 (1978): 912–24.
12. 'It might appear from some passages in the former part of Mr. Wordsworth's preface, that he meant to confine his theory of style, and the necessity of a close accordance with the actual language of men, to those particular subjects from low and rustic life, which by way of experiment he had purposed to naturalize as a new species in our English poetry. But from the train of argument that follows ... those sentences appear to have been rather courtesies of modesty, than actual limitations of his system ... I cannot, and I do not, believe that the poet did ever himself adopt it in the unqualified sense'. S.T. Coleridge, *Biographia Literaria*, eds James Engell and W. Jackson Bate (Princeton, NJ: Princeton UP, 1983), II, 69.
13. My characterization of this political transformation draws primarily on J.G.A. Pocock's discussion of civic humanism in *Virtue, Commerce, and History* (Cambridge: Cambridge UP, 1985) and Carole Pateman's treatment of political obligation in *The Disorder of Women: Democracy, Feminism and Political Theory* (Stanford, CA: Stanford UP, 1989).
14. Jack Lindsay discusses the difference between the normative feudalisms of England and France, where relations were established through binding oaths, versus Occitan feudalism, where the feudal oath was more matter-of-factly contractual. *Troubadours and Their World of the Twelfth and Thirteenth Centuries* (London: F. Muller, 1976).
15. 'The Rime of the Ancyent Marinere' is moved, for instance, from first place to twenty-third, and its spelling regularized. For the 1800 order of both volumes, and Wordsworth's de-emphasis of the archaic, see R.L. Brett and A.R. Jones (eds) *Wordsworth and Coleridge: Lyrical Ballads* (London: Methuen, 1963), 1–4, xli–xlii.

16. I am following Forrest Pyle's analysis of the Romantic imagination as figured by images of rupture and healing in *The Ideology of Imagination: Subject and Society in the Discourse of Romanticism* (Stanford, CA: Stanford UP, 1995).
17. For the influence of Ruskin's aesthetic application of medieval principles, see Michael Brooks, *John Ruskin and Victorian Architecture* (New Brunswick, NJ: Rutgers UP, 1987) and Roger Stein, *John Ruskin and Aesthetic Thought in America 1840–1900* (Cambridge, MA: Harvard UP, 1967).
18. Boston's pre-1850 private libraries included specialized libraries like the New England Historic Genealogical Society (1845) circulating libraries, 'Social Libraries' (composed of popular or practical books for the labouring classes, first proposed by Benjamin Franklin in 1731 as the 'Library Company'), Sunday School libraries, and the 'District' or public school libraries (first created in New York State). *Report of the Trustees of the Public Library of the City of Boston*, July 1852 (Boston, MA: J.H. Eastburn, 1852), 11–13.
19. Quoted in Peter Arms Wick's *A Handbook to the Art and Architecture of the Boston Public Library* (Boston, MA: Associates of the BPL, 1977), 45.
20. *Report of the Trustees of the Public Library*, 3.
21. Alan Shestack, Introduction to *Edwin Austin Abbey* (New Haven, CT: Yale University Art Gallery, 1973), ii. See E.V. Lucas, *The Life and Work of E.A. Abbey, R.A.* (London: Methuen, 1921).
22. Kathleen A. Foster, 'The Paintings' in *Edwin Austin Abbey* (New Haven, CT: Yale University Art Gallery, 1973), 4. Foster notes that in preparation for scenes in the 'Holy Grail' murals, Abbey went to the south of France for its Romanesque architecture, and to Bayreuth for a performance of Wagner's *Parsifal*. 'His studio was full of costumes, armour, antique fabric swatches and bits of old furniture, and his library was stuffed with art books, reference books, photographs and engravings' (p. 12).
23. As Foster notes, 'his concentration on *meaning* in art left little room for pure representation, and no space at all for art-for-art's sake exercises': Foster, 'The Paintings', 5. His style, in her view, is expressive of an escapist personality: Abbey rejected what he termed 'the "plain vulgarity" of modern life', and dedicated himself instead to 'a more inspirational imaginary world' (p. 5). This romanticization of the medieval is in stark contrast to Wordsworth's depiction of a contemporary and reformist chivalry, yet Abbey's strong foundations in British Romanticism – particularly through the work of B.R. Haydon – reveal how important the Wordsworthian vision was to Abbey's emphasis on morality in the Book Delivery Room murals.
24. For a highly detailed and complex study of Sargent's masterpiece, see Sally M. Promey, *Painting Religion in Public: John Singer Sargent's* Triumph of Religion *at the Boston Public Library* (Princeton, NJ: Princeton UP, 1999).
25. 'The Quest and Achievement of the Holy Grail. Wall Paintings in the Boston Public Library Installed in 1895 by Edwin Austin Abbey, R.A. An Outline of this Version of the Legend by Henry James'. Publication of the Boston Public Library, undated.
26. A fact noted by Homer Saint-Gaudens in his *The American Artist and His Times* (New York, NY: Dodd, Mead, 1941), 157, cited by Foster, 'The Paintings', 15.

10

Home (at Grasmere and 'On the Range'): Wordsworth and Owen Wister's *The Virginian*

James A. Butler

'That "Uncertain heaven received / Into the bosom of the steady lake", I should have recognized any where; and had I met these lines running wild in the deserts of Arabia, I should have instantly screamed out "Wordsworth!"' So asserted Samuel Taylor Coleridge, famously, of lines from 'There was a Boy', published in *Lyrical Ballads* (1800).[1] Given Coleridge's claim that he could identify so confidently Wordsworth's themes and phrasings, one wonders what he would have made of the following passages:

> (1) I wanted no speech with any one, nor to be near human beings at all. I was steeped in a revery as of the primal earth; even thoughts themselves had almost ceased motion.
>
> (2) [I]t has made me want to become the ground, become the water, become the trees, mix with the whole thing. Not know myself from it. Never unmix again.
>
> (3) The creature we call a *gentleman* lies deep in the hearts of thousands that are born without chance to master the outward graces of the type.
>
> (4) It is imagination that takes the load of fact, supplied by experience, and lifts it into universal truth.
>
> (5) Would I might prison in my words / And so hold by me all the year / Some portion of the Wilderness / Of freedom that I walk in here.
>
> (6) [T]he ancient earth was indeed my mother and ... I had found her again after being lost among houses, customs, and restraints.

Those concepts, those images, some of those phrasings seem so tantalizingly familiar: could they be new and early drafts of the sort that the

Cornell Wordsworth Series editors unearth from the poet's cluttered notebooks? No, the six passages all come from a very late Romantic, the American writer Owen Wister (1860–1938), as recorded in his journals and in his best-selling Western novel *The Virginian: A Horseman of the Plains* (1902).[2] These Wordsworth-like passages roam not the deserts of Arabia but the wildernesses of Wyoming.

The Virginian was a 'best-selling' novel in an absolutely literal sense, because one scholar writing in 1970 claims that the book 'may well be the most widely read American novel ever published'.[3] It was reprinted fifteen times within seven months after publication, fifty times in its first 33 years, and many times since. Five movies have been made, the most recent in 2000; 248 television episodes aired from 1962 to 1971. Those who on film or stage have portrayed the mythic character with no name but 'The Virginian' include Gary Cooper, Henry Fonda, Joel McCrea and Bill Pullman, each uttering the hero's immortal threat to the villain: 'When you call me that, *smile*!' Audiences not only screamed in terror at Boris Karloff's portrayal of the creature in *Frankenstein* but recoiled in indignation at his villain, Trampas, in *The Virginian*. Never out of print since 1902, more than a dozen editions of *The Virginian* are still available. A check of Amazon.com sales rankings for Oxford World's Classics shows Wister's *The Virginian* is outselling in that series and at that site *The Adventures of Huckleberry Finn, Alice's Adventures in Wonderland, Dubliners, Great Expectations, The House of the Seven Gables, Jane Eyre, The Scarlet Letter, Selected Tales by Edgar Allan Poe, Sherlock Holmes: Selected Stories, A Tale of Two Cities, Walden* and – yes – *Selected Poetry by William Wordsworth*.[4]

In *The Virginian*, Wister set the pattern (either for imitation or parody) for all subsequent Western films and novels, including his creation of such familiar elements as the strong, silent, cowboy of chivalric standards; the perky New England schoolteacher, Molly Wood, who gives up some of her Puritan principles in discovering 'I wanted a man who was a man'; the swarthy villain, wearing the requisite black hat in most film versions; and, most important perhaps, the epic gunfight where the hero unapologetically asserts in the dusty streets his right to take the law into his own hands.

The myths that Wister created are now so ubiquitous in the popular culture of the United States that readers and critics have treated them as indigenously American and not paid sufficient attention to their roots in British Romanticism. Our mythic cowboy cannot, after all, spend all his time riding horses, shooting villains and wooing the schoolteacher. The Virginian is, astonishingly considering the later history of the Western novel and film, a reader of such serious literature as Sir Walter Scott's *Kenilworth* (his favourite book), Jane Austen's *Emma* (his least favourite), Charles Dickens's *David Copperfield* and George Eliot's *The Mill on the Floss*. The tenderfoot narrator of the novel makes clear The Virginian's love for horses by quoting from and meditating on 'The Rime of the Ancient

Figure 9 Frederic Remington's illustration for 'The Game and the Nation' (May 1900 in *Harper's New Monthly Magazine*) used Wister himself as the model for the tenderfoot narrator of this story about The Virginian, thus providing a double portrait of the author (left) and his most famous character.

Mariner'. Among other Romantic authors implausibly referred to in works by Wister (who is, after all, chiefly a writer of cowboy stories) are Ann Radcliffe, Robert Southey, John Keats and Lord Byron.

'The mind of man' is, as *The Prelude* tells us, 'framed even like the breath / And harmony of music' (1805, I, 352–3). Individual notes contributing to that harmony are sometimes hard to distinguish, in music as in influence studies. But the case for Wordsworthian influence on Wister, both on his works in general and on *The Virginian* in particular, is clear, given the novelist's references to the poet. For example, in an important letter that has recently surfaced, Wister responds – in Wordsworthian and Shelleyan terms – to a stranger's inquiry about what was his favourite poem: 'Poetry is more than furniture, it is food. After Religion it is the best, the most intimate nourishment in strengthening the soul and mind of that happy man who has the appetite and digestion for it'. He then lists those few poems that 'hit [him] most intimately and left the deepest marks', including Wordsworth's 'The world is too much with us' and 'The Daffodils'.[5] In *The Virginian*, Wister has his hero consider the psychological effects of money, of 'gettin' or spendin' it', thus echoing the line 'Getting and spending, we lay waste our powers' from 'The world is too much with us' (272–3). Indeed, Wordsworth's sonnet anticipates the central theme of *The Virginian*: Wister in 1911 prefaced his novel with the statement that his book is 'an expression of American faith' that the country would survive its principal enemy, the excesses of those in Wall Street.[6] As for Wister's admiration of 'The Daffodils', the novelist presents in his preface to *The Virginian*, as we shall see, an account of memory very similar to the poem's depiction of the flashes of recollection on Wordsworth's 'inward eye'. In his short story 'Napoleon Shave-Tail', Wister has the commanding officer of a Western fort quote Wordsworth's 'We Are Seven' in advising visitors of the strength of his force:

> Seven commissioned males, sir. Our Major is on sick-leave, and two of our Lieutenants are related to the President's wife. She can't bear them to be exposed. None of us in the church-yard lie – but we are seven.[7]

Wister's letter to his mother (26 June 1891) further suggests his familiarity with Worthsworth. There Wister refers to line 15 of the poet's 'Elegiac Stanzas': 'the light that never was, on sea or land'. He did not identify the poem or author for his mother, probably assuming that such knowledge was the common currency of his family's very literate culture. But he added three words to the quotation, implying both the Wordsworthian base and the Wisterian elabouration of some of his Western themes. Owen Wister wrote, 'the light that never was on land or sea [*sic*], *except in Wyoming*' (*Wister Out West*, 116; italics added).[8]

One additional source of Wordsworthian influence on Wister is more biographical than textual. In 1898 Wister married Mary (whom he called 'Molly') Channing Wister, his second cousin once removed. About the time of his wedding, he began assembling his Western stories (with added material) to form *The Virginian*. In this new material he created a well-born New England schoolteacher and love interest, Molly Stark Wood, who journeys to Wyoming to educate the children of Bear Creek. Molly Channing Wister, herself of New England heritage and a civic leader of national significance, was one of the first women to serve on the Philadelphia School Board; after she died in childbirth in 1913, she was praised by the Philadelphia Superintendent of Schools as 'a great leader of educational thought and accomplishment'.[9] Her educational theories pervade *The Virginian*, and a tradition in the Wister family is that she was an active collabourator on the novel; a manuscript at the Library of Congress shows that she definitely helped to shape the 1904 stage version.[10]

Molly Channing Wister's educational theories are without doubt indebted to the writings of her great-grandfather William Ellery Channing, the Boston essayist, poet, abolitionist, Transcendentalist and 'apostle of Unitarianism'. Channing acquired a copy of *The Excursion* shortly after its 1814 publication and 'never read anything but Shakespeare more'.[11] Finding in Wordsworth 'a fountain of Spiritual life', Channing ranked him as 'the great Poet of our times', visited him at Rydal Mount in 1822 (producing an account of their conversation), and corresponded with the poet.[12] According to educational historian Lawrence A. Cremin, Channing was a pivotal figure in mid-nineteenth century educational theory, a man who 'campaigned for an expanded common school system in which better-trained teachers would employ more benevolent methods to encourage self-help and self-culture' and who contended 'that education ultimately nurtured the divinity inherent in every human being'.[13] Channing rightly identified *The Excursion* as his great influence, because his theory of education replicates the Wanderer's impassioned call for national education in Book IX:

to secure
For all the Children whom her soil maintains
The rudiments of Letters, and to inform
The mind with moral and religious truth,
Both understood and practised, – so that none,
However destitute, be left to droop
By timely culture unsustained, or run
Into a wild disorder; or be forced
To drudge through weary life without the aid
Of intellectual implements and tools;
A savage Horde among the civilized
A servile Band among the lordly free![14]

Molly Wister's sister Ella remembered that their childhood religious education consisted of readings selected at random from the Bible, attendance at Unitarian Sunday School, and exhortations to read the works of their great-grandfather William Ellery Channing (Haines 49). At the age of 17, Molly Wister began 11 years of teaching in the same Sunday School that she attended as a child. By her early twenties she was much involved at

Philadelphia's 'Evening Home and Library Association', which tried to keep teenage boys of the lower classes from the streets and the saloons, from becoming – in other words – a permanent 'savage Horde among the civilized'. Owen Wister wrote of her work at the 'Evening Home' in an essay published in 1895, the year in which the Commonwealth of Pennsylvania finally mandated universal education.[15] At the time of the Wisters' marriage, Molly, still in her twenties, served on the Philadelphia School Board and gave lectures, which her ancestor – and Wordsworth – would have liked, on the methods for using character education to civilize those burdened by severe poverty.[16] Fittingly, since her educational theories are based on Channing's (and, ultimately, Wordsworth's) principles, Molly Wister represented the family at the 1903 unveiling of her great-grandfather's statue in Boston's Public Garden (Haines 117).

Molly Wister would certainly have had some effect on the educational sections of *The Virginian*. The position on universal education advanced by Wordsworth and Channing and Molly Wister is, of course, the reason for teacher Molly Wood's trip west to Wyoming in the novel. And the call for a benevolent approach to teaching by all three theorists becomes the educational model in the new Bear Creek schoolhouse in *The Virginian*, even if we hear about the methods from the idle gossip of those who disapprove:

> 'I think she encourages a man some', said poor Nebrasky.
> 'Encourages? Because she lets yu' teach her how to shoot', said Wiggin.
> 'Well – I don't guess I'm a judge. I've always kind o' kep' away from them good women. Don't seem to think of anything to chat about to 'em. The only folks I'd say she encourages is the school kids. She kisses them.'
> 'Riding and shooting and kissing the kids,' sneered Trampas. 'That's a heap too pussy-kitten for me.' (*Virginian*, 110)

Given the number of connections between Wordsworth and the Wisters, it thus makes good sense to examine more closely the various parallels between the poet's work and *The Virginian*. My argument is that Owen Wister's creation of the mythology of the American West (one of America's pervasive cultural constructs) rests firmly on Romantic values. Indeed, it could be argued that one of the principal conduits for spreading Romanticism into popular culture is Wister's *The Virginian* and its multitudinous progeny. Any attempt to think about how Romantic and specifically Wordsworthian ideas reached the general public in the twentieth century must therefore consider the role of Owen Wister and his 'best-selling' novel *The Virginian*.

Born in 1860 into the bluest of blue-blooded Philadelphia families – his ancestors arrived in Pennsylvania *before* William Penn – Wister is a most unlikely person to have created the mythology of the Wild West. His grandmother, the actress and abolitionist Fanny Kemble, travelled in top literary circles, met Sir Walter Scott and knew Edward Trelawny (friend of Shelley and Byron) and Lady Byron. Young Owen was surely the only 14-year-old boy in America ever to receive as a Christmas gift from his grandmother an album of autograph letters, most of them written to her, from Sir Walter Scott, Charles Dickens, Matthew Arnold, Ralph Waldo Emerson, James Russell Lowell, Henry Wadsworth Longfellow, William Makepeace Thackeray and many others of similar literary importance.[17] Henry James had squired Owen's mother, Sarah Butler Wister, around Rome, and she inspired at least one Jamesian character.[18] A Phi Beta Kappa graduate in music and philosophy from Harvard, Wister played one of his original compositions for Franz Liszt, who thought he had 'un talent prononcé' (Payne 5). But Wister's physician father wanted a more practical career than a musical one for his son, and for two years the new Harvard graduate perched on a high stool below stairs at the Boston Union Safe Deposit Vaults calculating, over and over, interest at two-and-a-half per cent. 'Getting and spending we lay waste our powers', and the stress produced the eventual mental and physical collapse of Wister's powers. He began to suffer from dizziness, horrific dreams, hallucinations and week-long devastating headaches.[19]

In January 1908, a writer for the *North American Review* wrote that 'on every street, at every corner, we meet' people suffering from the same debilitating illness.[20] The sickness numbered among its victims Theodore Roosevelt, Edith Wharton, William and Henry James, Willa Cather, Virginia Woolf, Frederic Remington, Walt Whitman and Owen Wister, but the name of the illness is unknown to the general population today. That name is 'neurasthenia'.

Dr George M. Beard coined the word 'neurasthenia' in 1869 and popularized it in his 1881 book *American Nervousness: Its Causes and Consequences*. The various symptoms Beard identified – 'immobilizing, self-punishing depression', 'endless self-analysis', and 'morbid introspection' – came, he asserted, from the nature of post-Civil-War American life itself. Indeed, Beard wrote, 'American nervousness is a product of American civilization'.[21] The progress and potential of a country in the midst of rapid industrialization and of its great national expansion (both westward and through immigration to the crowded Eastern cities) energized and ultimately exhausted its peoples' psychic energies. For Beard, the screaming journalism of the popular press exacerbated the problem. Society's best and brightest were the ones particularly susceptible to neurasthenia during America's 'gilded age', because they were society's intellectuals; the stress caused by such intense thinking produced the illness. For Beard, neurasthenics needed something other than mental labour to recover from that 'endless self-analysis'.

This mental suffering is, of course, very familiar to readers of Wordsworth. We have, for example, the poet's declaration that 'We murder to dissect', as well as his own well-known diagnosis of 'endless self-analysis':

> Thus I fared,
> Dragging all passions, notions, shapes of faith
> Like culprits to the bar, suspiciously
> Calling the mind to establish in plain day
> Her titles and her honours, now believing,
> Now disbelieving, endlessly perplex'd
> With impulse, motive, right and wrong, the ground
> Of moral obligation, what the rule
> And what the sanction, till, demanding proof
> And seeking it in every thing, I lost
> All feeling of conviction, and in fine
> Sick, wearied out with contrarieties,
> Yielded up moral questions in despair
> (*TP*, 1805, x, 888–900)

In the Preface to *Lyrical Ballads*, Wordsworth offers an analysis of society's ills startlingly similar to that of Dr George Beard's emphasis on industrialization, rapid expansion of the nation and its population, and the overactive periodical press. For Wordsworth, our minds are blunted, made unfit for 'voluntary exertion', and reduced 'to a state of almost savage torpor' by the same causes:

> The most effective of these causes are the great national events which are daily taking place, and the encreasing accumulation of men in cities, where the uniformity of their occupations produces a craving for extraordinary incident which the rapid communication of intelligence hourly gratifies.[22]

Owen Wister knew enough of these causes for his own mental sufferings to transfer the maladies to his characters. The tenderfoot Easterner who narrates *The Virginian* comes to realize that 'merely the sight of the newspaper half crowded into my pocket had been a displeasing reminder of the railway, and cities and affairs' (*Virginian*, 374). In Wister's short story 'How Lin McLean Went East', Lin thinks he can return 'home' to the Boston and New York he knew as a youth but discovers in those cities only his 'deep hatred of the crowded, scrambling East'.[23]

Wordsworth had Dorothy and the west of England to help him recover from his mental breakdown; Wister had Dr Silas Weir Mitchell and Wyoming. In the 1870s, Mitchell (who preferred to be known as S. Weir

Mitchell) developed a treatment for neurasthenia that prevailed in both America and Britain until Sigmund Freud's theories produced more diverse and complicated psychic diagnoses. Like most members of Philadelphia's élite, Mitchell was related to Owen Wister, who dedicated his second novel (*Lady Baltimore*) to him and in 1914 gave his cousin's memorial address at the College of Physicians. Mitchell first outlined his treatment for neurasthenia in his paper 'Rest in Nervous Diseases', published in 1875. For Mitchell, the mental stresses caused by the times (he considered 'railroads' to be another one of those potentially debilitating features of the age) could be cured by massage, electrical stimulation, a fattening diet, and either bed rest or – if the patient were up to it – physical activity and a new environment. Not surprisingly, given the attitudes of the time, 'the rest cure' was more frequently prescribed for women and the vigorous 'camp cure' for men.[24] When Wister consulted his cousin in 1885, the doctor told the upper-crust Wister to go west: 'There are lots of humble folks in the fields you'd be better for knowing' (Payne 76).[25] The rest, as they say, is history – or the history of the Romantic Western.

Just one day after Wister reached Medicine Bow, Wyoming, in 1885, he wrote in his journal that the West was 'much more than my most romantic dream could have hoped'. And within a week of his arrival, Wister recorded that 'I'm beginning to be able to feel I'm something of an animal and not a stinking brain alone' (*Wister Out West*, 31–2).[26] In mining his several visits west for *The Virginian*, Wister merged that more than romantic dream and his newly discovered animal spirits to reimagine in American terms three great (and related) themes of British Romanticism: (1) the importance of the feelings and language of common people; (2) the opposition of nature to civilization; and (3) the revolutionary hopes for a new Eden, for a recovered paradise.

Like Wordsworth's Preface to *Lyrical Ballads* and his 1801 letter to Charles James Fox, Wister's main theoretical statement – 'The Evolution of the Cow-Puncher' (1895) – celebrates rural people and defends the language that they speak. Wister's palpable anxiety over what his social class had become ('merchanting themselves upwards to the level of family portraits and the cut-glass finish') finds relief through fellow feeling not with the well-off but with the heroic common cowboy. 'From the tournament at Camelot to the round-up at Abilene': in 'these wild men ... their fighting Saxon ancestors awoke ... for a moment and made them figures for poetry and romance'.[27] 'Men who do not wear fine Cloaths can feel deeply' argues Wordsworth, (*WL*, I, 315)[28] and Wister asserts the same for those who 'put aside their ... New York suits for the tribal dress' ('Cow Puncher', 610). Just as Wordsworth shows his readers how the sturdy and unaffected Cumbrian 'statesmen' (such as the shepherd Michael) embody virtues found less frequently among those whom the poet says are guilty of 'social vanity' (*LB*, 744), so does Wister pit Western America against the decadent East Coast.

The Virginian is in part a *Bildungsroman* in which the effete and over-rational Eastern tenderfoot learns to emulate the cowboys' natural and instinctual nature. 'In their spirit', wrote Wister of the cowboys, 'sat hidden a true nobility' and thus 'their figures took on heroic stature' (*Virginian*, 33).

Wister similarly exalts the language spoken by these cowboy equivalents of the Lake District 'statesmen'. Wordsworth, of course, wants 'to bring [his] language near to the language of men' and to avoid poetic diction (*LB*, 747). According to Wister in 'The Evolution of the Cow-Puncher', 'Ordinary words and phrases, freshened to novelty by the cow-puncher's wits, show his unpremeditated act of brevity, varying in aptness, but in imagination constant'. Then follows in Wister's essay a long, appreciative discussion of Western diction, concluding with the observation that the evocative language of the cow-punchers – some of the words perhaps 'of long standing and archaic repute' – has an eloquence which only 'that prudery which we carry as a burden along with the benefits of academic training' prevents from finding more general use ('Cow Puncher', 612–14). Thwarted by a Philadelphia-society upbringing, which would certainly qualify as Wordsworth's 'social vanity', Wister well knew the linguistic burden imposed by patrician prudery and academic training. Must fiction be, he asked, 'perpetual tea-cups'?[29] And in an 1893 poem, he questions whether 'Life's so indelicate' that it 'Must be concealed by fig leaves and by hymns' when it instead 'has a craving to parade undressed'. Against this 'sham', Wister wants to say 'damn!' but must say 'O sugar!' (*Wister Out West*, 253–4). Not for a quarter century after first publication of *The Virginian* did Wister and his publishers include the final word instead of a blank in the cowboy's all-purpose epithet 'son-of-a-bitch'.

The second Romantic impulse I wish to discuss, the opposing of nature to civilization, is chiefly rendered in Wister's journals by his setting the Philadelphia lawyer he became against the Western landscapes where he could escape from his gloomy 'office and driveling legalities' (*Wister Out West*, 201).[30] His exultant language in portraying the West would not be out-of-place in eighteenth-century British travel books. For example, Wister, sprawled across a train's cowcatcher to experience more intimately the mountainous scene, revelled in the landscape's 'splendid terrors', its 'precipices', and each 'new vista of cataracts'. At Yellowstone, Wister wrote that the ravine was 'at once romantic, exquisite, and wholly sublime', so much so that a travelling companion – eyes wide and mouth agape – became so emotionally overpowered by the sublime that she had to be 'helped to a log' (*Wister Out West*, 45, 127–8).[31] For Wister, the East in general and Philadelphia in particular (no less than London for Wordsworth) signified artificial rules, overbearing authority, and faceless isolation. Both writers also fled from the industrial revolution, occurring later in America than in Britain but bringing similar fundamental changes to the land and its people. Only escape from the cities thus made possible a

Figure 10 Frederic Remington's 'The Last Cavalier' illustrated the first appearance (in *Harper's New Monthly Magazine*, September, 1895) of Owen Wister's 'The Evolution of the Cow-Puncher', an article celebrating the heroic common cowboy as descendant of medieval knights.

free, spontaneous and social life, and *The Virginian* (like *Home at Grasmere* and *The Prelude*) opens with such a flight from an urban into a rural landscape. In those rustic spots far from the supposedly civilized cities, both Wister and Wordsworth found their literary themes. Wister described his subject – the American West – as 'the whole mystic and heroic pageant of our American soil; the only greatly romantic thing our generation has known, the last greatly romantic thing our Continent holds; indeed the poetic episode most deeply native that we possess'.[32]

Wordsworth and Wister, seeing the virtues of both people and landscapes of their chosen regions as imperilled, sound an elegiac note in their works. After all, by the time Wordsworth wrote 'Michael', 'the ploughshare has been through the ground' where the characters' cottage stood (l. 486); the departed shepherd and wife and son exist, like so much in Wordsworth, only in the poet's memory. In his preface to *The Virginian*, Wister tells us that the West of his 1902 novel is 'a vanished world', accessible now only to those journeys 'which memory can take' (*Virginian*, viii). But Grasmere and Western qualities, some still present and others recreated through memory, offer possibilities for a renewed human society, for a paradise regained. Thus my third example of how Wister brought

Romantic ideas into American popular culture is his use of Edenic imagery and millennial language.

Familiar to Wordsworthians is the poet's repeated use of such imagery and language, including descriptions of what he hoped for from the French Revolution. Many of Wordsworth's most millennial sentiments, however, are associated with his chosen Grasmere, including the promised 'coming of the milder day' (l. 175) in 'Hart-leap Well' as he journeys to his new Lake District home. The poem *Home at Grasmere* compares the poet's new dwelling-place to 'the bowers / Of blissful Eden' and claims that the mind can recreate there lost 'Paradise and groves / Elysian'.[33] When the tenderfoot in *The Virginian* first arrives at his chosen Medicine Bow, Wyoming, he employs comparable phrasing, finding in the West 'a pure and quiet light ... the air of creation's first morning' and 'a world of crystal light, a land without end, a space across which Noah and Adam might come straight from Genesis' (*Virginian*, 12–13). 'It's like Genesis', Wister wrote in his own journal when he first saw Medicine Bow in 1885, an emotional response whose importance for the author can be seen in his echoing it forty years later in one of his last Western stories: 'that crystal air that was like creation's first light' (*Wister Out West*, 29–30, 33).[34]

Clearly, the West for Wister represented as much of a fresh chance for his country as first the French Revolution and then Grasmere 'blessedness' had embodied for Wordsworth, a blessedness that the poet trusted would spread 'To all the vales of earth and all mankind' (*Home at Grasmere*, MS.B, II. 254, 256). America's previous attempt at revolutionary rebirth from the old European ways had, Wister thought, petered out by the late nineteenth century. His country's last chance was now its Western frontier: here was a new Garden of Eden, a new and final possibility for Genesis. In the West, Wister wrote in his journal, 'the future America is just bubbling and seething in bare legs and pinafores', adding his conviction that 'it won't be a century before the West is simply the true America, with thought, type, and life of its own kind' (*Wister Out West*, 29–30, 33).[35] In the final paragraph of *The Virginian*, the title character is no longer just a simple cowboy but has built upon those youthful experiences to become 'an important man, with a strong grip on many various enterprises' (*Virginian*, 503). The novel's hero therefore becomes the new Adam, the product of a successful revolution in sensibility, the inevitable child of a marriage of Democracy and Social Darwinism.

The Virginian is thus better seen as a revolutionary political and social manifesto than as an escapist cowboy yarn: What values of its Western cowboys deserve to be the values of all regions and people of the United States? How can those standards of behaviour be made universal? How does democracy enable heroic individuals of even lower social classes to rise to shape and renew society? When Wister began to publish his Western stories, that American apostle of realism – William Dean Howells – found much to praise but 'grieve[d] for some lingering traits of romanticism' in Wister's work.[36] Given the amazing popularity of *The Virginian* and that so many of Wister's values are indeed 'lingering traits of romanticism', I therefore argue for the novel's fundamental importance in transmitting Romantic ideas. *The Virginian*'s final sentence tells us that the hero 'is going to live a long while', and he has in fact done so, conveying his Romantic message to many millions in the century since its publication.

Two people, both anonymous, will have to represent the reactions of those many millions of readers who discovered or rediscovered Romantic ideals in Wister's work. The reviewer for the *New York Times Saturday Review of Books* had no doubts about what Wister showed in *The Virginian*, and we should have no hesitation in recognizing the Wordsworthian parallels: 'Simple men who live near to nature usually have poetic sensibility ... . Even those men whom we meet every day sometimes uncover to us unsuspected depths.'[37] The real influence of *The Virginian*, however, is not on cultured reviewers but on those ordinary men and women who found in the novel what may have been their most intense exposure to the ideas of British Romanticism. As a result of Wister's book, for example, the school authorities of the western states were flooded with applications from women who wanted to go west to teach just like Molly Wood in the novel. From Marblehead, Massachusetts, came this application from one rapt young woman who had absorbed Romanticism from Wister (but who might have benefited from a dose of realism about teaching and horseback riding):

> I long for life on the plains. I wish to get away from the world's conventions and dwell close to the heart of nature. I never have taught school, but my brother always has me help him with his lessons, and while I haven't any experience in riding, I am sure I can ride any horse in Montana with a little practice.[38]

The Library of Congress preserves many similar letters among the Owen Wister Papers. Those letters document how often *The Virginian* triggered Romantic conversion experiences in its readers, thanks to Owen Wister – and to William Wordsworth, a poet admired and drawn upon by Wister.

Notes

1. Samuel Taylor Coleridge, *Collected Letters of Samuel Taylor Coleridge*, ed. E.L. Griggs (6 vols, Oxford: Clarendon, 1956–71), I, 452–3.
2. The quotations are from (1) Owen Wister, *The Virginian: A Horseman of the Plains* (New York, NY: Macmillan, 1902), 374; (2) *The Virginian*, 12; (3) Owen Wister, *Owen Wister Out West: His Journals and Letters*, ed. F.K. Wister (Chicago, IL: Chicago UP, 1958), 36–7 (Journal entry of 21 July 1885); (4) *Owen Wister Out West*, 256; (5) *Owen Wister Out West*, 92 (Journal entry of 19 November 1889); (6) *The Virginian*, 375.

3. D.E. Houghton, 'Two Heroes in One: Reflections Upon the Popularity of *The Virginian*', *Journal of Popular Culture* 4 (1970): 497.
4. I accessed the USA site of Amazon.com on 7 June 2002; random checks on several other dates showed similar results.
5. Owen Wister to unknown correspondent, 10 July 1910, Wister Family Special Collection of La Salle University, Connelly Library, Philadelphia (R.T. Fallon Purchase Fund). On 5 July 1910 Wister wrote the Shakespeare scholar Horace Howard Furness about this request for his favourite poem from 'a gent from Oshkosh (really)' and to say that he selected poems 'which oftenest come unbidden to my mind' and 'dwell there least forgotten and most quoted' (Owen Wister Papers, Box 21, Library of Congress, Washington, DC).
6. Owen Wister, *The Writings of Owen Wister: The Virginian* (New York, NY: Macmillan, 1928), xxi.
7. Owen Wister, *The Jimmyjohn Boss and Other Stories* (New York, NY: Harper, 1900), 140.
8. For other influences on the novel, chiefly in the operas of Wagner, see G. Thompson, 'Musical and Literary Influences on Owen Wister's *The Virginian*', *South Atlantic Quarterly*, 85 (1986): 40–55.
9. M.G. Brumbaugh, 'Appreciations' in *Civic Club of Philadelphia Memorial Bulletin for Mrs. Owen Wister* (Philadelphia, PA: Civic Club, 1913), 31–2.
10. Ella Wister Haines indicated that her sister Molly played a significant role in the composition of *The Virginian*; see E.W. Haines, 'Reminiscences of a Victorian Child' (unpublished typescript, 1953), 54 (Wister Family Special Collection of La Salle University). On her contributions to the theatrical presentation of *The Virginian*, see Mary Channing Wister to Owen Wister (undated, but with an envelope postmarked 16 November 1903) in the Owen Wister Papers, Box 3, Folder 1902–03, Library of Congress.
11. *Memoir of William Ellery Channing*, ed. W.B. Channing (2 vols, London: Chapman, 1848), II, 95.
12. Channing to Wordsworth, 4 March 1835 (MS. A/Channing/1, Wordsworth Library, Grasmere); lecture delivered by Channing on 11 May 1841 (MS. A/B, W/1, Wordsworth Library). This material is referred to by kind permission of the Trustees of the Wordsworth Trust, Dove Cottage, Grasmere. For additional information on Channing and Wordsworth, see J. Beer, 'William Ellery Channing Visits the Lake Poets', *Review of English Studies*, n.s. 42 (1991), 212–16.
13. Lawrence A. Cremin, *American Education: The National Experience, 1783–1876* (New York, NY: Harper & Row, 1980), 33, 259.
14. I quote from the 1814 text of *The Excursion*, IX, 298–309; the entire speech of the Wanderer (IX, 292–418) is useful in understanding Wordsworth's educational theories.
15. See R. Duane, 'Mrs. Wister's Work at the Evening Home and Library Association', *Civic Club of Philadelphia Memorial Bulletin for Mrs. Owen Wister*, 44–7; and Owen Wister, 'Where Charity Begins', *Harper's New Monthly Magazine*, 91 (July 1895): 269–72.
16. The manuscript of Mary Channing Wister's address on 'Methods of Developing Character' is at the Historical Society of Pennsylvania, Philadelphia.
17. This Fanny Kemble-Owen Wister album is now at the Armstrong Browning Library, Baylor University, Waco, Texas.
18. Darwin Payne suggests that there are allusions to Sarah Butler Wister in James's *Roderick Hudson*, 'Madame de Mauves', and – as Mrs Westbrook – in 'The

Solution'; see *Owen Wister: Chronicler of the West, Gentleman of the East* (Dallas, TX: Southern Methodist UP, 1985), 16–17.

19. B.M. Vorpahl, *'My dear Wister': The Frederic Remington-Owen Wister Letters* (Palo Alto, CA: American West, 1972), 17.
20. This comment by H. Addington Bruce is quoted by T.J.J. Lears in *No Place of Grace: Antimodernism and the Transformation of American Culture, 1880–1920* (New York, NY: Pantheon, 1981), 50.
21. The account of symptoms is quoted from Lears, *No Place of Grace*, 47, 49. Beard's statement on the root cause of American nervousness is quoted in an article to which I am generally indebted for information on neurasthenia: G. De Brigard, 'Cowboys: A Thesis Excerpt', *Harvard Advocate*, 136, no. 2 (Winter 2001): 7–13. See also T. Lutz, *American Nervousness, 1903: An Anecdotal History* (Ithaca, NY: Cornell UP, 1991).
22. W. Wordsworth, *Lyrical Ballads and Other Poems, 1797–1800*, ed. J.A. Butler and K. Green (Ithaca, NY: Cornell UP, 1992), 746. All citations in this essay from the prose and poetry of the *Lyrical Ballads* will be from this edition.
23. Owen Wister, *Lin McLean* (New York, NY: Harper, 1898), 33–4.
24. Mitchell's prescription of the rest cure for Charlotte Perkins Gilman went spectacularly wrong, as is recounted in her short story 'The Yellow Wall-paper'. For more information on Mitchell, see J.P. Lovering, *S. Weir Mitchell* (New York, NY: Twayne, 1971).
25. Mitchell's advice was recorded by Wister in his Texas Journal under an entry listed as 'Miscellaneous Items: At the Hot Springs', Owen Wister Papers, Box 1, at the Library of Congress.
26. Journal entries of 3 and 8 July 1885.
27. Owen Wister, 'The Evolution of the Cow-Puncher', *Harper's New Monthly Magazine*, 91 (September 1895), 606, 604, 614–15.
28. Letter to Charles James Fox (14 January 1801).
29. Owen Wister, *Roosevelt: The Story of a Friendship, 1880–1919* (New York, NY: Macmillan, 1930), 29.
30. Journal entry of 29 April 1894.
31. Journal entry of 8 July 1887, and letter to Sarah Butler Wister, 11 August 1891.
32. F. Remington, *Drawings*, with introduction and verses by O. Wister (New York, NY: R.H. Russell, 1897), unpaged introduction.
33. William Wordsworth, *Home at Grasmere: Part First, Book First, of 'The Recluse'*, ed. B. Darlington (Ithaca, NY: Cornell UP, 1977); *Home at Grasmere* MS. B, ll. 123–4, 996–7). Wister's early journal entries could not have been directly influenced by *Home at Grasmere*, which first appeared in 1888. Sentiments similar to those expressed in *Home at Grasmere* appear, of course, in *The Prelude* and elsewhere in Wordsworth.
34. Journal entry of 6 July 1885; Owen Wister, 'The Right Honorable The Strawberries', in *The Writings of Owen Wister: When West Was West* (New York, NY: Macmillan, 1928), 179.
35. Journal entries of 2 and 6 July 1885.
36. 'Life and Letters' [Review of O. Wister, *Red Men and White*], *Harper's Weekly*, 39 (30 November 1895): 1133.
37. 'The Virginian', *New York Times Saturday Review of Books* (21 June 1902): 426.
38. Newspaper clipping, no source, no date (but *c.* 1903), Owen Wister Papers, Box 78, Library of Congress.

11

An Ethics of Wonder and the Cure of Poetry: Wordsworth, William James and the American Reader

Matthew Scott

> Life's nonsense pierces us with strange relation.
> (Wallace Stevens, 'Notes Towards a Supreme Fiction')

I

A black and white photograph in the book before me on the table shows a group of laughing men. One of them holds a kind of out-sized banjo on which the sun glints so starkly that it is pure white. Perhaps they are singing rather than laughing. Most of the rest of the image is a subtle chaos of the darker shades of grey but there is another white form in the picture and it is behind them, a ghostly presence of smoke. At first glance, the men may be recuperating after a strenuous day's partying with a little light music on the guitar. And yet, were the picture sliced to reveal only their faces, there would already be something in the manic masks to make me feel uncomfortable. To look down, moreover, is to see that one carries a gun in a way that speaks of an over-familiarity with its use. It points outwards to me, the viewer, but before my eyes can rest on it in the field of his vision, I apprehend something else that is far more terrible. Let me turn the page now. Another picture shows an elderly couple. They aren't laughing at all. I can hardly see their faces, shrouded in headscarves, just a frightened eye here and there, which betrays the simple, dark fear that death may be imminent. Behind them, in the grainy middle-distance is the burnt detritus of a massacre. They are being taunted by a hooded figure swathed in ammunition-belts. For them, I sense, it isn't important that I recognize the terror in their eyes. They are not looking for the gaze of the cameraman, imploring some distant viewer through him to end the slaughter. They are interested neither in me nor in how I feel, watching them at this frozen moment in time. For them, I am not there to bear witness to their suffering. They are absorbed in the moment of trying to stay alive.

There is something between these images of affected presence (the Christian killers pausing after their work) and of terrified supplication (the survivors trudging homeward to no home) that is united for me in the presence displayed at the downward pointing of that first gun. In the foreground, prostrate before her killer is a young Palestinian girl murdered during one of the early acts of ethnic cleansing that marked the beginning of the 1976 civil war in Beirut. In death, the British photographer Don McCullin captured her fate for a later audience.[1] Why, I wonder, do these and other similarly awful images appear to implore us to return our eyes to them? Are we indignant to see what they record? Do they inflame the imagination? Certainly, the images horrify and do indeed remain as a form of testament to human inhumanity, but they also perform another service, which is chastening to the sympathetic imagination of the viewer. Those who are about to die are, like the dead themselves, rather uninterested in the absent living. The forced posturing of the murderers, glib in their inglorious barbarity, is already hard to comprehend. But we can at least feel a hatred of it, speaking almost blithely at times of man's inhumanity. Images of suffering record nothing so clearly as the absolute failure of the imagination, our enviable failure to imagine what it is like to be about to die at the hands of another. Pain is, as Elaine Scarry has suggested, both the hardest of emotions to communicate and the hardest to imagine in another.[2] These are images of the unimaginable.

I turned back to these photographs by Don McCullin after reading a recent essay by Susan Sontag, *Regarding the Pain of Others*.[3] It may seem to be a strange starting point for a reflection on the reception of William Wordsworth. Let me begin by explaining why I feel that it is an appropriate point of departure. First of all, why consider these images rather than any others? In part, their haunting presence has something to do with their contemporaneity. If one of their disturbing aspects derives from the precise nature of what they represent, then it may be because we have conflict in the Middle East very much on our minds in the west at the moment. But it is not simply this alone. To put it unequivocally and yet a little crudely, these images disturb me deeply, and somehow I feel that it is appropriate that they should do so. My horror is evidence of their power to move, to affect, and yet this affective nature is difficult to explain. In some strange sense, what is essentially disturbing about them seems to relate to the fact that the way they attach themselves to me emotionally is obscure. A question is tacitly raised. What can we do when faced with a verbal or visual image that is affective and yet whose portrayed suffering we can do nothing to alleviate? These images horrify because and not merely in spite of the fact that they are historical There is something both intimate and distant about them, and it is this that moves me to discuss them.

We ought to be literate, visually, when it comes to images of barbarity in the Middle East, because suffering there is now very much our own concern. And yet should we perhaps be a little ashamed collectively that it *is* only now, when the impact of this suffering rears up to challenge the safety of our world, that they do have such a particular impact? In a significant sense, these images have the capacity to pull us, as modern western viewers, in two opposing emotional directions. On the one hand, the fact of their apparent historical relevance attaches them to the emotional baggage that is presently part of living as a concerned citizen in the post-9/11 world. Meanwhile, however, there is an equal or indeed even stronger sense of the impossibility of our empathizing with the plight of those represented. As we seek out the eyes of the dispossessed, it is at best a form of distant sympathy that is evoked, a sense of guilt and sorrow generated by the fact of the image's very remote nature, which reduces the precise individuality of the incident portrayed so that it becomes simply another piece of evidence to be adduced in order to justify some meek, indignant platitude about the terrible nature of human suffering. We are left with an awareness of our distance from the victims, and the failure of the imagination to accommodate such an image in any particularly meaningful way.

This sense of failure is significant because it raises questions about the ongoing historical resonance of any record of human pain. When confronted by suffering from the indistinct past, we may wish to ask whether such a failure of the imagination is in fact historical or absolute. Do we fail to achieve anything other than a distant sympathy because we are historically removed from the events portrayed? Or is there instead something intrinsically so remote about the condition of another person's pain that the best we can do as an exercise in sympathy is to record our inability to imagine it? We are at least in part conditioned to believe that we can appreciate the suffering of others because we are able, with the help of a significant effort of imaginative engagement, to put ourselves in their situation. Surely, however, there are circumstances that we simply can't imagine, those that become no less remote regardless of the quantum of effort on our part. There are limits to the imagination beyond which we need to rely on something else, a form of individual conscience that rests not with sympathetic understanding but rather with the recognition of a humanizing horror of incomprehension. As she looks at similarly affecting images of Russian soldiers killed during the invasion of Afghanistan, Sontag seems to suggest that where sympathy fails, a form of inchoate wonder is generated and it is in this that a connection between humanity inheres, awfully but palpably:

> These dead are supremely uninterested in the living: in those who took their lives; in witnesses – and in us. Why should they seek our gaze? What would they have to say to us? 'We' – this we is everyone who has never experienced anything like what they went through – don't understand.

> We don't get it. We truly can't imagine what it was like. We can't imagine how dreadful, how terrifying war is; and how normal it becomes. Can't understand, can't imagine. That's what every soldier, and every journalist and aid worker and independent observer who has put in time under fire, and had the luck to elude the death that struck down others nearby, stubbornly feels. And they are right.

As I first read this concluding passage, I had in my mind Wordsworth's early poem 'The Old Cumberland Beggar'. It is a work that made innovative claims about the supposed interdependency of sympathy and charitable action, and which, I believe, continues to be interestingly relevant to contemporary reflections on the aesthetic construction of sympathy.

Modern readers of the poem are immediately faced with a sense of their historical distance from its concerns, which are very self-consciously rooted in eighteenth-century arguments about the process of charity. Crucially, however, the object of the poem – the beggar himself – is already presented as an appreciably historical construct. Wordsworth tells his readers that 'The class of Beggars to which the old man here described belongs, will probably soon be extinct' (*LB*, 228). In so doing, he points precisely to the fact that his poem uses material that is likely to be foreign to the reader. And yet the poem asks us as readers to strive to imagine the plight of the beggar and to imagine moreover what it is to feel disinterested sympathy for someone whose plight we cannot fully comprehend. The sense of an unbridgeable gap between the poem's specific subject and the world of both the poet and his readers is a truism in the work, but it becomes, as I shall presently suggest, a virtue in the production of a humanizing affect. If Sontag makes a claim about the very limits of sympathy, as they are provoked in images of suffering that are simply beyond our understanding, Wordsworth seems to make an opposite or at least an intriguing and different claim, which suggests that the production of a form of fellow feeling that manifests itself as a simple sense of human solidarity has little to do with our understanding the specific circumstances of another person's situation.

This gap between the reader's understanding of the world and that suggested by the subject of the poem seems to me to be nowhere better dramatized than in the lyric 'We Are Seven', and it is to this that I would like to turn most immediately. The poem relies upon a pathetic collision between two rival ways of looking at the place of death within the construction of the individual's world view. To be more precise, it focuses upon the inability of a child to recognize that, on the terms of her adult interlocutor's apprehension of the world, the death and burial of her siblings must constitute their absolute absence from her world. I hesitate to use the expression 'world view' because it seems to aggrandize that which has widely been seen as the child's artless and slightly over-sentimentalized account of her situation. A recent reading by Peter de Bolla, however, has suggested that we should not approach this poem simply by looking at the gap between the two different accounts with a view to taking sides, but should instead take the work to be a serious attempt to deal with rival ways 'of naming and numbering oneself as part of the world.'[4] De Bolla's reading begins from the tacit suggestion that he finds his own apprehension of the world to be complicated; that he can himself on occasion 'sense absent persons as present'. It is this that leads him to propose that we should take the child's claims seriously, or at least that we should allow our reading to accommodate them as valid ways of expressing the conditions of her existence as she sees it.

Effectively, we witness within the poem a debate about both the world and the ways in which language describes it. The child's repeated insistence that 'we are seven' appears to name a particular state, upon the existence of which the adult interlocutor cannot agree. In simple terms, while a form of the fantastic conditions one speaker's world, the other abides by the rational. Moreover, in order for the adult adequately to sympathize with the child, there is a sense of urgency about the need for them to agree about the sadness of her situation. And yet, the child appears to unseat the adult in his attempts to interact with her, even to the point at which he appears to be simply unsympathetic. For this reason, he keeps returning to the question of how it may be that she can still be one of seven siblings if two have already died. With this in mind, he insists on reinforcing the distinction between life and death in order to press the issue:

> You run about, my little maid,
> Your limbs they are alive;
> If two are in the church-yard laid,
> Then ye are only five.'
> ('We Are Seven', 33–6)

As readers, then, we are faced with a desperate situation that is conditioned by the effects of infant mortality, but one whose resonance is in part vitiated by the fact of historical remoteness. Equally, the dialogue dramatizes a stark sense of the inadequacy of sympathy alone in ameliorating her circumstances and, in so doing, demonstrates that there is no simple and universal way of interpreting those circumstances. We may not be consoled by the child's refusal, 'Nay, we are seven!' but significantly we do, I think, have a sense that the affective quality of the poem emerges in spite, and perhaps even because of the fact that we are, as readers, alienated from the exact world view of either speaker. It is hard to read the poem without feeling the pressure of the child's insistent claim, and to do so is equally to resist the rational demands of the adult, with which our allegiance might ordinarily be expected to reside.

For this reason, it is perhaps worthwhile to return momentarily to the language of the poem itself:

> 'Sisters and brothers, little maid,
> How many may you be?'
> 'How many? seven in all,' she said,
> And wondering looked at me.
>
> 'And where are they, I pray you tell?'
> She answered, 'Seven are we,
> And two of us at Conway dwell,
> And two are gone to sea.
>
> Two of us in the church-yard lie,
> My sister and my brother,
> And in the church-yard cottage, I
> Dwell near them with my mother'. (*LB*, 13–24)

Part of the extreme pathos of the answer lies in what seems like an incipient rationalism in the child's answer. Four of her siblings live at a considerable distance from her, at sea and at Conway, and yet the surety of their continuing existence makes it apparently reasonable to count them among her extant family. The two in the church-yard are literally dead and buried, having no bodily form, and yet in terms of mere physical proximity to the church-yard cottage, their graves are closer to the child than the equally absent living. So the child is forced to wonder about the very nature of bodily absence and its connection to a form of continuing existence. Given Wordsworth's own constant preoccupation with the nature of epitaphic memorial and his use of vestigial symbols both natural and man-made, which resonate with the presence of the dead in poems such as 'The Brothers', 'Michael' and 'The Ruined Cottage', we should, I think, consider the child's confusion very seriously. For de Bolla, the poem radically complicates an adult sense of knowledge because it asks how the phrase 'we are seven' can constitute knowledge about the world in a way that has to do with something other than simply 'understanding what its primary referent might be' (de Bolla, 109) This is a useful point if we hang onto a sense of the divergent form of order prevalent in the child's world.

Under the terms of this reading, the apparently logical inclination to discriminate negatively against the child's form of understanding is complicated as we begin to sense two opposing forms of order. One may be characterized by its basis in wonder, the other in an increasingly specious seeming form of reason. I am moved to justify this opposition by placing significance upon the fact that the child is described as 'wondering', when she looks at the adult speaker. Her world is figured early on as one of the marvellous and, much as the adult attempts to correct the make-believe reality in which she exists, forcing it instead to conform to the ordinary, hers remains that which de Bolla terms a 'world of wonder'. Indeed, he reminds us that this childlike sense of wonder is abidingly Wordsworthian and inheres 'in a different habitus, an Emersonian one in which the question of founding a philosophy, a grammar of life, is intimately linked to finding in what Emerson calls the foundling of the child' (de Bolla, 109).

It is worthwhile to pursue this a little. The man, the speaker in the poem, attempts to control the voice of the child uncomfortably and, much as he recognizes her wonderment, his own incomprehension is itself a form of wonder beyond which he wishes to move, by speaking as it were definitively upon the child's experience. And, to allow these ideas to trespass momentarily upon my own experiences, if I feel equally uncomfortable sensing my wonder as I view those images of dying Palestinians, then perhaps it is because similarly I already control the conditions of their visibility even as I am absolutely removed from them. Something of Wordsworth's exemplary Romanticism inheres, I think, in the way in which implicitly he drives a wedge between two forms of wonder in this poem. One strives to overcome incomprehension; the other finds wonder as a humanizing end in itself. Emerson and Wordsworth, whose mundane beggar becomes an affective presence in the mind of his readers, both sought to make great claims for the ordinary. Wonder, in as much as it works to defamiliarize the commonplace, fills us with a sense of the need to care about the mundane. The connection between the two writers is highly suggestive, I think. In so far as 'We Are Seven' is really a poem about the gap that emerges between perceived reality and the articulation of an understanding of humanity's place in a world that eschews the form of logic upon which the adult speaker insists, the final sections of the essay *Nature* are especially resonant.

Harold Bloom suggested in *The Breaking of the Vessels* that Emerson's statement, 'The ruin or blank that we see when we look at nature, is in our own eye', formed part of a 'transumptive' chain of uses of the word 'blank' that goes back as far as Milton's *Paradise Lost*, and that includes a number of examples in Wordsworth.[5] There is something, I think, that is strikingly compelling about this word. As much as adult incomprehension is a form of blank wonderment, the trope also accommodates its childlike opposite. While Bloom attends closely to those in *The Prelude*, which Emerson could not have read at the time of *Nature*, the word does appear notably in Wordsworth's 'Ode: Intimations of Immortality', where its connection to the troubled growth of adult insight out of the naïve visions of childhood is apparent:

> The thought of our past years in me doth breed
> Perpetual benedictions: not indeed

For that which is most worthy to be blest;
Delight and liberty, the simple creed
Of Childhood, whether fluttering or at rest,
With new-born hope for ever in his breast:–
Not for these I raise
The song of thanks and praise;
But for those obstinate questionings
Of sense and outward things,
Fallings from us, vanishings;
Blank misgivings of a Creature
Moving about in worlds not realized,
High instincts, before which our mortal Nature
Did tremble like a guilty Thing surprized.
('Ode,' 136–50)

In both cases, it is pretty clear that there is a mistrust of any supposed knowledge of the world as far as it is the product of empirical perception alone. Certainly this is a later Wordsworth than the poet whom we confront in 'We Are Seven,' and is one more inclined to a mystical vision, the early stirrings of which are apparent in 'Tintern Abbey'. But even allowing for this, there is enough of a sense of the value of childlike wonder, and indeed of our need to strive after its remoteness in an act of empathetic understanding, to force an interesting comparison between the early poem and the Emerson who writes that 'Love is as much [the demand of the spirit] as perception.'[6] Moreover, the Wordsworthian valorization of wonder as it emerges in the reconfiguration of the commonplace, a defamiliarization of the ordinary that wills us to 'see into the life of things', (*LB* 'Tintern Abbey', 49) is very obviously present in Emerson's neighbouring statement that 'The invariable mark of wisdom is to see the miraculous in the common.' Indeed, the complicated relationship between facts and their poetic transformation into an ideal, a relationship that so preoccupied Coleridge in his criticism of Wordsworth's poetry, is pregnant in Emerson's conclusions to *Nature*. It is a matter that needs to concern any reader of Wordsworth, for whom so much of experience appears to exist only psychologically, and hence in subjective terms that are far closer to the child's reality than to that of the adult who appears to speak in the poet's voice.

Having said this, Wordsworth is never quite the poet that Coleridge would have him be, one for whom a retreat from the real into truths of the mind alone is enough. Usefully summarizing the problem, Seamus Perry has written recently:

> The most influentially mistrustful Romantic, though, must be Wordsworth, who is really two Wordsworths incongruously joined together. One is the poet whom Coleridge especially admired, an exponent

> of the egotistical sublime, to whom the daffodils beside Ullswater were as nothing compared with the ideal daffodils that continued dancing in the renovating space of his mind. But there is another one, with whom Coleridge felt rather less easy: 'There is, I should say,' he writes of that Wordsworth in *Biographia*, 'not seldom a matter-of-factness in certain poems.'[7]

It seems to me that Perry is probably right to point out an opposition between two Wordsworths (who clearly do battle in 'We Are Seven'), and we can sense how it intrudes problematically upon the persistent operation of sympathy in his poems. The beggar in the early poem is not, after all, just a pathetic idealization of his mind but is rooted in a specific place, belonging, we must recall, to a particular *class* of beggars. Are we then, as readers, to attempt to empathize with his specific subjects, regardless of any historical distance from us? Are we to search, in other words, for their facticity, acknowledging in so doing that historical suffering has force but is different in kind from any that we know, and is as such as critically remote from us as the very notion of sympathy that was current at the time? Or do the very subjects, by contrast, persist as far as they represent types of a common humanity that promote merely, and yet crucially, a fellow feeling of solidarity with others in our mutual struggle with existence? And are we to do so simply because we attain a sense from our reading that they too are human? What in any case would such a type of the human look like? We are now rightly troubled by this kind of essentialist conception of humanity. A central question about identity is begged, and under such conditions, specific historical and social oppressions surely begin to relinquish their emotional force. It seems to me that a profitable line of questioning may proceed precisely from the gap that emerges in my examples between verbal and visual images. Is the verbal image of the beggar easier to modify than the photograph with which I began? Does it act as a mental *aide-mémoire* to force other related but different images of dispossession upon my mind? Does the verbal image always obscure its facticity so that it is sufficient for a humanizing concord of affect that nevertheless tactfully occludes mimesis? I am not yet sure. For the moment, however, let us allow these questions to hang in the air as we return to Emerson, because the Emersonian answer to the dilemma posed by my reading of 'We Are Seven' seems to admit few of these relativist concerns.

At the extraordinary closure of *Nature*, Emerson suggests that we need to uncover a communality of feeling in the apprehension of the ordinariness of being alive, and it is figured as a form of wonder that casts a shadow over later nineteenth-century conceptions of the Romantic:

> What is a day? What is a year? What is summer? What is woman? What is a child? What is sleep? To our blindness, these things seem

> unaffecting. We make fables to hide the baldness of the fact and conform it, as we say, to the higher law of the mind. But when the fact is seen under the light of an idea, the gaudy fable fades and shrivels. We behold the real higher law. To the wise, therefore, a fact is true poetry, and the most beautiful of fables. These wonders are brought to our own door. You also are a man. Man and woman and their social life, poverty, labor, sleep, fear, fortune, are known to you. Learn that none of these things is superficial, but that each phenomenon has its roots in the faculties and affections of the mind. (Emerson, 49)

Emerson's affections of the mind are precisely those qualities that enable us to become moral beings concerned disinterestedly with the situations of others around us. The wonder of the blind man restored to sight with which he closes *Nature* proclaims a childlike vision of the world that 'cometh not with observation' alone and is one that we begin to sense in the Wordsworth of *Lyrical Ballads*, inhering thereafter in a tradition of American readings of the poems as a curative or therapeutic experience. As Emerson embraces a sense of wonder in the ordinary, he appears to complete a reading of 'We Are Seven' that denies force to the disembodied logic of the adult poet. It is a poem that above all dramatizes the failure of sympathy, precisely because reason is held up locally as more than a match for imagination. And yet what sustains in our reading is a sense of the conflict of interpretations. Emerson's community of humanity is felt bodily, in as much as the affections are physical. As our sight is cured, so is our body healed. It is a visionary moment that is felt in the heart, but such is its surety that we have, I think, certain difficulty following him now. Emerson, a keen reader of Wordsworth, would, one senses, deny the distance of his poetry. And yet, in order to understand the ways that Americans did read Wordsworth in the nineteenth century, we need to acknowledge that they are both as close to and remote from us as are the poems themselves. We can attempt to uncover past ways of reading but we need to ask ourselves fundamentally whether the force of those readings can be useful to us. If they are to be, then it is because we can harness them onto our own interpretative problems and challenge the feeling of immovability that the poems themselves present. With this in view, I would like, in the second part of this essay, to pursue my reading of Wordsworthian sympathy within this tradition, before turning back to some of the ideas with which I began.

II

At the start of this essay, I considered a number of images that are, though horrifying and affective, distressingly remote from my imagination as their viewer. I suggested that since I cannot conduct an effort of imagination that makes the suffering portrayed real to me, I have difficulty persuading myself that I feel a sense of useful sympathy for the victims. They dramatize 'an end of the imagination,' in Wallace Stevens's phrase, which is a state that he calls rather notably a 'blank cold'.[8] The pain of others is, in an integral sense, sublime because it is both emotively moving and yet tests the essential limits of our understanding, and hence our capacity for sympathy. Moreover, the remote nature of foreign experience is very much a concern of Wordsworth's, and it is manifest in his own attempts to describe a feeling of significant emotional engagement with others that is defined less by rational understanding than it is by instinct. The especial interest that we should find in Wordsworth's own interpreters, I shall now suggest, lies in the fact that it is there, and particularly in the tradition of American nineteenth-century readers, that we find this central Wordsworthian preoccupation emerging within the interpretative analysis of the poems themselves.

In his difficult fragment essay on '[The Sublime and the Beautiful],' Wordsworth extends the connection between blankness, or the failure of the imagination, and a sense of wonder or spiritual insight in ways that are instructive for the kind of opposition that emerges in my account of 'We Are Seven'. He is concerned in the work to examine the specific psychological effects of the sublime upon the mind and, although his subject is principally the effect of sublimity in nature, he also attends to man-made phenomena. In fact, his argument bears up interestingly in the analysis of his own poetry because in asking the question, 'What is the sublime?', he is really inquiring into the psychological effect upon us of external objects that excite both a sense of power and of incomprehensibility. In the essay, Wordsworth makes the perceptive point that analyses of the sublime – and he has in mind those of the British eighteenth-century tradition, which attempted to define all the various objects, natural and man-made, that had a claim to being universally sublime – had simply gone about the problem in the wrong way. The objective of the philosopher is 'to look into his own mind and determine the law by which he is affected'. (*Prose*, II, 357). The sublime is, Wordsworth writes, 'the elevation of our being,' and yet it is important to point out that different people are conditioned to find themselves elevated or moved by different objects, and that these change according to circumstances and knowledge. As such, he notes that someone who has been brought up in Lincolnshire will not find the Lake District, sublime, although it is, a universal site on past models, but will rather be greeted by 'a kind of blank and stupid wonder' (*Prose*, II, 358, 359). His point is that elevation or transport, the moving towards a new psychological space, is not merely the product of the impact of a universal affect, but is relative to the aesthetic apparatus that we have through learning, inheritance and local culture.

The blank wonder that Wordsworth identifies as the product of our encounter with unfamiliar external objects is a form of psychological blockage, which is resistant to the development of both sympathy and the enhanced moral agency that he sees as characteristic of the power of the sublime at its most renovating. Crucially, Wordsworth aims to discriminate between two distinct forms of wonder in this essay. If the former is stultifying, then the latter is fructifying, in a word that he employs so notably in the first draft of the spots of time episode in *The Prelude*. When he describes a child's understanding of the structure of a cloud moving from a fantastic belief in its solidity, 'taught by tales and pictures', to an apprehension of its evanescence, he notes that fear and wonder are replaced by awe and religious admiration. But awe alone is no end in itself. It is a passage from wonder to reflection and action promoted by a sense of the sublime that Wordsworth is determined to describe, and this is very much the product of feeling that we have objects and events before us whose force we can sense without our attaining a complete understanding of them:

> Power awakens the sublime either when it rouses us to a sympathetic energy and calls upon the mind to grasp at something towards which it can make approaches but which it is incapable of attaining ... or, 2dly, by producing a humiliation or prostration of the mind before some external agency which it presumes not to make an effort to participate. (*Prose*, II, 354)

Wordsworth's discrimination between the forms of wonder generated by a sense of incomprehension is vital to our understanding of his work, because it is clear that a form of inquisitive wonder is a prelude to the kind of reflection that enables us both to order the world on our own psychological terms and to admit a set of useful affects that helps us to feel instinctual sympathy for the world around us and solidarity with our fellows. In this sense, wonder is very much a curative emotion promoting reflection upon the human condition and upon man's situation in relation to a world that he cannot hope completely to comprehend. It is to the inheritance of this distinctively curative strain in Wordsworth's poetics that I now wish to turn. Specifically, this is with a view to identifying the growth to prominence of a particular topos that informs upon the creation and maintenance of an ingredient in the Romantic critical ideology within which we continue to read Wordsworth. In so doing, I hope to demonstrate something of the process by which an early critical response shades gradually into the creation of a cultural construct that is inherited by later readers.

My first landing-place is one drawn from James Humphreys who, as the publisher of the 1802 Philadelphia *Lyrical Ballads* and as Wordsworth's first publisher in America, was an outspoken critic of independence. The work of Joel Pace, especially evinced in a recent article in *Symbiosis*, has drawn our attention to the ways in which Humphreys was instrumental in acquiring a diverse American readership for the poems and continues to be interesting as an early interpreter of the work.[9] Casting Wordsworth's project in a distinctly political light, he notes in one set of advertisements to the *Ballads* that his publications are all 'calculated to instruct and amuse, and to instill and disseminate those Principles which cement society, and on which its general Happiness is founded'.[10] Another of his advertisements for the *Ballads* aligns the poems with his ministry and resonates with the language of social reform and amelioration: 'let not the name of Ballads give rise to prejudices in the minds of those who have never seen this work; for it is as much Superior to those things commonly known by that name, as happiness is preferable to misery.'[11] Humphreys' conception of Wordsworth is highly politicized but, it also connects with a wider concern to suggest the therapeutic value of reading to the labouring classes. 'I recommend it [reading]', he writes in *Town and County Friend and Physician*, 'as a medicine, which, by it's effects on the mind, will secure you from the attacks of some diseases which really originate [therein].'[12] Wordsworth's poetry is as such a socially benevolent force, whose work not only suggests the restorative power of nature upon the mind but also effects this restoration in the act of reading. The relationship between the community and the individual is to a large extent at the heart of Wordsworth's poetical project and, in the early decades of the nineteenth century, he was strongly associated with a number of important reformers. Particularly significant in the context of this essay was Dorothea Lynde Dix who, inspired by visiting the poet who was the author of 'The Idiot Boy', went on to campaign for the reform of mental asylums and the treatment of the mentally ill while working to rescue orphaned children from almshouses. Her connection to Wordsworth is interesting because she compiled several readers for the young, including *Hymns for Children* (1825) and *Garland of Flora* (1829), which included selections from his poetry. For these early readers, the emotional engagement of the reader by the poem is already theorized as a curative process and this is in itself an acute and sympathetic reading of Wordsworth's own poetic theory, which recurs as a presence in American responses to the poet.

Nowhere is this felt more strongly than in reactions to Wordsworth's greatest work. As we move into the mid-century, and following the publication of *The Prelude*, a startling anonymous review published in *Graham's Magazine* states:

> We believe that few metaphysicians ever scanned their consciousness with more intensity of vision, than Wordsworth was wont to direct upon his; and in the present poem he has subtily [*sic*] noted, and firmly expressed, many new psychological laws and processes. The whole subject of the development of the mind's creative faculties, and the vital laws of

> mental growth and production, has been but little touched upon by professed metaphysicians; and we believe 'The Prelude' conveys more real available knowledge of the facts and laws of man's internal constitution, than can be found in Hume or Kant.[13]

Few of the 1850 reviewers chose to think of the work as anything other than an autobiographical poem. *Graham's Magazine*, however, praises it for precisely those qualities that remain remarkable to us and implies that Wordsworth's ultimate intention, to produce a great philosophical poem, is fully realized in *The Prelude* itself. The insights of this reviewer are all the more interesting (and perhaps explicable) when one considers that contributors to the magazine included poets and authors such as Edgar Allan Poe, James Fenimore Cooper, Henry Wadsworth Longfellow, James Russell Lowell and William Cullen Bryant. Many of these contributors were sensitive to the aims of Wordsworth's verse. Lowell, for example, considered the poet to be one of the reformers who sought to bring about the 'eternal life out of which all tradition takes its rise', and the reviewer here suggests that the poem is not merely a description of the imaginative growth of the author but is also to be valued as a document of universal human interest.[14] The Wordsworth that emerges is therefore not the political poet of the *Ballads*, but one whose work attains a philosophical timelessness, which enables *The Prelude* to speak freshly to the reader even at the distance of many years. Nevertheless, in view of the fact that one of the poem's central subjects is the restoration of mental and imaginative health after a period of unhappy guilt, the review retains a trace of Humphreys' original assessment. If to describe the laws of mental growth is in part to affect a cure that which Wordsworth calls in *The Excursion* 'Despondency Corrected', then *The Prelude* is itself a therapeutic work.

Over the course of the nineteenth century, Wordsworth emerges for American readers as a poet of an essentially curative aesthetic and it is one for which the place of sympathy in this construction is both vital and vexed. It is time for us to turn to William James and to several texts that were written in the final years of that century. It is not only the interpretative light that James casts over Wordsworth in these essays that is of specific interest, although this coheres importantly with much in these earlier readings, but also the use to which he puts the poet therein. Wordsworth does not figure especially highly in James, but he is cited extensively in a late essay of 1899, 'On a Certain Blindness in Human Beings', versions of which he delivered to teachers and non-academic audiences over many years. Closely related to this, and an essay in which he again quotes from Wordsworth in support of his argument, is the second piece in *The Will to Believe*, 'Is Life Worth Living?' I will turn to these shortly. First, however, we should dwell briefly on a more famous essay in that collection, 'The Sentiment of Rationality'. There, as James is describing an attitude to the world that is emotional, anti-speculative and opposed to rationality, an attitude that is Romantic in the simple delight taken in a proximity to the wonders of nature, he slips a short quotation from Wordsworth into his argument:

> To religious persons of every shade of doctrine moments come when the world, as it is, seems so divinely orderly, and the acceptance of it by the heart so rapturously complete, that intellectual questions vanish; nay, the intellect itself is hushed to sleep – as Wordsworth says, 'thought is not; in enjoyment it expires'.[15]

Here again we encounter a Wordsworth of apparently acute psychological perception. His observation – that the mind contented is anti-speculative – is taken by James to be an aphoristic truth. And yet although Wordsworth is an exemplary Romantic, he is not brought to bear in the argument so much as he is used as justification for its conclusion. The quotation is slipped into the prose and appears to attain its conclusive weight simply by being tagged *to* Wordsworth. Moreover, in his essay, 'On A Certain Blindness in Human Beings', James appears to extend this reading somewhat, suggesting that Wordsworth had an acute psychological sense of moments of significance but that he lacked the rational ability to conceptualize such insights, relying instead upon the performative power of their declaration:

> Wordsworth [is] similarly full of this sense of a limitless significance in natural things. In Wordsworth it was a somewhat austere and moral significance – a 'lonely cheer'.
>
> To every natural form, rock, fruit, or flower,
> Even the loose stones that cover the highway,
> I gave a moral life: I saw them feel
> Or Linked them to some feeling: the great mass
> Lay bedded in some quickening soul, and all,
> That I beheld respired with inward meaning.
>
> 'Authentic tidings of invisible things!' Just what this hidden presence in nature was, which Wordsworth rapturously felt, and in the light of which he lived, tramping the hills for days together, the poet never could explain logically or in articulate conceptions.[16]

In spite of this anti-rational strain in Wordsworth, however, his work is directly associated for James with a curative and sustaining quality even as it appears to reside in significance over signification. He goes on: 'that inner life of his carried the burden of a significance that has fed the souls of others, and fills them to this day with inner joy' (Gunn, 275).

It is highly significant that James, following the example of John Stuart Mill, had himself suffered from a form of depression in his late twenties in which he evidently felt that he shared something of the despondency that Wordsworth describes in *The Prelude*. Moreover, in a letter from Henry James Sr to his younger son, there is a description of William's emergence from this state:

> He had a great effusion. I was afraid of interfering with it, or possibly checking it, but I ventured to ask what specially in his opinion had promoted the change. He said several things: the reading of Renouvier (specially his vindication of freedom of the will) and Wordsworth, whom he has been feeding upon now for a good while; but especially his having given up the notion that all mental disorder required to have a physical basis.[17]

It is tempting in the context of this essay to suggest that Wordsworth himself contributed to James's sense that depression could be cured by mental reflection not least because the period in question, the early 1870s, was one in which Wordsworth's reputation in America was at a height. The following year, 1874, would after all see Emerson (James Sr's long-time friend) produce his selection of Wordsworth for the *Parnassus* edition, which draws significantly on *The Prelude*. Furthermore, in James's essay 'Is Life Worth Living?' we are provided with some of the evidence to advance this claim. Russell Goodman has written of this essay:

> James writes that a philosophy is a reflection of 'a man's intimate character,' and it is certainly plausible to see James's position on the will, or right, to believe as a justification for his own life, particularly as it unfolded during his recovery from depression.[18]

In 'Is Life Worth Living?' James holds that in 'an enormous class' of cases 'the part of wisdom as well as of courage is to believe what is in the line of your needs' (Gunn, 238). Goodman nicely assesses this question: 'Whether life is worth living demands a reflection of this sort: "One confirms one's hypothesis by the very holding of it" ' (Goodman, 79). Meanwhile, James himself writes:

> If you surrender to the nightmare view and crown the evil edifice by your own suicide, you have indeed made a picture totally black ... But suppose, on the other hand, that instead of giving way to the nightmare view you cling to it that this world is not the ultimatum. Suppose you find yourself a very well-spring, as Wordsworth says, of –
>
> 'Zeal, and the virtue to exist by faith
> As soldiers live by courage; as, by strength
> Of heart, the sailor fights with roaring seas'.

> Suppose, however thickly evils crowd upon you, that your unconquerable subjectivity proves to be their match, and that you find a more wonderful joy than any passive pleasure can bring in trusting ever in the larger whole. Have you not now made life worth living on these terms? (Gunn, 238)

Wordsworth's 'strength of heart' is in a sense a synonym for James's 'will', and it is tempting to see something diachronically Romantic in the apparent similarity. Moreover, the writer who forms a key bridge between Wordsworth and James, and one to whom James appeals frequently is Walt Whitman, whose 'mere joy of living' (Gunn, 219) seems to proceed from a naïve, physical and emotional apprehension of the world around him. James tells us that '[h]e felt the human crowd as rapturously as Wordsworth felt the mountains, felt it as an overpoweringly significant presence, simply to absorb one's mind in which should be business sufficient and worthy to fill the days of a serious man' (Gunn, 277). The almost somatic connection to external reality that is felt by Whitman and Wordsworth, on James's account, follows in some key sense from the impression that their poetry lends us of a regeneration of wonder in the commonplace. In 'On a Certain Blindness in Human Beings', James describes this kind of insight as a realization of the existence of an 'essential divinity, or of eternal meaning ... embodied in the fields of vision over which [the] eyes so carelessly pass' (Gunn, 279). He goes on:

> There is life; and there, a step away is death. There is the only kind of beauty there ever was. There is the old human struggle and its fruits together. There is the text and the sermon, the real and the ideal in one. But to the jaded and unquickened eye it is all dead and common, pure vulgarism, flatness, and disgust. 'Hech! it is a sad sight!' says Carlyle, walking at night with some one who appeals to him to note the splendor of the stars. And that very repetition of the scene to new generations of men *in secula seculorum*, that eternal recurrence of the common order, which so fills a Whitman with mystic satisfaction, is to a Schopenhauer, with the emotional anaesthesia, the feeling of 'awful inner emptiness'.

The wonder that proceeds from this Romantic freshness of vision, an apprehension of significance in the ordinary, serves to idealize common reality and to provide a sense of there being a mystical order to the world around us that is therapeutic. By invoking Carlyle and Schopenhauer, however, James implicitly exposes a division in his conception of Romanticism. In contrast to this benevolent, curative strain of wonder, there is a speculative form, which is an unsettling emotion promoting reflection upon the human condition and upon man's situation in a world that he cannot hope completely to comprehend. This form of wonder comes to highlight the essence of human ignorance with disturbing, and even disabling, force.

James observes in his essay, 'The Sentiment of Rationality', that 'thought' cannot 'stand forever pointing at the universe in wonder; if its movement is to be diverted from the useless channel of purely theoretic contemplation' (*Will*, 75)[19] On his account, there is something of an unsettling irrationalism to this form of the emotion, which is a potential bar not only to action but to thought itself. Theoretical metaphysics is characterized for James by Schopenhauer's late Romantic 'ontological wonder-sickness'. (*Will*, 72) To wonder, for example, at the potential non-existence of the universe is to become lost 'in wandering mazes' of speculation, 'craving for further explanation' when the 'bottom of being is left logically opaque' (*Will*, 73).[20] As he censures the 'ontologic wonder' of Romanticism's heroes, Job, Hamlet, Faust and Sartor Resartus, James decides that in order to act 'we should pause and wonder as little as possible'. (*Will*, 75, 73)[21] The 'free motion' of thought is 'blocked in the purely contemplative path' (*Will*, 75) that has taken its inheritance both from Socrates' advice to Theaetetus that the 'sense of wonder is the mark of the philosopher,' and from Aristotle's declaration in *The Metaphysics* that 'it was because of wonder that men both now and originally began to philosophize.'[22] Wordsworth's vision of the world is, by contrast, one in which the opacity of being's truth is celebrated. Nature is, in its essence, beyond our comprehension, and yet we can feel a sense of its significance and of the significance of our connection to an obscure order of which we are part.

In *Pragmatism*, James declares that it is precisely in this sense of a mystical divine order within Wordsworth's world that his poetry's curative quality inheres:

> A world with a God in it to say the last word, may indeed burn up or freeze, but we think of him as still mindful of the old ideals and sure to bring them elsewhere to fruition; so that, where he is, tragedy is only provisional and partial, and shipwreck and dissolution not the absolutely final things. The need of an eternal moral order is one of the deepest needs of our breast. And those poets, like Dante and Wordsworth, who live on the conviction of such an order, owe to that fact the extraordinary tonic and consoling power of their verse. (Gunn, 50)

We may, I think, not wish to follow James in his instinctive sense of Wordsworth as a anti-speculative mystic bound first by a form of pantheism and then by Anglicanism, but it is nevertheless striking to see how this conception of the poet merges with earlier readings. Inasmuch as Wordsworth insists upon a restoration of the childlike vision of nature, his work is both a form of therapy, assuring us of the potency of an order beyond the scope of the individual mind, and productive of a deeply humanizing, because affective, experience that connects us to our fellows. These are bold claims but they deserve some concluding reflections. In the final part of this essay, I should like to turn briefly to two of the finest modern American readers of Wordsworth, in an attempt to return us to some of the ideas with which I began.

III

Thus far, much of this essay has sought to dwell upon forms of incomprehension and moments when the incomplete understanding of affective events within the world around us, even and perhaps especially those that confront other people, can nevertheless be productive of a kind of valuable emotional experience in us, which I have been describing as a form of sympathetic wonder. At the back of my mind throughout, I have had a poem, Wordsworth's 'The Old Cumberland Beggar', and a sense of its particular resonance as a work that is concerned with the ways in which human beings look at one another:

> Him from my childhood have I known, and then
> He was so old, he seems not older now;
> He travels on, a solitary man,
> So helpless in appearance, that for him
> The sauntering horseman-traveller does not throw
> With careless hand his alms upon the ground,
> But stops, that he may safely lodge the coin
> Within the old Man's hat; nor quits him so,
> But still when he has given his horse the rein
> Towards the aged Beggar turns a look,
> Sidelong and half-reverted.
> ('The Old Cumberland Beggar', 22–32)

Something of the poem's psychological interest seems to me to be caught in this kind of moment, which appears to describe a form of human interaction that resists customary reciprocal acknowledgement. The beggar elicits the attention of passers-by, and appears to engender a form of sympathy or concern in them. There is, however, no sentimentalized response from him in turn, which might afford this charity some special social validation by virtue of his gratitude and the concomitant progress towards mutual good feeling. That kind of exchange would, as David Bromwich has pointed out, have been very much in line with the kind of advocacy of sentimental charity, like Adam Smith's, of which Wordsworth was rather suspicious.[23] In fact, the poem is really very little concerned with dialogue at all and there is nothing in it that hints at significant communication. Yet it suggests an experience of human affirmation. In these few lines, there is contained an extraordinary density of reflection upon our idea of sympathy, especially as it is inherited from the eighteenth century. The poem comments with a dignity of purpose upon a common human bond of solidarity existing between us that is remarkable, not least as it is not the product of mutual understanding, and still less of mutual self-interest.

It occurs to me that much is contained in the word 'seems' in the second line above: 'he seems not older now'. I wonder whether this tells us something significant about the operation of sympathy in the poem. Of course, we surely know (just as did Wordsworth himself) that the beggar is far older now than he was in those earliest childhood memories. The poet was entering his late twenties when he began this poem and so his first experiences of the beggar cannot be less than twenty years earlier. Implicit in this aside is of course a statement about the relative speeds at which we age, but there is something more significant than this in the tacit acknowledgement of a distance between their two minds that no amount of mature reflection can bridge, even though the beggar has become, as a site of memorial reflection, Wordsworth's own intimate. And so it seems natural that we should ask whether Wordsworth is interested in the beggar *per se* and how he feels. In essence, I rather think not. Instead, he is interested to record how his own inability to trespass upon the consciousness of the beggar, other than cursorily, may make affect his feelings towards himself. Wordsworth, it seems to me, wants to record the way in which the failure of his sympathetic imagination actually serves to force a moment of self-analysis that asks him about his own humanity. It is for this reason that Wordsworth's description of the watching beggar as 'A silent monitor' ('The Old Cumberland Beggar', 115) feels like such an admonishment: in a condition of plenty, it is simply impossible for one to imagine absence. David Bromwich has written:

> The beggar is an emblem of alienation. Yet he sponsors the feeling of belonging to humanity that none of us would do without. It is a quiet suggestion of this poem, which becomes unmistakable when one reads it alongside other poems by Wordsworth, that any life at all, when its conventional accretions have been burned away, might become the sort of monitor that the beggar's is. (Bromwich, 38)

The poem serves as a general reminder of the potential for sorrowful persistence in the human condition and presses us to ask how we may morally improve all the facets of our lives through a greater consideration of our common human bond. There is no allowance made for a simple, single, directed act of giving that may ameliorate one man's condition and provide temporary solace for an uneasy conscience. This is a poem about communication with oneself, about how our feelings for others change us. 'If one looks at the short poem "Old Man Travelling" ', Bromwich writes as though to press my point further, 'one sees how consistent was Wordsworth's denial that a feeling *about someone* becomes deeper by pretending to be a feeling *from the other person's point of view*. The man in that poem has been "led / To peace so perfect, that the young behold / With envy what the old man hardly feels." That is, they see in him the image of a tranquility that may have nothing to do with his experience of himself.' In Bromwich's statement, there is, I think, a tacit assertion of the kind that Wallace Stevens provides in his wonderful poem, 'The Plain Sense of Things': 'Yet the absence of the imagination had / Itself to be imagined' (Stevens, 503). If we recognize the cold blank that resides within us when we cannot imagine the plight of another human being, then is this failure not in a key sense also its own imaginative act of humanizing wonder? This is a question that surely confronts us today with renewed force.

In the fifth of his Wellek Literary Lectures on 'The Fateful Question of Culture', Geoffrey Hartman argues that a disturbing paradox is operative in the concept of the sympathetic imagination. Drawing upon Wordsworth's project for the expansion of human sensibility through a benevolently connective poetry of sympathy, Hartman declares: 'the more successful an expanding sensibility becomes, the more evidence we find of actual insensibility.'[24] His paradox is, in fact, not merely locally operative but inheres in the central doctrine that underpins his account of modern cultural morality; a doctrine holding that the moral end of artistic representation is to enable human beings to understand the circumstances of others and to feel sympathy or at least collective empathy accordingly. Hartman is concerned to describe the present vicissitudes of this doctrine, out of which his paradox is born. In so doing he moves in his discussion from poetry to film reportage, presupposing in the process that an important aspect of Wordsworth's own poetics is the intention to document and represent the actual conditions of suffering in his subjects, even if not actually to claim to understand that suffering. Placing these very different media in a related context implicitly involves Hartman in an aesthetic argument about the nature and value of representation, and it is with this that I wish to end.

Where there are victims suffering at the hands of others, we may suppose that there is considerable insensibility, present certainly in their torturers and potentially in those who do not intervene to save them. Suffering and insensibility in these terms may be said to exist in proportion to one another. To the extent that we uncover evidence of their suffering as we become more concerned to understand the plight of others, Hartman's maxim is self-fulfilling. If the camera and the newsreel are the modern organs of suffering's transmission to an audience increasingly eager to sympathize with others, then they are also the media by which we produce an ever-expanding body of evidence reminding us of the persistence of insensibility. As such, the paradox is less an integral condition of sympathy than a description of its operation in a world of technological development, a world in which we record and report on that suffering with growing ease. Yet Hartman's paradox resists such simplistic reduction. Moreover, in focusing upon the audience itself, he questions the very capacity for sympathy in a culture that is saturated with images of suffering. If Wordsworth's humanizing project relies upon one group of people making known the suffering of others through communicative media to a third party, then the price of a global news media eager to exploit our emotional engagement in the immediacy of suffering is that this suffering will become commonplace. Sympathy furthermore relies upon the engagement of our imagination with circumstances that are quite unfamiliar to us. It is of course eminently possible to feel sympathetic towards those in circumstances that we know, but an equal caveat applies: as often as sympathy seems to require an inequality of circumstance, it also demands that we make an effort to understand situations that are radically unfamiliar to us. Beneath any ongoing commitment to the value of sympathy, there cannot merely be the matter of commiserating with those in circumstances that we know, nor indeed the recognition of 'just desserts', though it is interesting to reflect on whether it is possible to judge and sympathize simultaneously. Rather, I think, its value lies in the potential for our achieving human intimacy with persons and events that are foreign and distant from us.

At this point, the importance of Hartman's aesthetic argument must intrude upon the discussion, for he provides a succinct and devastating declaration of the power of mimesis to reduce an audience to a state of critical and ethical paralysis. Indeed, we may recognize his description of contemporary modernity with renewed unease in the wake of recent history for it is one in which cultural experience is dominated by the immediacy of the photographic image. But his argument reaches beyond or behind a familiar reaction against the proliferation of images and their part in the demise of the reading public. Instead, he looks to assess the implications of a transformation in Western cultural literacy by which the dominant medium of the communication of suffering, the literary text, has been replaced with the moving visual image. Implicit in this change, he argues, there is an attendant aesthetic transition from the epic fantasy of the poetic text to the stark realism of film, which is further complicated by an expansion from the local to the global in the horizons of our conscious awareness. The presence of global images of suffering that call for our attention imposes a sense of sympathetic responsibility upon us that simply cannot be met, with 'feelings that cannot be acted on, and a resentment that may actually shut the doors of perception that the romantic revolution in sensibility wished to open wide, on all creation, all creatures, in an infinite, nonenvious expansion of the humanitarian convenant'.

This is a chastening vision of our growing inability for sympathy and it is articulated with very conscious reference to Wordsworth, whose project of aesthetic realism ultimately articulates itself as something of a humanitarian concern on Hartman's terms. The Wordsworthian belief in the grounded nature of poetic representation by which art suggests the specific reality of the circumstances of others leads, through technological advancement, to a reliance upon media that require no attention on the part of the audience. As human suffering is presented to us through the direct medium of film, we become immediate consumers, unaware of the fundamental strangeness of the mediated vision of art. And yet it is only through a consideration of this strangeness that we achieve the form of awareness, combining a sense of intimacy and distance, through which art's moral purpose is achieved. This is a useful tension that Hartman will later describe as a form of wonder.[25]

Nowhere in the lecture series does he refer to the figure of Walter Benjamin who seems to stand so obviously behind its central thesis.[26] Instead, through a careful handling of sources Hartman presents the distancing effect of Wordsworth's poetic form as a benevolent product of Romanticism's ambivalence towards mimesis. As much as it is Wordsworth's intention to present us with images of suffering grounded in reality, these are valuable specifically insofar as they are verbal and hence in need of modification in the mind of the reader:

> Photographs of the dying, the mutilated, the mute, the devastated are harder to *modify* than verbally mediated pictures. Utopian visions dim. Snapshots of ordinary or happy life are increasingly like promotional inserts, ads that persuade us to buy life, to go on living [my emphasis]. (*Culture*, 144)

Moreover, while Hartman exposes a concern with the forms of concentration present in our interaction with different media, he also implicitly valorizes one form of aesthetic engagement over another. By privileging the intimacy of the reading experience over the immediacy of film, he suggests that it is through recognition of the strangeness of aesthetic experience that we become emotionally engaged with representation. There is admittedly a troublesome tacit assumption in Hartman's argument that the forms of poetic representation employed by Wordsworth can be reasonably discussed in comparison with those of film reportage. But more important than this is the fact that he appears to make Coleridge's criticisms of Wordsworth's supposed poetic theory from *Biographia Literaria*, into a virtue and strength.[27] Poetry, in as far as it is mimetic, relies upon techniques of representation that modify the ordinary, drawing attention to the transformation of language and experience in the process. Poems are not merely documentary records of the suffering of others. We may say in fact that the *techne* of writing intrudes benevolently upon the practice of imitation:

> The consciousness of a link between sensitivity and desensitisation has always been there *in art*. The art of art allows strong feelings to emerge,

> even toward what is strange and estranged, for 'things silently gone out of mind' or 'things violently destroyed.' The binding together of differences into a harmonious 'empire' is never given up. In art this is accomplished by an economy of form or by limits of representation that keep the spectator of the suffering (oneself or others) from being overwhelmed. (*Culture*, 144)

As such the argument contains a discreet statement about the technique of mimesis that privileges the formal distance of the poetic representation over the apparent immediacy of the film image. Immediacy, on his argument, promotes not intimacy but a mixture of shock and diversion that prevents emotional engagement.

I have suggested that Hartman's lecture is strongly indebted to Benjamin. Although its conclusions are very different, it is also, like Benjamin's famous essay, concerned with asking how modern culture can achieve benevolent social ends. By emphasizing a distinction between film and poetry, Hartman encourages us to think about the ways in which distraction and concentration relate to one another in aesthetic experience, where concentration upon the work of art is central to the growth of our structures of feeling and humanitarian understanding. Insofar as his sympathy paradox is operative, Hartman's conclusions actually have more in common with Romantic or eighteenth-century concerns than with Benjamin, and he ends with a rather hesitant plea for aesthetic education that would be characterized by the 'intense individual contemplation that marks art criticism at its empathetic best' (Hartman, 344–5). Addressing forms of representation that appear to hide their artifice so completely that they are present to us as mere spectacle, Hartman's diagnosis of a condition of inattention present in our interaction with the medium of film is a reiteration in part of Benjamin. Film reportage is an extreme example of a medium in which we easily accept representation upon its own terms. Nevertheless, Hartman's contention is more widely applicable if we are to continue to ask about the social value of cultural activities and, more importantly, about our capacity for investigating and interpreting the forms of representation characterized by such activities. And behind the thoughts of this elderly American scholar, viewing with certain mistrust the progress of his adopted nation's culture as it slouched towards the millennium, there are questions about the limits of sympathy that were raised by a young English poet two centuries earlier in a different political climate. They have failed to go away.

Notes

1. *Don McCullin* (London: Jonathan Cape, 2003), 230–1, 236–7.
2. See Elaine Scarry, *The Body in Pain: The Making and Unmaking of the World* (New York, NY: Oxford UP, 1985), esp. 27–59, 161–80.

3. Susan Sontag, *Regarding the Pain of Others* (London: Hamish Hamilton, 2003).
4. Peter de Bolla, *Art Matters* (Cambridge, MA: Harvard UP, 2001), 104.
5. Harold Bloom, *The Breaking of the Vessels* (Chicago, IL: University of Chicago Press, 1982), 79.
6. Carl Bode (ed.) *The Portable Emerson* (Harmondsworth: Penguin, 1981), 49.
7. Seamus Perry, 'In Flesh-Coloured Silk', *London Review of Books* 25, no. 23 (4 December 2003): 16–18.
8. *The Collected Poems of Wallace Stevens* (London: Faber and Faber, 1955), 502–3.
9. Joel Pace, 'A Publisher's Politics: *Lyrical Ballads* (Philadelphia, PA, 1802)', *Symbiosis* 7, no.1 (April 2003): 35–55 and 'Wordsworth and America: Reception and Reform' in *The Cambridge Companion to Wordsworth*, ed. Stephen Gill (Cambridge: Cambridge UP, 2003), 230–45.
10. Patrick Kelley, *Elements of Book-Keeping* (Philadelphia, PA: James Humphreys, 1803), 208.
11. *Relf's Philadelphia Gazette and Daily Advertiser*, 16 January 1802.
12. James Humphreys, *Town and Country Friend and Physician* (Philadelphia, PA: James Humphreys, 1803), 323.
13. *Graham's Magazine*, 37 (1850): 322–3.
14. See Perry Miller, 'International Romanticism' in Henry David Thoreau, *Walden and Civil Disobedience*, ed. Owen Thomas (New York, NY: Norton, 1966), 283.
15. William James, *The Will to Believe and Other Essays in Popular Philosophy* (New York, NY: Dover, 1956), 27.
16. William James, *Pragmatism and Other Writings*, ed. Giles Gunn (Harmondsworth: Penguin, 2000), 274.
17. Ralph Barton Perry, *The Thought and Character of William James* (Boston, MA: Little, Brown, 1935), I, 339–40.
18. Russell B. Goodman, *American Philosophy and the Romantic Tradition* (Cambridge: Cambridge UP, 1990), 79.
19. See also Ross Posnock, *The Trial of Curiosity: Henry James, William James, and the Challenge of Modernity* (New York, NY: Oxford UP, 1991), 27–53.
20. See also John Milton, *Paradise Lost* (II, 561). In his 1929 lecture on ethics to the Heretics Society in Cambridge, Wittgenstein remarks: 'To say "I wonder at such and such being the case" has sense only if I can imagine it not to be the case. ... But it is nonsense to say that I wonder at the existence of the world, because I cannot imagine it not existing.' See Ludwig Wittgenstein, *Philosophical Occasions*, ed. James Carl Klagge and Alfred Nordmann (Indianapolis, IN: Hackett, 1993), 41–2.
21. Tony Tanner detailed the importance of the place of wonder to later conceptions of Romanticism in his early examination of nineteenth-century and modernist American literature. See Tony Tanner, *The Reign of Wonder: Naivety and Reality in American Literature* (Cambridge: Cambridge UP, 1965), esp. 1–15.
22. See Aristotle, *The Metaphysics* (α, I, 982b), trans. Hugh Lawson-Tancred (Harmondsworth: Penguin, 1998), 9, and Plato, *Theaetetus* (155d) in *The Collected Dialogues*, ed. Edith Hamilton and Huntington Cairns (Princeton, NJ: Princeton UP, 1961), 860. For a suggestive discussion of the importance of Plato and Aristotle to later definitions of wonder, see Philip Fisher, *Wonder, The Rainbow, and the Aesthetics of Rare Experiences* (Cambridge, MA: Harvard UP, 1998), esp. 9–17, 40–5.
23. David Bromwich, *Disowned by Memory: Wordsworth's Poetry of the 1790s* (Chicago IL: University of Chicago Press, 1998), 23–43.

24. Geoffrey H. Hartman, *The Fateful Question of Culture* (New York, NY: Columbia UP, 1997), 144.
25. Geoffrey H. Hartman, 'Benjamin in Hope', *Critical Inquiry* 25 (Winter 1999): 344–7.
26. Specifically I am referring to the end of 'Das Kunstwerk im Zeitalter seiner technischen Reproduzierbarkeit' ['The Work of Art in the Age of Mechanical Reproduction'] (1936), reprinted in Walter Benjamin, *Illuminations: Essays and Reflections*, ed. Hannah Arendt (New York, NY: Schocken, 1969), 217–252.
27. I refer to the argument of Chapter 18, in which Coleridge addresses the opposition between poetry and prose. See *The Collected Works of Samuel Taylor Coleridge, Volume 7: Biographia Literaria or Biographical Sketches of My Literary Life and Opinions*, eds. Walter Jackson Bate and James Engell (2 vols, Princeton, NJ: Princeton UP, 1983), 58–88.

Index

Printed in the United States
50919LVS00001B/168